Mike,
Enjoy the story.
people, yesterday, today, and tomorrow.
Ralph Story Bat
Major USMC (Ret)

AN AMERICAN SHAME

AN AMERICAN SHAME

The Abandonment of an Entire American Population

(Revised)

Originally a flag of distress was used on the cover of this book. Section 8 of the U.S. Flag Code reads in part: **"The flag should never be displayed with the union down, except as a signal of dire distress in instances of extreme danger to life or property." Guam fit the bill, and still does.** However, some individuals failed to understand the Flag Code of the United States, and judged the book by first sight of its cover. Without reading its content, some individuals took one look at the cover, and called the book Un-American. They rejected it. By not looking inside the cover, they became, in a sense, another American shame. So, based on the recent passage of the Guam War Reparations Act in Congress, and to allay the concerns of my fellow Americans, and some U.S. government officials, I flipped the flag, on the front cover, over. Now, perhaps, just perhaps, they may look inside the cover of this book to discover its important message for all Americans.

MAJOR RALPH STONEY BATES, SR., USMC (RET)

ISBN-13: 9781533320568

ISBN-10: 153332056X
Library of Congress Control Number: 2016908146
CreateSpace Independent Publishing Platform
North Charleston, South Carolina

This book contains both fact and fiction, with the oftentimes fictitious conversations and actions used primarily to support fact while telling a story of a people during the Japanese occupation of Guam. Certain characters, whose names are not known, have been given fictitious names in order to maintain a story-line that supports known historical events. Fictional names, dreams, and conversations are just that, and any resemblance to actual people or events is purely coincidental and unintentional.

This book is dedicated to the actual heroes of the Second World War on Guam after the Japanese invasion and before the Americans returned with a vengeance. The sacrifice, dedication, and love for the United States of America of many in this captive population were profound and boundless. Some of them would give their lives because of it. In the vernacular of the United States Marine Corps, they were Semper Fidelis, first, foremost and forever.

This work is also dedicated to the soldiers, sailors, Coast Guardsmen, and Marines who removed the yoke of oppression from the people of Guam in July 1944. And, to the United States citizens of Guam today, as they struggle to find the rightful earned place for their island in the sun and with the other American people.

And, especially to one particular citizen of Guam, my good friend and fellow Marine Adolf Peter Sgambelluri, or as we all know him—SGAMBY—without his participation, guidance, and support, this book would not have been possible. The above photo is of my friend, Sgamby.

Major Ralph Stoney Bates, Sr., USMC (Ret)

There is a place on the American island of Guam called the Manenggon Valley. It is sometimes referred to, by some, as an island within an island because it is surrounded by rivers and streams. It is a peaceful place, immersed in tropical beauty. But, it was not always so. When the Japanese occupied Guam during World War II, thousands of American civilians—men, women, and children, were driven from their homes and villages, and were marched at gun and bayonet point into a prison enclave, surrounded by machine-guns and guards in this Manenggon Valley. Hundreds of others were forced into similar, yet smaller concentration (death) camps located farther south on the island. Many of these Americans died on these forced marches and while they were held captive inside the confines of these *camps.* Hundreds of others died from disease, starvation, and wanton murder.

Manenggon exposed the depth of man's inhumanity to man. Even today, many elderly American Guamanians shudder at the mere mention of the name Manenggon. It was Guam's version of the Bataan Death March. Only these captives were not captured military men. They were all American civilians who had been abandoned by their country.

In October 2015, my wife and I drove to the center of the Manenggon Valley accompanied by a survivor of the World War II death march and this death camp. The survivor who accompanied us had been forced to go there as a small child, along with her mother and thousands of others, who were driven like cattle to await their Armageddon:

In 1944, **Rosario Flores Leon Guerrero** was that mother, marched day and night, carrying her small child, *herded* into the valley of death at Manenggon. We met her on Guam. This is her story:

> *I was eighteen when the Japanese invaded. We left Agana and went up to our farm in Yigo to escape the Japanese. They were rounding up the pretty, young Chamorro girls to force them into being sex slaves to the Japanese soldiers. I wanted to avoid that.*
>
> *I had a boyfriend. He was Catholic, while I was a Baptist. Father Duenas advised me to marry my boyfriend, and I did. Shortly after, I became pregnant.*
>
> *You know, I was married three times* [to the same man], *first in a Baptist ceremony, then later in a bombed out chapel in Agana, we had a Catholic ceremony, and a bit after the liberation, we had a more formal, traditional Catholic ceremony.*
>
> *I was seven months pregnant and had a ten-month-old child when we were ordered from Yigo for the long march to Manenggon. I had been sheltered from most of the horrors of the war, but now I would become part of those horrors. I had heard of the tortures, executions, and rapes. But I had yet to actually see any.*
>
> *It was early July 1944, and early in the morning when we were forced out of our home and marched toward Maimai with only the clothes on our back. Reaching Maimai in early evening, we spent the night in the open. The next morning we heard gunfire. The Japanese were edgy. Their tone and mannerism changed. They were nervous. Very nervous.*
>
> *We left Maimai and marched on toward Manenggon. We met others from different villages. It became a river of people. Everyone was weeping, while at the same time trying to encourage each other. "Do not fall out," it was repeated, "the Japs will kill you." The news of executions, beatings and murder of those who fell out were rampart along the way.*

My feet were swollen, and very painful, and my baby Rosie was hungry and thirsty. She was only ten months old, but she was skinny and feverish. My cousins took turns carrying Rosie. No one dared stop.

Some people were carrying their dead child. They couldn't stop to bury them and they didn't want to drop and abandon them. It was tragic. Awful!

We reached Manenggon in the afternoon. We heard about a group of men from Agat who were forced to march toward Manenggon and were never heard from again. Everyone was wondering what was going to happen to us. We found a spot on the ground, cut some banana leaves to lie on and lay down in the open.

I don't remember how long I was at Manenggon, maybe two or three weeks. I'm not sure. I remember when the Japanese came and took several young men to carry supplies for the Japanese up toward Yigo. I never saw them again. Rumors said that they were killed by the Japanese.

People in the camp shared what we could find as we looked straight into the barrels of those machine guns that the Japanese had set up pointing right at us. Interestingly, I didn't see a Jap soldier from where I was located. Family and friends tried to isolate me from the Japanese soldiers.

Finally, one day: "Man mattu I Amerikanu! Man gaigi esta!" (speaking in Chamorro) *Americans were sighted. Americans had arrived.*

We were given food and water. We were asked to march again; this time toward Sumay. The Japanese had scattered. We were being guarded by Americans. We were marched for two days. There were so many dead bodies, the stench was overwhelming. We passed by body after body in various stages of decomposition. What struck me as strange is that the people were quiet. Some were crying and refusing to be comforted. For a people who cherish socializing, laughing, and singing, it was unusual. It was out of place. I suppose that we were still in shock.

American soldiers were everywhere. They gave us canned food, but we drank from the river, after boiling the water. As I said, dead bodies were everywhere, including the river.

Despite the poor living conditions, people were so happy. Everywhere I looked there were tears and quiet reflection. Reuniting with family members, or accepting the realization that some had died, while others were never found, lost forever.

The thing that will stay with me forever is the dead babies. All through that march to Manenggon, babies were dying. They were dying because they could not be fed, could not be cared for. They died in the arms of loved ones, and they would not let the body go. They carried their child with them, sometimes for days. They were hanging onto their babies for days. They kept praying for a miracle. Those memories will continue to haunt me for the rest of my life.

I will also never forget the liberation. I will always remember the liberation.

The above interview was told to the author and researcher in the presence of her daughter Rosie, and Rosie's husband, our long-time good friend and fellow Marine, Lt. Col. Adolf Sgambelluri, USMC (Ret)

Lyn Bates (L) and Rosie Sgambelluri (R) beside a river in the Manenggon Valley, Guam

Today, a monument (below) in front of the Governor's Complex on Guam, depicts the desperation of an entire population being marched, as many believed, to their death.

Photos made by, and property of Lyn Bates

A rendition, (drawing) given to the author while on Guam in 2015, by a person unknown. Since it was handed to the author, apparently to assist us in researching our novel, we intend to use it as such. It depicts Chamorros herded by Japanese in Guam's "Death March" of 1944. Photo property of author

TABLE OF CONTENTS

ENDORSEMENTS

Geri and I never in our wildest dreams ever thought that Ralph Stoney Bates and his wife Lyn would enter our lives in such a dramatic way. Although others in the past have attempted to tell the story of the Chamorro people, no one can even come close to their perspective, told so well in this historical novel.

Carl Gutierrez
Former Governor (D) of Guam

This book is an excellent presentation of an untold story of an unknown people, the Chamorro of Guam, that have shed their blood and tears for a United States of America that has yet to reward them within the halls of Congress, the chronicles of American history, and the laudatory assessment of an American ideology. As I closed the manuscript after reading the contents, I remarked, "Finally, the full story of the Chamorro people and of Guam and all Guamanians has eloquently been told." This book should be a very good educational tool. The people of Guam will remember their heritage more clearly, thanks to Stoney and Lyn Bates.

Joseph F. Ada
Former Governor (R) of Guam

Ralph Stoney Bates has captured the strength and courage of the Chamorro people during the Japanese occupation of our island. And, of the bewilderment that those same people of Guam feel at the response of the United States government toward the suffering, loyalty, and adulation of an American island society. That society has been so proud of the United States of America, over the seas and across the years. It is the same America that has promised so much to others wanting to come to its shores, and so little to those of this island that actually shed its blood and tears for the America it loves. This is a must read for any loyal American, especially those who have fought for the honor of defending its way of life. It is a wake-up call for the United States Congress. Well said!

Frank F. Blas, Jr.
Senator, 33rd Guam Legislature

Through his novel, Ralph Stoney Bates has found the voice of the people of Guam, especially those who lived the occupation during the war in the Pacific.

Robert Underwood, President, University of Guam
Former Guam Representative to the United States Congress

Marine Major Ralph Stoney Bates is a.writer of unparalleled dimensions. In this novel, he truly tells the tragic story of the Chamorro of Guam, during and after the Japanese occupation. It further outlines the often unspoken and mostly untold truth of the attitude of the government of the United States toward those who shed their blood and tears upholding the honor of American values and ideals. This book should be utilized in the high schools, colleges, and the University of Guam as a powerful teaching instrument. And, the War in the Pacific Museum would be well advised to maintain this book ready for the public.

Juan Blaz
Sergeant Major, U.S. Army, (Retired)
Military Consultant and Historian of Guam

FOREWORD

No author is better suited to tell the story of Guam's Chamorro people—*An American Shame: The Abandonment of an Entire American Population*—than Major Ralph Stoney Bates, Sr., USMC (Ret). He has the background, ability, and heartfelt need to tell of the Chamorro past, and lay out their aspirations for the future. Yes, this can be, and will be for many, a disturbing and challenging book. Its contents will be readily dismissed by some, but compelling facts will resonate with readers, generating an awareness of the selfless sacrifices of Guam's Chamorro and clearly demonstrating the United States' failures in providing the hard-earned opportunities so richly deserved by the Chamorro. Therein lays a possible blessing this book will bring to the Chamorro people.

A former enlisted Marine, or "Mustang" officer, Major Bates's interest in the Chamorro was kindled during early tours and visits to Guam while a United States Marine, combined with an enduring, longtime friendship with fellow United States Marine and Guamanian, retired Marine, Lieutenant Colonel Adolf Peter Sgambelluri, who, with his family, survived the brutal Japanese occupation during World War II. In his first book, an anthology titled, *Short Rations for Marines,* Major Bates included a short story about Sgambelluri's father on Guam during the occupation.

In his second book, a highly-successful historical novel, *A Marine Called Gabe: The Life and Legend of John Archer Lejeune, The Greatest Leatherneck of*

Them All, Major Bates developed a unique, finely-honed ability to create and deliver attention-gaining prose in a powerful narrative, combining fact and fiction to tell a story. Building on his experiences with *Gabe*, and understanding the necessity for in-depth research as a foundation for *American Shame,* Major Bates and his chief researcher, wife Lyn, stayed more than six months—living on the island of Guam, among the Chamorro of World War II, and/or their descendants. Interviewing and associating with former governors and congressional representatives to the U.S. Congress, current elected officials, military historians, educators, and most importantly, many Chamorro citizens of Guam, their early determination to produce this book was strongly reinforced and *American Shame* became a fervent, personal mission.

Readers will clearly benefit from the enthusiastic reception and openness of the people of Guam, and particularly the Chamorros who greeted the Bates' during their research. They were brought into the families, almost adopted, as they gained insight into Guam's historical association with the United States—first as a U.S. colony, through the time it was dominated by a U.S. Navy military governor, then in World War II where Japanese atrocities, including beheadings, beatings, and rapes were endured and up to today's efforts for Chamorro (and Guam) self-determination.

Major Bates writes: *It is a challenging and controversial novel as intended. But, hopefully it will have some measure of insight to a people that remained loyal, to this day, to a country, and an ideal that had abandoned them in their darkest hour.*

Certainly, mistakes in our United States-Guam relationship have been made. The journey has not been without major bumps, but as America focuses more on the Western Pacific and Guam's strategic importance gains greater significance each day, the timeliness of Major Bates' effort may well serve the United States, Guam and the Chamorro people very well. It's not too late.

Colonel Walt Ford, USMC (Ret)
Former Marine Corps Association
Publisher, and Editor, *Leatherneck*
Magazine

PREFACE

The following is believed to be historically factual, based on readings, research, and beliefs of the author:

The people of the United States Territory of Guam are stratified when it comes to talking about the war years, especially the Japanese occupation of their island. Some talk willingly, some hesitantly, and some simply don't. There is still some bitter resentment over issues of that era, and its aftermath. Fortunately, oral histories have been collected over the years, starting in 1981, from survivors of the Japanese occupation. Most of the transcribed oral histories are accepted as truth by most, while others believe some of the oral statements to be a bit exaggerated or that the story teller was "confused." Some talk of the resistance network or *underground* while others say there was no such group. The important thing is that the stories are recorded. They *are* recorded for all to see. The willing participants were allowed to tell it as they lived it.

Historians long into the future will have access to these priceless documents to draw their own conclusions. These people of Guam, as they lived under various forms of abuse and control, did what they could to survive. Some believed the propaganda of the Japanese and thought the Americans would never return to Guam. Many believed in their hearts that they would return. A few, in the underground network, knew for a fact that the Americans were returning. Indeed, as the Americans returned, many of these people of Guam contributed directly to the success of the Marines, sailors, and soldiers who recaptured this island, freeing its inhabitants from virtual slavery and possible total extermination.

While the stories revealed in this novel through this writer and other sources are believed to be true, there will be those who will not accept them as such; however, the stories are as close to the truth as extensive research has allowed. There will always be disagreements, differences in opinions, and misunderstandings. Times, places, and events conform to the writings and stories of others and to documented oral interviews on file at the University of Guam and other locations. For this historical-novel, the author takes no liberties with the known facts *as presented.* He does take liberties to fill in what we do not know. The lost shaded conversations, the unknown precipitating events that caused these documented actions to take place, the internal emotions and feelings of those who had loved ones brutalized or killed right before their eyes—these things must be told, and retold. Why? Simply because these remarkable stories of this remarkable society of captives needs to be balanced with history and to be known and remembered by all Americans, actually the entire world, not just Guam, not just America, the world needs to hear them. We begin in the beginning:

This author's Marine Corps career took him to the Western Pacific often. Duties, temporary additional duty, trips, stops, deployments, and stays in Japan, Taiwan, Philippines, Okinawa, and places in between, including fifteen months in a place called Vietnam, are very familiar to him. And, twice his family joined him in serving various assignments on Okinawa, coupled with travelling throughout the Far Western Pacific. There were good times, sad times, and times of stark terror. All these images are now long ago. Most memories fade with time, while others remain sharp and more in-focus as time goes by. Yet, as time changes and lives move on, it has become his personal crusade to locate evidence of some of those unsung heroes of the Pacific War on Guam and write about them—before memories and their accompanying emotions fade. Why Guam? Because they are the last of an

American civilian generation since the American Civil War that actually experienced war, up close and personal. They were more than deeply involved spectators caught in the clash between the military might of two opposing factions. They were victims of that war.

The author states:

> *I served in the Marines with one of the sons of the man who is a subject of this novel. He is Adolf Peter Sgambelluri, a Marine Corps Lieutenant Colonel, Retired, who with his family in his youth, survived the Japanese occupation. Through Adolf, or "Sgamby" (with a y), as I know him, I learned bits and pieces of the exploits of his dad—over a long, long process of time. After our mutual retirements from the Corps, I lost contact with Sgamby for a time. While continuing to pursue a law enforcement career after retiring from the Marines, I worked in a couple of Sheriff's Departments, one in New York, the other in Florida. After I retired from the Broward County Sheriff's Office in Florida, which was an ordeal worthy of another book at another time, I wrote articles for newspapers and magazines which ultimately led to the writing of a book, my first book.*
>
> *My first publication was an anthology of true short stories and Sgamby (I had found him) provided me a short story about his dad. It was published in my anthology,* "Short Rations for Marines."
>
> *My second book was about another somewhat forgotten Marine, of whom only three books have been written. He is Lieutenant General John Archer Lejeune,(pronounced luhjern) our 13th Commandant of the Marine Corps. John Lejeune laid the foundation that allowed for the building of a mighty amphibious force that drove the forces of the Japanese Empire back across the Pacific to the very doorstep of Japan. Had it not been for John Lejeune, the Marine Corps of WWII and the Marine Corps of today might never have been. There would never have been the mighty Corps of amphibious assault Marines dominating the point of the spear and propelling those who wielded it across the Pacific. Oh yes, perhaps eventually we would have defeated the Japanese with*

the American army and navy forces, but John Lejeune's Marine Corps made it happen at a more rapid pace. That's a fact. That book is titled "A Marine Called Gabe."

After, the publishing of "A Marine Called Gabe," *I assisted another author, who had died before finishing his writings of a book titled* "Back Step," *a military-history, science-fiction novel about a Marine Master Gunnery Sergeant who, during a freakish accident between science and nature, back steps in time from the 1980s to the 1760s.*

This book is my fourth enterprise at writing books about unique individuals and events that deserve to be in the forefront of history. This is a historical novel about ordinary people of Guam accomplishing some extraordinary things. They are somewhat obscured not only by the uniqueness of their endeavors, but also the shadows of history, the remoteness of Guam, and the passage of time. It is about some extraordinary and exceptional people and the love and loyalty that they had, and still have, for this United States of America. It is so unfortunate that seemingly it appears their love and loyalty has never been returned.

My experience as an historical-fiction writer is sharply focused. In my first historical-fiction work about the life and legend of John Archer Lejeune, I placed myself into the psyche of John Lejeune, in his times, and in the circumstances of the moment, in order to make interesting fiction support the known facts. The process is to make history come alive, accurately. So it shall be in this novel. My style of writing an historical-novel is to gather as much information about the subject matter as possible, such as times, places, people, and events. Then, every attempt is made to document those times, places, people and events, from various official archives, personal memories of comrades, friends and relatives, and various other sources. And, once all is in place and the collected data is completed, in short, the sum of the story is believed to be factual, then, opinions, verbal dialogue, individual beliefs, etc., are conjured and added to the facts in order to tell a story—always guided by the facts. The story makes these facts become more alive. Thus a piece of historical-fiction is born.

The created conversations, activities, and emotions surrounding the known facts must be developed to convey a believable story that is not only interesting to the reader, but also has a tendency to always support the known facts. That's my goal. There are some readers and authors who believe that a historical novel should: "reflect its historical period so well that the story could not have occurred at any other time in history."

Defining the Genre: What Are the Rules for Historical Fiction? by Sarah Johnson

That is my belief also. Keeping the story in the historical time-frame of its occurrence in order to have the conjured fiction merge with the known facts of the time is essential to good story telling. Combining fictional conversations and thoughts with known historical events highlights and amplifies the events and the people who lived them.

For this novel, my wife Lyn and I visited Guam in November 2014. Guam was our home away from home while we researched the times, places, and people of Guam to conjure images going back to before, during, and after the Japanese occupation. Thus, the novel began. Then, in July 2015, we returned to Guam to live and work for almost five months in order to absorb the feeling of Guam and its people. We crawled into people's memories inhaling the air and emotions surrounding events seventy-odd years past. We absorbed more than time at the Micronesian Area Research Center and the Spanish Archives, within the University of Guam; we tried to capture the feelings of dozens of the survivors of a ruthless occupying force by reading their priceless oral testimonies retained within the files of the university and with personal interviews. We also came across colorful anecdotes of the occupation times that made life more bearable by giving people a chuckle to ease the tension of those times.

After days within the walls of the University of Guam, we travelled slowly around the island, briefly and frequently stopping and talking to people cutting coconuts for tourists, selling merchandise in small village stores, serving food and drinks in cafés, or just cleaning the yards of

seaside homes. We attended commemorative and memorable events and festivals, listening, observing, and chatting with newfound friends. We explored World War II sites where blood was shed and lives were lost by victor, vanquished, and those caught between the two. We entered public and private museums dedicated to keeping memories of World War II on Guam alive. And we read dozens of books, articles, letters, notes, written oral interviews of World War II survivors, and a lone diary kept in two small notebooks written by one William Gautier Johnston who did not survive the war, but his diary did. We were assisted by many local citizens of Guam and many of their elected and appointed officials, during our brief stay and met many more on-line, via emails, after we returned. These trips to Guam were absolutely necessary to taste the flavor and feel the climate of the times of Guam, now and then. We had to experience Guam as the people of Guam feel it. And, we did. The one thing that eluded us was the American military/naval commander on Guam. She refused any audience with us, thus supporting the claim by many of Guam's citizens of aloofness, a siege mentality, of a "behind the fence" attitude of many of the American military/naval commanders on Guam. They tend to see themselves as not part of the Guam community. Right or wrong, the admiral certainly came across in that manner to this author.

As a result of our time on Guam, we discovered that some people are desperately trying to forget the occupation by the Japanese. They don't want to talk about it. Others are making sure that we will never forget. They have talked about it and have given oral interviews. For many, it is as alive today as it was over seventy years ago. The stories vary, but most of the discussions and readings underscored the mercilessness of the times. Oh sure, there were some interesting, lighter moments: The fly count, the "crippled" individual, the soap telegraph, all to be explained later in this novel. But, most of the stories were dramatic, heart rending, and a shocking revelation of man's inhumanity toward his fellow man.

For this writing, we begin by pulling one example of many, many documents related to the occupation. What follows is but one oral interview that we found on file and on-line. It is included in this novel in the original format to set the stage for the times and conditions on Guam between December 1941 and July 1944.

An oral statement:

I am Manny Merfalen to represent my father, deceased, my brother, deceased, and my sister, also deceased, and myself. I'm going to stay away from the process of internment and the process of forced march.

I'm going to get to the point of brutality that was sustained by both my father, my brother and my sister, as well as myself. I'm going to start off with my sister. One morning, we were visited by a few Japanese and an interpreter and the Commissioner of Dededo. At the present time, their title is Mayor. They introduced themselves to be the representative of the police, and the reason for their being there was because of my sister being married to an American Navy man. The interpreter was sort of rushing the investigation, and he thought that, when I was delivering the question to my mother, he thought that my mother was the wife of the American Navy man. I had my sister in hiding.

And the question, the first question that came out, was where is the American? My mother cannot answer that because she doesn't know what he was talking about. So immediately went and told my sister to come out, when the next question was told to my mother, if you didn't tell the truth, you would all be executed. This is in regards to my brother-in-law being an American, and they thought that we were hiding an American.

So the question went on repeatedly to my sister, and my sister was only giving them negative answer. Each time they're not satisfied with the answer, it was followed with a blow in the face, not with the palm open, but with the fist closed, to my sister's face every time she gave a negative answer. This went on for almost an hour, and they finally decided to leave, leaving my sister with a puffy face, bleeding through the mouth and nose.

And then the following day, the same people came, informing my mother that we have to deliver my sister down to the Agana police station for more investigation. My mother ordered me to accompany my sister to the police quarters. I turned her in, and the same interpreter that came to Dededo the day before was there waiting for my sister.

The other two Japanese who came with him wasn't there except for an additional man who was there in the police station. He ordered my sister to sit, and then turned around and looked and told me to get out. But I didn't want to leave my sister alone because I wanted to see what they were going to do to her. So I walked out the door, and did not leave. I stood just outside the wall of that police station listening to what they were going to do next.

By coincidence, they were moving her into the next room, but I cannot help but watch in through the window just across from where she was standing with the interpreter and another man in that room. They were tying up her hands in front of her, and there was a chair just before her and she was told to get on the chair. So they strung up my sister to the beam of that building and I watched her dangling on that rope.

Then the questions started. The same line of questioning was repeated that she was answering negatively when she was questioned the day before up in Dededo. Every time she gave an answer, it was followed with a whip, about a yard long whip, instead of a beating with the hand. I can see through the window flashes of blood. Her dress is soaked with blood. She wasn't crying, but I can see tears dripping through her face. That makes me so angry. I had to run away from there as far as I go.

And when she was unconscious before I left that place, the interpreter who was doing all the whipping instructed the man inside with him to bring a container of -- well, I thought maybe a container of water to wake her up. When I was watching through the window, they poured this container of liquid over her head, then she started screaming. And what it was, it's not water, but it's gas. I can smell the fume of that gas coming out through that window from a distance of maybe 15 feet. So I started moving away from the building. I was crying. As far as I can go from 100 feet away, I can still hear my sister yelling.

I went to my mother and told her what happened. The following day, they dropped my sister off in Dededo. She cannot eat. She won't eat. She won't talk for weeks. And then the investigation stopped. The more of the concentration - - the most of the concentration of the investigation was concentrated on the subject of my sister being married to an American Navy man, but what can she give other than to say no because there's no way that she can give any information with pertaining to the military and the activities that my brother-in-law was doing. Her husband never told her anything about the Navy anyway, to begin with.

The next day we were all sorted out in groups. My two brothers, all the other sisters were assigned to areas where they were supposed to be doing some work. And I was put together with my older brother and my father digging pits for making charcoal. And three weeks after that, one morning I reported to work on the same side, my brother and noted that my father wasn't there.

My father disappeared for the entire day. The following day, my mother found out that my father was in the hospital. We got more information about the situation, and we found out that the day he was missing from the site where we were working, he was down at the police station in Dededo being beaten up by the securities, ending up with multiple broken bones in his body, then ending up in the hospital.

Lastly, about three weeks just before the activities of the American airplanes started coming in more often, we were on an ammunition and supply detail for some command in Mangilao for the military and, at the time, there was a plane flying over us. We were told to disperse with what we have on our shoulder into the jungle. My brother, being a heavy smoker, he took out his cigarette and light it, and momentarily when the supervisor of that crew saw the light, he yelled at one end of the group of people where we were and, in no time, he was there already yelling at my brother. I couldn't help watching him, what he was going through, and he was brutally kicked, hit with a stick, knocked down unconsciously.

Then I try to render help to give him comfort when an officer and three other men was approaching. About that time, they were lifting him up, as I was holding my brother on one arm, and the officer drew his sword out. I thought he was going to cut my brother's head, but then he waved at me, placing the blade on my arm, left arm, and moving me to move away. So those two men in uniform held my brother's arm in a position where he can have access to the head of my brother, but then he didn't do it. He withdrew his sword back into the scabbard, leaving me with a slash on the gut about an inch and a quarter scar, permanent scar that was inflicted by the sword. And at that time, they tied my brother's arm and dragged him behind a horse, and that was the last time I see of him.

The above interview is from "Real People. Real Stories." It was a weekly testimonial series provided by the Office of Guam Senator Frank F. Blas, Jr. The testimony of Manuel Mafnas Merfalen is recorded in the Guam War Claims Review Commission public hearing held in Hagatña, Guam, on December 8, 2003. This story is sponsored by the community involvement of Calvo Enterprises, Inc.

While editing this book in South Carolina, it was discovered, with deep regret and intense sadness, Manuel Mafnas Merfalen died on Guam on 1 January 2016. He is buried at Our Lady of Peace Memorial Gardens in Windward Hills, Yona, US Territory of Guam.

Soon after our arrival we met Senator Frank Blas, Jr. on Guam. He is a fascinating man, a Chamorro who cannot understand why museums and memorials exist all around America, and it is reasonable and proper, in remembrance of the Jewish people the Nazis tried to exterminate, yet not one place in the fifty United States of America is dedicated to the Chamorro of American Guam who were enslaved, tortured, maimed, murdered, and prepared for extermination by the Empire of Japan. Indeed, it appears that America has ignored it. To say it is baffling would be a gross understatement.

My researcher, proof-reader wife and I read, discussed, and analyzed dozens of oral interviews such as this one. It was astounding to grasp what savagery the population of this American island had to endure during the Japanese occupation. They were, and are, a remarkable group of American men and women, who risked torment, brutality, torture, and death each day by sometimes simply being disrespectful to their captors, or being loyal, or assumed to be loyal to their country, the United States of America. Even for possessing American money, an American flag, or a radio, the punishments were severe.

For Guam, the entire population became entwined pawns in the war in the Pacific. For many who actually lived it, actually experienced the war *up close and personal*, their scars may, with time, fade; but their emotions will remain with them until they die. That's why writing about their experiences, their memories, their emotions, and their exceptional love for America and Americans is important. To have their exploits, their personal stories move from shadow to light is the goal of this book. If possible, there should be a book written that would encompass them all. But, that is quite impossible. The plan, with what time is left to us on this earth, is to reveal as many exceptional stories and events as research, resources, and time will allow, and to write of, or otherwise reveal, their exploits, their journeys, and their purpose. To tell the stories of their personal loyalty and devotion to their families, these United States, and to the soldiers, sailors, and Marines who returned to free this society of captives from a tyranny they will never forget.

However, one can walk through only one door at a time; therefore, the portals must be taken one at a time. Seldom can a single person collect facts more efficiently than several persons. My researcher and I have read numerous publications revealing the times of the Pacific War on Guam. Assistance has been recruited from many people of Guam to provide the best support for this novel. Unlike many previous authors who have written about the plight of these Americans of Guam, this is the first time, in my knowledge, that an "outsider" a mainlander, has written of their burden that many still bear. We deeply respect the Chamorros and appreciate their support and endorsements, and have treasured their writings and oral histories. We will further recognize and thank many of them at the conclusion of this novel. Walk with us on this journey. Walk together with us!

INTRODUCTION

There is a real, factual story here, told through the medium of a novel, a story of an island and of a people on that island. In this book, the people and events are developed fully by utilizing the medium of historical-fiction to highlight the known facts. Conjured conversations, thoughts, dreams, and beliefs are developed with a tendency to support the factual events of history. Real stories are told in more precise detail, with the hope that history will come alive in the mind of the reader for a deeper understanding of the trials, tribulations, and spirit of these unique people. This book will lay the groundwork for introducing the people, what they did and how and why they did it. There will be overlapping views and conflicting views, because the real people involved see and remember things differently. But, again, the stories are real. They are an amalgamation of what has become the foundation of Guam today. This book will also outline a debt, not yet paid in full, a debt owed to the people of Guam by the other people of these United States of America. The future of Guam and its people rests squarely on the shoulders of these people of the United States. Let the events contained herein tell you why. The future honor of the United States depends upon it.

The following contains historical fact as revealed in intensive research and underscored by the beliefs of the author:

Guam is an island in the Pacific Ocean. It is one of several islands making up the group known as the Mariana Islands. The United States won

Guam as a war prize after the Spanish-American War in 1898. At first, it was just a colony. The term *colony* is a land title the Americans swore they would never again use, nor would they ever have one. America was once a colony of Great Britain. The colonist fought the British for independence to become the United States of America, and then, in 1898, the country that had won independence established colonies of its own. Because of their abhorrence of the word, the Americans chose to refer to those areas as *territories.* Guam's people, the native Chamorro, became U.S. nationals, not citizens of the United States. Not yet. Ultimately, Guam became an unincorporated territory of the United States. Actually, though Washington would disagree, it's still just a colony. But, what do they know? What do they care? Why should they care? What follows answers those questions.

After Guam was captured from Spain, the Navy Department was ordered to manage the island and its people and to defend it if necessary. It was useful to the American Navy with its expanded world-wide role. It served as a coaling/resupply station for ships of the American Navy, and eventually, it became a link in the chain of communications across the Pacific Ocean. In the 1930s, it became a stop-over station for Pan American Airways flying boats, fondly referred to as *clipper ships* in respectful memory of the fast vessels of the same name that sailed during the mid-nineteenth century until replaced by steam propulsion. One popular route was a course sailing from America to the Orient, across the wide Pacific Ocean. They called the sailing vessels that traversed it the *China Clippers.* It had reduced the time for getting to the Orient from several months to a mere five or six-weeks. These more modern Pan American Airways flying-boats guaranteed passage to the Orient in five or six days. Hence the use of the term—*clipper ships,* was a popular reference to their modern flying boats. Guam was a popular stop-over location.

Guam was also a popular duty station for sailors and Marines. Indeed it was staffed and treated like a colonial possession by the United States government. It wasn't much different than the British in Singapore and Hong Kong, the Dutch in Indonesia, the Portuguese in Macau, or the French in Indochina. On Guam, the duty hours for the sailors and Marines began early in the morning, about four or five days a week and ended about noon. As the sun would raise high in the sky, the island inhabitants began to relax and slumber in the heat of the day, often riding out frequent cloudbursts inside the protection of their bamboo and thatched roof huts. So it was with Marines and sailors. Duty was easy. People were friendly. Life was good!

The naval officers, usually accompanied by their families, lived in spacious homes staffed by native workers who cleaned, cooked, and served the occupants. Maids cleaned the homes, did the laundry, and made the beds. Cooks prepared and served the meals. Some households employed nannies to watch over young children, freeing the occupants for more social endeavors. Enlisted men lived in comfortable barracks with servant "house-boys," who washed and pressed their clothes, shined their shoes, made their bunks, kept the barracks spotless, and perhaps sometimes cleaned their rifles for inspections. Life was good!

They raised the flag in the mornings, lowered it in the evenings, had an occasional inspection or parade, and wiled away their time swimming, fishing, golfing, or hanging out at their favorite watering-hole. They enjoyed the company of locals; in fact, many of the sailors and Marines were married to locals or had a steady local girl-friend. Ah, yes, life was good!

At one time, there were heavy artillery pieces installed on the island, along with a Marine aviation squadron, both designed for the defense of Guam. However, officials in Washington decided they didn't need such instruments of war, and they subsequently removed those assets. After all, the world was at peace, and our nearest neighbor was a friendly Japan, just north of Guam by only a few miles. The folks in Washington didn't want to appear belligerent to our friends—the Japanese.

Life was good!

Then, war arrived!!

On the mainland of the United States, and in most of its territories, memories of events of World War II are fading fast. Attendance at Veterans Day and

Memorial Day functions grows smaller as attendees grow older each year. Nationally, Pearl Harbor Day remains somewhat in vogue, and the European D-Day is remembered by some, but as a combined nation, we fail to adequately remember or pay much attention to other significant events of those demanding war years and the graphic events that characterized them. That is, unless we happen to be one of the vanishing survivors of that war, or we reside in Hawaii where the sunken USS *Arizona* and the anchored USS *Missouri* garner thousands of visitors each day, or we visit or reside in one of the island battlegrounds, like the Unincorporated United States Territory of Guam.

On a Sunday morning, 7 December 1941, the American Territory of Hawaii (the island of Oahu) suffered through ninety minutes of aerial warfare imposed upon the American people in a surprise attack by the Japanese. It was a horrific ordeal of bombing, strafing, and torpedo launches, causing destruction of property and the loss of many lives. "Remember Pearl Harbor" became a rallying cry of the War in the Pacific.

On the American Territory of Guam, the American population suffered through two days of aerial attacks, followed by a ground invasion, and nearly thirty-two months of brutal occupation, barbarism, torture, and wanton murder, at the hands of forces of Imperial Japan. In 1944, the population endured months of bombings, naval barrages, and an invasion by American forces to recapture the island and liberate the population from Japanese control.

On Guam, the native Chamorros vividly remember World War II. It directly and dramatically affected their lives forever. It permanently changed Guam and the people of Guam—forever! It was 8 December (7 December in the Western Hemisphere), the day Japanese aircraft started dropping bombs on them and strafing the streets with machine gun fire. And, they unmistakably remember the fateful 10 December, the day Japanese forces came ashore virtually unchecked, to invade, capture, and occupy their island—making them captives in their own homeland.

They also remember, embrace, and celebrate 21 July, Liberation Day, as they call it, when in 1944, the Americans came back to Guam with a vengeance. Yes, on Guam, memories are constantly jogged and kept alive. Almost daily, the people of Guam and visitors to the island drive along the four-lane highway appropriately named Marine Corps Drive past invasion beaches where the Japanese, and later the Americans, swept ashore: the former to enslave them; the latter to *free* them.

On Guam, one can still see, touch, and feel the pillbox emplacements, the bomb craters, the gun mounts, the guns, and the scars and notable remembrances of war on their little island. Public and private war museums are visited each day, while plaques and monuments dot roadways all around the island providing notice that something remarkable happened here. Rusted hulks of machines of war are often visible to both the curious and the indifferent passersby. Many still harbor visible and invisible scars born from the time they were alone and defenseless as a society of captives, hoping and praying for the day the Americans would return or perhaps believing they never would.

WW II fuel truck, still there in 2015. Photo made by and property of Lyn Bates.

Exploits abound regarding American exceptionalism and storied heroism, during America's War in the Pacific in the early 1940s. Early in that war, after the sudden unprovoked attacks by Japan, the defense of Wake Island, Corregidor, Bataan, and Pearl Harbor created instant heroes forever documented in the history of a grateful nation. Then just a bit later, Doolittle's surprise bombing raid on Japan from "Shangri-La," followed by the mighty naval Battles of the Coral Sea and Midway, and the first land offensive by Americans (the Marines) at Guadalcanal, created more legends and more heroes out of ordinary, every-day people, who performed extraordinary deeds.

As the war progressed in places like Tarawa, Bougainville, Saipan, Iwo Jima, the Philippines, and Okinawa, news blared from radios and glared from Fox Movietone News in theaters and from newspaper headlines sweeping across America. Men like Evans Carlson, Robert McCard, "Howlin' Mad" Smith, Luther Skaggs, "Manila" John Basilone, Louis Wilson, Ira Hayes, "Bull" Halsey, and "31 Knot" Burke, became household names. Dozens of places and hundreds of names were woven into the fabric of our nation's history. All of them, the extraordinary heroes of the Pacific War, deserve every accolade bestowed upon them. They are forever defined by the word – *heroic.* None were born heroic, but all achieved the wanted or unwanted title. By their heroic deed, each added his name to honor and fame.

But, there are other heroes—the unsung heroes; those men, and a few women, who fought personal battles, not seen or heard of by associates, friends, or fellow countrymen. Often they waged silent, clandestine, and lonely battles against the enemy. For some, it was a last defiant act of bravery. More often than not, their activities were known only to a few, very few. And sometimes, those significant efforts were known to God alone. Yes, there are many stories of these people and events that have never been told to a wider audience than perhaps just family and close friends. There are hundreds, if not thousands of them. Most of these people and their stories, unfortunately, have just faded away—their souls committed to God, their stories lost to the shadows of history. This novel focuses on some of these people, just a few who lived and experienced the war up close and personal. It is also a story of an amazing group of Americans, the people on the American island of Guam—the Chamorro.

Many young American boys had idyllic dreams during the early 1900s and perhaps even today. From the early 1900s until about the 1960s, to live on a tropical island of unsurpassed beauty, inhabited by friendly natives, surrounded by beautiful women, listening to locals singing and playing enchanting music, leading a life of some work, some play, and total blissful solitude, was an absolute possibility for a few adventuresome people. Some of these adventurers included some fortunate American sailors and Marines who happened to be assigned to duty on Guam. The *natives*, as most Americans called them at that time, were the Chamorros, the people of the Mariana Islands in the far-off Western Pacific Ocean. To be assigned to duty on a tropical island was indeed almost every young man's dream, and Guam fit that description perfectly—the magical lure of the tropical seas conjured in their minds, had been generated by movies, books, and stories, mythical and factual, plus a radio show that was a powerful influence.

Asan Beach looking north 1930 era
Photo Property of George Taylor, Chamorro Island BBQ, Chamorro Village, Hagåtña, Guam

From the 1930s through the 1960s, many of these young men were enchanted, as was this author, by a simple, yet compelling radio program titled *Hawaii Calls*. It was beamed across the airways into living rooms, bedrooms, and treehouses of young boys holding an RCA battery radio up to one ear, listening to the sound of the surf on a faraway island and the music that followed.

> *Hawaii Calls was a radio program that ran from 1935 through 1975 that featured live Hawaiian music conducted by Harry Owens, the composer of* "Sweet Leilani." *It was broadcast each week, usually from the courtyard of the Moana Hotel on Waikiki Beach but occasionally from other locations, and hosted by Webley Edwards for almost the entire run.*
>
> *The first show reached the West Coast of the continental United States through shortwave radio. At its height, it was heard on over 750 stations around the world. However, when it went off the air in 1975, only 10 stations were airing the show. Because of its positive portrayal of Hawaii, the show received a subsidy for many years—first from the government of the Territory of Hawaii, and then from the State of Hawaii. The termination of the subsidy was one of the reasons that the show went off the air.*
>
> Wikipedia: Hawaii Calls

It was the sound of the waves washing upon the shore, the captivating voice of the announcer relating the temperature of the air and the temperature of the water, along with the soft, rhythmic, swaying South-Sea music that created images of a tropical paradise occupied by friendly natives who would welcome you with open arms. Many young American men would dream. Some would act.

> Indeed, in addition to the Hawaiian Islands, other such places did and still do, in fact, exist. Unknown to many Americans, the American Virgin Islands, the Azores of Portugal, French

> Polynesia, the Federated States of Micronesia, American Samoa, the Philippines, and of course Guam and its native population Chamorro, beckon. Guam was, and still is, America's Western frontier on the other side of the world. To most of these young American boys, they were "*. . . those faraway places, with strange sounding names, calling, calling me . . .*"
>
> From a song sung by Margaret Whiting, 1948

It is believed by most professionals who study this sort of thing, that both the Native American Indian and the Chamorro of the Mariana Islands originated from somewhere in Asia thousands of years ago—the Chamorro from Southeast Asia, the Native American from North-Central Asia. With that said, there remains controversy as to the Native Americans' entry into the American continents by land or by sea. One theory is that some Native Americans have an "across the Pacific" origin as did almost all Pacific islanders. Interestingly, both suffered the same fate from foreign invaders of their homeland.

Guam's people, the Chamorros, have lived as a society of captives, which ended in the early 1950s with the passage and enactment of the Organic Act by the United States Congress. Their captivity began long before that. The Spanish arrived in March 1521, had a great misunderstanding with the mostly naked Chamorro natives, and departed. They returned for good in 1565 and began introducing and imposing Christianity upon the native population, starting in 1568. After an extended period of warfare between native Chamorro and the Spanish, in conjunction with a severe reduction of the Chamorro population due to the introduction of European diseases like smallpox, Spain ruled the lives of the indigenous population of the Marianas, which included Guam, until 1898. It was a period of time just over 300 years. That is longer than the United States has been in existence.

The smallpox epidemic of 1856 caused the deaths of over 5,000 Chamorros, sixty percent of the total population at that time. Much like the native populations of the Americas during the European arrival and dominance, disease and the use of warfare, isolation, and relocation by arriving European intruders (conquerors), gradually reduced and subjugated the native populations, molding them into a more permissive society. They gradually became more acceptable to the dominant European ruling population.

In the early years of the Americas, many of the Native American tribes were *allowed* to occupy only *approved* dwelling areas as long as they displayed *proper* attitudes, thereby causing less of a problem to the ruling, dominant population. However, native Guamanians (Chamorros) were not, in a sense, confined to reservations within their own land like the Native American Indians. But, like the Native American Indians, the Chamorros were relegated to a lesser societal class than those of the conquering nation(s). And, the Spanish, like the [European] Americans, made extraction and relocation of whole populations into an actual art-form. At one time, the Spanish relocated the Chamorros from the islands of Tinian and Saipan to Guam for better control by their military forces. Similarly, at one time, Native Americans were relocated from their traditional homelands to "Indian Territory," in the current state of Oklahoma or to other Indian reservations for better governmental control. In short, population control was a government practice that evolved into a rather sophisticated system (art-form) in some societies.

People of Guam (Chamorros). Photo from Guampedia.com

The original inhabitants of Guam are believed to have been of Indo-Malaya descent originating from Southeast Asia as early as 2,000 B.C., and having linguistic and cultural similarities to Malaysia, Indonesia and the Philippines. The Chamorro flourished, as an advanced fishing, horticultural, and hunting society. They were expert seamen and skilled craftsmen familiar with intricate weaving and detailed pottery-making who built unique houses and canoes suited to their region of the world. The Chamorro possessed a strong matriarchal society and it was through the power and prestige of the women, and the failure of the Spanish overlords to recognize this fact, that much of the Chamorro culture, including the language, music, dance, and traditions have survived to this day.

Guam-OnLine.com

Prior to 1950 and the passage of the Organic Act, making all Guamanians U.S. citizens with partial citizenship rights, all the native people of Guam were classified as U.S. nationals since 1898.

Although all U.S. citizens are also U.S. nationals, the reverse is not true. As specified in 8 U.S.C. § 1408, a person whose only connection to the U.S. is through birth in an outlying possession (which is defined in 8 U.S.C. § 1101 as American Samoa and Swains Island (which is administered as part of American Samoa), or through descent from a person so born, acquires U.S. nationality but not U.S. citizenship. This was formerly the case in only four other current or former U.S. overseas possessions.

* *Guam (1898–1950) (Citizenship granted by an Act of Congress through the Guam Organic Act of 1950.*
* *the Philippines (1898–1935) (National status rescinded in 1935; granted independence in 1946; United States citizenship never accorded).*
* *Puerto Rico (1898–1917) (Citizenship granted through the Jones–Shafroth Act of 1917).*
* *the U.S. Virgin Islands (1917–1927) (Citizenship granted by an Act of Congress in 1927).*

The nationality status of a person born in an unincorporated U.S. Minor Outlying Island is not specifically mentioned by law, but under international law and Supreme Court dicta, they are also regarded as non-citizen U.S. nationals.

In addition, residents of the Northern Mariana Islands who automatically gained U.S. citizenship in 1986 as a result of the Covenant between the Northern Marianas and the U.S. could elect to become non-citizen nationals within 6 months of the implementation of the Covenant or within 6 months of turning 18.

The U.S. passport issued to non-citizen nationals contains the endorsement code 9 which states: "THE BEARER IS A UNITED STATES NATIONAL AND NOT A UNITED STATES CITIZEN." on the annotations page.

U.S. Nationality Law

Native Americans at Carlisle School Photo from Carlisle School Website

> *In 1817, the Cherokee became the first Native Americans recognized as U.S. citizens. Under Article 8 of the 1817 Cherokee treaty, "Upwards of 300 Cherokees (Heads of Families) in the honest simplicity of their souls, made an election to become American citizens."*
>
> *However it was with restrictions that Cherokee became American citizens. Factors establishing citizenship included:*
>
> 1. *Treaty provision (as with the Cherokee)*[All Cherokee were granted]
> 2. *Registration and land allotment [later] under the Dawes Act of February 8, 1887* [If the Cherokee owned land]
> 3. *Issuance of Patent in Fee simple to Natives* [If a Cherokee actually applied for and was granted a patent]
> 4. *Adopting Habits of Civilized Life* [Acted "civilized"]
> 5. *Citizenship by Birth (minor children)*
> 6. *Becoming Soldiers and Sailors in the U.S. Armed Forces*
> 7. *Marriage to a U.S. citizen* [A white person]
> 8. *Special Act of Congress*
>
> Wikipedia Native American Citizenship

Then something intervened: After the American Civil War, the Civil Rights Act of 1866 stated, "all persons born in the United States, and not subject to any foreign power, <u>excluding Indians not taxed</u>, are hereby declared to be citizens of the United States."

[And today we seem to totally ignore the **"subject to any foreign power"** clause.]

The opening paragraph of the bill removing American Indians as citizens is as follows:

> *Be it enacted by the Senate and House of Representatives of the United States of America in Congress assembled, That all persons born in the United States and not subject to any foreign power, excluding Indians not taxed, are hereby declared to be citizens of the United States; and*

such citizens, of every race and color, without regard to any previous condition of slavery or involuntary servitude, except as a punishment for crime whereof the party shall have been duly convicted, shall have the same right, in every State and Territory in the United States, to make and enforce contracts, to sue, be parties, and give evidence, to inherit, purchase, lease, sell, hold, and convey real and personal property, and to full and equal benefit of all laws and proceedings for the security of person and property, as is enjoyed by white citizens, and shall be subject to like punishment, pains, and penalties, and to none other, any law, statute, ordinance, regulation, or custom, to the contrary notwithstanding.

In short, the United States, because of a conflict in the two laws, took American citizenship away from the Cherokee.

The Indian Citizenship Act of 1924, also known as the Snyder Act, was proposed by Representative Homer P. Snyder (R) of New York and granted full US citizenship to America's indigenous peoples, called "Indians" in the actual Act. (The Fourteenth Amendment already defined as citizens any person born in the US, but if "subject to the jurisdiction thereof." The latter clause excluded anyone who already had citizenship in a foreign power such as a tribal nation or a foreign nation). The act was signed into law by President Calvin Coolidge on 2 June 1924. It was enacted partially in recognition of the thousands of Indians who had served in the armed forces during World War I.

There is a kinship in the similarity among American Natives and the Native Chamorros of the Mariana island of Guam. The Chamorros have survived as equals on Guam due to their strong familial ties, their overt loyalty to the United States, and their dominant numbers within the population. North American natives have survived by blending into the culture of the dominant population or by maintaining customs and traditions within the confines of granted reservations.

A careful reading of the 1866 bill reveals the mention of "territories" in the United States. But, it says territories *in* the United States. Those were the only territories the United States had. The United States had no territories outside the United States at that time.

The Spanish ruled Guam, the other Mariana Islands, and several Caribbean Islands, in addition to the Philippines, until the aftermath of the Spanish-American War in 1898. As a result of the Treaty of Paris, after the end of the war, Spain ceded the Philippines, Guam, Puerto Rico, and Cuba to American control, thus ending Spanish rule of Guam. However, Spanish influence remained as American rule administered by the United States Navy took over.

Although the populations on Guam became American Nationals when the United States took possession of Guam, it took fifty-one years for the people of Guam to gain quasi-American citizenship. It was much longer than when the people of the Virgin Islands (1932) and Puerto Rico (1917) were granted quasi-citizenship.

Throughout the times of Spanish rule, their galleons and later the more modern ships of Spain and many other countries brought hundreds of immigrants from the Philippines and Mexico to Guam. During that time, small numbers of other Pacific islanders, including Japanese and Taiwanese, migrated to Guam. Guam was a stopover anchorage for Spain's ships sailing from the coast of Mexico to Manila in the Philippines. It is believed by some that, due to the prolonged influx of Spanish (Mexicans) and Filipinos, the pure-blood Chamorro have long disappeared, and all Chamorros are of some mixed bloodline today. This concept remains very controversial. But their culture, language, and identity of the people called Chamorros remains strong.

The Spanish influence especially that of the Catholic Church steadily molded the native Guamanian population. They were given Spanish names, usually after baptisms, and Christianity dominated the lifestyle of the indigenous populations. Throughout the dominance of Spain, and the subsequent rule of Americans, the Chamorros maintained their cultural bond. World War II and the Japanese invasion and occupation of Guam tested the strength of that culture as no *thing* and no *one* had ever tested it. That culture not only survived, but also became stronger.

Before World War II, Guam was a far-away paradise. It was occupied by its native Chamorro, some naval government civilian workers, a few wealthy travellers who had crossed the Pacific on Pan American Airways' flying boats (Clippers), a few employees of the airline, a few expats, some construction workers, a few oil company employees, and a whole bunch of lucky sailors and Marines guarding America's island frontier.

One of the lucky sailors was a man named Giuseppi Marcello Sgambelluri, a native of Italy and a naturalized American citizen. A lucky Marine was William Gautier Johnston, a native of Alabama, reared in Tennessee, and a far-sighted teacher and writer. Another lucky sailor was Chester Carl Butler, a native of Texas, and a great innovative businessman. Each of these men would choose to live on Guam, marry a charming Chamorro woman, and begin to raise a large family. Sgambelluri was the first American man to marry a Chamorro woman. One member of each of these families would become prominent in the resistance and defiance of the Japanese occupation of their native land.

One of these "resisters" was one of the sons of Marcello Sgambelluri. He was Adolfo Camacho Sgambelluri, or "Sgambe," as he became known. Another was the wife of William Gautier Johnston whose name was Agueda Iglesias Johnston, and a third was the wife of Chester Carl Butler, Ignacia Bordallo Butler. Singularly and jointly with other Chamorros, they defied, deceived, and confounded the Japanese throughout the brutal occupation of their homeland. These three, and other Chamorros such as Jose Torres, Vicente Chargualaf, Jose Reyes, Antonio Artero, Juan Pangilinan, Angel Flores, Joaquin Limtiaco, and others, such as Ms. Riye Dejima, a Japanese woman living on Guam, and Tomas Tanaka, a half Chamorro-half Japanese man, lived their lives on the edge. And there were many more, always near summary execution or worse; they listened to clandestine radios, collected and passed on valuable information, protected the six American sailors who were hiding from Japanese occupiers, protected each other, enhanced morale, and kept the spirit of America alive in the hearts and minds of a society of captives. Many Chamorros actually actively rebelled against the invader-occupier by killing Japanese soldiers as the American invasion forces landed on their island. For many of these brave Chamorros, it became kill or be killed. There were no other choices. These are just some of the many unsung heroes of Guam that occupy the pages of this book and the hearts and minds of the people of that American island.

To appreciate the plight of the captives on Guam, one must realize that the Japanese had the power and were prone to use it. Resistance was a highly risky endeavor, punishable by death, including sometimes the death of one's immediate family.

These people, these natives, these Chamorros, these Americans looked death in the eye—and death blinked. Some would say they were foolish. Others would say they were brave. Today, we should say that they were intense, determined, patriotic Americans. We should also remember that they were among America's bravest of the brave during our War in the Pacific. To justify that statement, let us look at the actions of two brave Chamorro men on the morning of the Japanese invasion.

Yes, let us just look at two men and one incident from the dozens of men and women and hundreds of incidents known and unknown that occurred during the most abusive and violent occupation on American soil and of American people in history. Let us look at these two men, these two Chamorros, these two Americans, to gain some appreciation and to understand and acknowledge their deep love and devotion to their country—the United States of America:

The Japanese Navy Special Landing Force (Marines) landed quickly and quietly on Guam at about 0330 on 10 December 1941, and immediately descended onto the capital city of Agana.

Since 1898, each day at 0800, the American flag was raised at the naval base in Piti, the Marine Barracks at Sumay, and the governor's residence in Agana, adjacent to Plaza de España. Navy-Marine Corps-trained Naval Insular Guards and Bandsmen participated in the flag raising and lowering. It was a routine that never changed and never faltered. These two Chamorro Insular Guards participated in this daily routine event. They would do so a final time.

After a brief exchange of gunfire at the governor's house in Plaza de España and the quick surrender of the Americans, larger numbers of Japanese troops poured into the city of Agana. After the gunfire died away, and before sunrise, a Japanese officer and two enlisted men from the naval landing force came upon an unexpected and unbelievable scene. It was the sight of the American flag still flying atop the flagpole in front of Plaza de España, in the pre-dawn morning. We will never know why, but the flag was indeed flying. As previously mentioned, usually "colors," as raising and lowering the flag is called, goes off precisely at 0800 and at sunset each day. But, during the bombings, invasion, and rifle and machine-gun firing, things got a little off-schedule.

In the early morning pre-dawn hours, two of Guam's Chamorro Naval Insular Guards had apparently raised the American flag, no one knows when or why, yet there they were. These two insular guards were still standing at attention at the base of the flagpole, appearing to be standing guard over the site. Some have said they were ordered to do so, while others say they did it on their own. Then, there are those who say their action was a myth. It really doesn't matter. The flag was up and flying and these two men were present.

Initially, the Japanese officer seemed stunned, then perplexed, and eventually angry. Just minutes earlier, the Americans had surrendered to Japanese forces, yet here was the American flag still flying high. Perhaps the Japanese officer was insulted? Perhaps! We don't know. What we do know is that he was overtly infuriated.

Stories vary as to what happened next, but all versions seem to agree that when the Japanese officer, holding a Japanese battle flag in one hand and waving his sword in the other, gestured to Naval Insular Guardsman Angel Flores to lower the American flag and raise the Japanese flag—Flores refused. He looked the Japanese officer in the eyes and simply shook his head, "No!" Standing nearby was Vicente Chargualaf, who had apparently assisted in raising the flag that morning. He stood at attention and made no move. He seemed to ignore the exceptionally incensed, Japanese officer. Screaming something in Japanese, the officer raised his samurai sword, further threatening Flores. His rage rising, he pointed to the flying American flag and again gestured for it to be lowered, while holding up the Japanese battle flag in his non-sword hand, indicating that it was to be raised. Flores and Chargualaf shook their heads side to side while still standing at the position of attention. They displayed no fear. Their hands were down beside their thighs. They stood ramrod straight, tall, and proud.

Both had been taught since grade school that the American flag should never be lowered until sunset and that it should never touch the ground. They knew the flag was a symbol of America, and America should not be disgraced. They believed what they had been taught. They stood their ground.

The Japanese officer went virtually spastic. He yelled and waved his sword above the head of Flores as two accompanying Japanese naval landing force enlisted men came running to his aide. The officer then swung his sword at Flores's head. Flores ducked, but he didn't see the enlisted man, perhaps avenging the perceived insult of his officer, before it was too late. The Japanese infantry-sailor stabbed his bayonet into the chest of Flores, twisted it before withdrawing, as he had been taught, to create more internal damage. Flores collapsed as the naval infantryman again shoved his bayonet into his dying body. A second naval infantryman rushed toward Chargualaf from his blind side and thrust his sharp bayonet through his body. Both Flores and Chargualaf were mortally wounded. Chargualaf died the next day. Flores died a day later.

The Japanese officer ordered the two Japanese enlisted men to lower the American flag and to raise the Japanese battle-flag. Once this task was completed, they spread the American flag across the ground, formed a circle around it and shined flashlights onto its surface, completing a pre-arranged signal to the overhead aircraft that they had captured the capital of Guam.

The actions of these two Chamorro men, non-citizens, unable to control their own destiny, subject to all of America's laws, volunteer members of an Insular Guard Force, sworn to defend America and Americans, paid a salary half of what an American sailor of the same rank or rating was paid, subject to the same rules and regulations as American sailors and Marines, unarmed and unafraid, displayed an unbridled loyalty to America and its flag that cost them their lives on that fateful day. They would not be alone. They would be followed by many, many more. Although they were held captive for thirty-one months, most Chamorros admirably adhered to an innate sense of patriotism in support of a country that had abandoned them in their darkest hours.

The United States Navy awarded citations to Angel Flores and Vincente Chargualaf on 22 May 1978. It was Armed Forces Day—thirty-four-years after the Americans liberated the island from the Japanese.

> And then there was this: On Guam, during a 2012 ceremony that consisted of an unveiling of old photographs of the WW II days: . . . *Hope* [the author of the article] *cited photos of Mr. and Mrs. Angel Leon Guerrero Flores and Mariquita Quitugua Flores. Angel Flores, according to Cristobal, died at the age of 31 at the hands of a Japanese solder* [naval-infantry] *after refusing to lower a U.S. flag and replace it with the Japanese flag.*
>
> 26 October 2012, Marianas Variety [MV Guam News]

Thus is the opening chapter of the lives of a society of captives in their own homeland and of their loyalty to America and all that America stood for in a world of churning violence. While meatless Tuesdays, gasoline and sugar rationing, tin can and war bond drives were common to Americans on the mainland, all Chamorros of Guam, like many of the men of the mainland who were marching off to war, began paying the price of liberty with their very lives.

The Chamorro of Guam, unknown, unseen, and unheard, boldly maintained the hope, dream, and promise of life, liberty, and the pursuit of happiness in an American land far from the shores of mainland America. They never lost hope and faith in the America they loved. They held to a firm belief that America and its people would not further abandon them. In faith, in hope, in dreams, and in song, they prayed for America's return to Guam.

These are the men and women on an island in the Pacific, before, during, and after the Japanese occupation of their island—performing documented and undocumented feats of unbelievable bravery and downright audacity. They often faced death but never dishonor. Some have been briefly recognized, while most others have not. A few performed feats of bravery which will forever be sealed in the shadows of history. Some are well known but not widely disseminated. Some had choices—others did not. Some were brutally slain by their captors for their loyalty to America, and some were slain for no reason at all. They are part of America's greatest generation. Many are already gone from this world—all are waiting to be recognized.

BACKGROUND

The following contains facts, opinions, and beliefs as revealed via research:

After two days of bombing and strafing military and civilian targets, in the pre-dawn early morning on 10 December, between 400 and 500 Japanese Naval Infantry (Japanese Marines, or *Rikusentai)* had landed at Dungas Beach north of Agana around 0330. Once ashore, they moved quickly in the direction of Agana. A small number of American sailors, most unarmed, a few Marines, and the Chamorro Insular Guard Force waited near the governor's house in the Plaza de España. This would be the only organized defense by force of arms against the Japanese ground invasion of Guam. For some strange, unknown reason, the governor had instructed that only Chamorros of the Insular Force would man the Lewis Guns (.30 caliber machine guns), further, his instructions were to fire on the Japanese for about twenty minutes, and then to cease fire and surrender, according to a diary kept by William Johnston. The military governor had already instructed the senior staff and commanding officers that he would surrender. He knew, or felt, that there was no hope of repelling the invaders, and no relief or support was on the way. Only a few knew the facts. None were Chamorro who made up over ninety percent of the population of Guam in 1941.

As Japan bombed Pearl Harbor and Japanese forces stormed across the Pacific and Southeast Asia in early December 1941, the people of Guam, and the United States military forces assigned to defend them, were the first Americans to fall under control of Japan. In other places, outnumbered and overwhelmed, Hong Kong resisted until Christmas Day. Wake Island's fighting Marines (assisted by a few Chamorros from Guam) resisted until 23 December. Though not outnumbered, but definitely out-maneuvered, the British at Singapore held out until 15 February 1942. In the Philippines, though outnumbering the invaders, but not out-fighting them, Generals MacArthur and Wainwright's forces fought delaying actions until May 1942. Even the Dutch East Indies (Indonesia) resisted until 9 March 1942. However—Guam fell on 10 December, a couple of days after the bombing of Pearl Harbor, and just a couple of hours after the Japanese landed their invasion forces on the island. Unlike the Marines of Wake and Midway Islands, the Marines assigned to defend Guam, stationed at Marine Barracks, Guam, complying with the governor's order, offered no resistance, no defense against the Japanese ground forces, other than scattered, unorganized skirmishes. Those Marines were angry, very angry at the governor and his order to surrender. They wanted to fight. But there were no plans to defend Guam, and almost everyone knew it. That is except the Guamanian people, the Chamorros.

Guam's Insular Force composed of mostly native Chamorros, along with a handful of Marines and sailors of the governor's staff, offered the only somewhat *organized* armed overt defiance toward the Japanese during the early morning invasion. Only at Plaza de España was there *organized* armed resistance to the invading Japanese Army and Naval Infantry, not at the Marine Barracks, not at the naval base, not anywhere else on the island. There were no sandbag emplacements. No trenches or foxholes. No barbed wire, established fields of fire, final protective fire lines, nothing that would resemble a prepared defense. It lasted only a short time. Then, during the brutal occupation that followed, native Guamanians—the Chamorros, suffered agonizingly under Japanese rule. America either forgot about them or never knew of them.

What is Insular? The dictionary definition states:

* Relating to, or constituting an island.
* Living or located on an island.
* Suggestive of the isolated life of an island.
* Circumscribed and detached in outlook and experience; narrow or provincial.

Actually it's more than that. An Insular Force or Insular Guard is also people. Guam's Insular Force was only a small group compared to the insular forces in the Philippines and Puerto Rico. After the end of the Spanish-American War, the U.S. Navy in the Philippines, Guam, and Puerto Rico used the men from the local population to assist them in the management of civil government affairs. The Navy called them their *Insular* Force. Insular meaning concerned only with local (isolated) matters. They were used much like the natives/citizens in the areas of the Banana Wars in the Caribbean and Central America. They assisted the Navy in their civil (and in some cases, military) duties.

> ***The Insular Patrol Force came into* [formal] *being on 5 April 1901. President William McKinley formalized an ad hoc arrangement already informally in place in the Philippines and Guam, by formally creating the Insular Force of the U.S. Navy, authorizing the Secretary of the Navy to enlist up to 500 natives of Guam and the Philippines. The force was unique, in that the men enlisted to serve only in their home areas, "to which they were particularly adapted or suited." They served on some ships, but only when that ship was assigned to that local command area. The force grew slowly, in part owing to the drawdown of forces after the Philippine Insurrection ended, but by 1906 there were 285 Filipinos and 28 Chamorros from Guam in the Insular Force.***
>
> The Insular Force: Adapting to Local Conditions,
> US Naval History Blog.

Naval Insular Forces received military training, usually conducted by Marines; they were guards in certain situations, they performed ceremonial duties, they were policemen, and there was even an Insular Band. Their actual duties were established by the Naval Governor. For a time in the early 1900s, young able-bodied men were drafted into the Insular Force. All young men had to serve. In the 1930s they became a purely voluntary group. Then, in 1940, as war-talk intensified, the Insular Force was dramatically increased. They swore an oath, signed enlistment papers, and were paid by the United States government. Of course, their pay was one-half the pay of a sailor or Marine of the same grade. Clearly, they were not equal in status.

Guam Chamorro Insular Forces march in review, circa 1938 or '39
Image from University of Guam, MARC files.

This Insular Force would stand front and center before the war, at the opening of hostilities at the beginning of the war, and in the aftermath of the war during and after the liberation of Guam by the American forces. It would assume several titles, Insular Patrol, Insular Force, Insular Police, Chamorro Combat Patrol, and others. In each case, its composition is primarily Chamorro males. But it is important to realize that there were others, other Chamorros who risked their lives and the lives of their families defending America and American ideals, under exceptionally dangerous conditions, that were not part of the Insular Force.

Guam and its people had been *set-up* by the United States to be expendable. The Washington Naval Conference was really a disarmament conference in disguise. It had been called by President Warren Harding, conducted in Washington, D.C., between 12 November 1921 and 6 February 1922, with nine nations participating—the United States, Japan, China, France, Britain, Italy, Belgium, Netherlands, and Portugal—regarding interests in the Pacific Ocean and East Asia. The Conference was conducted outside the auspices of the League of Nations, and its primary focus was to limit construction of navy ships and naval armaments. Some of the participants had to actually cease construction of ships in order to comply with the provisions of the treaty. Part of its provisions would establish a Western Pacific zone of islands and waters free of military and naval build-up. It was based on the belief that all nations could agree and actually cease, or prevent any arms race by dismantling the various existing navies' man-of-war vessels and weapons. The idea was to make all nations equal so one could not dominate the other. Great idea *if* everyone complies. The agreement also stipulated that the United States and Japan would not fortify islands in the Western Pacific.

As a result of the Treaty of Paris ending World War I, Japan had acquired all islands previously occupied by Germany, before losing the Great War. The Japanese acquired numerous Pacific islands during and after the war. The United States had, many years earlier, acquired and occupied Guam, Hawaii, and the Philippines in the Pacific.

The United States maintained allegiance to the provisions of the agreement while Japan ignored it. In 1936, Japan formally withdrew from the treaty and banned all westerners from many of its islands as its military build-up began in earnest. There is a popular belief among some historians that the famous secret mission of Marine Lieutenant Colonel Earl Hancock "Pete" Ellis was conducted to look for Japanese fortifications that would have been in violation of this agreement. Not so. Ellis departed on his mission on 4 May 1921, and died on 12 May 1923. He departed before the Washington Naval Conference convened and died just fifteen months after it concluded. Ellis was concerned with the *intentions* and *attitudes* of the Japanese whom he believed were destined to conduct war with the United States, and he wanted to observe and mark littoral features for possible amphibious landings by American Marines, on Japanese held islands, in case of war with Japan. Ellis and Marine Commandant John Archer Lejeune envisioned strong defense battalions of Marines guarding America's frontier islands, and a strong amphibious assault force of Marines to attack and capture the Japanese islands once war came. They considered war with Japan to be a foregone fact—and that was in 1921. (See *A Marine Called Gabe.*)

There were some feeble attempts to enhance the ability to defend Guam, but the U.S. Congress disapproved all request from the Navy Department until 1941 when a construction contract was awarded to improve *existing* facilities on Guam. Of worthy note is the fact that the Great Economic Depression began in the fall of 1929 and lasted through most all of the 1930s. Like most of the world economies, the United States was deeply affected by the sudden, swift, lengthy economic downturn. It severely limited military spending.

Pete Ellis did have an earlier connection to Guam. Then, Captain Ellis, under orders that were based on a special assignment established by the Joint Army/Navy Board to study the defense of Guam in 1914, as ordered, reported to Guam. Since war had broken out in Europe, both German and Japanese warships had been observed in the waters around Guam, and considering Guam's proximity to the other islands of the Marianas controlled by Germany, there was a concern for the security of this new American possession in the far Western Pacific. After Ellis arrived, he reported to then governor-designate Captain William J. Maxwell, U.S. Navy, and was assigned several duties such as the governor's secretary and aide-de-camp, along with duties as the chief of police, registrar of the civil government, and intelligence officer.

It was also during this period, while his fellow Marines were occupying the Mexican city of Vera Cruz, when Pete Ellis's health began to deteriorate. Many historians and military history buffs believe that this was the beginning of a long slide toward his premature death in 1923. Interestingly, Ellis was on Guam as the first shot was fired by Americans in World War I. It was a U.S. Marine who fired the first shot at Germans in World War I only two hours after President Wilson signed the Declaration of War document: On 7 April 1917, Corporal Michael B. Chockie, USMC, fired across the bow of the SMS *Cormoran*, a small German man-of-war held captive in Apra Harbor, Guam. That ship is still at the bottom of Apra Harbor.

The results of the Washington Naval Conference actually left the American island of Guam totally defenseless and led to the easy invasion and occupation of Guam by the Japanese. The Navy was forced to remove previously installed coastal artillery from the island and recall a Marine aviation unit. Japan fortified her islands, while America abided by the treaty. American naval power in the Guam portion of the Western Pacific was no match to the Japanese naval power. And, the Congress of the United States was aware of it. Washington didn't want to antagonize our *friends* the Japanese.

However, one interesting positive result ensued from the Washington Naval Conference—it unintentionally gave us our first aircraft carriers. Although the USS *Langley* was the first American aircraft carrier, which was constructed over the hull of a converted collier (a coaling ship), the USS *Jupiter* in 1920, the Washington Naval Treaty caused the cancellation of two partially built battle-cruisers *Lexington* and *Saratoga.* Their hulls were then converted to the aircraft carriers CV-2 and CV-3. *Langley* was CV-1. In those days, the battleship and the battle-cruiser were the dreadnaughts of the oceans of the world. Not much thought was devoted to the newfangled aircraft carrier, and very little thought given to the submarine. To the admirals, battlewagons were the dominant kings of the seas. Besides, there weren't many aircraft carriers around at that time, and many American admirals questioned the wisdom of having them at all.

In World War I, the Navy explored the use of aviation, both land-based and the envisioned ship-based airplane. However, the Navy came perilously close to abolishing its own fledgling aviation program in 1919 when a famous (or infamous) comment made by William S. Benson, our first Chief of Naval Operations, became public. Benson said to the world that he could not "*...conceive of any use the fleet will ever have for aviation,*" and he set about to abolish the Navy's new-fangled aviation arm. It was the timely assistance and intervention of the Assistant Secretary of the Navy, Franklin D. Roosevelt, who reversed the decision because he believed naval aviation might someday be "the principle factor" at sea, with missions to protect its own fleet, bomb enemy warships, scout enemy fleets, and map enemy mine-fields. No wonder that particular Navy Secretary would become President of the United States one day. He had vision.

In addition, at that time, somewhat akin to our modern times, there existed within some significant segments of the population this naive belief that if the United States disarmed, the other nations would follow suit. Such thinking made great nations weak and weak nations more powerful. Unpreparedness for war is a sign of a weak nation. Unpreparedness for any war is the sign of a confused nation, and ignorance of the potential for wars is also a sign of a confused nation. Its leaders presume to read the minds of potential enemies. If that confused or unprepared nation is insignificant on the world stage, it's possible to get away with it. Other nations will ignore you. But, if that nation is front and center on the world stage, it's flirting with disaster. Great nations, great armies, and great leaders must, in fact, lead, or they will be led by others. The great World War II General George Patton said it most simply—"lead, follow, or get the hell outta the way." The United States chose to get outta the way—Guam was on its own.

Guam is the largest island in the Micronesia group of islands in the Western Pacific. It is at the southernmost tip of the Marianas, with a modern (2010) population of around 161,000 people, thirty-seven percent being Chamorro. Today, the island is an organized, unincorporated territory of the United States. The native people, the Chamorro, have occupied Guam for close to 3,500 years. The first foreign controlling occupants were the Spanish, arriving to colonize in 1668. Americans occupied and controlled Guam after the Spanish-American War in 1898. The Japanese seized and occupied Guam in December 1941. Thirty-one agonizing months later, they were driven out, captured, or killed by the violent American invasion in July 1944. Almost as a sign of an apology, in 1950, all citizen-residents of Guam were made United States citizens, with partial citizenship rights, revealed in this novel. Finally!

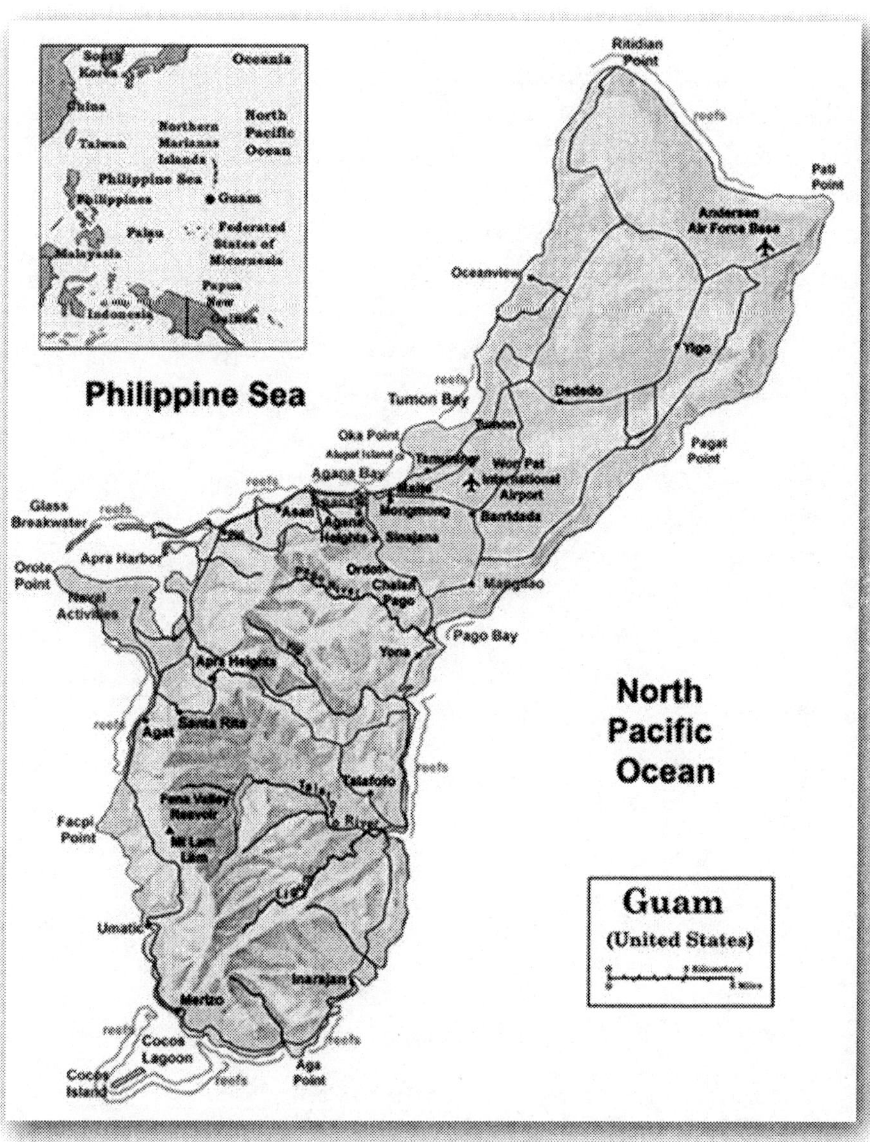

Guam is a beautiful, peanut shaped, tropical island four to twelve miles wide and approximately thirty to thirty-five miles long, surrounded by colorful coral reefs, teeming with marine life. It's mountainous in the southern part of the island and has a somewhat dense and very lush tropical jungle inland with mangroves along some of its coastline. There are numerous white sandy beaches in several areas and stark limestone cliffs dropping to the sea mostly in the north. It is a place on earth where one can choose to escape from the modern world and immerse one's self in a time and place hundreds of years and thousands of miles away from the hectic surroundings of modern, complex, fast-moving society. And, that can be done in a short drive. One might remark that Guam has it all.

It has luxury hotels, high-end shopping plazas and stores, a vivid nightlife, and some of the best dining establishments in the world. It also has more mom and pop merchants than big-box stores, more local eating joints than chains, and a local culture that is appealing for the simple pleasures of life. It possesses awesome scenery, deep, thick jungles, almost inaccessible beach coves, rivers, ancient structures and a people called Chamorro. It is a far-away slice of America that still beckons. Still calls.

Indeed, it is a far off slice of America no longer surrounded by Japanese held islands, but rather surrounded by American held islands. It is a slice of America, held at arm's-length by the government of mainland America.

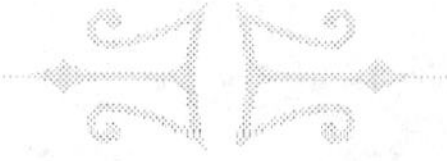

THE CHAMORRO

The following contains factual data, assumptions based on conversations with individual Chamorros on Guam and intensive reading of all listed reference material:

The native population of Guam and indeed much of Micronesia, especially the Mariana Islands, originally came from Southeast Asia around the time the Egyptians were building the pyramids. They are most closely related to other Austronesian-speaking natives in the Philippines and Taiwan, as well as the Caroline Islands i.e., the many languages of Southeast Asia and the islands of the Pacific. The Chamorro people had been in the Marianas a long time before Ferdinand Magellan, a Portuguese explorer sailing for the Holy Roman Emperor King Charles I of Spain, accidently bumped into Guam.

The Chamorros of the Marianas had their own unique language, customs, hierarchy, societal structure, and traditions dating back thousands of years. Then the Spanish came. Spain ruled. Guam changed. Chamorro culture has, over the past 300 years, acquired noticeable influences from the Spanish, American, Filipino, and Japanese immigrant populations, as well as the presence of fellow Oceanic (mostly Micronesian) group populations. After the defeat of the Spanish in the Spanish-American War, Spain sold the other Mariana Islands to Germany. The United States didn't want them. The influence from the Germans living on the islands up until 1918 is evident primarily in the Northern Marianas and today is revealed only in the form of certain given names and family surnames and a few blue eyes in the former German colonies.

The people of Guam are more supportive of American standards and ideals than many of those living in the fifty States are aware of. It is especially true of the American military:

> *The influence of the American military on the Guamanians has been nothing short of amazing, or perhaps another word would be—phenomenal. The military enlistment rates are higher in the Marianas than in any other place in the Western Hemisphere. On Guam, the enlistment rate in the American military is around 14 per 10,000; by contrast, the State of Montana, which has the highest per capita enlistment, has a rate just half that, with approximately 8 people per 10,000.*
>
> Guampedia

Yet, a dichotomy does exist: Not too long ago, a young American soldier arrived home to Guam from one of our most recent wars in a distant foreign land. He arrived in a wooden casket, draped with an American flag. A guard of honor escorted his remains, and local dignitaries honored his return home, arriving at the airport in a dignified, appropriate manner that all such military war casualties deserve. He had served his country honorably and given his life, not only defending America, but also in giving the people in that foreign land where he died the right of all free people to choose their own destiny. The right to vote for their leaders, the right to own property, the right to prosper by the sweat of their own brow, the right to receive benefits from the government that is imposing taxation upon its citizens, and the right to disallow their government to take away their personal property without due process of law. These are the rights that young soldier fought and died for. Rights he could not have in his own country, the United States of America—as long as he lived on Guam. Before this young man entered the military service of his country, and had he lived to return as a military veteran, he was and would have been ineligible to vote for his commander-in-chief, the President of the United States, the person who sent him to that war. He would be required to pay taxes but would not receive the full benefits of that taxation. For example, he would pay tax for the Affordable Care Act but would not be eligible for its benefits **(see the following website- www.com.gov/CCIIO/Resources/Letters/Download/Letter...) for clarification.**

And, chances are that the land he was born on, the land his parents and grandparents owned and lived on, at one time had been much larger; now, portions of that land have been seized by the United States government and compensation was, either never paid or grossly underpaid for that seizure. Compounding this unjust situation, his dad is a military retiree from the United States Army and also is not entitled to all military veterans benefits.

Where this young soldier is buried, and where his father lives, American flags fly from masts and standards throughout the land, *The Star Spangled Banner* is sung with more gusto than at an Irvin Berlin concert on the 4th of July, and pride for America is firmly rooted in the heart and mind of every living soul. Indeed, here the World War II population, those Tom Brokaw forgot to write about in his book *The Greatest Generation,* the grandparents of this young soldier, were abandoned by their government to face imprisonment, brutality, torture, and attempted extermination by the forces of the Empire of Japan during thirty-one months of agony—from December 1941 to July 1944. They too are *The Greatest Generation*. Brokaw, like most Americans, simply didn't know.

Yet, in spite of the suffering of this population, their love and pride in America knows no bounds. And even though limited U.S. citizenship was granted this population by the U.S. Congress after the war, no holocaust museum has ever been dedicated to the remembrance of their suffering and attempted extermination. Full citizenship rights have never been granted to these Americans, Congress could take away the citizenship of this entire population literally with the stroke of a pen. They have all the requirements and demands of citizenship, but not all of the rights of, and privileges of, citizenship.

Yet, they continue to march to the sound of the guns when America calls. They wear their "veteran" caps or display their "veteran" automobile tags as badges of honor, with pride, and they stand proudly with infectious dignity when *Old Glory* marches by during their Liberation Day parade on 21 July. That is the day America's mighty amphibious fleet arrived to drive the Japanese from the only heavily populated, seized, and occupied American land during the Second World War. They *liberated* these previously abandoned Americans who were the last innocent civilians caught between opposing military forces on American soil since America's Civil War.

As this novel was being written, we drove along Marine Corps Drive, past preserved beaches where unopposed Japanese forces came ashore to enslave Guam's American population, and thirty-one agonizing, brutal months later, America's military and naval might swept ashore, opposed by fanatical Japanese defenders, to *liberate* that American population. Later we drove along Army Highway and turn again onto Vietnam Veterans Memorial Highway toward a valley called Manenggon, where more than 8,000 men, women, and children were driven like cattle to be confined in a killing field enclave awaiting their fate. Only the rapid advance of American liberating forces prevented the implementation of a Japanese-style—*final solution.*

This is Guam, America's far-western outpost, occupied by the guardians of the outer limits on America's frontier. The first to see the sun rise over American soil are *the people of Guam.* As recently deceased Brigadier General Vicente "Ben" Blaz, USMC (Ret) once told a session of the U.S. Congress about the people of Guam, *"equal in war, unequal in peace."* That statement appropriately describes these American military veterans and retired military, residing here—being short-changed. They do *not* have the same citizenship and veterans benefits as American military veterans in the fifty States.

This is an American national disgrace, a national *shame*, that the American people should require correcting.

The Chamorros were, and still are, fiercely loyal to the United States. They endured with resentment the occupation by Japan as they protected the six hiding sailors, especially the sailor George Tweed, with their lives against the attempts of the Japanese authorities to find and kill him. That is a documented fact.

Another little known fact about the Chamorro of Guam during World War II, are the previously mentioned Chamorros from Guam who worked for Pan American Airways on Wake Island in 1941. Following the attack by the Japanese, the Pan Am employees were to be evacuated along with the passengers of a Pan Am Clipper flying boat, on its way to the Orient that had turned around, returning to Wake, and had survived the first Japanese attack on Wake unscathed. The Chamorro workers for Pan American Airlines were initially allowed to board that get-away plane. Then they were involuntarily removed; in short, they were kicked off the airplane to make room for lighter skinned people. They were left behind and, therefore, volunteered to assist the Marines defending the island. Major James P.S. Devereux, the Marine commander, put rifles in their hands and ammunition in their pockets and said, "Go kill Japs." They fell with a rifle in their hands. Ten Chamorro civilians were killed in action by the Japanese while fighting for the Marines on Wake Island. They were fighting alongside American Marines. Those who survived were taken as prisoners of war to Japan, along with the Marines and other civilian construction workers, for the duration of the war. Few writers of military history present that fact.

The Japanese retained some civilian workers to be used as slave labor on Wake Island. As American forces closed in on Wake in 1943, the Japanese commander, Japanese Rear Admiral Shigematsu Sakaibara, ordered the execution of all civilian construction workers. He marched them to the isolated tip of one of the islands, blindfolded them and machine-gunned them to death. All, except one man who survived. That unknown man marked a coral rock, still there today, carving the message ***98 US PW 5-10-43*** near where the victims had been hastily buried in a mass grave. This unknown

American was soon recaptured and beheaded. Documents found on Wake Island, at the surrender of the Japanese garrison, document that fact. That Japanese officer, who ordered the mass murder and personally beheaded the surviving construction worker was tried, convicted, and hanged by the Americans in 1947 on Guam. Much of the evidence against the admiral came from some of his own officers who had left notes objecting to the order to murder the civilian captives.

None of the society of captives on Guam knew of the murder of the construction workers on Wake Island. Since 10 December 1941, Guam was hidden from the world—they were alone. It was as if a curtain had been drawn around Guam, leaving it isolated, completely alone in the vast Pacific Ocean owned by Japan. They had to somehow survive. They would remain on their own until July 1944—thirty-one brutal, terrorizing months later.

What is bewildering is why the OSS (Office of Strategic Services) never contacted the very pro-American Chamorro of Guam. They conducted secret submarine contacts with friendly forces, imported secret radio equipment for receiving and transmitting communications with Allied Headquarters in the Philippines, Indochina, and China, organized and equipped resistance elements, and conducted a host of other secret contacts with anti-Japanese elements; yet no *one*, no-*thing*, ever *attempted* to contact the Guamanian people, the Chamorro of Guam, throughout the entire Japanese occupation. Why?

SGAMBE

The following contains factual data revealed by research:

Most events in history have a long trail from their origin to the actual events or person who made a unique contribution to the annals of history. One of our stories begins in Italy long before the turn of the 20th century. The region of Calabria in Italy is part of the geographic toe of the Italian boot. It is a mostly mountainous region and the closest part of Italy to the island of Sicily. Though mountainous, for the most part, it is actually an agricultural region in the valleys at the bottom of the mountains. It has a perfect climate for growing things, cold snowy winters and warm dry summers. Because of its climate, citrus fruit orchards dominate the lower valleys between the mountains.

Giuseppi Marcello Sgambelluri was born in the village of Siderno di Marina, a town on the coast in the Calabria Region of Italy. This stout, adventurous Italian, like many of his fellow citizens at that time, immigrated to the United States in the late 1800s, residing initially in Albany, New York, and finally settling in Endicott, New York. He worked at the Endicott-Johnson shoe factory in the tannery section. At the outbreak of the Spanish-American War, out of loyalty to his new country, he enlisted in the U.S. Navy, completed boot camp at Mare Island, California, and ultimately sailed to take part in the occupation of the newly acquired island of Guam in the far Western Pacific.

> He loved the island and its people, the Chamorro. He was still on the island in 1903 when Lieutenant Commander William Sewell, the third American Governor of Guam, made the first of many future attempts to diminish the Spanish influence and elevate the American influence on Guam. In his efforts to *Americanize* the island population, Spanish music was his first target. He ordered, among other things that *They [Chamorros] are to learn to read music . . . and play (band) instruments instead of maracas, mandolins, castanets and Spanish guitars.*
>
> Guampedia: Guam Music

The governor's order applied to all children on Guam between the ages of eight and fourteen while they were attending school. The curriculum had a long-range plan. It was envisioned to become popular among the young people so as to eventually replace the Spanish influence in music. At about the same time, U.S. Navy men stationed on the island also formed a band to play American style music. Within that Navy band was Marcello Giuseppe Sgambelluri. He was to have a long-lasting, positive influence on the people, culture, and history of Guam that continues to exist today.

> *Sgambelluri was sent to Mare Island, California to procure instruments for the band and brought back saxophones, trumpets, tubas, trombones, coronets, clarinets, flutes and the like. He gave lessons to students twice a day. The first concert by the native Chamorro brass band was held in the kiosk in the Plaza de España with Governor Sewell and his entire staff in attendance.*
>
> Guampedia.com: Band Ensembles

After serving his time in the Navy, he took his release from naval service, choosing to remain in the new American territory of Guam, settling down and marrying a young Chamorro lady by the name of Joaquina Deza Camacho. Their union produced nine children. One of the boys was born on 2 July 1912. They named him Adolfo Camacho Sgambelluri. They called him Sgambe.

As a young man, Sgambe attended public school. The Collins School was first established in the early 1920s by Doctor Tom Collins. He was brought to Guam by U.S. Navy Captain Adelbert Althouse, then the Governor of Guam. Collins made fundamental sweeping changes in the education system.

> *The nature of the changes was dramatic. Ten new schools were added between 1922 and 1926 and enrollment increased by 800 to 2,837. Teachers increased in number from twenty-nine to 108 and approximately 25 percent of all educational expenditures were in education in comparison to the 10- to 20-percent figure of the first two decades.*
>
> Guampedia: Education During the U.S. Naval Era

Sgambe was to benefit from those changes. After attending the Collins School, young men often attended the Guam Institute, which was located in the Jose P. Lujan House. Sgambe graduated school at the age of seventeen.

Jose Lujan, a Chamorro, built the two-story house with the idea of renting it out to U.S. Naval officers, making some good money. In fact, some naval officers were his first occupants, after he and his wife moved out. But, a school was needed, and Jose provided it. Some historical writings suggest that it was possibly the first house on Guam with indoor plumbing.

> *For a long period of this building's life it* [Lujan House] *housed the Guam Institute, one of the first private schools during Guam's Naval Era, run by Nieves Flores. Archbishop Felixberto Flores (the first Chamorro archbishop), the first Chamorro Chief Judge Joaquin Perez, Governor Ricardo Bordallo, and other prominent local figures were all students at this school.*
>
> Guampedia: Lujan House

Sgambe joined the Guam (Insular) Police in 1933 and remained with the police department until 1950, even though the Japanese occupied Guam for nearly thirty-two months. After the war, he was the first Guamanian to attend the famed FBI National Academy at Quantico, Virginia. Attending the FBI National Academy requires an extensive background check. Only a highly select few may traverse its halls aboard the Marine base at Quantico. After his FBI training, he was appointed Immigration Inspector and Acting Assistant Chief of Port Security. Eventually, he rose to be the Chief of Customs and Quarantine in 1955. He held that position until retiring in 1971.

But the true test for Sgambe came during World War II. When almost all Chamorro civil servants were called back into service by the conquering Japanese authorities, Sgambe went back to work at the police department. The broad term we would use today to describe Sgambe would be *double-agent* or *undercover agent*, a role he would assume, and one that would consume him during the Japanese occupation. His first self-imposed responsibility was to safeguard as many Guamanians as possible from death or torture by the Japanese authorities, and he had to do that without compromising his role as "policeman" *for* the Japanese occupiers.

To safeguard his activities, he set up a system of clandestine contacts with only a select number of people whom he trusted explicitly; most were his very close friends, and he chose to pass critical information to only them about pending Japanese activities. Through this system, no one else knew anything about Sgambe, except that he was nothing more than a Japanese controlled "flunky." Some of his "friends," indeed most of the Chamorro population of Guam, despised him. He carried that burden with him while feeding information to the proper sources to protect his people of Guam. But only that small few knew Sgambe's true role.

Indeed, it was a small few. One was Mrs. Agueda Johnston, another was Joaquin Limtiaco, a third was Tomas "Tommy" Tanaka, and there was Jose Flores—and they told no one else. It was the only way he and his extended family could survive. However, sometimes, when opportunity and timeliness merged, when he had no other choice, he passed vital and timely information to others outside his inner circle that he also felt a loyalty to and trusted implicitly, but he always brought Agueda and Joaquin, and sometimes Tommy and Jose, into the circle of clandestine information flow. All along, he was a loyal American, appearing to work for the Japanese, saving Chamorro lives. In order to do what he was doing, in order to protect the people of Guam, he had to appear loyal to the Japs. Any suspicion of disloyalty would mean his instant death and that of his family. If his activities had been terminated, many more Chamorros would have been brutalized, tortured, or killed. In this capacity, he witnessed many things he could not control. These *things* would weigh heavily on him all his life.

In his book *An Island In Agony*, author Tony Palomo interviews and writes of Adolfo Sgambelluri (and others), and in one section he allows Sgambe to tell his story of the capture and execution of three American sailors. I will not repeat the words of Sgambe contained in that book, nor will I repeat the narrative of that author. Rather, in this novel, I will re-describe the events simply to make an effort, a noble effort, to describe how he must have *felt*, how he might have *acted*, and what he must have *thought* during and after this horrific mind-numbing ordeal.

WAR COMES

The following contains a mix of researched, developed, factual data, and conjured conversations designed to support the facts and to provide a story flow:

Tension mounted as the stale, dank air grew warmer. For a Monday morning, it was unusually quiet. Faces revealed anxiety as the group of armed men milled around, some in small clusters, talking quietly. Anticipation tugged at reason. Fear was controlled by a universal sense of camaraderie with a tinge of honor and duty thrown in, plus an occasional off-colored joke that helped relieve the uneasiness. Soon, as expected, footsteps echoed across the Plaza as the gathering of men began to fall into a loose semblance of a military formation as if practiced to perfection over a protracted period of time. As the echo of footsteps ceased, they came to the position of attention without command.

"Okay, men. Stand at Ease! Now listen up. Hear this good! This morning, the Japs have bombed our naval base at Pearl Harbor, in Hawaii Territory. I'm not going to pull any punches with you. You all know, we're a small island surrounded by Jap islands. We will probably be next. Hell, you can bank on it. You men with families, I want you to take off and get them settled safely. If you want to return to help out preparing to defend the island, meet up here in two hours. If you want to remain with your family, I understand. You're a quasi-military guard force. You are not Marines. It looks like we're at war with the Japs. Marines and sailors are expected to defend the island. You are not expected to fight Japs. I'm just asking that you help with the immediate preparedness for defense against air attack. Then, follow your conscience. Protect your families. Now hurry. You know what to do. We don't have a lot of time."

Marine Captain Charles Todd, the appointed chief of police was addressing his "police force," also called the Guam Insular Patrol, or Insular Police, made up of Marines, sailors, and local Chamorros, Guam's native population.

The news was not unexpected. The military governor of the island had been ordered to destroy all classified material on 4 December. And, Japanese photo recon aircraft had been spotted flying over the island for weeks in the form of "friendly" flyovers from Japanese island locations to the north of Guam. The destruction of classified material, by burning, had been completed by 6 December. Things had been tense. Almost two months earlier, the military governor of the island, U.S. Navy Captain George McMillin, ordered all military dependents and all U.S. construction workers off the island. On 17 October, the dependents of the American military personnel on the island, minus Mrs. Ruby Hellmers, one very pregnant navy wife who had been ordered to remain in the Navy hospital on the island, were evacuated to the United States by the Navy transport USS *Henderson.* They were followed a few days later by most all of the 1,000 construction workers who had been sent to improve military facilities. Those improvements were *a bit late.*

"Questions?" the captain asked.

"Captain, Sir."

"Yeah Sgambe?"

"Sir, word around the island is that Jap spies are being transported from Saipan, as we speak, to slip onto the island. I think the word's good. It's going to happen. What do you want us to do about that?"

"I'll get to that in just a few. Right now, you stay here, Sgambe. You two, Roberto and Taitano, the rest of you, dismissed! Go! Take care of your families."

The men broke ranks and stood talking among themselves for a few seconds, and suddenly, roughly half of the twenty-eight men began to walk or run in different directions. The other half reformed their ranks.

The captain looked a bit perplexed. "All right, you people, I still see a lot of married folks out there. I said git! Now move it!"

"All due respect, Sir, one of the Chamorros, Ramon Camacho, replied, "We just worked it out. Our families will be alerted by others. Then, the men will come back here in two hours. All we gotta do sir, is git them outta town. Git into the countryside, the jungle, caves, ranches, small villages, anywhere but here. Hide our families. Then, we can fight Japs."

"I told you men, you're civil policemen. I want you. . ."

Again, Ramon spoke, interrupting the captain, "Please, Sir, Captain, we are Chamorros, yes, but we swore an oath, an allegiance to the United States, an allegiance to the Marines also. When those Japs bombed your Pearl Harbor, we became *Marines*. If this is war. . ." he paused as in deep fleeting thought, "We fight beside you, Sir!"

Captain Todd's puzzled appearance instantly transformed into a look of pride standing before his small police force. "All right people, give me a minute to talk to the governor."

He walked a few steps to a field phone, a left-over from The Great War, placing the receiver to his ear and holding it between his head and shoulder; he spun the crank to activate a similar phone on the duty desk in the governor's office. After a few seconds, he spoke, "Let me talk to the captain."

After another short pause, he spoke again, "Sir, the Chamorros will defend the island with us." There was another extended pause, "When shall I place all the Japanese nationals in the jail?"

The response could not be heard.

"Yes sir. Wilco!"

Again, a slight pause, listening, turning slightly, and glancing at his small band of locals still in formation, he continued, "Consider it done, Sir. Out!"

After the brief conversation, he placed the receiver back in the box and again slowly turned to face the men still in formation, now standing at attention.

It was 0800 on 8 December 1941. At about 0545 that morning, Governor McMillin had been informed of the Japanese air raid on the U.S. Navy base on the Territory of Hawaii. He immediately informed his staff officers and the Marine Barracks. He had remained in his office, going over the plans, such as they were. A Navy commander and a chief petty officer were reviewing a map of Guam that lay atop a table next to the duty desk. To the man, the earlier expectation had suddenly become reality.

"The rest of you men, get out there and evacuate as many people as possible from Agana. I think bombs will start falling very soon, and we need to have everyone in protective positions." Todd looked sternly at his mixed force of sailors, Chamorros, and Marines. "We are at war, men. Let's act like it." He paused, looking with pride at his band of Chamorros. "Okay, get on it. Meet back here at 1500. Dismissed!"

The men began to walk away, in different directions, moving toward previously discussed locations to prepare the local population for protection from attacking aircraft and worse—attacking Japanese ground forces.

Three men remained in the plaza standing beside the Marine captain, and a few other Marines and a Navy chief petty officer stood nearby. "Sgambe, I want you and the two Juan's, Roberto and Taitano, to git out there and round up every Jap on the island and lock 'em up. Put 'em all in jail. Got me?"

"Yes Sir! Consider it done," Sgambe replied. "And, what you want me to do with the prisoners we got in there now?"

"Turn 'em loose."

"Aye, Sir!" Sgambe smiled, saluted, and departed with his two cohorts.

As the three Chamorros began to walk from the plaza, the first of many explosions was heard in the distance. The men picked up their pace. The first bombs fell on Guam on 8 December, the day of the Feast of the Immaculate Conception. Guamanians were preparing for a traditional Catholic celebration including an outside parade. Hundreds of people would be outside or in church. Overhead, Japanese aircraft could be seen in the clear, almost cloudless morning sky. Sgambe glanced at his watch. It was 0827. War had arrived on Guam. Thirty-two months of Hell had begun.

"Let's split up. We'll get the job completed faster," (speaking Chamorro) Sgambe stated matter-of-factly.

As Japanese aircraft continued their unchallenged assault on the Marine Barracks, the Piti Naval Yards, the Pan American Hotel, the Standard Oil facilities, and the minesweeper USS *Penguin,* which carried the largest guns on Guam, Sgambe and his two companions started and completed their mission of confining Japanese citizens living on Guam. Based on the size of the jail and the number of Japanese nationals, they decided that only the men would be confined.

"I'd better call Captain Todd." (speaking Chamorro) Sgambe picked the telephone up and listened for an operator. Quickly, he realized that the phone was dead. He stopped off at a business that had a telephone and that phone too was dead. Later, he would discover that the lines had been cut. Someone on Guam had cut the telephone communications system. Messages by runner became the norm. The Chamorro population would learn of wars' arrival by a rain of death from the skies as bombing and strafing aircraft wearing the rising sun bore down on them.

He decided to complete their mission. They were polite but firm. Mostly, they simply ordered the Japanese in broken Japanese or Pidgin English to report to the jail. However, based on their prior intelligence gathering, there were a few whom they personally escorted to the lock-up.

"Mister Shinohara, Sir, I must ask that you accompany me to the jail. We are under attack by Japan, and I am sure you understand this necessity," Sgambe offered.

"Yes. I understand," Frank Shinohara replied.

In short order, the jail was full of Japanese residents of Guam, while surprised, but overjoyed previous residents of the jail were freed and ordered to go home and safeguard their families.

As the day progressed, the minesweeper USS *Penguin* was sunk after its gunners apparently shot down one Japanese aircraft. Another aircraft was hit and damaged. That aircraft was last seen trailing smoke, heading north rapidly, and losing altitude. Its loss was never confirmed. The two harbor patrol boats YP16 and YP17 were damaged and/or scuttled, thus eliminating all armed Navy surface vessels. All day, specific targets were hit by the attacking aircraft, as were targets of opportunity. Streets in Agana, military facilities, and any and everything came under falling bombs or strafing machine guns of the Japanese Empire. They even strafed villages of no military value. Eight or nine aircraft seemed to be in the skies, swarming like bees, all day long. Two of the first casualties on Guam were Chamorros working for American Airlines.

In the small isolated villages, Japanese aircraft would bear down on anything moving. Men, women, and children scurried about, looking for shelter, any shelter to escape the unchallenged rain of death from the skies. Casualties were mounting. Nerves were frayed. Families were torn apart. Fear and determination gripped the island. Some were in total panic mode, while others attempted to prepare for the expected invasion by Japanese forces.

"What will the Japs do to us?" was the most common question, and "Will the Americans send more Marines?" was the second question most often asked. "I don't know," was always the answer. But someone did know.

The Navy captain, who was also the appointed governor, did know. He was aware that there were no contingency plans to defend Guam. Only recently, in early 1941, had there been any second thoughts of defending the small, isolated Wake and Midway Islands. These islands were United States possessions. Thoughts of defending Guam were brief, but those thoughts quickly faded. Congress did not want to antagonize the Japanese.

Hawaii, Wake, and Guam were part of a string of refueling/rest areas for Pan American Airway's flights across the Pacific to the Philippines and sometimes China. Guam was the last stopover before Manila. Guam was also, in addition to being a refueling station, a naval resupply and equipment base. Plus it had a radio-relay station for wireless transmissions and an American telephone/telegraph cable relay station on the island for transmitting other forms of communication across the Pacific. The civil rationale of these radio locations was commerce, especially air travel, while the military concept was that Hawaii, Midway, Wake, and Guam also offered protection of sea lanes to the Orient, especially to the Philippines, by the United States Navy.

The governor knew what was expected of him in case of war with Japan; he was to burn everything and hightail it out of there. There was no help coming. That was the strategic plan from Washington. Never mind the 25,000 people of Guam living under America's jurisdiction and protection. Apparently, to the war planners, they were expendable pawns on the chess-board of war.

There had been considerable activity on and around Guam prior to the Japanese attack on Pearl Harbor. In November 1941, Japanese navy radio communication's traffic, monitored in Hawaii, the Philippines, and Dutch Harbor, Alaska, increased from locations in northern Japan. That told those who were doing the monitoring that a large number of warships were gathering and beginning to move northeast. Guam communications would have been aware of that event. They couldn't break the code, but they could monitor the traffic. Guam had been alerted early-on about the very real possibility of hostilities with Japan. They had evacuated dependents and construction workers, burned all classified documents, and the naval governor had held a meeting with senior naval officers regarding plans to surrender the island to the Japanese, *prior* to the Japanese attack on Pearl Harbor. Some of the information came from official sources, but a great deal of weight was the *Chamorro Telegraph* among Chamorros in Saipan, Tinian, and Rota, and those on Guam.

Naval Intelligence knew that two large fleets of Japanese ships were on the move from Japan, one toward the northeast (possibly toward Hawaii or the West Coast of the mainland United States) and the other south (possibly toward the Philippines or Dutch East Indies). They actually did not know their destination. That is until 6 December when the following message was deciphered at Dutch Harbor:

> *Nagumo's ships (flagship Akagi) had reached a point (on December 6, 1941, Hawaiian time) about 600 miles north and slightly west of the island of Oahu, in Hawaii Territory. The skies were cloudy, with a wind of about 20 knots. At 0530 the task force received a message from Yamamoto conveying the gist of his reply to the Emperor's rescript.*

Shortly thereafter he "respectfully related" the rescript itself. Thereupon all officers and men "firmly determined to fulfill the responsibility entrusted them by the Emperor, by destroying the U. S. Pacific Fleet with utmost efforts.

Day of Deceit, by Robert B. Stinnett.

There were other warnings, other transcriptions both military and diplomatic, that should have alerted the United States to the planned Japanese attacks. All were treated in amateurish regard by the highest levels of military and diplomatic enclaves. Codes were being broken, alerts were being fed in by foreign diplomats, word was being sent to various places, *except, perhaps to Hawaii.* But one thing remains obvious, even to the casual observer: *The United States government had already decided to let Guam and its Chamorro population fall to the Japanese.*

But it was different for little Wake Island, 1,500 miles to the east of Guam. It (Wake) had different plans for the attacking Japanese.

In 1935, Pan American Airways had built a small village for their personnel to provide service to their flights on its U.S./Philippines/China route. The village was the first human settlement on the island. The Pan Am employees planted gardens and imported other food and water supplies, via an occasional visit by a freighter and their frequent clipper flights from the U.S. mainland. Those commercial clipper flights to Manila via Pearl Harbor, Midway Island, Wake Island, Guam, and on to Subic Bay (Manila) took about four days, and they were running about two flights each week. Also, SS *North Haven,* a 15,000-ton merchant ship occasionally provisioned each island that the clippers used as stopovers on their four to five-day flights across the Pacific.

In January 1941, the United States Navy established a military base on Wake Island. Then in August, they established the first permanent military garrison. The 1st Marine Defense Battalion, totaling 449 officers and men under Major James P.S. Devereux, was settled in to defend the small atoll. The island also had sixty-eight U.S. Navy personnel and about 1,221 civilian workers from the construction firm of Morrison-Knudsen Corporation.

This sudden increase in population was in addition to the already present Pan American airline employees. Some of those employees were Chamorros from Guam.

The Marines came to fight. They were equipped with heavy armament, six 5 inch/51 caliber (127 mm) cannons, twelve 3 inch/50 caliber (76.2 mm) M3 anti-aircraft guns, eighteen Browning M2 .50 caliber heavy machine guns, and thirty heavy, medium, and light, water or air-cooled Browning M1917 .30 caliber machine guns. In addition, each Marine carried his 1903 Springfield rifle, or a .45 caliber sub-machine gun, or a .45 caliber semi-auto pistol. The Marines had arrived on the atoll short in personnel strength, but loaded for bear. They were missing some critical items like range finders for their big naval guns, heavy explosives such as anti-personnel mines, beach fortifications, and the like. What they lacked in equipment and personnel, they made up for in sheer guts and ingenuity.

On 28 November, Commander Winfield S. Cunningham, USN, reported to Wake to assume overall command of the island's naval forces. With him were eight Navy officers, fifty-eight sailors, and fifty-one Marines of VMF-211 (ground crew), arriving aboard the USS *Wright*. The VMF-211 ground crews were delighted seeing that everything was apparently ready at the airfield, and so was the new island commander. However, upon close inspection, protective revetments for protection of aircraft had not even begun. Protection of fuel storage areas had not been completed. The aircraft were to be sitting ducks.

On 4 December 1941, the rest of Marine Fighter SquadronVMF-211 arrived on Wake Island with 12 F-4-F Wildcat fighters flown by Marine pilots arriving from the USS *Enterprise*. Ground crews had arrived a few days earlier. They had no spare parts. They had barely arrived in time for the war. The American aircraft carrier USS *Enterprise* had sailed close enough to the island to launch her Marine aircraft for the final leg to Wake. Then she turned around and headed back to Pearl Harbor and was still at sea when the Japanese attacked.

As the Japanese first attempted to land a force on Wake, the defenders of Wake Island put up such a fight that they sunk the first Japanese surface warships of the war and repulsed the first landing attempt by Japanese Marines. The battle of Wake Island became part of Marine Corps lore. Guam would not. Not then. Interestingly, almost all writings about the defense of Wake Island, especially those by such noted historians as Robert J. Cressman, (*A Magnificent Fight: Marines in the Battle for Wake Island*), fails to mention the contribution to defending the island by the Chamorro airline workers of Guam. Even the Hollywood version of the movie *Wake Island* shows Caucasian civilian construction workers assisting in defending the island—but not the Chamorro.

In addition to resources provided for the defenses of Wake, the Midway Islands started to receive military personnel and supplies in the form of the U.S. Navy beginning to build airfields and a submarine base in September 1940. Marine air and ground units, and the Army Air Corps bombers eventually arrived and were present on the islands for the naval Battle of Midway in 1942. Midway and Wake were heavily defended, but not to the degree that had been earlier suggested by the Marine Earl "Pete" Ellis in 1921. His prophecy began to ring true, while his suggestions were ignored.

Similarly, in the Philippines of 1941, considerable War Department interest in defending the island nation from attack by the Japanese was generated. Interestingly, the build-up for the defense of the Philippines continued in spite of a 1940 agreement that, if war came with Japan, only holding actions would take place while defeating German and Italian forces would take top priority. In the months before the bombing of Pearl Harbor, massive additional military personnel and supplies poured into the Philippines from the United States. So much was devoted to defending the Philippines that the senior man in charge, Douglas MacArthur, called back to active duty by President Roosevelt, finally had to say that he had enough. Perhaps he did, but he certainly squandered what he had in his amateurish concept of defending the Philippines.

Reasons abound regarding the fall of the Philippines. Pick one, or more of these: A belief by the President of the Philippines, Manuel Luis Quezon, that the Philippines could somehow remain neutral, and MacArthur may have tacitly supported that belief. Remember, before he had been recalled to active duty with the United States Army, MacArthur had been a field marshal with the Philippine Army, working for the president of the Philippines. He never resigned from that position. Another: After news of the attack on Pearl Harbor was transmitted to MacArthur's headquarters, MacArthur was asked, by his Army Air Corps commander, to approve a pre-emptive strike by B-17's and P-40's against Japanese airbases on Formosa. The Army Air Corps commander was convinced that he could catch the Japanese aircraft on the ground and destroy most, if not all of them. That approval was apparently "staffed" to death. The decision was delayed until it was too late. By not striking first with his B-17 bombers and P-40 Warhawks at the Japanese on Formosa, MacArthur ended up having his aviation assets out on the ground, out in the open, like sitting ducks for the Japanese first strike to be able to destroy fifty percent of them in the Philippines. MacArthur had a nine-hour window after the attack on Pearl Harbor, but he wasted it. And a third: During the evacuation of Bataan, and the retreat to Corregidor Island, many of the critical supplies were left on Bataan to fall into Japanese hands. These are just a few of the tactical blunders made in the Philippines. After bombs rained down on the Pacific fleet at Pearl Harbor, the U.S. military in the Philippines was simply not prepared for the arrival of the Japanese, even though the assets were available to put up a sustained defense. But, in the final analysis, the American and Filipino ground forces did hold out longer than anyone expected without an Air Force or a Navy to support them.

The question for readers is—Why did the United States decide to defend the Philippines, and also Midway and Wake Islands— the latter two essentially just large sand spots in a larger ocean, and not Guam, with a population of almost 25,000 American civilian Chamorros, and hundreds of westerners, a naval hospital, a Navy base with a deep-water port, a Marine barracks, a communication station, and a vital link in a defensive chain of islands from Alaska to the Philippines? Each of these locations would have been on the forward edge of the battle area in a war with Japan.

Guam and Malta were two vital islands in a unique location near our World War II enemies. Properly defended, they could withstand assaults and become a thorn in the side of the opposition, severely hampering their long range plans for conquest. Japan, including the Northern Marianas, was near Guam, and German occupied territory and Italy were near Malta. The British decided to defend Malta, while the Americans decided to abandon Guam. Defending Malta interrupted Axis plans for the conquest of North Africa, while abandoning Guam opened the door to the Philippines, New Guinea, and Dutch East Indies for Japan.

The Navy Department had been asking for years for improvements of Guam's defensive posture, only to be ignored by Congress. But as war between the United States and Japan grew more inevitable, the Philippines and Wake and Midway Islands were rapidly mobilized for defense against Japanese attack. It would seem to the casual observer that the evacuation of military dependents and civilian construction workers from Guam, in October 1941, should have been followed with a rapid build-up of defenses on Guam. Instead, the Japanese were allowed to walk ashore without firing a shot, and the only opposition by fire was by Chamorros and a few sailors and Marines around the governor's house in Plaza de España, the power generating station, and a few other isolated locations. Not exactly an American military tradition. Not exactly the Alamo.

Everyone on Guam, military and civilian, was *shamefully abandoned* by the United States government. The military and various civilian personnel were taken away as prisoners of war, while Chamorro and mixed-blood (mestizo) residents were left to fend for themselves. An entire population of United States Nationals had to adapt, overcome, and survive, each in their own way, against the might of the Japanese Empire.

THE JAPANESE ARRIVE / DEATH BLINKED

The following contains factual data combined with conjured conversations, which may have occurred, designed to support the known factual data related to Sgambe and the American surrender of Guam:

In the early morning darkness, "Sgambe" had secluded his family and was returning to Agana to pick up additional supplies early, before he had to report to the Plaza. Even though they expected it, they were unaware that Japanese forces had already landed on Guam.

As Sgambe and three of his friends, the Untalan's—Luis, Jesus, and Vicente—were walking in the San Antonio area discussing where they might obtain additional food and clothing for their families, the unexpected happened:

"This place looks like a ghost town," (speaking Chamorro) one of the men remarked.

"Yeah! Look, most of the stores are dark and doors are open. They look abandoned. Let's just take what we need quickly and get back," another responded.

"Let's look for some canned goods."

"Good idea."

"Want to split up, or. . ."

"Quiet! I hear voices." Sgambe whispered.

"It's Japs."

"Let's get outta here!"

They turned to move into the shadows of a building, when they inadvertently ran right into a platoon of Japanese concealed by camouflage and darkness. They didn't know it at that time, but this same platoon had earlier indiscriminately and without hesitation or provocation, shot up a civilian vehicle, a jitney loaded with young civilian Chamorros, most of who were killed.

Twenty or so Japanese naval infantrymen shouted menacingly and pointed bayoneted rifles inches from their faces and chests, as the four raised their hands above their heads. For the first time in his life, Adolfo Camacho Sgambelluri knew what it was like to face certain death, a sudden swift death at the hands of the invaders.

Instant fear gripped the four men as they were prodded with bayonets held by screaming Japanese invaders, lusting for more blood. There was no question in anyone's mind what was going to happen next. The Japanese troops lined the four men up against the wall of a nearby house, preparing for a summary execution. Sgambe, his nerves on edge, frightened beyond belief, knew that he was going to die. He just knew he didn't want to die standing like a zombie in front of a wall. As the Japanese stepped back in obvious preparation to organize into a firing squad, he whispered to the others that they would, all together, break into a run, in different directions, as soon as he yelled. He had picked a swamp he knew was nearby as his destination. On the run, he reasoned he and the others had a slight chance. Standing against that wall, they had none. His adrenalin rush had reached a boiling point. "Now!" he shouted. They went for it.

Off they went, not in different directions, but all heading in the direction of the swamp. Their sudden action took the Japanese by surprise. In the few seconds it took them to recover, Sgambe was halfway to the swamp, running like a madman, darting left and right, ducking and jumping. With his heart beating like a snare-drum and his raw throat gasping for air, he waited for the bullets to catch him in mid-stride. But when the fusillade arrived, somehow it missed him. Running faster than he ever had in his life, he entered the formidable swamp right beside his friend Vicente. Two were wounded and survived while Vicente and Sgambe were somehow missed by the fusillade.

In the swamp, running or walking through the mud at the bottom of the water or walking over dry spots or "islands" of semi-dry-mud lumps of earth was like walking through a field of thick glue. It refused to let go of their feet as they sank into the muck, and made a sucking sound when their strength overcame its grip. Every time they put a foot down, it would hold on, and when they attempted to lift their feet it would literally suck the shoes and socks right off. Sgambe lost a shoe in the sucking mud, exposing him to the long, stabbing thorns on the roots of the gado plant or spiny yam. Those spines can penetrate the sole of a shoe. Adding to his problems and pain, he had somehow smashed his thumb while pushing through lemonchinas, another thorny bush designed to stab and torment anyone attempting to walk or run through it. And there were other, sometimes more dense but not as deadly, undergrowth that defied penetration; however, he bulldogged his way through them and he cheated death, for the first time. It would definitely not be the last. And, that second time would come quickly. Very quickly!

After getting away, covered with perspiration, dirt, and mud, with an aching shoeless foot, and a bleeding, throbbing thumb, he found a house that he recognized and obtained assistance from a friend. After getting a loaner pair of shoes to wear, he got back out on the road in order to quickly get back to the Plaza in Agana, and almost immediately, he saw the lights of an automobile approaching. Tired as he was, he was still very concerned about getting additional provisions for his family before he would figure out what else he needed to do just to survive in this new world that had supplanted his little island paradise. But, he had to report at the Plaza first. His feet still hurt from the thorns, and walking was difficult. He made a foolish decision.

When he heard the whine of a car engine behind him, his first instinct was to get off the road, but instead, he reasoned Japanese troops would not be driving cars. It must be a local, he thought. He stood, in plain view, and waved at the automobile for it to stop. It did, along with a second automobile that he failed to see, behind the first. They were both loaded with scouring Japanese troops. "Out of the frying pan, into the fire," he thought. Again, he was suddenly surrounded by bayonet wielding Japanese.

"Damn, why did I get out on the road?" he whispered, almost aloud, to himself. The Japanese soldiers were pointing their rifles at him and poking him with the tips of razor sharp bayonets. "I ain't going without a fight," he uttered to himself as he prepared to jump the nearest soldier, knowing that it would lead to his instant death. He would die on a lonely road, alone, with half a dozen menacing Japanese troops cutting his body apart with their bayonets.

Then, suddenly, he heard a familiar voice speaking in Japanese. It surprised him. Turning his head toward the speaker, to his amazement, he saw his friend Jesus Okiyama, a Nisei. Apparently, he quickly reasoned, Jesus appeared somewhat in charge of the Japanese search party. Or, at least, he was assisting them. They were looking for American military stragglers.

"Be still! Don't move, Sgambe!" Jesus shouted in English and immediately launched into Japanese, as he pushed his way between the frenzied troops and his friend. After a brief and somewhat heated verbal exchange between the soldiers and Okiyama, Sgambe was told that he could leave.

The Japanese lowered their rifles and shouted additional taunts at him, which he did not understand, though he knew the implications, he slowly turned, his hands still above his head, and walked out of the glare of the headlights toward the protective darkness.

As he slowly walked away nervously, he turned his head back to view the two vehicles starting up and the soldiers reloading. As the vehicles geared up and started to move with the reloaded passengers of death, he turned his head back and continued to walk in the direction of Agana, half expecting to be stopped again, but miraculously the two cars sped by him, with laughter and more obvious taunts emanating from the car's occupants. He watched their tail lights disappear before his heart slowed down and his breathing returned to normal. For a second time, he had looked at death and cheated it. He struck out for the Plaza.

The first and only pitch battle took place at 0445 in Plaza de España in Agana, as Japanese troops encountered Captain Todd's lightly armed Insular Force of Marines, sailors, and Chamorros. They had picked up a few Lewis machine guns and a few rifles, which had firing pins in the bolts, unlike the previous rifles that had their firing pins removed by order of the governor. As Japanese troops appeared in view, the Chamorros and a few Marines and sailors opened fire and initially stopped the Japanese force cold. Two of the Chamorros manning one Lewis gun were Pedro Cruz and Vicente Chargualaf, both Naval Guard members. A teen-age civilian, Roman Camacho, wanting to support his countrymen, fell to the ground beside them and began to feed the guns with ammo canisters.

There were no prepared fighting positions, no sense of command and control, fire discipline, or selected fields of fire. No Marines were brought up from the Marine Barracks at Sumay to augment the Insular Force. Nothing!

As this brief fire-fight was ongoing, an additional 5,500 men of the Imperial Japanese Army, under Major General Tomitaro Horii, made landings on the island at three separate locations. This information was relayed to the governor.

The governor weighed his options, checked his known casualty figures, and finally decided that his original plans were solid. The Marine Barracks at Sumay, consisting of 145 men under Marine Lt Col William McNulty, the Insular Force Guard, consisting of 246 men, many unarmed (some unarmed by the governor), the Guam Insular Patrol (Police Force), consisting of roughly thirty Chamorros, the unarmed naval hospital sailors, another handful of Marines, and more unarmed sailors could not defend Guam from attacking Japanese forces already ashore. To do so, he had reasoned, would cause heavy casualties. His only warship had been sunk, leaving numerous sailors who had survived available, but they were unarmed. And, he knew the American civilians and native population would endure the brunt of the casualties. He decided at that point that he had put up enough of a "defense," and further fighting was futile. As expected and as planned, he would surrender his forces to the Japanese, as he has stated, to prevent the additional loss of lives to an overwhelming Japanese force. It was 0545, 10 December 1941.

As the firing continued around the Plaza, someone blasted the car horn of a car parked near the governor's house, three times in rapid succession. No one knew who did it or why. But then, the firing suddenly stopped. (In his book *Captive of the Rising Sun*, Rear Admiral Donald Giles says he was the one who blew the car horn.) During the lull, to everyone's amazement, someone speaking English shouted from the Japanese side of the Plaza, "Send over your captain."

Commander Donald Giles and Chief Boatswain Robert Lane, behind the pillars at the entrance to the Plaza, had a quick conversation.

"You know the captain has decided to surrender, don't you Boats?" Commander Giles asked.

"I heard, Sir. Long time ago, I heard," replied Chief Lane.

"Want to go with me?"

"Yeah! We step out into the open and get our asses shot off," quipped the chief.

Giles appeared stoic.

"Coming over!" the chief yelled suddenly.

"We will not fire!" a voice echoed back from the street.

"Hold your fire!" yelled the commander.

Together, they discarded their pistols, stepped out into the open, waited briefly, and marched over to the Japanese side making contact with the Japanese naval commander. Several Japanese Marines pointed their bayonetted rifles at them, terrifying the two men, before a senior officer commanded them to stop. In the company of Commander Hiroshi Hayashi of the Imperial Japanese Navy landing force, they were taken to the naval port to make contact with the Japanese commander of the Guam invasion forces. Commander Giles offered his surrender to the Japanese commanding general. Then they returned to the Plaza and entered the governor's house, accompanied by armed Japanese Naval Infantry. Captain McMillin had already been captured and was dressed only in his underwear.

Confusion reigned as the Japanese shouted at the Americans in Japanese, sometimes pointing their rifles in a hostile gesture at the Americans. Sgambe, still wearing loaned shoes on his throbbing feet, spoke to Captain Todd who had been stripped to his underwear, "Sir, I think I can tell them where to find interpreters." He paused as one of them pointed his bayonetted rifle at him. *"Dozo!"* he uttered and proceeded to indicate through gestures, and some basic Japanese language he had picked up from friends, that there were Japanese in the jail who could interpret for them.

The Japanese commander spoke with two of his troops, which resulted in their pushing Sgambe out of the room with the points of their bayonets. Sgambe was surprised when, once outside the house, one of the Japanese said "Okay Maline (Marine), we go hoosegow," indicating that he was to lead them to the jail. He assumed they wanted to find the jail and Sgambe had the keys. Once he understood, he motioned for the two of them to follow him. They were back within a few minutes with a weeping Japanese female and her husband, who was removed from the jail.

Captain McMillin offered his formal written surrender, and Japanese Naval Infantry Commander Hayashi accepted the surrender of American military and naval forces on Guam. In the "McMillin Report," made in 1945 after his release from prison in Manchuria, Captain George McMillin describes the surrender and provides a copy of the surrender document as follows:

Government House, Guam
10 December 1941
From: Governor of Guam
To: Senior Officer Present, Commanding Imperial Japanese Forces in Guam
Subject: Surrender.

1. ***I, Captain George J. McMillin, United States Navy, Governor of Guam and Commandant, United States***

Naval Station, Guam, by authority of my commission from the President of the United States, do, as a result of superior military forces landed in Guam this date, as an act of war, surrender this post to you as the representative of the Imperial Japanese Government.

2. ***The responsibility of the civil government of Guam becomes yours as of the time of signing this document.***
3. ***I have been assured by you that the civil rights of the population of Guam will be respected and that the military forces surrendered to you will be accorded all the rights stipulated by International Law and the laws of humanity.***

(S) G.J. McMillin (Summary of Enclosure 2, as amended by oral information from Captain G.J. McMillin.)

After his release, Captain McMillin also offered his praise for the conduct and action of the Chamorro Insular Force personnel. They manned the machine guns and other defensive positions that repelled the initial advance of the Japanese. Too bad that few in America have really taken note of this fact.

There were periodic and widely scattered skirmishes around the island before all military personnel received word of the surrender. Very angry and very disappointed Marines (apparently except their commanding officer who knew of the surrender decision), awaiting the arrival of the Japanese near the barracks, reluctantly discarded their weapons and prepared for the worst at the hands of the Japanese.

Many publications related to the defense of Guam tell a story of Marines taking up defensive positions at the rifle range and engaging in a pitch battle with Japanese ground forces. No evidence can be found to support that thesis. Apparently, it's not so. It seems to be pure fabrication. There had been no organized defense plans involving the Marines of the Marine Barracks. It is a fact that Marines fired upon Japanese aircraft that were bombing and strafing the island indiscriminately. They may have hit one or two of them. But, the Marines were not moved to the capital for defense, nor to the naval base at Piti; indeed they had remained at their barracks at Sumay. As the Japanese landed in numerous locations and the order of surrender was disseminated, it almost became an "every man for himself" type of situation. All knew of Nanking and the atrocities committed by the Japanese against Chinese soldiers and civilians, including small children, and they expected the worse. Many of the Marines had encountered the Japanese while on duty in various places in China. Word of the surrender reached the Marines before the Japanese landing forces reached them. They were not a happy lot. They hated the surrender order. But they complied with it, although several individual Marines took to the jungle with their weapon and ammunition with intent of conducting a fight as a guerilla force. Within a week or two, most had surrendered or been captured by searching Japanese patrols.

Excerpt below is from: The WWII POW Experience in the Pacific, Robert E. Winslow; Sergeant Major, USMC (Retired) (1939-1970) Internet posting April, 2007, and printed in Martin Boyle's publication:

> *Several miles away at their now bypassed defensive positions on Orote Peninsula, most of the 125 men of Marine Barracks, under the command of Lieutenant Colonel William K. McNulty, were told to prepare for surrender. But Marines are not trained for surrender, and the prime scuttlebutt had it that the Japanese took no prisoners. Several small groups of enlisted Marines gathered ammunition, weapons and food and took off into the boondocks, prepared to wage guerilla warfare against the Japanese. PFC John Breckenridge was in a group of nine who went to the hills and remained there for about eleven days. After being informed by friendly natives that the Japanese had not massacred any prisoners and intended to take them to Japan, and that any Marines left on the island would be shot on sight, they turned themselves in.*

Martin Boyle and two other Marines were captured by a Japanese patrol after two weeks in the bush. Boyle recalls several other bands, one a group of fifteen led by Sergeant Jim Holland. Before the month was out, all the Marine holdouts either turned themselves in or were captured by Japanese patrols.

Martin Boyle, *Yanks Don't Cry*

Primarily from his memory, over three years later, Captain McMillin gave this full report after his release from prisoner of war status in September 1945. It is as follows:

(corrections and notations are in brackets)
SURRENDER OF GUAM TO THE JAPANESE
By George J. McMillin, Captain, USN
11 September 1945
From: Captain G. J. McMillin, U.S. Navy
To: The Secretary of the Navy
Subj: Surrender of Guam to Japanese

1. *On 8 December 1941, I was serving as Governor of Guam and Commandant of the Naval Station, Guam.*
2. *At about 0600, on 10 December 1941, I surrendered the island and military and naval forces located there to the senior officer present, Imperial Japanese Forces in Guam (Enclosure 1).*
3. *Since that time, and until 20 August 1945, when we were informed by Russian forces occupying the Mukden, Manchuria area that we were free, I have been a prisoner of war in Japanese hands. A report of my prisoner of war experience will be made in separate correspondence. The following report on the circumstances of the surrender of Guam is made from memory more than three and one-half years after the event. All notes made at the time were destroyed when the Japanese started periodic*

searches of personal effects, generally removing written matter. Dates and times mentioned are Guam dates and times.

4. *The political situation in the Pacific was assumed to be tense during the summer of 1941. After an effort extending over several months, arrangements were finally made to evacuate all dependents, including civilians, from Guam. This evacuation was completed on 17 October 1941, with one exception, Mrs. J. A. Hellmers, the wife of John Anthony Hellmers, Chief Commissary Steward, U.S. Navy. Mrs. Hellmers was expecting to be confined for childbirth before the transport "HENDERSON" was due in San Francisco. All precautions possible were taken to be prepared to carry out the mission assigned to the Station, and to prevent surprise. The Station ship "GOLD STAR" was in the southern Philippines, and on the day preceding the start of hostilities was loaded and ready to proceed for Guam. On 7 December the Commander in Chief Asiatic Fleet ordered the ship to delay sailing for Guam on account of the serious international situation. A warning message was received from the Department about 4 December. This was the first information from the Navy Department regarding the international situation. On 6 December classified matter was destroyed by burning, in accordance with instructions received from the Navy Department.*
5. *About 0545, 8 December, a message was received which had been originated by the Commander in Chief, Asiatic Fleet, to the effect that Japan had commenced hostilities by attacking Pearl Harbor, prior to a declaration of war. Steps were taken immediately to evacuate the civilian population from Agaña, and from the vicinity of possible military objectives* [no warning was given to civilians. They were at church celebrating the Feast of the Immaculate Conception when aerial assaults began. They were caught by surprise.], *in accordance with a plan previously prepared. All Japanese nationals*

were arrested at once, and confined in jail. All navigation lights were ordered extinguished. Schools were suspended, and church gatherings prohibited. The civil population had been previously instructed about what they should do in air raids. The Bank of Guam was ordered to remain closed. All activities were ordered to take station for carrying out the assigned mission, but instructions were issued that no destruction was to start without specific orders from Government House, or when it was definitely apparent that the Japanese were on the Island.

6. *The U.S.S. PENGUIN had been on patrol off the Harbor entrance during the night. This nightly patrol of the PENGUIN or a Y.P. boat had been in effect for about six months. The PENGUIN was informed by radio, and instructed to remain outside the Harbor prepared for air raids.*
7. *The Insular Force Guard (about 80 natives of Guam), a force that was authorized for enlistment in April 1941, were assembled in the Guard Headquarters on the Plaza in Agaña. The U.S. Marines (less about 50 on duty on patrol stations throughout the island, plus police and Government House detail) were at the Marine Barracks, Sumay.*
8. *Enemy planes appeared from the direction of Saipan shortly after eight o'clock, and the first bombs were dropped on the Marine Reservation and vicinity at 0827. The Marines were in barracks, or on their normal duties throughout the post. Several were injured running across the golf course, for protection in the surrounding thickets. The Pan Air Hotel kitchen received a direct hit, and several native employees were killed. An attack was made on the U.S.S. PENGUIN outside the Harbor; the ship gallantly fought, but was soon in a sinking condition. Ensign White, U.S.N.R., was killed by machine gun fire at his station on the AA gun. The PENGUIN had the only guns on the Station larger than a .30 caliber machine gun. The ship was abandoned in a sinking condition, and sank*

in deep water off Orote Point. There were several men injured, but all of the crew succeeded in getting ashore on life rafts, bringing Ensign White's body with them. The Captain, Lieutenant J.W. Haviland, 3rd, U.S. N., was wounded. A complete list of dead and wounded is attached (Enclosure 2). The Navy Yard, Piti, was badly strafed and bombed, with considerable damage to material. The U.S.S. ROBERT L. BARNES was strafed and bombed at her buoy in the Harbor. Several leaks were started in her hull. The radio station at Libugon was strafed and bombed during the day. One bomb wrecked a civilian house near the Naval Hospital, and not far from Government House. The house had been occupied by Tweed, G.R., radioman first class, U.S. Navy. The greatest number of planes seen at one time during the day was nine. They generally came in at an altitude of about 1500 feet.

9. *Bombing was discontinued about 1700, and not resumed until about 0830 the following day. A report came in that a native dugout had landed about daybreak near Ritidian Point, the northern end of the island, and that about eight Japanese from Rota had entered the island. The patrol and police arrested and brought in three men who admitted that they were natives of Saipan, that they had relatives in Guam, and that the Japanese had sent them over to act as interpreters when the Japanese landing force arrived. These men were identified by reliable natives of Guam as residents of Saipan. The men said the Japanese would make their landing the next morning (Tuesday), in the vicinity of Recreation Beach, to the eastward of Agaña. This proved correct, except that the landing was made on Wednesday, 10 December. I asked these men why they gave me this information. They replied to the effect that the Japanese had treated the natives of Saipan like slaves, and that they had determined to tell what they knew, even though they would be shot should the Japanese find out about it. I was*

not inclined to accept the story at the time since I thought it might be a trick to have the Marines moved from Sumay to the Beach during the night, in order that they might make a landing in the Apra Harbor area without opposition. The three informers were locked up in jail, where the Japanese found them two days later.

10. *Bombing continued on Tuesday,* [Tuesday would have been 10 December]*11 December. No surface ships were seen until the next day when the landing was made. Considerable additional material damage was done at the Marine Reservation, Pan Air Installation, Standard Oil tanks (which had been set on fire by bombs on Monday, 10 December), Navy Yard, Piti, and Libugon. Lookout stations at Ritidian Point were machine gunned, also the villages of Dededo, Inarajan, Merizo, and Umatac. A bomb possibly intended for Government House, or the Communications Office, struck an old Spanish house across a narrow street from the jail, where all the Japanese residents were confined. The house was demolished and the Japanese badly shaken, but they were protected by the concrete walls of the jail. They begged to be released, but were kept in confinement until the invading force released them the following day. During the bombings, the planes were kept under fire as much as possible by .30 caliber machine guns and rifles. There were reports of planes being damaged and shot down, but none of these reports were verified. Another bomb wrecked a civilian house about fifty yards to the eastward of Government House. Another fell in Government House gardens.*
    (dates are incorrect)
11. *The U.S. Marines at the Marine Barracks, Sumay, took up a field position in the butts of the rifle range, under Command of Lieutenant Colonel William K. McNulty, U.S.M.C.* [Not true]
12. *About 0400 on Wednesday, 10 December, I was informed by the watch that flares had been seen in the vicinity of the*

beach to the eastward of Agaña (Recreation Beach, Dungas [Dungca's] Beach), and it was thought landing operations were in progress. There were no defenses at this point, or at any other point on the island. Orders were immediately sent to all stations to carry out the mission assigned. About 0445, shooting was heard in the San Antonio district (east of the Plaza), and fires were observed. The Insular Force Guard took up defense positions in the Plaza, with no equipment except a few .30 caliber machine guns and rifles. The Japanese approached rapidly through the San Antonio district, and approached the Plaza on the narrow street alongside the Naval Hospital and Cathedral. The Insular Force Guard stood their ground, and opened up a fire with machine guns and rifles hot enough to halt the invading force for a short time. The situation was simply hopeless; resistance had been carried to the limit. At about 0545, three blasts were sounded on the horn of an automobile which was standing in front of Government House. This was not a prearranged signal to cease fire, but it seemed to have been understood by both sides, and firing stopped immediately. The Japanese shouted across the Plaza from the Cathedral, "Send over your Captain." Commander Donald T. Giles, the aide for civil affairs to the Governor, and Chief Boatswain's Mate Robert Bruce Lane, U.S. Navy, stepped out. They were marched through the San Antonio district, and made contact with the Commander of the Naval landing force, returning about a half hour later to the Plaza with the Commander.

13. *I was captured in the Reception Room of my quarters about twenty minutes after the cease firing signal. The leader of the squad of Japanese who entered my quarters required me to remove my coat and trousers before marching me into the Plaza, where officers and men were being assembled, covered by machine guns.*
14. *At about 0645, Commander D.T. Giles returned with the Japanese officer to the assembled group in the Plaza.*

15. *Commander Giles identified me as the Governor of Guam. The Japanese Commander, Commander Giles, and myself entered Government House. Members of the Japanese guard were armed with rifles and fixed bayonets. None of the Japanese group spoke English. I was able to indicate that Japanese local residents were confined in the jail across the Plaza. Shinahara, Shimizu, and Mrs. Sawada were sent for. Mrs. Sawada was very emotional and in tears. Shinahara did the interpreting. The Japanese officer identified himself as Commander Hayashi, Imperial Japanese Navy. After a short discussion, he asked if I was ready to sign papers. I told him I was prepared to surrender the post, and after further discussion, I wrote and signed a letter of surrender, (Enclosure 1). Shinahara informed me that I was to remain in Government House until further orders. I remained there with Commander Giles and Chief Yeoman Fariss [Fariss], until about 2030, without food. About 2030, Commander Giles and myself were ordered to leave immediately for the Naval Hospital, and were only permitted to take a few toilet articles. I found that the Guam officers were assembled there at the Suzana Hospital. Two days later, officers were removed and confined in the K.C.K. Catholic Church Building. I was permitted to remain at the hospital. The others in this hospital group were Captain Lineberry, Medical Corps, Medical Officer in Command Naval Hospital; Lieutenant Commanders H.J. Van Peenen, and T.I. Moe, Medical Corps; Commander D.T. Giles, and Pharmacist Daul.*
16. *A description of the period of confinement in Guam, as a prisoner of war, will be submitted in separate correspondence. The magazine at the Marine Barracks was destroyed; at the Pan Air Installation about 4,000 barrels of gasoline fell into the hands of the Japanese because the adjoining Standard Oil tank installation was on fire, and these Pan Air tanks could*

not be reached. The Quartermaster's Storehouse and contents were burned. Considerable damage to the storehouse and stores had been done at the Navy Yard., Piti. One of the Y.P. boats was destroyed by fire, and the other one practically so. The motive power of the small craft had been generally destroyed. The U.S.S. R.L. BARNES was damaged and leaking considerably, but had not sunk. The 5,000 barrel fuel oil tank which had been completed a short time before had been filled with fuel from various sources. No oil had been used from the tank because the piping had not been completed. This tank was set on fire and destroyed by H.H. Sachers, a civilian employee of the Public Works Department. A recommendation will be written under separate cover on Sacher's action in this case. The automotive transportation on the island fell in the hands of the Japanese practically intact. The large diesel trucks which were used by the contractors were destroyed.

17. *The Insular Force Guard which had been organized beginning in April 1941, proved themselves to be a valuable asset, even though they were green troops. They stood their ground in their short action in the Plaza, until they were called back. I consider that these fine natives are entitled to recognition for the showing they made on this occasion. A list of all naval personnel serving in Guam on 8 December 1941, is attached hereto as Enclosure 3. A list of all casualties, dead, wounded, and missing, is attached as Enclosure 2.*
18. *It is estimated that the Japanese landing force consisted of a naval battalion (first wave) of about 600 men, followed by Army troops of the strength of a reinforced brigade (about 5,000 troops).*
19. *Officers and men assigned to the Stations on this occasion generally performed their duties in a satisfactory manner. Recommendations for special mention where such is considered warranted, will be made in separate correspondence.*

G. J. McMILLIN, Captain
U. S. Navy
Encls: (HW)

1. *Ltr. Of Surrender dtd. 12-10-41.*
2. *List of Deceased and Wounded.*
3 *Personnel on Guam on 12-8-41*

(S) G.J. McMillin (Summary of Enclosure 2, as amended by oral information from Captain G.J. McMillin.)

U.S. Casualties

Enclosure 2 indicated a total killed in the Jap invasion of Guam as follows: (1) 13 officers and men of the U.S. Navy and Marine Corps; (2) 4 members of the Guam military; (3) 1 American and an estimated 40-50 civilians.

Enclosure 2 indicated a total wounded as follows: (1) 37 officers and men of the U.S. Navy and Marine Corps; (2) 8 members of the Guam military; (3) an unknown number of Guam civilians.

C.L. DuVal.

DECEASED

American Military [2 Officers, 11 EM]
Bright, Lieutenant Graham P. (SC) USN
White, Ensign Robert Gabriel USNR
Smoot, Malvern Hill CMM 271-52-43 [RG 24 Box 3]
O'Neill, Frank James BM1c 328-23-72 [RG 24 Box 3]
Fraser, Rollin George BM1c 311-09-65 [RG 24 Box 3]
Pineault, Leo Joseph Cox 204-44-61 [RG 24 Box 3]
Ernst, Robert Walter SM3c 381-29-69 [RG 24 Box 3]
Hurd, Seba Guarland SM3c 337-14-86 [RG 24 Box 3]
Schweighhart, John GM1c 228-29-54 [RG 24 Box 3]
Bomar, William W. Jr PFC
Burt, William H. PFC

Anderson, Harry E. Corp
Kauffman, John M. Jr PFC [Modified per Official Marine Roster created from enlistment records, USMC, Bureau of Personnel, 11 Mar 1942]

American Civilian [1]
Kluegel, John "Jack" [CPNAB, Public Works employee]
Guam Military [4]
Cruz, Jesus Cruz NS2c
Flores, Angel L.G. "
Chargualof, Vicente Cruz "
Sablan, V.S. "
Guam Civilians [3]
Camacho, Ramon
Mendiola, Ignacio
Untalan, Jose Castro

LIST OF WOUNDED AT GUAM, INCLUDES ONLY THOSE MARINES NOT ON DUTY AT THE MARINE BARRACKS
[39 Military (includes 5 Chammoro Guards) and 4 civilians - 43 total]
NAME RATE DATE OF WOUND AGENT LOCATION LENGTH OF TREATMENT
Lieut. J.W. Haviland, 3rd 12-8-41 Bomb fragment Left forearm 6 weeks
Ensign E.A. Wood 12-8-41 Bomb fragment Back 3 weeks
Allen, D.A. GM3c 12-8-41 Bomb fragment Both legs, Rt.arm, Rt.shoulder 1 month
Hanzsek, J. MM1c 12-8-41 Bomb fragment Left wrist 2 days
Camillo, A.J. QM1c 12-9-41 Bomb fragment Left shoulder 1 day
McKenzie, L.W. F2c 12-8-41 Bomb fragment Back of head 3 weeks
Young, J.R. CRM 12-8-41 Bomb fragment Left side 1 day
Haskins, T.T. S2c 12-10-41 Bayonet Head (top) 1 day
Hale, E.E. EM2c 12-8-41 Bomb fragment Right upper chest none
Ballinger, R.W. PFC 12-10-41 Bayonet Back 10 days

Moore, H.C. SGT. 12-8-41 Bomb fragment Chest
Legato, A. CPL. 12-8-41 Bomb fragment Face and head
Rathbun, L.E. RM2c 12-10-41 Machine gun Left leg 2 days
Nixon, H. C. PFC 12-8-41 Bomb fragment Back 2 places 3 weeks [see roster for notation]
Nichols, G.E. CPL 12-8-41 Bomb fragment Both lower legs 1 month
Spellman, E.J. PVT 12-8-41 Bomb fragment Right thigh 1 week
Whitaker, K.F. CWT 12-8-41 Machine gun Left lower leg 1 day
Ratzman, E.M. S1c 12-8-41 Bomb fragment Punc. Int.
Wilson, R.E. EM3c 12-8-41 Bomb fragment Punc. pubic region
Zimmer, R.W. F2c 12-8-41 Bomb fragment Leg
Gwinnup, R. H. EM1c 12-10-41 Machine gun Both legs [feet] permanent damage to feet
Allain, J.A. MM1c 12-8-41 Machine gun Rt. leg
Tattrie, N.s. MM1c 12-8-41 Bomb fragment
Blaha, Joseph Henry CY 12-10-41 Rifle & bayonet Right leg & chest short right leg as a result
Cepeda, Francico Sablan NS2c
Sablan, Antonio Cruz NS2c 12-8-41 Lac. scalp
Meno, Jose NS2c 12-10-41 Bayonet Back
Sablan, Jose Santos NS2c 12-10-41 Bayonet & bullets
Limfiaco, Vincente Acfgelle [Aflagui] NS2c 12-10-41 Bayonet & bullets Leg
Santos, Jose C. Civ. 12-9-41
Hughes, Wm. Rufus Civ. 12-10-41
Hughes, Jaquin Untalan (wife of above Hughes) Civ. 12-10-41
San Nicolas, Magdalena Limtiaco Civ. 12-8-41
Magelssen, Walter S1c 12-8-41 Machine gun Leg
Chargualuf, R. OC1c 12-8-41 Bomb fragment Back
Perez, J.A. MM1c 12-8-41 " " Back
O'Brien, R. W. CBM 12-8-41 " " Left forearm
Lumpkins, Floyd F1c 12-8-41 " " Neck, jaw & hand
Babb, J.W. (*) Pfc 12-8-41 " " Leg amputated

** At Sumay Barracks*

(Summary of Enclosure 3)

U. S. Forces and Civilians located on Guam at Outbreak of War

Enclosure 3 indicated that the following U.S. forces and U.S. civilians were on Guam as of 8 December 1941:

274 officers and men of the U.S. Navy under Captain George J. McMillin, USN, Governor of Guam: (2) 153 officers and men of the U.S. Marine Corps under Lieutenant Colonel William K McNulty, USMC; (3) 247 members of the Guam Insular Forces, of which about 100 comprised the Insular Force Guard; (4) 134 U.S. civilians.

The principal U.S. vessels at Guam were, the minesweeper PENGUIN, commanded by Lieutenant J.W. Haviland, III, USN; the ROBERT L. BARNES, an immobilized tanker, commanded by Lieutenant J. L. Nestor, USN; and two YPs (district patrol vessels).

The U. S. Naval Hospital at Guam was commanded by Captain W. T. Lineberry, MC, USN.

C. L. DuVal

In the book *Captured, The Forgotten Men of Guam*, completed and edited by Linda Goetz Holmes, author Roger Mansell and Goetz describe the death toll of Japanese invaders as somewhere between one and 100 or 200. In other publications, it is stated that only one Japanese invader was killed during the invasion. No one really knows; however three boxes of Japanese officers' ashes and fifty boxes of Japanese enlisted men' ashes were taken on the same ship hauling American prisoners to Japan. This is stated in several published sources and a diary kept by William Johnston. One thing is clear. There were casualties on both sides. Most of the information regarding the Japanese invasion of Guam and its aftermath could not be told until after the Americans retook the island in 1944. For months, no one in America knew anything about what had happened on Guam in December 1941. Very clearly, it garnered little news attention and little interest. Guam, and its population, had been written off.

The aforementioned diary was written in two small, brown-covered notebooks by William Gautier Johnston of Alabama, an early 1900s American Marine on Guam. He was reared in Tennessee and later became a civilian resident of Guam. Johnston provided invaluable information about the capture of Guam. He kept the diary from the day after the initial bombing until just before he died in captivity. In his diary, he wrote that sixteen American civilians, Marines, and sailors were buried, apparently killed in the initial invasion. There were many, many Chamorros killed. Some of the dead were on the Insular Force, some were just kids out for a ride, and others were killed for just being in the wrong place at the wrong time.

In the Plaza later that morning, as American military and naval personnel were being searched and processed by their Japanese captors, a Japanese soldier, in full public view, bayonetted a Marine, splitting his stomach open. The Marine was PFC John Kaufmann. There were several witnesses who stated that there was no apparent reason for the killing of that Marine. Some have speculated that it could have been because he was slow in complying with instructions; others say he cursed the Japanese. Yet another story was that he had an involuntary twitch in one eye that caused the Japanese to think he was taunting them. No one really knows; however, Johnston states that the Marine refused to bow to the Japanese and called them "yellow bellied bastards." He died instantly. Word spread quickly that this was going to be a brutal, inhumane occupation by the Japanese.

There were several different military organizations on Guam. All ultimately came under the naval governor. They were the Marine Barracks, the Naval Hospital, the Communications Station, the Naval Guard Force, which encompassed the police department, and the Naval Insular Guard. Marines and sailors, along with Chamorros, were part of the Naval Insular Forces. All were ordered, by the governor, to surrender to the Japanese invasion force. Few expected the protection of the Geneva Convention.

As we moved into the late 1940s, many questions began to be asked by military and civilian planners, writers, and historians. Some were perplexed that the governor had surrendered so quickly. It remains unclear if these surrender orders were handed down from higher headquarters, or if, in his own mind, he knew his defense forces were totally inadequate. The surrender of Guam is something the United States military does not like to talk about. Again, as a reminder, some writings have suggested that the Marines at the Guam Marine Barracks fought Japanese ground forces as an organized defense network. That is simply not true. Future writers, who happened to be on Guam at that time, state clearly that the order to surrender came to the Marines before Japanese forces arrived at the Marine Barracks. The Marines and the USS *Penguin* put up a defense by firing at Japanese aircraft and may have shot down or severely damaged one or two of them. By the time the Japanese invasion force arrived at the Marine Barracks, the order to surrender had already been issued by the governor. The Marines, minus a few who disappeared into the jungle, complied with the surrender order.

As my wife and I conducted research into the events, we wondered aloud whether or not the communication, relative to burning secret and confidential documents and surrendering, had been communicated down to the ranks. It appears that the answer is: No! We also noted that the governor had failed to destroy or hide the roster containing the names, ranks, and assignment locations of all military and naval personnel.

Imagine how the civilian population of Guam must have felt when all American military dependents and civilian construction workers were evacuated in October 1941. Many people, or even most of the population, would have thought that the Marines would now defend against any attack on the island. The burden of concerns and plans for civilian military dependents had departed as they sailed away. It is possible that the local population wondered, “When are reinforcements coming?” They were unaware that the United States was preparing to defend numerous locations in the Pacific, everywhere from the Philippines to the Midway Islands, but not Guam. Why?

Picture yourself as a Chamorro on Guam, working for the American Navy. You watch as a large transport ship pulls into the harbor, and it proceeds to embark all the American civilian dependents of U.S. military personnel stationed on Guam, except the one female in the hospital. This is followed by another ship that on-loads almost 1,000 American civilian construction workers who arrived only a few months ago. Like the American dependents, they just sail away. Yet, no additional military personnel arrive. And, all this is occurring in October 1941. This has got to rattle your cage. As an aside, there is a persistent rumor, still being heard on Guam, that there was to be a third Navy vessel to arrive before Christmas to evacuate all U.S. military personnel from Guam. If factual, it would have left only the American Nationals (the Chamorros), and a few western civilians alone on Guam to face the Japanese. True, or not true, it remains a rumor.

Meanwhile—nothing else on the island changes. The flag goes up, the flag comes down. Bands play and the Insular Guard marches in review, still carrying those rifles marked "Do Not Fire." They can't fire them anyway. The Governor has ordered the removal of the firing pins. They are in his safe. Is he afraid of an armed rebellion of Chamorros, *or* is it that he wants no armed resistance against what he knows is coming?

The American military continued to behave as a colonial power in an occupied colony, holding social functions for the clipper-ship passengers arriving aboard the flying-boats. No defensive positions are prepared, no requests for guns, ammunition, or supplies are issued, and no warning orders promulgated to the civilian population. The only exception seems to be that the local Insular Police Force is ordered to establish a coastal-watch for "infiltrators" from the Northern Mariana Islands.

As the Japanese land on Guam and move toward the capital city where the governor is located, why does he order the Chamorro Insular Guard to man the machine guns? These Insular Guards are the same men who had been issued Springfield rifles with no firing pins. These World War I Lewis Guns, the machine guns, members of the insular forces have never fired before. Why are the Marines not brought up to defend the capital, or even the Navy base at Piti? Both were strategic positions. Years earlier, Marine Lieutenant Colonel Pete Ellis outlined a plan for the defense of Guam. Why was it not followed?

It appears the Chamorro were not the only ones abandoned on Guam to face the fate of the conquerors.

⚜

After the Russo-Japan War (1904-05), Japan threw away the rule book on "proper" treatment of captives in war. It seems, based on writings at that time and since, that they felt the terms of the peace treaty, forced on them by America had somehow made them appear to have lost, instead of having won that war with Russia. Thereafter began a slow, but steady slide toward an anti-western attitude and a rising militarism that dominated pre-war and World War II Japan. They began to consider themselves superior to any and all westerners. They began to treat westerners with contempt. During the War in the Pacific, Asia, and South-East Asia, no one was exempt from their beast-like treatment. Military, civilians, old, young, men, women, and children, including babies, were all viewed as sub-human objects. American Nationals, and the American citizens of the American territory of Guam were no exception, they were brutalized unmercifully. The late 1800s and early 1900s saw a perversion of the Bushido Code of Samurai chivalry, and gave rise to a national militarism in Japan. It taught that to compensate for failure, ritual suicide was a way to "save face." It also gave rise to despising the western white race that would manifest itself in prisoner of war camps throughout the war zone controlled by the Japanese.

It should be made clear that all Japanese were not brutal to their captives. At least one of the Japanese officers on Guam was an American citizen who was visiting his relatives in Japan when the war broke out. He was drafted into the Japanese Army and eventually ended up on Guam. As the Americans began their invasion, this Japanese-American visited a Chamorro whom he had befriended. Early in the occupation, a group of Japanese soldiers were harassing a Chamorro farmer. They were taking the pigs and chickens and requiring the family to give them their recently harvested crops. This officer stopped that activity by telling the soldiers the farm was under his personal protection and that the property they were stealing belonged to the emperor, through him. If they did not stop, they would be severely punished. They never bothered that particular farm again. That officer gave the Chamorro a small American flag that he said he had carried on his person since he arrived on Guam. He said to the lady farmer, "No Japanese will survive the battle against these Americans. Please, you keep this flag." Adolf P. Sgambelluri has that flag. It was given to him by his aunt, the lady farmer.

Most of the enlisted Japanese had only one uniform. They had to remove it occasionally in order to wash and dry it. In a northern village, a senior enlisted soldier, a sergeant perhaps, would come to this one particular home and request permission to wash his clothing. The lady of the house, a Chamorro, would give him permission to do so. The Japanese man would strip, wash his garments, and hang them to dry, while the lady of the house remained in another room so as not to view a naked soldier. When his clothes were dry, he would dress, thank the Chamorro for the use of the wash facilities, leave a few yen as payment, and depart.

There were other isolated events during which Japanese soldiers and sailors showed compassion to the plight of the Chamorro, but it was not the norm. Also, not every Chamorro of Guam resisted and defied the Japanese. Some knew the Americans were returning. Some did not know that fact. All were simply trying to survive in a world turned upside down. Methods of defying authority came in complex ways, some rather humorous. When they were ordered to turn in a cup of dead flies each day to Japanese authorities, in order to control the fly population imported by horses brought from Japan, or face punishment, half the cup was filled with grass and leaves. Dead flies were on the top. One Chamorro faked a crippling condition, pretending that he could not walk. He never walked when Japanese were around. He escaped "work" details and possible death in this manner. When he saw the first American Marines in 1944, he jumped up and ran to meet them. One did what one had to in order to survive.

In the immediate aftermath of the United States' entry into war, in Washington, D.C., and London, England, a decision was made from a list of options. American armed forces would first and foremost assist Great Britain in defeating Nazi Germany to "save Europe." The United States, as a neutral nation, had been supplying Russia and Great Brittan with war supplies and tacitly supported their war effort against Germany. After the attack on Pearl Harbor and the United States' declaration of war on Japan, Germany and Italy declared war on the United States; subsequently, the United States declared war on Germany and Italy. In spite of the attack by the Japanese, the mind-set of the Americans and the British was — let's defeat Germany and Italy first— save Europe and the Europeans, then, and only then, would they consider joining Australia, the Netherlands, China, and New Zealand in defeating Japan in the Pacific, and Asia. America did not think it had the military strength, nor the industrial production capacity to fight a two-front war. One war-front across the Atlantic against Germany and Italy, and another war-front across the Pacific against Japan seemed to be simply too much. Therefore, the initial strategic concept for the Pacific War became a process of establishing a defensive chain of islands, such as Samoa, Hawaii, French Polynesia, and New Caledonia (they sided with the Free French government in exile), Midway, and Fiji, to stop the advance of the Japanese. Along with Australia, the Netherlands (Holland), and New Zealand, the Americans would hold the Japanese advance until Hitler was defeated. Such as it was, that was the plan. And, it was a reasonable plan considering that the United States had been an isolationist society since the end of the Great War, and just like the time period before our entry into World War I and the Korean War, military preparedness was woefully inadequate.

We may assume that the Japanese had thought the Americans would react exactly that way. As such, they began preparations to cut Australia off from the United States. Indeed, without any offensive move against Japan, Australia, and New Zealand would have been cut off. Japan had moved into the Solomon Islands and was planning to take Port Moresby through the Owen Stanley Range in Papua, New Guinea. From Port Moresby, the

Japanese could have had unrestricted access to attack Australia by air, and combined with a naval assault from the sea while maintaining air superiority, could have invaded Australia.

Had it not been for Admiral King of the U.S. Navy and Commandant Holcomb of the Marines, convincing President Roosevelt to open an offensive thrust in the Solomon Islands, that earlier strictly defensive plan would have prolonged the Pacific War by years, and possibly doomed Australia to invasion by Japan.

Had the Japanese been successful with their plans for capturing Port Moresby (Operation MO), they would have used that success as a springboard to their overall plan for capturing New Caledonia, Fiji, and Samoa (Operation FS) to add to their outer defensive chain of islands.

Note, that in the Pacific, only Guam was left out of the Americans' plans for defense against Japanese attack. The defense of the island was considered, discussed, and abandoned. As bombs and tracer rounds rained down on the population of Guam, the only proffered instructions that were passed to local civilians were, "Get out of Agana, go hide, and if you have a radio, camera, or weapon, hide it. Hide it well. Don't get caught with it by the Japs." In short, all knew the Japanese would take Guam and its 25,000 inhabitants. But, even with all this confusion and inability to defend Guam, most people on the island strongly felt that the American Navy would return in just a few weeks to "kick the Japs out." The locals trusted the U.S. Navy, and all of them were told over and over again of the fighting prowess of the U.S. Marines—told mostly by the local Marines. Locals could repeat the stories of the famous battle of Belleau Wood, the various campaigns of the Banana Wars, and tales of China duty, especially the Boxer Rebellion, sometimes relating and repeating those stories word for word. They were completely confident in the U.S. Navy and of the U.S. Marine Corps to protect them.

But, on the evening of 8 December 1941, the U.S. Navy on Guam consisted of a sunken mine layer and two damaged and destroyed patrol boats, and the Marines of the Marine Barracks were not organizing for a defense of the island. Apparently, from numerous sources, it has been suggested and written in other publications, that their commanding officer, a hero of the First World War, had become more interested in social functions than military fighting functions. From the little information uncovered, there were no defense plans drafted, or field exercises conducted, that were designed for defense of the island. Apparently, he made it a point to meet and socialize with the passengers of the clipper-ships passing through Guam, leaving his executive officer to accomplish the military requirements. The bombings caught them completely by surprise. The civilian population that had learned to depend on the protection of the American naval forces found themselves in a panic.

Many locals began to collect food and a few belongings and head for one of the many ranches, or isolated villages on the island. There, they reasoned, they could hide out until the American Navy returned to recapture Guam—surely, in just a few weeks. Guam had ample water. Numerous streams ran through the island, and rainfall can be counted on most of the time. Fruit grew in abundance on vines and trees. Shelter and clothing would be important items to obtain. Canned goods would not require preservation, so packing canned food and clothing was of immediate priority.

But on 8 December, in the evening lull, ammunition, such as it was, was distributed to the Insular Police Force, as well as a few 1903 Springfield rifles. Almost all of the rifles were stamped with that inscription "Do Not Fire." Indeed, many of them had no firing pins. Remember, the firing pins were in the governor's (some reports were stating that they were in the colonel's safe) safe. After all, we don't need accidental discharges or a rebellion supplied with American rifles—that seemed to be the thought process. Most of the Insular Force policemen were armed with pistols only. With the sinking of the minelayer, USS *Penguin,* the largest guns remaining on the island were .30 calibers. Soon they would be facing a Japanese invasion force with massive firepower and overwhelming numbers just over the horizon. They awaited their arrival.

Although the aerial bombing and strafing by Japanese aircraft continued all day, Sgambe and the other Chamorro policemen conducted evacuations, locked up Japanese nationals, secluded their own families, conducted "lights out" drills, and combed the area for Japanese or Saipanese infiltrators and sympathizers. As they performed their rehearsed and last-minute assigned duties, they became less frightened and more determined. The strafing by aircraft of "the rising sun," was especially effective at killing virtually anyone caught in the path of the stream of projectiles, or fragments from exploding bombs. Though their shooting and bombing accuracy was lacking, the Japanese were highly indiscriminate in their choice of targets.

All public facilities were closed, as were banks, stores, and transportation facilities. Panic gripped the civilians on the island.

That night, members of the Insular Force picked up three of eight Northern Chamorros (Saipanese) who had landed on Guam from Saipan or Rota. These Chamorros had excellent Japanese language skills and were to be the interpreters for the onrushing Japanese forces. They landed on a couple of deserted beaches in the north on the night of 8 December 1941. The other five Chamorros (Saipanese) were reported *missing* by the Japanese Navy after the occupation began. All three of the captured ones said that the Japanese would land that following morning, and that they had been sent over as interpreters because the Japanese knew they would easily capture the island. It didn't happen the next day; however, at 0830 that next morning, the air raids continued. The island was now unable to do anything except fire at the aircraft with machine guns and rifles and shake a defiant fist at the Japanese pilots.

Armed defense of the island from ground assault would last no more than a few minutes. War had arrived and Guam would be changed—forever!

GUESTS OF THE "SONS OF HEAVEN"

The following contains factual data derived from numerous sources and conjured conversations designed to support known facts in order to facilitate a story:

On 10 January 1942, all American military and civilian prisoners, including Sgambe and his father Giuseppi Marcello Sgambelluri, were being held temporarily in the Saint Vicente de Paul building at Agana. Eventually the American military, civilian residents, and foreigners (westerners), were evacuated to prison camps in Japan and Manchuria, all except a handful of Chamorro police and Insular Guardsmen, Chamorro civilians, including Sgambe, and six sailors who took to the jungle rather than surrender. Five were eventually caught and killed outright, but Radioman George Tweed evaded the Japanese for almost the entire occupation with the help of many Chamorros, including Adolf C. Sgambelluri, Agueda Johnston, wife of William Johnston, Joaquin Limtiaco, Juan Pangelinan, Antonio Arterio, Tomas Tanaka, and many, many others who risked their lives concealing him from the Japanese. It was a gutsy, controversial call. Some of the Chamorros wanted to give Tweed up to the Japanese to prevent further torture and killing of those suspected of harboring him. In the end, even though torture and death were possible and in fact happened several times, many of the Chamorros protected Tweed.

The military and civilian prisoners from Guam, including Sgambe's dad, Marcello, William Johnston, Chester Carl Butler, and other residents of Guam, were loaded onto the Japanese ship *Argentina Maru* and transported to Japan. With the mostly male military and civilian prisoners were five female Navy nurses and one female Navy dependent and her new-born baby. Initially, they were sent to the prison camp Zentsuji on the island of Shikoku. Most would remain there for almost four years. Eventually, most of the civilian prisoners of war were confined in Kobe, Japan. The five female nurses, and Mrs. Ruby Hellmers, wife of Chief Commissary Steward John Anthony Hellmers, and her infant daughter, Charlene, were eventually repatriated. It was the only repatriated prisoner operations by Japan during the entire war. There are many stories about life in Zentsuji, and one of the examples of life as a military prisoner of Japan is told by Robert O'Brien, who came to Guam in the 1930s.

> *He married Marie Santos Inouye, a woman of Chamorro and Japanese descent, and they had four children, Patricia, Joseph, Henry and Robert. He participated in the short-lived defense of Guam and became a prisoner of war. O'Brien survived four years in a prisoner of war camp in Zentsuji, Japan. . .*
>
> www.guampedia.com/robert-obrien-u-s-prisoner-of-war

Robert O'Brien, born in 1908 in New York, came to Guam in the 1930s with the U.S. Navy. Some 560 people were taken by the Japanese as prisoners of war from Guam: 274 officers and men of the U.S. Navy under Captain George McMillin, 153 officers and men of the U.S. Marine Corps under Lt. Col William McNulty and 134 U.S. civilians (nurses, priests, businessmen, etc.) who happened to be on Guam when the Japanese captured the island.

Robert O'Brien's brother had constantly asked him about his experiences of getting captured and being a prisoner of war. It took over ten years for him to finally open up in a letter to his brother. In 1958, he finally responded to Bill's inquiries about what had happened to him during the war. After some hesitation he wrote a detailed letter telling his war story. The letter was put away in an attic at his brother's home in Michigan, only to be found recently. Both men had passed away many years earlier. The content of the letter has been altered, in brackets, only for the purpose of clarity and brevity. None of the original wording has been removed. Only partial excerpts from his letter follow:

> *My gosh, Bill, I wish I could write you a concise but clear story of my 48 months plus a few days as POW. As you know, I have seldom mentioned much about that phase of my life. Matter of fact, I have never felt it was worth telling about. However, you have mentioned it several times and I have always ignored your queries. But after this last letter from you, I have decided to give you a brief outline. Many incidents have slipped my memory now. So it is only a sketchy story.*
>
> *To give you just a few brief points, I will start from the beginning. On December 6, 1941 our ship, the USS* Penguin, *left Apra Harbor, Guam on a routine patrol, our main objective being to be on the lookout for Japanese subs. The situation was such at the time that we felt it wise to be on the lookout for snooping Japanese, though we really had not the slightest idea that a war was imminent. We didn't even have our guns unlimbered or ammunition at hand, the ammo being still in the magazines down below. Ours was to be just a "routine patrol," with orders only to observe and report what we saw. We spotted nothing, though for days we had been seeing high flying planes which we all presumed to be Japanese from Saipan, 120 miles away.*
>
> *Matter of fact, we had a big beach party planned for that same afternoon, our annual ship's beach party. The day was also a big holiday for the whole island, being the Feast of the Immaculate Conception. As soon as we dropped the hook and got moored to our buoy in the harbor, even before the first boat from the beach had reached the ship, (we were about four miles out from the dock), we sent about one third of the crew*

ashore in our whaleboat, part of them heading for Recreation Beach to make initial preparations for our afternoon beach party, the rest on various assignments, the only pharmacists mate being among them, as he had some business at the hospital.

You see, Guam had no real defense force at the time. The 125 Marines here were primarily for internal security and training of the local police force. I was able to get out of the hospital right away, as most of my scratches were pieces of shrapnel, none of which had hit a vital spot. I still carry a few pieces around just as souvenirs.

I took over a half of the defense force. That is, I took over half as the NCO in charge, at the Plaza in Agana, as that was the selected spot for our last stand as we called it.

The Japanese did not attempt to land until early on the third day. Then[they] bombed and strafed us the first two days and nights. It was a bit annoying as we had only two Lewis machine guns, World War I vintage with pan feed, thirty round[s] to the pan, and about 100 rifles stamped on the stocks, "Do not shoot." They were given to Guam for use in training a militia and were actually dangerous to use. But we used them. I shared a 45 with seven other men. If I got it, number two took the gun; if he got it, number three took the gun and so on. By now we were ready as we could be and were deployed in the grass, behind bushes mind you, in the Plaza. A bush couldn't stop a beer can, but we had nothing else, and for some reason nothing had been done early enough to make sand bag emplacements. I guess the shock of the war starting without any forewarning had really fouled up what little organization there might have been.

Well, that was the lowest moment in my life when we received the order to destroy whatever weapons were still serviceable and fall back to the so-called Palace (so named because of the Spanish days). But orders were orders and we did as we were ordered. A Marine Officer (the Chief of Police on Guam) was given the unenviable task of making the surrender offer to the Japanese. Surprisingly the Japanese ceased fire and soon surrender was arranged. A mighty low moment.

Anyway, the troops were so shaky that they ran us through a double line of troops, a gauntlet, Indian fashion; and swiped at us with bayonets and gun butts. One unfortunate lad right behind me was killed. Others lost part of their scalp; one bled to death later from a bayonet cut across the back. One of our wounded, who had been shot through both ankles, was used as a kicking target on his ankles. One poor guy later lost his mind.

And then they stripped us naked and made us lie in the sun until 1100 that morning without medical attention, or even a little water. These were bitter moments for the old timers among us. Before the day was over, they herded us into a building and permitted us to get back some clothes and then the next day we were all locked up in the Cathedral and served two skimpy meals a day. A few brave Guamanians managed to smuggle in a little food and medicine.

Near Christmas time, the Japanese let Maria come to the Cathedral for a short visit to bring me food and cigarettes. Later events showed she needed this worse than I did. Since she was married to an American service man, she was barred from our home, and couldn't even get in to pick up cooking utensils or anything. The Japanese had moved into our house, using it as an officer's quarters.

Just before we left Guam for Japan on the Argentina Maru, Maria was allowed to see me once again and this time she was permitted to bring the children. She already showed signs of the hardship she was suffering, being force[ed] to live wherever she could find someone able to take her in. Everyone was in bad shape by the end of that first month, because the island was thoroughly disrupted and the Japanese were reorganizing the island as they wished. No crops were being grown. Business was at a standstill, and very few people had enough food. They had to fall back on the Japanese; and the families of the American service men were naturally at the bottom of the list.

The Japanese even had the gall to suggest to Maria that her troubles would be over were she to submit to being placed in a Japanese Army, "Entertainment Group." Well, Maria has a mind of her own and a temper that matches any good Irish temper any day. I guess she didn't improve her standing with the Japanese when that suggestion came up. Actually, Maria lived in eighteen different places during the war, and these were only temporary spots permitted her use by the charity of those who had the places. Maria and the four had it pretty tough.

But to get back where I was: We were kept in the Cathedral for about a month. Then the Japanese marched us five miles to Piti and into the Argentina Maru, a troop transport (she had been a liner but was now a troop carrier) and off to Japan. We went in tropical clothing being told that where we were going no warm clothes were needed. (We didn't have any anyway.)

We soon landed in Japan in the dead of winter. I have only a hazy recollection of those first weeks there. It was rugged trying to get used to the sudden change in climate on soup only, three times a day (horse bones with Chinese cabbage and miso). We had the trots so bad that the toilet facilities had to be tripled in the first three days. Then when they had us pretty low (They were cagey, those characters), they commenced to treat us better and gave us bread and some solid food and put us in Japanese discarded army uniforms, World War I or older, I believe.

You should have seen us taller men in those short-legged pants and small coats. My pants reached my knees and the coat sleeves reached my elbows. I laugh lots about it now, but boy, that was sure hard to take to have to accept a Japanese uniform at the time, especially so soon after having been in our own uniforms. I think we all had a guilty pang over that, but self-preservation had taken hold of us and the pride of uniform did not keep us from accepting anything to keep from freezing.

Even then it was so cold for all of us that we doubled up at night when trying to sleep under blankets made out of paper (yep, they were made from paper and the Japanese threatened to shoot anyone who let water get on them). A break for us was the appointment of an old retired Japanese Colonel as head of the prison camp and the old boy had a heart and soon we had some small coal stoves for heat. And we soon were permitted to take a bath (did not have one from the time we left

> *Guam until a month after our arrival in Japan) and three meals a day of rice and soup as our fare. . . .*

The letter continues and can be found on Guampedia, Robert O'Brien.

In the book *Captured: The Forgotten Men of Guam*, Roger Mansell and Linda G. Holmes vividly describe life at Zentsuji amid savagery, starvation, and murders. The Japanese treated western prisoners as inferior human beings, at best, and insects, at worst. Their book is an awesome read.

Many of the men of Guam, who were not Chamorro or mixed-blood men, like Robert O'Brien, were transported to Japanese prison camps for the duration of the war.

Sgambe and his dad, Marcello, were being held in captivity while awaiting transportation to Japan where they were destined to become prisoners of war. On the day they were being processed for movement, Mrs. Sawada, a Japanese national who had been living on Guam for many years, noticed Dorthea Sgambelluri, who had been her language teacher and had taught her English. She also noticed an English speaking Japanese officer, whom she recognized, supervising the loading of civilian prisoners onto trucks for transport to waiting ships in the port.

Sgambe's wife, Dorothea, who was standing at a distance, as ordered by the Japanese officer, waved at Mrs. Sawada as she approached.

"What is going on Dorothea? Why is your husband and his father over there with the American prisoners?"

"They are taking them to Japan as prisoners."

"Is he not Italian?"

"Yes, his father, he was born in Italy, yes."

"I don't understand this! Wait here! I'll talk to the officer."

As Mrs. Sawada approached the officer, he immediately recognized her as one of the friendly Japanese assisting his occupation forces.

"Good morning Mama-san," the officer said in English and smiled at Mrs. Sawada.

Good morning, Sir. I see you are holding two of my very dear friends, she stated, matter-of-factly, in Japanese, smiling at the officer.

Mrs. Sawada pointed to the two Sgambelluri's, Adolfo and Marcello, and continued to address the officer in the Japanese language, even though the officer was speaking English to the captives, and to her, *Sir, those two men are very friendly to the Japanese community here on Guam. The younger one is a policeman and has always treated us with respect, and the older one is his father.*

"They are American prisoners, and they are going to Japan to be confined. They may be repatriated later. They'll get good treatment," he assured.

Mrs. Sawada switched to English, "Sir, I believe, if you will check, you will find that they are Italian. Is not Italy aligned with Japan?"

"Not matter. Why you interested?"

"You will need people who will assist you here. The young man is a policeman, as I stated. He can be valuable to you. And is not the name Sgambelluri of Italian source? What will happen when they get to Japan, and they find out that you sent to prison two Italians, your allies? Will they not question that?"

The officer now devoted his full attention to Mrs. Sawada. "You stay here," he issued.

The officer walked over to the truck and ordered Sgambe and Marcello off. "You two, off the truck, get off. Now! He looked directly at Sgambe. "You policeman here?" he asked.

Sgambe bowed to the officer, "Yes sir, I am."

He then looked directly at Marcello, "You speak Italian?"

"Marcello replied, "Yes, I do." He looked directly to the officer, "Why?"

The officer slapped Marcello across the face. "You show respect. You bow."

Marcello slowly bowed – slowly and slightly.

"You Italian?"

Marcello stood up straight and thumped himself on the chest with his fist, "I am 'Merican!" He announced in his still broken English with a strong Italian accent. "A (he paused) Merican!" he emphatically repeated.

Sgamby spoke in Chamorro, "Christ's sake, Dad. Don't tell him that. Let them leave you here."

Marcello responded also in Chamorro, rather forcefully. "No! I am A-Merican. You stay here. Take care of Sgambelluri families. Look out for all Chamorro. I go with other A-Merican."

"Dad, don't be a fool. Tell them that. . ."

"You!" the Japanese officer shouted, pointing at Marcello. "Get on truck! Get on truck! Now!"

"Dad, don't be stupid. . ."

Sgambe was suddenly slapped across the face by the officer, "You!" he pointed at Sgambe, "go to police headquarters, go, now!" For emphasis, he placed a hand on his holstered pistol. "You go now!"

In Chamorro, Marcello spoke as the truck pulled away, "Take care of our family, son. Take care of our people. Do anything you must to protect them."

Thus, Sgambe was retained as a policeman on Guam. Eventually, he was assigned to work with a Northern Chamorro from Saipan, Jose Villagomez. Villagomez was a devout supporter of Japan and the Japanese. He did not like Sgambe, nor did he trust him.

Sgambe had to win Villagomez over to make his double-agent role successful. He did that by volunteering to translate English to Chamorro and Chamorro to English for Villagomez. Villagomez's superiors thought that it was Villagomez doing the translations. They praised him for his efficient language skills. Villagomez ate it up. Sgambe now had him just where he needed to have him.

As time went by, Sgambe could insert a word here or a phrase there and mislead the investigators in order to protect many Chamorro from the Japanese style of *justice.*

But with several Japanese/English-speaking officers and teachers on the island, and Chamorros from Saipan, it was a very risky pastime. Sgambe would need to be very careful and very brave just to stay alive.

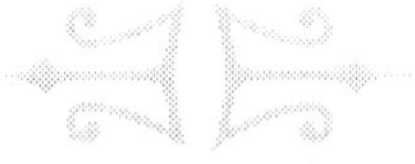

IGNACIA BORDALLO BUTLER

The following contains actual conversations that took place during our stay on Guam plus conjured conversations during the Japanese occupation of Guam designed to support the known facts:

"It is important to me to cement my grandmother's legacy," so stated Gerard A. Champion, grandson of Ignacia Bordallo Butler. As the current owner/operator of Butler's, Inc., the oldest business on Guam, Champion continues to uphold the honesty and fairness exhibited by his grandmother and grandfather.

Ignacia's husband, Chester Carl Butler, was born in 1884 and reared in Texas. He came to Guam as a sailor, fell in love with the island and its people, and decided that Guam would be his home. He remained on Guam after his discharge from the Navy. He was to become a very successful businessman. He and his wife, Ignacia, started Guam's first soft-drink business with a flavored seltzer-water, which became a very popular soda on Guam. In addition, they produced a root beer and a ginger ale, which the Chamorro called "ginga." He also was a pioneer of many other "firsts" on Guam, such as organizing the first Elks Club, and the first Chamber of Commerce, and founding the first club of Rotary International on Guam.

Chester's wife, Ignacia Bordallo Butler, was born on 13 November 1897, to Baltazar Bordallo and Rita Pangelinan-Bordallo. Baltazar was originally from Saucelle, Spain, a region between Madrid and the Portuguese border, and moved to Guam where he started a cattle ranch. He and Rita married and they had five children.

After Ignacia Bordallo, the oldest of their children, completed her schooling in Agana, she was sent to the Philippines for her high school education and to earn a teacher's certificate. On Guam, at that time, females rarely attended high school. She returned to Guam at age seventeen and met Chester Carl Butler, a former Navy man from Fort Worth, Texas. They fell in love, much to the initial displeasure of her parents.

Ignacia was a Catholic and Chester a Baptist, which normally would have been a big obstacle to marriage, but their love-bond was strong, and magnetism prevailed over tradition. Chester converted to Catholicism. They were married on 8 January 1915. As a wedding gift from her father (he had come-around) they were given a building in downtown Agana. Originally, the intention was to use it as a school, but they converted it to a store. They called it Butler's Emporium, which in addition to housing their soda and ice cream business, became a dry goods store. This was their first enterprise. Through the years, their businesses grew and diversified. Eventually, they owned the second movie theater on Guam, a trading company, the first radio station, and an emporium that sold all the major magazines of the day such as *Life, Look, Time, Post, Newsweek,* and *Collier.* But their grand prize was in gaining a Coca-Cola franchise in 1923. They brought into Guam the new product simply called Coke. Chester had travelled to Atlanta, Georgia, and had obtained a franchise from the new Coca-Cola Company. On Guam, Coke sales soon skyrocketed. Their Coca-Cola bottling plant was the first ever overseas, as was their franchise.

The Butlers were, in every sense of the word, partners. Each considered the other an equal. They did everything together. She was every bit as astute and business-savvy as her husband.

Sensing that war was a strong possibility, the two of them began to plan ahead as to what they should do to protect their family and their assets. They dispatched some family members to California and transferred some monetary assets to a San Francisco bank, as word of the American dependents preparing to depart Guam was revealed. They were simply being prudent by choosing to err on the side of caution.

When war did come to Guam, Chester was taken away as a prisoner of war, along with other civilian westerners and military personnel. This left Ignacia alone with several businesses to run under the watchful eyes of the Japanese. Before his departure for Japan, where he would be placed in a prison facility, Chester was held in temporary confinement, along with other Guamanian westerners, inside different buildings in Agana. Ignacia would visit him and bring him food and personal items. These visits would not last long.

"What will I do without you, my husband?"

"You will do what is necessary to survive. Do not overtly defy the Japanese. The American military will be back. One day. It might be a few months, or even a year, but they will come. Be alive for me. You do what is necessary to live through this. America will prevail."

"I will be here, but I hate the Japanese for taking you away. You are not military. I will forever hate them. It is simply wrong."

"Pretend to do otherwise. I know you, and I know that you will despise them, and you will defy them. Do it secretly. Make fools of them, but do it in a silent way. You be here for me when I come back. And, I will come back. Believe it. Have faith in me."

"I believe what you say. I believe in you. But, hear me, my husband. I will get my revenge for what they do to you, in my own way. They will never know."

The Japanese allowed her to continue in business but required her to accept only Japanese yen as payment. Of course, the Japanese would sometimes just take what they wanted from her store without paying. Her resentment grew. Because of her contacts and clandestine radio reports, she was aware that the yen was soon to be worthless after the Americans returned, and rather than turn in her American currency for yen as the Japanese had ordered, she buried it in her back yard. As another defiant act, many times she would sell to locals and accept their hidden American currency for payment, which she would also keep hidden from the Japanese.

Throughout the occupation, this feisty Chamorro defied the Japanese at every turn; however, she was careful not to go too far. Because she was selling merchandise to Japanese, she was given a little leeway, but very little. She also provided foodstuff and clothing for the hiding American sailors. If caught, she knew the consequence would be her death.

Eventually, loose talk about George Tweed, the lone Navy man holdout, caused suspicions to be aroused. Tweed became an irritant and then an obsession for the Japanese. Japanese authorities brought Ignacia in for questioning several times, and a few of those times she was subjected to physical beatings with hands and sticks, as the Japanese suspected almost every Chamorro who had married an American of being subversive and of supporting the American Navy holdouts. One particular time, Pedro Martinez and Ignacia were brought in by the Japanese for questioning about the location of Tweed, the elusive American sailor. As they struck her with their hands, or a long bamboo stick, she would fight back, screaming, clawing, and biting. For anyone else, such resistance would have meant death or severe torture, but for some reason, the Japanese admired the gutsy five-foot-two Chamorro.

Another example of her acts of defiance was that she hid all her Coca-Cola syrup, claiming she had run out of the product just before the Japanese arrived on island. She kept it hidden in her warehouse throughout the Japanese occupation. She never sold Coke to the Japanese, but she would occasionally smuggle a sample to members of the underground network that she fully supported. A bottle of Four Roses bourbon sometimes accompanied the bottles of Coke. She even refused to wear the cloth identification tag the Japanese required all Chamorro to display. Ignacia had no intention of helping them track her movements. She simply would not wear it.

"Mrs. Butler, we are fully aware that you have produced and sold Coca-Cola for years. All we ask is for you to continue to produce the beverage and sell it to our soldiers of Imperial Japan," so stated Lieutenant Watanabe, an English-speaking Japanese officer of the Guam occupation force.

"Sir," stated Ignacia Butler, bowing slightly to the officer as demanded by the occupation officials, "I must again state that I have no syrup to produce the drink. It was to be delivered before the end of December, but obviously that cannot happen now."

"I am hearing that some locals are still able to obtain the drink, even now. How could that be if you cannot make the drink?"

"I do not know, sir. I said I have no syrup for making the drink. I notice that your officers have sake to drink. You must have it stored somewhere. Perhaps some of the people have stored some Coke. I don't have any, with . . ."

"Are you being insolent, Mrs. Butler? Do you wish to be questioned at the police station?"

"No sir. It is just that you are aware that the bottling plant has not been in operation since you have arrived to liberate us from the westerners. If I had the required syrup, I would gladly produce the drink. I just don't have it. You may search any of my property, if you wish," she stated, looking him directly in the eyes, "I would never lie to an officer of Imperial Japan."

The officer smiled, "If you do, you shall die, Mrs. Butler."

"I am fully aware of that sir," she replied, still looking him directly in the eyes. "I would never be so foolish," she paused briefly, "Sir!"

"No, you would not be." The officer smiled again, turned his back to her, and walked away, not seeing, as she bowed toward him, her fingers crossed behind her back.

Mrs. Butler was fully aware of the clandestine network of Chamorros who listened to the secluded radios finding news of the war, and she was aware of the soap-a-graph code network written inside soap bar wrappers originating with Mrs. Johnston. She knew that the Americans were getting closer and closer to Guam in their progress across the Pacific. Mrs. Ignacia Butler knew what she was doing during the Japanese occupation and she enjoyed doing it. Feisty, is an excellent word to describe Ignacia Butler.

In time, though, the Japanese came to respect her strength. Butler's granddaughter, Donna Champion, writes of her grandmother's position during World War II:

'I understand that the Japanese assigned an identification number to every person on Guam when they took over the island; however, my grandmother was never given a number. They knew who she was. She was indomitable and, I think, they respected this quality in her.'

www.guampedia.com/ignacia-bordallo-**butler**

When the Americans began their pre-invasion bombardments of the island, it was her property that seemed to be in their cross-hairs. That bombardment was one of the most intensive of the war, up until that time. Battleships, heavy cruisers, and land and carrier based aircraft pounded the island unmercifully.

The Butlers' businesses were virtually destroyed by the American pre-invasion bombardments of Guam. The Coca-Cola plant was wiped out completely. Compounding the problem, as the American military consolidated their forces on Guam, much of the Butler's properties were simply confiscated for military use. The military paved roads, constructed airfields, and established military camps and headquarters facilities anywhere they saw fit. After all, a war was still being waged against Japan. That was the military's primary concern. Everything else was secondary. And, at that time, everyone understood and accepted that fact.

Some assistance did come from the naval forces to Ignacia. As the island was being secured and fighting Japanese stragglers became routine, the U.S. Navy assisted her in rebuilding her Coca-Cola plant. Of course, they also wanted to purchase the product from her. That plant went back on-line, producing the beverage much like it did when it became the very first assembly line bottling plant outside the United States mainland. The American military thought it wise to get it into production again. The Butlers were very happy to begin selling their Coke to the American military and to the local population once more.

Just over a year later, after the surrender of the Japanese, Chester was freed from his prison in Japan, and he returned to a destroyed business network. The two of them, with family assistance, started to rebuild. Having much of their holdings in the hands of the American military compounded their recovery. However, the very serious immediate problem facing them was that the Coca-Cola Company had thrown the ball game, and walked off the field.

Their major problems came from the Coca-Cola Company of Atlanta, Georgia. The Coca-Cola Company had, for some reason, voided their franchise, and refused to pay the Butlers their earned commission. As stated earlier, America and Americans had "written off" the Guamanians and Guam. Perhaps the Coca-Cola Company had also written Guam off. Who knows, but once Guam was liberated and the war was over, you'd think that Coke would have honored their past franchise. They didn't. The Butlers had to sue the mighty Coca-Cola Company in order to get their franchise reinstated. They won an out-of-court settlement against Coke and maintained their franchise.

Unfortunately, due to Chester's confinement as a POW in Japan throughout the war, his health had failed. He died in February 1952, a little over six years after his release from captivity.

While he was alive, he never received compensation for his land and businesses that were confiscated by the American military. Ignacia rebuilt their businesses as best she could, and, with her son, James, continued to manage them for years. After the war, the Butler's store was moved from Agana to Sinajana. As she grew older, with her head held high, she sold most of her holdings including the Coke factory.

For years after the war, Ignacia did all she possibly could to assist others in recovering from the damage the war had dealt them. She made interest free-loans when possible, assisted churches in recovering from the ravages of war, and continued to grow her businesses. Gerard said, "She was tight with her money but generous to a fault in helping others. She was a class act," he added.

Years earlier, before his death, her husband, Chester, had given her a three-carat diamond ring. When money got a bit tight, she gave it to the

Catholic Church who auctioned it off for funds to assist others in recovering and recouping their war losses. Her grandson, Gerard, came across the person who had bought that ring at auction ten years ago and bought it back. It is now "on loan," as he calls it, to Gerard and his wife. One day, he will sell it and give the money to charity. "That's what my grandmother would have wanted," he said.

Once, when Gerard was assisting his grandmother at the store, a woman returned a treadle sewing machine that she had bought from Butler's Inc. She wanted her money back. Gerard said to her, "Grandmother, she bought this machine four months ago, and you're giving her money back? You're losing money."

Ignacia replied, "I may be losing money, but I'm gaining a loyal customer."

In 1987, Ignacia Butler, known to all as "the Grand Lady" in business circles of Guam, retired at the age of eighty-three and turned the businesses over to her grandson, Gerard Champion, of California.

When we visited "Gerry" on Guam in August 2015, he related to us that, at the time his grandmother asked him to run the business, he was teaching school in California and was quiet comfortable continuing to do that. He liked teaching. But, when that little five-foot-two, grey-haired Chamorro grandmother looked at him with those pleading brown eyes and said, "Gerry, I want you to take over the business and run it for me," he couldn't refuse her. He said, with a twinkle in his eyes, "I melted. I've been on Guam ever since."

After she retired, she moved to California. From there, she travelled far, wide, and frequently. Her excursions knew no bounds.

She died in California on 18 April 1993, at the age of ninety-five, leaving a legacy few can match. She and her husband are buried together at Holy Sepulcher Cemetery in Hayward, California.

Ignacia Bordallo Butler and Chester Carl Butler, of Butler's Inc., remains with the distinction as the oldest continuing business on Guam today, and celebrated 100 years of continuous business while we were on Guam.

Guam - Chester Carl Butler and Ignacia Bordallo Butler were honored for being pioneers in Guam's business community and for their contributions to the development of trade and commerce in Guam. Chester Butler is a co-founder of the Guam Chamber of Commerce, while Ignacia Butler was known as the "Grand lady of Business". They owned several businesses including Butler's Coca-Cola Bottling and K6LG Guam's first radio station.

Grandson Gerard Champion accepted the award on their behalf, saying, 'I'll never forget the kindness in her heart, and the good that they did for our island.'

www.**guam**pedia.com/**chester**-carl-**butler**

When asked what he remembers most vividly about his grandfather, Gerard related this: "I was at my grandfather's house in California. I was maybe five-years-old. I had climbed up on a water fountain in the house, and it broke and I got scared and hid under my grandfather's desk. While under there I found a nickel. I put it in my pocket. Eventually, I had to face my grandfather about the broken water fountain. He asked me what I intended to do about it. I reached into my pocket and took out the nickel and told him that I would pay for it. I handed him the nickel. He took it, then, he took me in his arms, gave me a big hug, and put the nickel into his pocket."

When asked to share a memory of his grandmother, he responded, "Other than her kindness and her business sense, two things come to mind. First, I remember as a small boy, when she would come from Guam to California, she would take me and wrap her arms around me and squeeze me tightly, and I would inhale her aroma that I loved. Later, I called it the Guam smell. It was a combination of the Guam mildew or moisture, combined with the smell of the betel-nut, lime, papula leaf, and ground coral so common with older Chamorro. Though later in life, my grandmother did forego the chewing of the betel nut. Even today, whenever I think of my grandmother, I still sense the aroma. Second, she was never on-time for anything. She was always late. She lived on Island Time. That means *whenever* I get to it. I remember in California, she was on her death-bed, and all her family had gathered around, Grandmother said, 'I'm going to die tonight.' I told everyone that grandmother would not die tonight because she had never done anything on-time. Grandmother died late the next day. True to form, she was always late. But, she was a grand lady to the end."

Ignacia Butler is an American hero of World War II and a genuine hero of Guam. She stood her ground, tall and proud, but, she stood not alone. . .

HUNTING TWEED, SGAMBE, AND JAPS

The following contains factual data developed by research, and from a collection of old, undated, news accounts written by war correspondents during World War II:

All of the American military and civilians on Guam were eventually accounted for, including the six sailors who had fled into hiding because they were convinced that the Americans would retake the island within a few short weeks or just a couple of months. Radioman First Class Tyson, Yeoman First Class Yablonsky, Chief Aerographer Jones, Chief Machinist Mate Krump, and Machinist Mate First Class Johnston, were eventually caught and killed by the Japanese. The first three who were caught were tortured and beheaded. The next two were immediately shot dead. George Tweed was the only one who survived, thanks to the many Chamorros who constantly protected and secluded him, provided him with food, water, clothing, and companionship, and who endured torture, rather than give him up to the Japanese.

When the Japanese invaded, there was no definitive plan for defense. Since the naval governor controlled the Insular Guard and the police force of Guam, he ordered that the Insular Guard would man defensives around the governor's complex at Plaza de España. It was a weak defensive plan, but at least it was a defensive plan. There were no plans for defense at any other location on the island. It is simply a fact.

Some of the sailors and Marines, for many reasons, could not, or would not surrender to the Japanese. Some with permission from their superiors, some without permission from their superiors, simply fled into the dense jungle of the island and either prepared to conduct guerrilla warfare against the Japanese or prepared to hide from the Japanese until the American Navy came to their rescue. All were convinced that it was only a matter of weeks, or at the most, a few months away.

As we look back at the situation from our modern position today, it was a naïve, ridiculous belief. But, in December 1941, on Guam, it had merit. After all, the American fleet was believed to be the most powerful in the world. They did not realize that much of that fleet now sat at the bottom of Pearl Harbor. And, most of the elusive holdouts were convinced that to surrender would mean torture, and murder at the hands of the Japanese. They were partially correct.

Eventually, most all of the holdouts would give up or be captured by Japanese patrols. Only one would hold out until the American Navy did return two years and seven months later.

That single holdout, Radioman First Class George Tweed would live at the cost of numerous Chamorro tortures and deaths. Francisco Ogo, Manuel Aguon, Juan Cruz, Juan and Joaquin Flores, Jesus Reyes, Wen Santos, Tommy Tanaka, Jose Luhjan, Wen Santos (for a second time), Francisco Pangelinan, Juan Prez, Juan Pangelinan, Antonio Artero, and others, each stepped up to defy the Japanese. They entered the deadly game in which the losers died. And there were others, other brave men who moved the sailors from place to place, paved the way by securing agreements, and passing supplies of food, health and comfort items, and clothing to assist and safeguard the remaining six sailors.

At first, when picked off the island by the crew of a passing destroyer, George Tweed seemed to relay a slightly different story of survival. In his first few interviews, appearing in magazine articles and newspaper accounts, and after surviving Guam and returning to the United States, Tweed never mentioned his assistance from the Chamorros. Articles from archives in Navy and Army published magazines support that fact. In the publication *Yank Magazine* in September 1944, an article written by Cpl. Tom O'Brien and a later one in a similar Navy magazine article, failed to mention the Chamorro assistance that allowed Tweed to survive thirty-one months on Japanese occupied Guam. However, in later interviews, after the liberation of Guam, he does mention the "natives" who helped him evade the Japanese. Indeed, he praises many of them.

In his book, told by him to the writer Blake Clark, Tweed does credit the loyalty and assistance that he received from the Chamorros. He also wrote of one Chamorro, he had planned to kill—Adolfo Sgambelluri. After the Navy made a wartime film about the exploits of "The Ghost of Guam" as Tweed was coined, he ultimately returned to Guam to personally thank some of those who assisted him, perhaps encouraged by the Navy—somewhat belatedly. Guam was secured in August, and the articles appeared in September 1944. Security of confidential information about Guamanians could not have been the reason for not mentioning the assistance by Chamorros in the first few magazine articles.

When Tweed returned to Guam with a Chevrolet vehicle, donated by the automobile company, as a gift to Antonio Artero, the last person of many who had secluded and protected him, there were large demonstrations protesting his visit. It was the first mass demonstration by Guamanians regarding anything in their history. They were extremely upset about the contents of his book, *Robinson Crusoe, USN.*

Initially, when the Japanese conquered the island, all Chamorro civil servants, including the former Insular (police) Force, were *questioned* very harshly by the Japanese. As the Japanese took control of the entire island and set about establishing what they believed to be total control over the population, Sgambe was retained as a policeman. Perhaps this was due to his fair yet firm dealings with the population of Guam, including Japanese, and perhaps it was his Italian sur-name or the fact that he was half Chamorro. This time, he was ordered by the Japanese occupation forces to *keep an eye* on the Chamorro population, and to report suspected subversive activity to the authorities. This *assignment* would place Sgambe in a role that saved many Chamorro lives, but would label him as a Japanese sympathizer to his fellow Guamanians—for many years to come.

Even today there are some that do not believe Sgambe's true role.

And, after the Americans re-captured Guam, he would voluntarily "walk back into the lion's den," at his request, to further assist the American forces. He was to be the proverbial "fly on the wall," in prison with Japanese suspected of war crimes. This unselfish act of bravery would further entrench him as a Japanese sympathizer in the hearts and minds of an island population that had endured barbaric treatment by these Japanese occupiers for almost thirty-two months. Alone, he wore the scarlet letter and the scorn of a people for many years—just to serve his country and his island people.

Interestingly, Sgambe would later assist the Marines in securing the holdouts on Tinian and in the surrender of Rota to the Americans. He acted as interpreter and as an advisor to American Marines. The Chamorros of Tinian, Saipan, and Rota were pro-Japanese. Marines could not trust them. Sgambe would pave the way, acting as interpreter, guide, advisor, and also as an investigator. Then, Sgambe would briefly join the Guam Combat Patrols to assist in hunting down the evasive, defeated, yet dangerous Japanese forces hiding on Guam. The Guamanians relished this particular duty. They would seek revenge, and they would extract it.

From a newspaper clipping titled "GUAM COUPLE HUNTING JAPS FOR VENGEANCE," the names of the author and the newspaper are unknown. It was apparently written in 1944. The following are excerpts from that newspaper article:

"None were more effective and efficient than a Chamorro couple, Felicano and Louisa Santos—each armed to the teeth.

Louisa remembers when the Japanese came to her home just before the Americans landed.

Come with us, the Japanese said. We will take you to a place where you will be safe from the American bombs, according to Louisa.

He led Louisa, her mother and her sister, along with twenty-five or so others to a big bomb crater. *It was like a big foxhole,* Louisa recalled.

At the urging of the smiling Japanese soldiers, they all jumped, walked, or crawled into this big crater supposedly to be safe from the American bombs.

Go ahead and sleep, one of the English speaking Japanese said. *We will watch over you.*

It started to rain.

Suddenly there was a burst of machine-gun fire, Louisa related.

When I fell, I fell under a bunch of falling bodies. Ramon Garrido fell near me. He was alive but bleeding. The Japanese came into the crater and cut his head off. Manuel Cherfours, Principal of the Merizo School, was hit with a sword. He fell and remained very still. Then it started to rain harder. It was a very hard drenching rain, she paused, a tear ran down her cheek and she brushed it away with a stern blank-stare, straight ahead, *he lived,* she finished.

After a long, silent pause, she continued, *my sister suddenly said to me that we must get out of here. Our mother is dead,* she said. *We lay still as the rain grew more intense. Then the Japs started to leave. My feet were hurt from a grenade or gunfire, I started to crawl. A man, Thomas Cruz, helped me crawl away.* Again she paused briefly and swallowed, brushing her hair away from her face, she blurted, *my sister died.*

Felicino and Louisa lived at the edge of the jungle near the 77th Infantry Division command post. They are armed with a couple of *found* M-1 carbines that must have been *discarded* from a Marine supply point, along with a couple of bandoliers of .30 caliber ammunition.

They hunt Japanese holdouts.

Feliciano gave Louisa a smile, turned his head toward the listening group of reporters and remarked admiringly, *my pistol packin mama.*"

And, so it was, after the liberation of Guam in 1944, and for several years thereafter.

SGAMBE'S BURDEN

The following contains factual data, conjured conversations, and author-designed dreams, utilized to support and enhance known facts:

Dorothea, if ever you hear that I have been arrested, or if I go missing, protect our family first. Take Adolf, Joseph, Giovanni, Wilfred, and Robert and go inland, quickly. Don't take time to gather food and clothes. Just go. Drop each child off at a different ranch; make it a different trusted family, and go hide. The Marines and the Navy will be back. I know they will, but. . .

Adolf, don't talk like that. You frighten me. I believe in you. Even though I don't know the details, I. . .

Asagua-ho! The children first. Our family must survive. Must survive. Must survive. . .

"Sgambe!" His eyes snapped open. He tensed. After a short pause, he heard it again, "Sgambe! (in Chamorro) Wake up!" He shook his head to clear his thought process. He had been dreaming, several dreams with the same ending, and he shook with a foreboding fear that one of them may come to be.

The voice was that of Villagomez, the Saipanese investigator for the Japanese police on Guam. He was the one who seemed to be watching

Sgambe most of the time now. And, he was Sgambe's boss. To his close friends, Sgambe called Villagomez *the Jap lover.* The Japanese had imported him from Saipan. He was a Chamorro. A *Northern* Chamorro. A Saipanese.

It was early afternoon on 11 September 1942. Sgambe had worked most of the previous night and was catching a few precious hours of sleep. When he departed work at the police station in Agana early that morning, he noticed some unusual foot traffic of Japanese military in and out of the building. Something was up. He just didn't know what it was.

As usual, he tensed, his throat went dry, and he faked a smile as he replied, "Yes! I'm awake. What is it?" (speaking Chamorro) he responded.

"Report to Chief Shimada. At once, Sgambe!" (in Chamorro) the Saipan native almost shouted at him. The imported Chamorros treated the Chamorros of Guam as unwanted step-children. Clearly, the Northern Chamorros sided with the Japanese. They favored the Japanese occupiers over the Chamorros of Guam. He didn't respond to Sgambe's smile and added a curt, "Now!"

"Okay, okay. I'm on my way." Sgambe allowed his feet to drop to the floor as he rubbed the sleep from his eyes.

Villagomez turned and began to walk away. Soon, he was out of sight.

As he pulled his shoes on, Sgambe wondered what was up. It had to be important for the Jap lover, Villagomez, to personally bring him the message. Fleetingly, the thought that they were on to him passed through his mind. He often wondered what he would do if the Japs ever caught on to his double-role. He had made a decision early-on that he would resist the Japanese, but in his own way. He had to protect his family and the people of Guam. He had to do it his way. But, if he were discovered or even suspected . . ., he shook the thought from his mind. Oh, he had formulated a plan of sorts. He would be killed, of course, but he had carefully planned for his wife to take the children and flee into the interior. They would be taken care of just like the elusive American sailors had been. The children would be farmed out to other families in order to conceal and protect them. Just hold out 'til the Americans return. They will be back. He had already heard over the clandestine radios of the Japanese fleet being destroyed by the American Navy near the Midway Islands, and most recently, he listened with awe to the radio announcer telling about American Marines fighting Japanese in the Solomon Islands. They'll be back. He just had to survive—with his family intact.

He could simply discontinue his double-role and just do as he was told by the Japs. That would be easy, and it would be the wise thing to do. But, he knew he couldn't do it. He had to fight the Japs any way he could, and this was the best way he knew. But, one mistake, just one, and he knew that he would be a goner. He didn't want to think about it, but his family would be goners too. He took pride in the fact that he had already safeguarded several Chamorros from certain torture and possible death at the hands of the Japanese. And they, both the Chamorros and the Japs, were none the wiser.

He chuckled to himself as he recalled when the Japanese were tipped off that F. B. Leon Guerrero, a Chamorro, was an American sympathizer. It created a buzz throughout the police department, and they had begun discussions about arresting him. To plant the seed, Sgambe, matter-of-factly, without emphasis, and as casual as he felt appropriate, let it leak through the police department that Leon could not possibly be an American sympathizer because he was always in trouble with the naval governor for anti-American activities, and he had constantly refused to obey the governor's rules and regulations. "Everyone knew that," Sgambe would say.

The Japanese authorities decided they had better things to do. Leon was not arrested. Or, stated in another context, Leon was still alive.

At another time, Sgambe saved Felix Wusstig from arrest, or worse, by the Japanese. Felix had threatened a Nisei with a rifle. He threatened to shoot him, a capital offense. The Nisei told Japanese investigators that he was threatened with a rifle. Sgambe got the Nisei's wife, a Chamorro, to tell investigators that Felix had a pistol and didn't threaten anyone with a rifle. She didn't know where the pistol came from. The investigators assumed both were lying. The case was dropped after Felix denied the entire matter.

Sgambe would also warn those with clandestine radios when the Japanese planned to conduct a surprise search for hidden radios. They always stayed one step ahead of the searchers.

On his way to the police station, Sgambe, was turning over in his mind the various possibilities for his summons to report to the chief of police. None of them were good.

"I'm here to see the chief," (speaking in Chamorro) Sgambe told the desk attendant as he entered the station.

"Chief wants you back here at seven o'clock today," the sergeant said (in Chamorro).

"What's up?" Sgambe asked.

"Seven. Sharp! Dress in dark clothing," the sergeant replied rather testily, nodding toward the door in a gesture of dismissal.

Sgambe started back toward his home deep in thought about this unusual situation. As he passed one of his close friends, he made eye contact without visual indication to anyone else and whispered as they passed on the street, "Something's up! Seven, tonight. Be careful."

He spent a fitful day thinking about what would happen at seven o'clock. He kept rolling various scenarios through his mind, dismissing one after another, and then recalling them, again and again. He formulated what he would do if he were arrested at 7 p.m. Should he tell his wife to assemble the children and go into the interior as planned? Maybe he should. All day, he vacillated from one situation to another, one plan to another. Perhaps he should remain quiet. Act casual. He returned to the police station a little before seven.

He had to run through a torrent of rain the last few yards before entering the police station. "Okay. Here I am," (in Chamorro) he announced, cheerfully, as he entered the station. Inside, he saw several interpreters from Saipan and a Jap officer by the name of Kimura talking with the Saipanese. A couple of Jap soldiers were standing nearby. Sgambe nodded to them, "*Kombowa*," he announced. They simply glared at him.

Finally, one of the Saipanese turned to Sgambe, as if to acknowledge his presence for the first time, "Come back after eleven o'clock," he said in Chamorro.

"What time after eleven?"

The Saipanese did not respond.

"I'll just wait here then," Sgambe replied. "I'll just go upstairs and relax," he added.

He was anything but relaxed. But, he did pretend to sleep.

Before long, he fell into a fitful nightmarish sleep. He tossed and turned, moaned and groaned, and dreamed a horrible dream:

It came just at sunset as a short, heavy, raucous cloudburst. Heavy rain fell in windswept streams creating pools where raindrops danced like soldiers on parade. The night emerged as a cool, still, quiet, evening. Everything always felt and smelled, so fresh after a rain. Later, as the evening grew darker and shadows pushed aside the light of day, Dorothea tucked her boys into bed. Before she retired for the night, she stepped out onto the porch and inhaled the sweet fragrance of the air blanketing her island home. She wondered almost aloud what her husband could be doing that was keeping him at work so long.

She reentered the home, now chilled by the night air, and put out the single light muted by a paper bag draped as a makeshift shade surrounding the bulb. Dark curtains were hung over each window as she closed and shuttered the front door, and shortly thereafter, drifted into a light slumber. Occasionally she had awakened, listened to the familiar sounds of the night, and drifted back to an incomplete sleep.

It was the sound of automobile or truck engines that first alerted her. Then silence. Relaxing, she began to drift off again.

"Come out! Come out now!" the voice of a Japanese officer demanded in near perfect English.

Dorothea had awakened as the trucks quietly pulled up near the front of her home. But, it had been quiet for almost a minute. She dismissed the noise as a dream. The loud voice caught her off-guard. Her husband had been called into work earlier that evening. That was unusual. At first, she thought that something had happened to her husband. An accident? Perhaps he was hurt. Or worse. But, suddenly, she stiffened as she drew a sharp breath that caught in her throat. She knew!

Awakened by the noise, Adolf, her oldest child ran into her bedroom, "Mama, what's going on? There are many Japanese soldiers out front? I'm frightened."

"Hush child. It's nothing. I'll see about it. You go get your brothers and go out the back door. Run as far and as fast as you can. Do it quickly and quietly. Remember what we have talked about many times. Time is now, son. Go quietly. Go quickly!"

Dorothea instinctively knew that Sgambe had been found out. Now they had come for her. But, she was hoping against hope that her children would be spared. She had, over time, instructed her oldest, six-year-old, Adolf, what to do if this ever happened.

Adolf ran into the back bedroom to gather his younger brothers and slip out an unmarked, makeshift door in the rear of the home. His memorized instructions were to run to a nearby farm. He knew the way. She needed to give them time to slip out and get away.

"I'm coming. Just a minute! Please!"

"Come out this instant, Dorothea!" (speaking in Chamorro) It was the voice of the despised Northern Chamorro (Saipanese), Villagomez. "You come out. We spare your children," he demanded matter-of-factly.

"I'm coming out. Please don't hurt my children. They are asleep." (speaking Chamorro)

She peered through a slightly open curtain and looked out the window to see about a dozen Japanese soldiers, and an officer, armed with the ever present samurai sword and pistol, standing beside Villagomez. As she moved and opened the door, the headlights of two vehicles came on suddenly, bathing her in bright, blinding light. As she brought her hand up to shield her eyes, she caught sight of what appeared to be a man on his knees, on the ground. He was covered with blood, and a hood was over his head, but she recognized her husband immediately. His white T-shirt was in tatters from apparent lashings. She flung the front door open.

"My Sgambe!" (in Chamorro) she screamed.

She had taken only one or two steps until she was grabbed roughly by two burly Japanese soldiers who immediately drug her from the front porch onto the ground a few feet away from her husband. She fell to her knees. She was petrified. Her entire body went numb. She opened her mouth to scream, but nothing came out.

A Japanese soldier yanked the hood from Sgambe's head. His face was a bloody pulp. One eye was hanging from an empty socket. His mouth was gagged by a bloody cloth. A rope was strung around his neck and she couldn't see where the other end travelled. His hands were manacled across his chest and his arms drawn back far enough to insert a stick in front of his elbows with the stick running across his back. The ends of the stick protruded a foot on each side holding his arms back in a grotesque physical impairment of arms and chest. His good eye was wide from fear as the Japanese officer standing over him drew his sword and faced him. Suddenly the officer exposed a wide, sinister grin as he turned away from Sgambe and moved toward, a still kneeling, Dorthea, paralyzed with fear.

As Sgambe realized his wife was about to be beheaded, right there, this instant, in front of him, he screamed a silent scream as he unsuccessfully fought his restraints, ripping his flesh against the handcuffs and ropes, almost breaking the stick. . .

"Sgambe! Sgambe! Wake up, Sgambe. We're ready to go." (in Chamorro)

The Saipanese investigator shook Sgambe awake. "Hey, man. You must be having a bad dream. You were moaning and groaning. Wake up! Come on! We gotta go." (in Chamorro)

Waking in a cold sweat, shaking, and frightened, Adolfo Camacho Sgambelluri slowly and weakly rose to his feet. "Yeah, man. Just dreaming, I guess," (in Chamorro) he mumbled, as he started walking toward the stairs and began to unsteadily descend from the second to the first floor of the Agana police station that housed the police department of the Occupation Government of Imperial Japan.

"Hey, man, where we going?" (in Chamorro)

"You'll find out. Let's go." (in Chamorro)

Downstairs were about a dozen or more men. Saipanese, Japanese soldiers, and the Japanese officer he had seen earlier, appearing to brief the assembly of men. The briefing went on for a while. It was around one in the morning when Sgambe was ordered to mount the cargo bed of a truck with several other men. They departed the police station taking the Senator Gibson Highway out of Agana, followed by two other vehicles loaded with Japanese soldiers.

"What's going on?" Sgambe asked one of the Saipan interpreters.

"We're going to get some Americans tonight. They're in the jungle, and we know where they are."

Sgambe felt a tingle throughout his body. It became difficult to breathe. Clearing his throat, he nervously asked, "Why am I here?"

"The Japs want you as an interpreter."

"I'm no good at interpreting American. I don't speak good English. They should get Juan (Roberto) for this."

"You're it, Sgambe!"

As the truck, followed by a small convoy of vehicles, continued to travel down the darkened roadway, Sgambe's mind was considering all the possibilities. *Had they caught the Navy men? Do they know about me? Am I going to be killed?* He began to feel sick to his stomach.

"Would you tell the Japanese officer that I am not a good interpreter?"

"Why you trying to get out of this, Sgambe?" he pointedly asked.

"I'm not. It is simply that there are better interpreters for English than me. That's all," Sgambe explained. Then, he decided that he had better keep his mouth shut. *This is not going to be good,* he thought to himself.

It was early in the morning, somewhere around four or five o'clock, when the convoy came to a stop. All dismounted the vehicles as one of the Saipanese approached Sgambe. "Now! You will stay by me, and if you hear a shot, or any shooting, I want you to yell in English, 'Hands Up!' Do you understand?"

"Yes. Where we going?"

"You stay with me. Got it?"

"Got it."

They began to walk a narrow single-file trail into the jungle.

After a few minutes, the single file of men suddenly split into two files. One went left, the other to the right. They seemed to know exactly where they were going. Sgambe was hoping against hope that they were on a "wild goose chase," and that they would not find any of the six American Navy escapees.

Shout "hands up!" in English. Sgambe didn't like the sound of that. The Saipanese Martin Borja was standing right beside him. Borja was always eyeballing Sgambe. He had no choice but to do what he was told.

They suddenly halted, and Sgambe stood looking into a streak of dawn. It was deathly quiet. They waited.

Around dawn, from somewhere up front, suddenly a shot rang out. It immediately startled him, but, he quickly recovered. "Hands up!" Sgambe shouted through a parched, dry throat.

To his utter dismay, and, later to his deep sorrow, the runaway sailor Jones emerged from the trees, followed by Yablonsky and Krump. Sgambe's heart sank and then began to beat wildly. His nerves were on edge, but all he could do was exactly as he had been told. He felt totally helpless, exhausted, and spent. He drew short, shallow breaths. He knew he was to act as an interpreter. He had to translate Chamorro to English and English to Chamorro. Others interpreted from Chamorro to Japanese and Japanese to Chamorro. Why? Why him? His lips tingled. He felt frozen in time.

It began simply enough. Simple questions were asked and responded to by the three sailors. The Japanese officer, Kimura, looked like the cat that had just swallowed the canary. He looked smug, defiant, like he had just won the war. By their looks and the brief words from the three Americans, Sgambe could tell that the three sailors had resigned themselves to the realization that this was their last day on this earth. Sgambe could barely speak. The sailors were obviously aware and accepting of their fate. They knew what was coming. They never begged. They never wavered. And, bravely, they lied through their teeth in their response to questions the Japanese posed. They protected those who had harbored and safeguarded them to the end. *I am proud of them,* Sgambe thought—almost aloud. He felt sick to his stomach.

Kimura walked by Sgambe and looked him in the eyes. Sgambe forced himself to lower his eyes and drop his head as his heart pounded in his chest.

He had to stand there, next to Borja, and observe as the Japanese took turns beating and choking the men. The sailor's hands were bound behind their backs. They were helpless. The Japanese took great pride in beating up the Americans. These "Sons of Heaven" little barbaric scavengers of low life had to *prove* their superiority to any westerner, especially Americans. Sgambe tried to have a reason to look the other way. But he could see the Jap lover closely watching him. He steeled himself for what was to come.

The Japanese savagely beat and kicked the three sailors while they were manacled. Some of the Japanese soldiers would cut the skin of the sailors with bayonet tips, causing pain and bleeding.

Kimura ordered one hand and arm of each sailor released from restraint. Then, the Japanese ordered him to tell the Americans to take the shovels and to dig their own graves. He did as he was told, and silently swore that one day either he would kill Kimura, or he would dance on his grave. One hand and one arm of each sailor having been released from restraint, they began to dig silently. Soon, they had complied, by finishing shallow graves in the soft soil.

Sgambe considered all his options. There were none. *I can die with them, or live to remember them. I will tell the world of this time, this place, these people,* he swore to himself. *Just remember all these names,* he thought. *One day. One day!*

The Japanese officer and a couple of Saipanese conversed briefly, and Sgambe was told to tell the men that they would be given the opportunity to write one last letter to their families. This, of course, was a guise to see if the men would write any incriminating information.

Silently, the men wrote to their loved ones back home, knowing their letters would never be delivered.

After brutal beatings and being taunted by their smug captors, the three sailors were sitting on the edge of the graves, their re-manacled arms wrapped around their knees, and their heads bowed. Sgambe knew what was next, and it sickened him to the point of almost throwing up. Instead, he tensed his throat muscles to hold it down. It was with profound sorrow and intense fear that Sgambe saw the Japanese officer, Kimura, take out his sword and swing it into the neck of Krump. It took two swings to behead him. Sgambe said that Krump actually seemed to tell Kimura to 'swing again,' when the first blow failed to kill him. Sgambe winced with each blow of the sword as each sailor was thus beheaded. The only words uttered by one of the sailors were, "Goodbye, boys." This scene would haunt Sgambe until his last days on this earth. "One day," he hissed, through clenched teeth, as laughing and smiling Japanese soldiers stabbed, and slashed, with their bayonets at the apparent lifeless bodies that had fallen into the open graves. As the graves were being covered, Sgambe swore a silent oath that he would somehow live to make them pay. And, one day—he did.

Once each sailor was partially or fully beheaded, and dirt thrown over the bodies, soldiers continued to thrust their bayonets into the bodies several more times.

When the three sailors' bodies had been covered with dirt, Borja, the Saipanese interpreter, was heard to say, "This will be a lesson to some of you." Sgambe bowed his head, and as tears welled in his eyes, then quickly dried, he shook with anger-combined with despair.

With the death of the first three sailors, that left Tweed, Johnston, and Tyson still evading the Japanese, and still being assisted by numerous Chamorros and others. Invariably, some of those assisting the American sailors were suspected by the Japanese and several were arrested, beaten, and tortured, then released. Eventually, Tweed separated himself from Johnston and Tyson and struck out on his own. Some say that Johnston and Tyson had decided to split from the indiscreet Tweed. None-the-less, it would be a fortunate decision for Tweed.

To make sure the Japs would pay for their brutal crimes, Sgambe verbally passed on information about the murders of the American sailors to his trusted confidants.

Furthermore, I was instructed that it meant my life if I should expose the incident to any native. But I did make it known to many whom I believed American all around, so they might tell the story to the proper authorities if I did not live to see the Americans back to Guam. Some of them were Dr. Ramon Sablan, Mrs. C.C. Butler, Mrs. A.I. Johnston, Mr. Luis Untalan, Mr. B.J. Bordallo, Mrs. C.J. Torres, Mr. Vicente R. Palomo and many others.

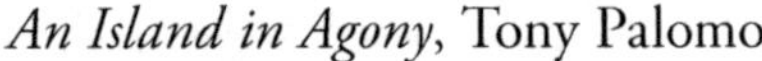

An Island in Agony, Tony Palomo

Photo above of a young Sgambe, photo provided from his son, Sgamby

By telling his story of the execution during the Japanese occupation to others, Sgambe risked his life to ensure that the Japanese would pay for their murders of the three American sailors. This act combined with many, many others, during and after the Japanese occupation, placed Sgambe in the role of an American hero of World War II.

This one man was not the only person to defy the Japanese occupiers in the Pacific, but he was the most unique. His style of defiance to Japanese authorities while supporting and defending his family and contemporaries placed him in circumstances that tore at the very fabric of duty and honor to one's people and to one's country. His defiance was right under the nose of the Japanese authorities. He walked a path few, if any, walked during the most horrific times ever experienced by a people. These were American people, held captive and brutalized by an evil, dogmatic empire. Atrocities committed by numerous Japanese, especially upon prisoners of war and indigenous people of their conquered territories, are fairly well documented. So well documented, in fact, that there must have been hundreds, if not thousands of undocumented atrocities from Burma to the Solomon Islands and all places in between. We may never know, but we can make rational assumptions, based on the collective savagery of all those well documented instances, in China, the Philippines, Wake Island, and other areas conquered by the Japanese early in the war. Japan violated international law, treaties regarding warfare, and common rules of modern civilized combatants. As time goes by, many memories and emotions do tend to fade. For Sgambe, they never did.

CONSOLIDATION

The following contains known facts developed by research:

On the morning of 10 December 1942, with the Japanese landing force of naval infantry accepting the surrender of all American military forces on Guam, and the three separate landings of almost 5,000 Imperial Japanese Army forces on three sides of the island, Guam was, in effect, captured American territory. In the hands of the Japanese, they immediately renamed the island Omiya Jima (Great Shrine Island). Initially, the Imperial Army Occupation Forces managed the island for a short time. Imperial soldiers were housed in schools and government buildings mostly in Agana. Chamorros were ordered to bow to all Japanese. Teachers were brought in from Japan, and the Japanese language and customs began to be taught. Automobiles, radios, and cameras were confiscated, and food rationing was placed in effect upon the Chamorro population. Any native caught with a weapon would be killed. Speaking English was forbidden. Yen became the currency. Possession of American currency was a serious crime. Forced labor was instituted, and young women were forced into prostitution as "comfort women" for Japanese troops and officers.

In March 1942, the Imperial Navy took over the management of the island. They were a bit more lenient, allowing the population to grow food and make products for trade. Social activities were allowed, but only to reinforce the "spirit of Japan," with games and songs. Children were allowed back into schools which were operated by Japanese rules. Discipline was still strict, but treatment was better under the Japanese Navy's administration. It was as if the Japanese thought and told all that they would be there for a thousand years. And, indeed they thought just that, for a few months. However, as the war progressed, in early 1943, with Japanese troops being driven back across the Pacific toward Japan, the Imperial Army returned to Guam in anticipation of defending it from the advancing Americans.

Most of these army forces were withdrawn from Manchuria. They were tough, hardened combat veterans. Social activities stopped, the schools were closed, and all Chamorros over the age of twelve were forced to work for the Japanese occupiers. They dug fortifications, built airfields, grew or raised food, and reinforced the interiors of caves on the island for defensive purposes. All this demanding labor was at the point of bayonets. No payments were rendered except for meager food rations.

But, the Americans were on the move. From the initial landings on Guadalcanal, and the retaking of Alaskan islands captured by the Japanese, to the assaults up the Bismarck Archipelago, the Armed Forces of the United States were on the offensive against the Empire of Japan. The U.S. Army's bombastic Douglas MacArthur was given command of the Southern Pacific forces, often referred to as the Southwest Pacific Area, and the Navy's calculating Chester Nimitz had command of the Central Pacific forces, also known as the Pacific Ocean Areas. For the most part, MacArthur was leapfrogging along the length of New Guinea, landing usually in unopposed areas, heading toward his "I shall return" Philippines, while Nimitz was storming straight across the central Pacific, assaulting small islands with frontal assaults on heavily defended beaches to get within bomber range of Japan proper.

It was working. America's industrial might had exploded. Planes, tanks, ships, various ammunitions, and guns were coming off the assembly lines as fast as possible while Japanese industries could not keep up. With America continuing to maintain rigid standards for training pilots, gunners, mechanics, submariners, engineers, and even scientists—everyone was deep into the war effort. Entire populations lent their support, from Eddie and Joe infantrymen to the Manhattan Project engineers and scientists, and even the iconic "Rosie the Riveter." All America was in the war. Standards were increasing, not decreasing.

America stormed across the Pacific in a series of amphibious assaults from the sea, pioneered by a generation of Marines in the 1920s and 1930s. They were now on the doorstep of the Japanese home islands. They had grown in tactics, technology, and determination. They were the finest amphibious forces the world had ever known—and, they were heading for Guam.

As the Americans began to invade Saipan, the Japanese on Guam became desperate. Air raids began on a frequent basis. In preparation to defend the island, thousands of Chamorros were driven from their homes and force-marched into the jungle areas to be confined into hastily prepared prison camps, ringed with machine guns; furthermore, they continued to be impressed into harsh, forced-labor gangs in order to continue constructing defensive positions for the "Sons of Heaven." With little food, water, and clothing, plus the inhumane treatment by the Japanese—many Chamorros died.

As anticipation of an American invasion intensified, the Japanese harbored a phobia about the locals "signaling" the American Forces. As mentioned, their initial solution was to assemble as many of the population as they could and march them into Manenggon Valley and various other isolated valleys on the interior of Guam to be confined, isolated, and starved in these crude, make-shift prison camps. In these *camps*, mass murders of selected groups prevailed as if some insane desire to exterminate witnesses of their *occupation tactics* seemed to be their additional focus. Indeed, earlier a directive from Imperial Headquarters had instructed Japanese commanders to eliminate their prisoners if American forces appeared to be in a position to overcome Japanese defenders. It is strongly believed that the Japanese forces were preparing for genocide against the entire Chamorro population on Guam.

While Sgambe was feverously working his dual role, his wife, Dorothea, managed to protect and feed all five of their children, Adolf, Joseph, Giovanni, Wilfred, and Robert (ages three to seven), even as they were being marched to one of the many barbed wire, machine gun guarded enclosed prison camps in the interior of Guam's dense jungle. Like her husband, she walked a tightrope to maintain her family, keep them safe, and have them survive intact. Likewise, Agueda Johnston and her children were herded into the Manenggon Valley to starve and suffer under the watchful eyes of the Japanese guards. Joaquin Limtiaco and his family were herded into the valley to starve awaiting the American invasion they knew was coming. And, there were others. Thousands of others—hundreds of families were moved into several tightly controlled areas surrounded by machine gun positions, with the guns pointing directly at them as an ominous signal as to what was to come.

My friend Adolf Peter Sgambelluri vividly remembers the Manenggon Valley. He remembers going to the river to get water for drinking or bathing, only to find the water contaminated with human waste. "You could see it floating down the river," he said. He was the oldest son; therefore, he bore the duty, the responsibility, and the tradition of acting as protector for his family. His dad, Adolfo Camacho Sgambelluri, was still defying and confusing the Japanese authorities. It was a strained time for the Chamorros on Guam.

Regardless of whether Guam was ruled by the Japanese Army or Navy, beheadings and other forms of execution were common. Torture was administered at the slightest hint of rebellion or disloyalty. The continuing evasion of Radioman George Tweed of the U.S. Navy also caused much more torture and a few more deaths of the resisting Chamorros. The Japanese were frustrated that they could not track him down and kill him. It became a deadly contest between the Japanese occupiers and the Chamorro protectors of Tweed. Through all this, for almost thirty-two months, Sgambe worked to protect as many people as he could, all the while mistrusted by the majority of Chamorros and watched closely by his Japanese and Saipanese overseers.

It's not unusual to find survivors of the Japanese occupation of Guam who simply do not want to relive the experience. Perhaps they don't want to recall moments of stark-terror, or for some, the memories of days when they simply didn't think the Americans were going to return to Guam. Many simply hunkered down into a survival mode in order to survive every day, one day at a time. Certainly it happened, but, there is little talk of it today.

There doesn't seem to be any single answer as to why some talk freely, while others will not discuss it. It is an individual thing. But the choice seems to also affect their descendants. To justify that statement, a specific testimonial that we extracted from Guam's public files explains how, but not why, many are affected even today.

Oral statement of Jose Quinene Cruz, who was sixty-three-years-old in 2003. As a child, he survived the occupation. He would have been born around 1940, and would have been around four-years-old on Liberation Day in 1944:

> *I come here really with a bit of a hesitation. I cannot measure to the atrocities that have been reported or that have been experienced. However, I come on behalf of the spirit of my grandmother, Librada Cruz Quinene, my mother and my father, Anna Quinene Cruz and Jose Reyes Cruz. If I have time, I will probably tell you about my own father-in-law and mother-in-law who refused, or hesitate really, to talk about the war. But, I have experienced them experiencing the nightmare.*
>
> *My name is Dr. Jose Quinene Cruz. I hail from Malesso', but I'm now living in Barrigada Heights. I am married to Teofila Sholing Perez and I have four children. I come as a child, or actually, the recollection of a child. The only recollection that I have because my mother and my father and my grandmother refused to talk about the war years, they really, truly believed that God will forgive and that God will bring justice.*
>
> *That, I thought, was very interesting. But I was always bothered that they befriended the Japanese when they later came to their home.*

I was the one who was experiencing the injustice because I saw that there really was, as part of my own upbringing and my own thinking. But, my mother and my father would always say, "Shut up. Do not say anything. It is done."

My only recollection from my grandmother and my father and my mother was one morning, when I was playing out in the rain, it was raining real hard and I told my mother, "I wish God would stop this rain." She told me, "Son, if the rain didn't stop, you would not be born." That's the only time when she spoke about the war. With further query, I said, "Mom, why, what happened?" She said, "I was in a firing squad with Nana," my grandmother, "and your father and two other siblings. We were there because when the taicho came," because my grandmother was the one who was massaging the taicho.

Well, the taicho came and Nana was not there, they burned their house because they were out in the ranch. They burned their house. When they came back, they found out that their house was burned. Then, they were actually corralled to go to the river right next to where the Malesso' Church is. They were lined up to be killed.

It rained and it rained and it rained. Because of the meticulousness of the Japanese, they actually did not kill them. My mom said we just slowly slipped out because they were enjoying themselves probably thinking that they'll kill them. So, that is my major recollection.

The other recollection that I have is really living in Malesso' and going and pasturing my cows right near where Faha is. You probably saw that. But, I always wondered how come there was a cross. When I asked, my father would say, "It's finished." You know? Let bygones be gone.

I further was an emcee for some of the celebrations in the Tinta and the Faha celebrations on July 15 and 16 in Maleso. To this day, I remember that the greatest feeling that I have was we were honoring the Americans for liberating us. It was never instilled in me that we were actually honoring the bravery of the people of Guam who were killed.

I had an uncle who was killed, my father's oldest brother. The memory that my father told me was only that he was a handsome dude.

He was a handsome man. That was not the word of my father, that's my modern word. That he was really a very industrious person. I wanted to ask my dad, "Tell me some more." I could not meet him. My father again said, "He is dead. Let him rest." I was deprived of my uncle.

I come here because I think the deprivation that I feel is really the deprivation of some of our loved ones. My uncle would've probably gotten me really, really advancing with a confidence that he actually had to the family. He was killed because of his stature. He was killed because he was a tall man, he was a big man. I'm a big person and my father's smaller than I am. I always told him, "Gee, if I only known Uncle Kin, I probably would actually measure up to him."

My other recollection is that I always saw my uncle Kin's children, who were without father and mother when I was growing up. No one ever told us really what happened. They continue to actually, my cousin, Jose, continue to be there representing his father. But, as a child, I actually then asked how come they don't have any mother and father. Again, my parents say, "Well, they were killed in the Japanese time and that's all that we know." Any recollection, or memory really, of any fond memories that I had, I was really deprived of that.

In addition, I think one of the things I can say about my mother is that she subsequently bore her oldest daughter on September 1944. But, subsequent to that, she had two miscarriages. I believe that was part of really the impact of war. Because Nana was forced to work for the Japanese. But, again, Nana would never talk about it. In that working, Nana, I think, was affected. But, she did not want to talk about it.

So, it's now my recollection. I'm sorry Nana is dead, and I cannot actually ask this. But, as I look at the atrocity and I hear the atrocities that are really bought, I actually say that there are other hidden atrocities, continuing atrocities that even to this day.

The atrocity that I bring is really the atrocity of being deprived of the memories of all of our heroes, all of my people, all of my elderly and all of the people who have merited.

I close really with a nightmare that my mother-in-law and father-in-law actually had. That one, I vividly experience. When Pop is about 80, 79 years old, he was starting to have Alzheimer's. When he leaves the house, there was one time when it was really a heavy rain. I think it's part of the recollection of the war, Pop, we found him hiding under one of the bushes. We asked him, "Pop, what are you doing?" He said, "The Japanese are coming."

My mother-in-law, who is still living, who is 93 years old, the only recollection that I have was that she was marched to Barrigada with her newly born son and forced to march, to carry the son who is just newly born. He was born on July 3rd, I think, 1943. Momma now refuses to talk about it. But, we hear it in the nightmare that she sometimes experiences. We hear it when she tells us she's afraid because the Japanese are coming.

Those are memories of the living. But, the memories of the dead I carry. I carry the deprivation of the memories that actually was not shared with me.

The above statement is from Real People. Real Stories. It was a weekly testimonial series provided by the Office of Senator Frank F. Blas, Jr. The testimony of Jose Quinene Cruz is recorded in the Guam War Claim's Review Commission public hearing held in Hagåtña, Guam, on 9 December 2003. This story was sponsored by the community involvement of The T-Factory.

AGUEDA IGLESIAS JOHNSTON

The following contains factual data, plus conjured, paraphrased, or edited conversations designed to support known facts:

There were others on Guam who defied the Japanese at the risk of their own lives and that of their families. William Gautier Johnston was a United States Marine assigned to Guam early in the 20th century. He was born in Athens, Alabama, in 1880, and graduated college in Tennessee. He attended two years of law school at Vanderbilt University. Soon the adventurous side of him took over, and he decided to join the U.S. Marines. After being assigned to Guam, the Marines put the college educated Marine to work teaching school to the Chamorros. That's where he met Agueda.

While teaching school, he met and fell in love with a young, local Chamorro woman, also a teacher, and at an earlier time, she was one of the students in his English language class. Her name was Agueda Iglesias [later] Johnston. She was eighteen-years-old when she married the tall Marine. It took some doing. It wasn't simple at all.

At that time, Navy Military Governor William Wirt Gilmer had outlawed marriage between military personnel and Chamorros on the island, believing the Chamorro people to be inferior. This same governor imposed other restrictive rules, eventually drawing the attention of the Secretary of the Navy. Among his rules were bans on whistling and smoking. He also required all Chamorros to carry identification cards. And, the most ridiculous order of all was to require each Chamorro to bring five rat heads into his sanitation department each day or face a hefty fine of twenty-five cents a day. Eventually, the Secretary of the Navy, Josephus Daniels, had Assistant Secretary of the Navy, Franklin D. Roosevelt, personally direct the rescinding of the Navy governor's "exceptionally restrictive orders."

William Johnston and others had petitioned Washington for relief from the ridiculous orders of this naval governor, but Johnston didn't wait for a solution to come from Washington. He found the solution. He resigned his commission in the Marines and became a civilian in order to marry his sweetheart, Agueda. Today, the name Agueda Johnston has been revered by generations of Guamanians.

Agueda was born in Agana in 1892 and grew up on a small farm in Finaguayog-Machanano. She was an only child. Schooling took place around the farming cycle. Crops came first. But, the young child loved to read. She was reading constantly, and she loved being in school. *"I was always happiest while in school,"* she had said in a *Territorial Sun* newspaper article dated 16 October 1966.

When she was between the ages of nine and eleven, Agueda was fascinated by the American Marines parading in Plaza de España. They were so tall and handsome. She conversed with them mostly in sign language, accented by a broken Chamorro-English pseudo language, combined with some household Spanish. To improve her communication skills, she then enrolled in an American school at age twelve primarily to learn English as she continued attempting to better converse with the Marines. It was not a simple task of just walking into the school, enrolling, and having a seat in the classroom. As a female, it was very difficult to get into the school, but, she did. It was her daunting determination that carried her through. She learned quickly, and she was very good at speaking and writing English, so good in fact, that she was selected to actually teach her new skill to others. She was paid thirty-two cents a day to teach school. She taught English to other Chamorros at the same time she was learning to improve her English. She ultimately became a teacher. It would grow from there.

One of her instructors was to become her future husband. Like the Navy governor at that time, her mother did not approve of her courtship with William. But, she eventually came around. After her marriage to William, also teaching in the same school, Agueda quickly acquired his traits of strong self-discipline and overt boldness. She was indeed both. In American terms, she was a "tough cookie." Those characteristics stayed with her all her life.

Today, Agueda is more than a household name on Guam. The name is spoken with great respect. Interestingly, she is noted for being a great educator, yet she never formally finished high school. Today, there is a middle school on Guam named after her.

In addition to their involvement in the education system, the Johnstons were successful business people on Guam. They had a movie theater, and a beauty shop, managed by Cynthia, their eldest daughter. Marian, the next to the eldest daughter, was engaged to an American sailor, from the USS *Penguin*. They also had a flair for making unique island soap on the side (managed by a son). The soap was a salt-water soap, very popular with the Navy. It was also popular with the Japanese occupiers of Guam. Their unique soap was composed of a mixture of caustic soda, coconut oil, and salt water.

At first the Japanese paid for the soap. Later, they just ordered Mrs. Johnston to simply produce it, and then they just took it. Locals also continued to purchase the popular soap. Many of the local families had only hidden American dollars and coins, which was forbidden by the Japanese. Possession of American currency was almost a sure death sentence; however, Mrs. Johnston would take American currency from the locals to sell her soap. She took Yen from the Japanese, but the soap she sold to them was inferior to that which she continued to sell to the Chamorros. It gave her a smug sense of satisfaction.

Before the Japanese invasion, William was working for the Navy Administration in public works projects. He and Agueda were considered well-to-do residents of Guam when the Japanese invaded. That invasion shattered their dreams and their lifestyle. At first they retreated to the north, or the interior, to their secluded ranches. The term "ranch" could mean a sturdy home or house, or it could mean a plot of land with a lean-to shelter. For the Johnstons, it was a plot of land with a nice home. Then, word came that they had to physically go to Japanese headquarters in Agana to formally surrender. On the way into Agana, they passed numerous bodies lying out in the open on the roadway. That was when William began to keep a diary, with his entries being chronicled up until near the date of his death as a prisoner of war in Kobe, Japan.

This author and the researcher of this novel have read those original diaries cover to cover. His description of details during the first few weeks after the Japanese occupation, and during his confinement in Japan, are astounding. Especially when one considers that the Japanese prohibited the recording of such accounts with threats of torture or death.

When the Japanese invaded Guam, although William was no longer an active duty Marine, he was taken as a prisoner and confined on Guam awaiting transport to Japan as a prisoner of war. Agueda and their children were held among the society of captives on Guam throughout the occupation. And, she would become a gifted, clandestine operator defying the Japanese throughout the occupation. Indeed, she may well be called the actual leader, or organizer, of the resistance network on Guam during the Japanese occupation.

The Japanese took over the Johnston's magnificent seventy-year-old house, Agueda's extensive antique collection, and all her silver and china. She and her children moved to the family ranch in the hills and began to survive from the soil and the food animals of Guam.

Their daughter Marian was a strikingly beautiful young lady of twenty-two years in age. Agueda feared for her at the hands of the Japanese who were taking many of the young Chamorro females as sex slaves. They called them *comfort women*. At first, Marian would hide in the outhouse when the Japanese came around the Johnston ranch. Japanese abhorred out-houses. It didn't make sense to use them when all one had to do was to use old Mother Earth, as appropriate. It worked for a while, but they had to come up with another guise to be used while still playing off the phobia of the Japanese. Knowing this, Agueda devised a scheme; she told Marian to cough constantly while in the presence of any Japanese. She then spread the word that Marian had contracted tuberculosis. The Japanese also had a phobia about that particular disease. It caused the Japanese to steer clear of their home. Marian was forever safe, but Agueda's problems were just beginning.

The six American sailors, who had refused to surrender to the Japanese, took to the jungle during the initial stage of the Japanese invasion. They went into hiding to await the American fleet that they assumed would be weeks, if not days away from destroying the Japanese and returning to Guam. Initially, they were but an irritant to the Japanese and to the Chamorros. But eventually they became a symbol of defiance toward the Japanese and a symbol of hope for the Chamorros. Most, but not all of the Chamorros felt that as long as the American sailors remained elusive and alive they were effectively defying the Japanese and inspiring hope that the Americans would return to save their heroic sailors.

But America, at that time, had no plans of returning to Guam. Indeed, most all of America didn't know or care anything about Guam. Guam had a curtain drawn around it. Unlike the Japanese occupied Philippines, Indochina, or China, no attempt was made to find out the situation on Guam. Guam had been written off. Guam was forgotten.

To support that bold claim let us look no further than Hollywood. The motion picture industry tends to establish what is popular in the minds of the movie-going audience. During World War II, patriotic films were very popular. On 11 August 1942, the movie *Wake Island* came to the American movie screen. On 3 June 1943, the movie *Bataan* was released. *Gung Ho*, a movie about the Makin Island raid by Marines was also released in 1943. These were patriotic movies designed to stir the war effort on the home-front. There was no movie about Guam. That is, not until 1962, long after the end of World War II. That movie was almost purely fiction. *No Man Is an Island* distorts and modifies the plight of George Tweed's hiding on Guam. They even substituted the language, using the Tagalog language of the Philippines instead of the Chamorro language of Guam. All-in-all, it again misrepresents to the American public the real activities on Guam during the Japanese occupation. There were just too many real people, doing real things, on the real Guam, for Hollywood to have made such a "dog" as this movie.

A real movie, with real facts, could have been made, if Hollywood and America had gone to the trouble to have those facts revealed. Remember, this movie was made in 1962, and Hollywood could have produced a movie that highlighted the heroic activities of many of those people defying the Japanese and feeding and protecting the American sailors on Guam. The intent of this novel is to reveal those facts. Agueda Johnston was a real person of Guam. Her story is real. Agueda's mission, during the war, became to protect the American sailors and to keep the spirit of America alive within the society of captives. So too did dozens of other Chamorros on the island of Guam.

Even today, as 7 December approaches, people gather all across America to "Remember Pearl Harbor" and those who can visit the Arizona Memorial in Hawaii, to pay respect to all the fallen on that "day of infamy." But, only on Guam, or in any Guamanian community anywhere, do they remember Guam. They remember those killed and tortured on Guam. They realize they are rapidly fading away, and they want to ensure the establishment of their legacy for all Americans to see. Unfortunately today, they are remembered, only and almost exclusively, by their Guamanian descendants.

Boldness during the Japanese occupation was risky. Agueda took risk. Accepting American dollars was risky. In fact, it was a crime, but if she refused American dollars, it would tacitly tell all Chamorros that she did not believe the Americans were returning to Guam. Therefore, she felt that she had to accept the American currency from the Chamorro. There were some days when she would have several American dollars and coins in her possession. Each day she would take the American money, hide it in a pocket sewed under her dress, and, at the appropriate time, remove it from the slit in her dress, and secure it behind a large framed photograph of one of her sons. That photo and its frame hung on the wall in her living room. Late at night, she would remove the money and take it outside to be buried in her garden at a special place known only to her. After the liberation by the Americans, she had over three-thousand greenbacks hidden, each with a picture of George Washington on the front.

Many times, Japanese officials, soldiers, inspectors, policemen, and Saipanese [collaborators] would stand, making laudatory comments while admiring the photograph in its ornate frame, still hanging on her wall, stuffed with American currency. Agueda knew possession of that currency brought the penalty of death. Again, it gave her a smug satisfaction.

There was one issue regarding her soap that the Japanese never discovered. There were secret messages written inside the paper wrappers covering the soap bars—messages like, "American fleet defeated Jap fleet at a place called Midway," or, "American Marines fighting Japs on Solomon Islands." Agueda sent her messages out based on input from specific Chamorro underground members. As the leader, or coordinator, she was the only one who knew all the underground operatives.

One of the other secret operations on Guam was the functioning of several clandestine AM/FM radios, secluded from the eyes and ears of the Japanese. At secret locations, men and women would gather to hear news of the progress of the war beamed in from Australian and some American commercial radio stations. The listening times and locations were a carefully guarded secret. Possession of a radio would lead to a death sentence. But, the information was a crucial factor in keeping morale alive, as many Chamorros had given up on the Americans. It was the only link the society of captives had to the outside world.

When the Japanese gathered the people of Guam together and told them that the Japanese fleet had destroyed the American Navy fleet in a place called Midway, and when the Japanese told them that their forces were victorious over the American Marines in the Solomon Islands, Mrs. Johnston and her "soap-a-graph," knew the real story.

Also concealed under Mrs. Johnston's soap wrappers were written instructions concerning the time and location of the next "listening" of the radio, and news of the advancing American invasion forces getting closer, and closer to Guam. Additionally, there was other important news disseminated only to a few trusted people. If those messages were discovered, Mrs. Johnston and her children would have been arrested, tortured, and beheaded. Instantly!

Mrs. Johnston was also a contact for Sgambe and Limty. If they had a vital and immediate message to get out, they would often pass it to her. And, she would send it out further, sometimes by the secret "soap-a-graph." The supply of soap lasted throughout the war.

When the first three American sailors were caught, brutalized, and beheaded, Agueda feared that they may have told of her involvement in the resistance network. Sgambe assured her they had taken that secret to their graves. He never told her how he knew. It bothered him too much.

Mrs. Johnston also talked often with Henry Pangelinan, an old Chamorro friend who, like Sgambe, was a member of the Japanese police department. Henry had lived in Saipan and spoke perfect Japanese. He and Mrs. Johnston were friends.

One day Henry showed up at her house, drunk.

"I know I am drunk. But I must tell you that we killed three American sailors this morning at Taihagan," he started to cry. "Ski, Krump, and Jones, they were beheaded." (speaking Chamorro)

"Oh, God, Henry! Were they tortured? Were they questioned about me?"

"They were only questioned about the other American sailors," he paused, "they taunted and abused them. They were given cigarettes and a note paper to write a last message to their families. The Japs thought that they would write something incriminating. They died without revealing anything." Henry paused, "It took two cuts of the sword to behead Jones. When the first blow cut him, it didn't sever his head, so he said, 'cut one more time, please.'"

[Actually, it was Krump, not Jones who took two blows of the sword.]

Henry's revelation did little to calm Agueda's concerns, but she continued her dangerous, clandestine activities.

Agueda I. Johnston, photo property of Linda Taitano Reyes, Agueda's granddaughter

Five weeks later, the capture and execution of two other sailors caused her to question her decision to continue engaging in such a dangerous endeavor, but she still did not stop.

This left George Tweed as the last holdout. Agueda stayed involved. She furnished Tweed with magazines, cigarettes, food, drink, and occasionally dresses, which he wore as a disguise to travel into Agana to see his friends and companions. She would also provide information on hiding places throughout the island that she knew about. She knew the island very well. Once, he actually came, in disguise, to a party at her ranch house, with Japanese present. But the primary means of communication between Tweed and Johnston was by an exchange of written letters. She was playing a very dangerous cat-and-mouse game. This was one hell of a brave lady.

When the Japanese took her husband to the prison camp, from which he would never return, it solidified Agueda's unqualified loyalty to America. It would never fade. That is one of the reasons she protected Tweed. It may have been the only reason that she protected him.

After Tweed was moved to his last hiding place, she continued to supply him with support, and they continued to exchange letters. Then, it caught up with her.

There was a knock on her door.

"Who is it?" she asked in Chamorro.

Kempeita! (Japanese military police) was the response. "You have been keeping the sailor Tweed. Come with us, and bring your family!"

Agueda was stunned. She couldn't breathe. "I have done nothing. I don't know Tweed. Is he that American sailor?" she asked.

"You come. Now!" was shouted.

Agueda and three of her children, two sons and a coughing Marian, who happened to be home at that time, were taken by the Japanese authorities, with a Saipanese interpreter, to the old Spanish Tribunal Building on the north side of the Plaza.

They arrived about four o'clock.

"You!" The policeman pointed at Agueda. "Upstairs. Just you! Now!" (in Chamorro)

Agueda was frightened, not so much for herself, but her children. Were the Japanese going to kill or torture her children in front of her eyes? What would she do?

She climbed the stairs and entered a room they called the "court-room," and before her eyes, on a desk, were a rifle, a club, and a stick with long knotted rawhide thongs, or strips attached. She knew what was coming, and she steeled herself.

"Please, me only. Not my children," she whispered a prayer.

She fought an instant urge of wanting to confess to anything to save her children, but, at the same time she wondered how much she could take. The blood drained from her head. Her heart was beating so hard that it hurt her chest, and her throat went dry and raspy. They were going to beat her, whip her, and after her confession, they were going to shoot her—and perhaps her children. She almost fainted.

There were three men in the room, the Japanese chief of police, a man now holding the whip, and Jose Villagomez, the Chamorro from Saipan, a Jap lover who acted as an interpreter for the chief, all wearing stern expressions.

"Johnston, do you know why you are here?" the chief demanded via Villagomez.

She heard him but was too petrified to respond.

"Do you know where Tweed is?" he shouted and was echoed by Villagomez.

Her lips moved as she croaked out a "No, sir. No!"

Suddenly, she was grabbed forcefully by two of the men and forced to bend forward over the back of a large chair. She clenched her hands around the bottom of the chair and gritted her teeth as lash after lash split her muslin dress and the flesh of her back wide open. She held back her screams, closed her eyes and groaned, and jerked with each violent damaging blow. Her dress continued to split along with her flesh, and she could feel the blood running, staining her dress, and dripping onto the floor.

"Do you know who has seen him?" asked Villagomez in Chamorro.

"No," she replied as faintly as she could to hide the pain and anger building inside her.

At first, she knew that she could not take any more lashes. Then, suddenly, she was lashed five more times. With each blow, the anger rose inside her, along with the searing pain of the blows.

Again she responded, "No!" and "No sir!" to each additional question. By the twenty-fifth blow, she was numb. Blood flowed down her body and pooled onto the floor. Her back was a raw sore. She was on the verge of passing out and praying for it to come quickly. All she could do was groan. Her head was jerked violently upright.

Finally, she spoke, "I don't know where he is, but I will help you look for him. Please!"

"You lie. I am sorry that you refuse to tell me what you know about Tweed. It is my duty to force you to tell. By fire if necessary, you will tell," the chief said, through Villagomez.

"Sir, I cannot tell you what I do not know. No torture can make me tell what I do not know."

She must have passed out. Agueda found herself alongside her two sons, ages twenty-one and twenty-nine. Her daughter, age twenty-two, was standing off in a far corner, still feigning a cough under the gauze mask the Japanese required her to wear. Four men now stood before her. Agueda wondered, what if they began to beat the children? What will I do? Will I break? It will cause the death of Tweed, yes; but it will also cause the death of dozens of Chamorro families. "How far does patriotism go?" she asked herself, "how far?" She stood trembling between her two sons who were holding her up. Their hands were stained with her blood. She could see anger mixed with pleading in their eyes.

George Tweed. This is the man for whom several have been tortured, two beheaded, and now my life endangered. What will I do? God help us all! she thought almost aloud.

The man with the club shook it in her face and yelled in Japanese while Villagomez yelled in Chamorro. "Go home! Tell no one what has happened here. Work with Japanese government to find Tweed. Remember, we are not through with you yet."

The Johnstons bowed politely and departed the building, and made a slow, painful trip back to their home.

Other than asking Antonio Artero, who was the person now hiding Tweed, to tell Tweed to stop writing to her, to stop sending her letters, she continued with her clandestine activities which included helping Tweed.

In response to her request, Tweed wrote her again. This time, he wrote to threaten her.

Much of the information regarding the torture of Agueda came from her hand written statement, and her type-written statement about Mr. Jose Villagomez, prepared by Agueda Johnston. Both items found at the Spanish Section of the University of Guam's Spanish Archives in a file marked—Agueda I. Johnston.

The following letter was written by George Tweed to Agueda Johnston perhaps carried by Mrs. Artero from one to another:

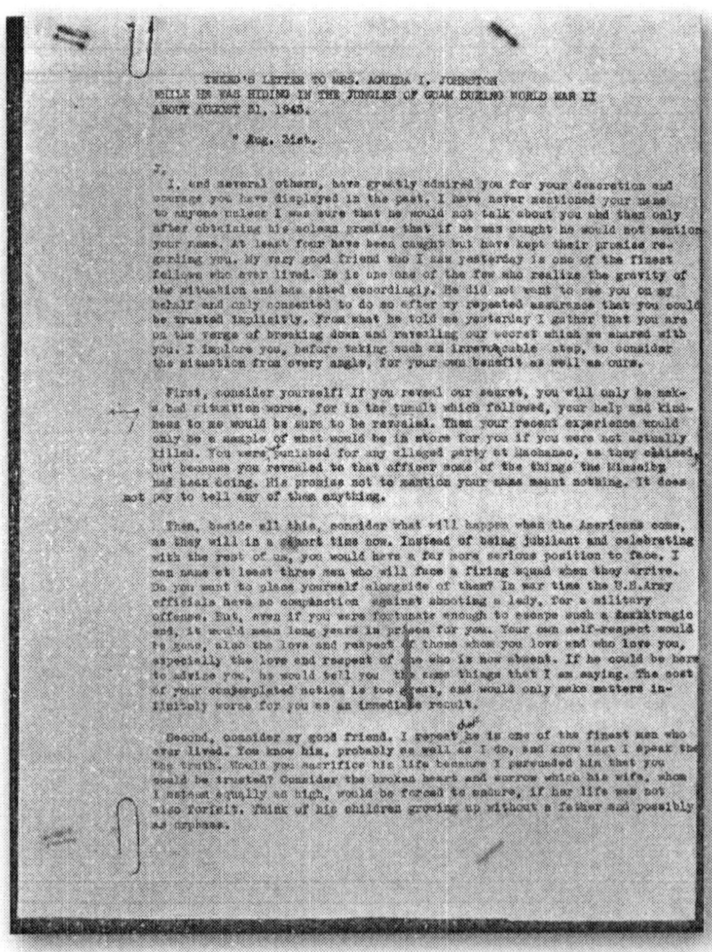

TWEED'S LETTER TO MRS. AGUEDA I. JOHNSTON
WHILE HE WAS HIDING IN THE JUNGLES OF GUAM DURING WORLD WAR II
ABOUT AUGUST 31, 1943.

" Aug. 31st.

J.,

I, and several others, have greatly admired you for your descretion and courage you have displayed in the past. I have never mentioned your name to anyone unless I was sure that he would not talk about you and then only after obtaining his solemn promise that if he was caught he would not mention your name. At least four have been caught but have kept their promise regarding you. My very good friend who I saw yesterday is one of the finest fellows who ever lived. He is one one of the few who realize the gravity of the situation and has acted accordingly. He did not want to see you on my behalf and only consented to do so after my repeated assurance that you could be trusted implicitly. From what he told me yesterday I gather that you are on the verge of breaking down and revealing our secret which we shared with you. I implore you, before taking such an irrevocable step, to consider the situation from every angle, for your own benefit as well as ours.

First, consider yourself! If you reveal our secret, you will only be making a bad situation worse, for in the tumult which followed, your help and kindness to me would be sure to be revealed. Then your recent experience would only be a sample of what would be in store for you if you were not actually killed. You were not punished for any alleged party at Machanao, as they claimed, but because you revealed to that officer some of the things the [illegible] had been doing. His promise not to mention your name meant nothing. It does not pay to tell any of them anything.

Then, beside all this, consider what will happen when the Americans come, as they will in a short time now. Instead of being jubilant and celebrating with the rest of us, you would have a far more serious position to face. I can name at least three men who will face a firing squad when they arrive. Do you want to place yourself alongside of them? In war time the U.S.Army officials have no compunction against shooting a lady, for a military offense. But, even if you were fortunate enough to escape such a ~~xxxx~~tragic end, it would mean long years in prison for you. Your own self-respect would be gone, also the love and respect of those whom you love and who love you, especially the love and respect of one who is now absent. If he could be here to advise you, he would tell you the same things that I am saying. The cost of your contemplated action is too great, and would only make matters infinitely worse for you as an immediate result.

Second, consider my good friend. I repeat that he is one of the finest men who ever lived. You know him, probably as well as I do, and know that I speak the truth. Would you sacrifice his life because I persuaded him that you could be trusted? Consider the broken heart and sorrow which his wife, whom I esteem equally as high, would be forced to endure, if her life was not also forfeit. Think of his children growing up without a father and possibly as orphans.

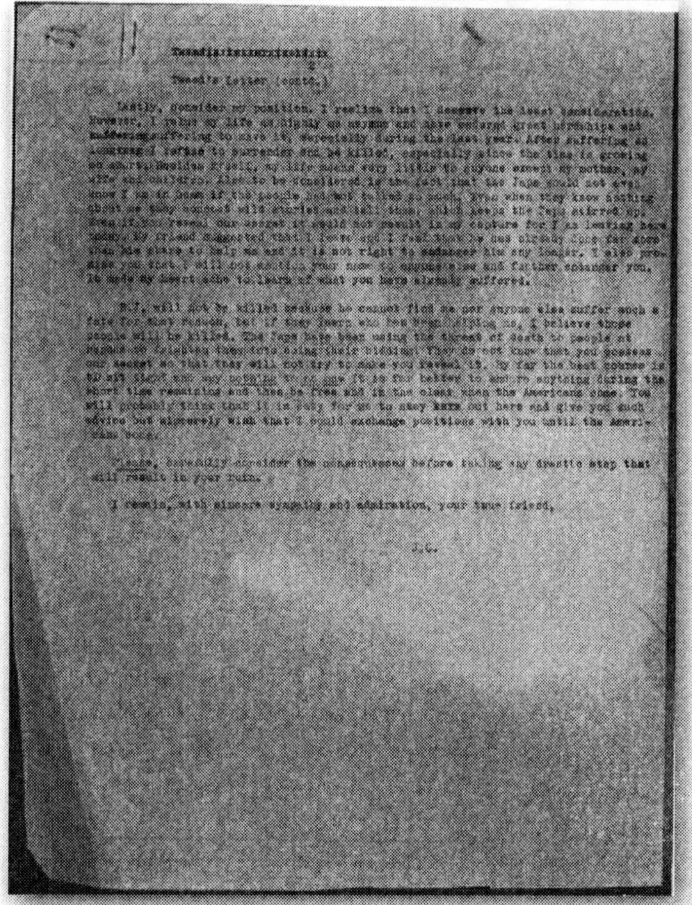

2

Tweed's Letter (contd.)

Lastly, consider my position. I realize that I deserve the least consideration. However, I value my life as highly as anyone and have endured great hardships and suffering to save it, especially during the last year. After suffering so [illegible] I refuse to surrender and be killed, especially since the time is growing so short. Besides myself, my life means very little to anyone except my mother, my wife and children. Also to be considered is the fact that the Japs would not even know I am in Guam if the people had not talked so much. Even when they know nothing about me they concoct wild stories and tell them, which keeps the Japs stirred up. Even if you reveal our secret it would not result in my capture for I am leaving here today. My friend suggested that I leave and I feel that he has already done far more than his share to help me and it is not right to endanger him any longer. I also promise you that I will not mention your name to anyone else and further endanger you. It made my heart ache to learn of what you have already suffered.

R.J. will not be killed because he cannot find me nor anyone else suffer such a fate for that reason, but if they learn who has been helping me, I believe those people will be killed. The Japs have been using the threat of death to people at [illegible] them into doing their bidding. They do not know that you possess our secret so that they will not try to make you reveal it. By far the best course is to sit tight and say nothing to no one It is far better to endure anything during the short time remaining and then be free and in the clear when the Americans come. You will probably think that it is easy for me to stay out here and give you such advice but sincerely wish that I could exchange positions with you until the Americans come.

Please, carefully consider the consequences before taking any drastic step that will result in your ruin.

I remain, with sincere sympathy and admiration, your true friend,

J.C.

Tweed's letter property of the Spanish Archives, University of Guam

The unlikely Agueda Johnston grew into her role by her assimilation of her husband's Marine Corps traits, and the arrest and detention of her husband by the Japanese that infuriated her by the fact that the Japanese were confining people who were civilians, not military, based on the color of their skin. For a while, she brought food and small comfort items to her husband's place of detention, items like small notebooks, pencils, handkerchiefs, clothing, and similar items.

On one of her visits, while her husband was being held in detention, Agueda informed him that the Japanese commander had requested that she provide him and his staff with an entertainment, a party with food, drink, and music for an evening. She was told that it was common knowledge that she was the one who could provide a lavish evening of entertainment. She didn't want to do it. So she told William of the request, and that she was going to refuse. William advised his wife that survival was now the paramount mission, and to deny the request would lessen her chance of survival.

"Do it!" he told her. "The children can play musical instruments, you can provide good food, and break the bar open. Treat them well. It will cause them to accept you. That is important to your success in defying them. Use your wits, not your emotions, to deal with the enemy."

She followed his advice.

Being "friendly" with the Japanese helped her manage the resistance network, but now it was much more dangerous to continue. Yet, she did continue. She relished the position and the activities. Clearly, she is an American hero of World War II.

Linda Tiatanio Reyes, granddaughter of Agueda,
With the author, Ralph Stoney Bates
Photo property of author

Tweed was promoted and decorated for his survival on Guam. He would never have survived had it not been for the support of the Chamorros, including Sgambe, Joaquin Limtiaco, Agueda, Juan Pangelinan, Antonio Artero, Tommy Tanaka, and many others. The Japanese may have conquered the island of Guam, but they never conquered its people. The resisters of Guam could have done much more to protect the Chamorro people, had it not been for Tweed. This story is not another story about Tweed. Though Tweed and the other five sailors are part of this story, but it is about a man they called Sgambe, a lady called Agueda, a lady called Ignacia, a man called Limty (Limtiaco), a man called "Tommy," and of many others, "the unsung heroes of Guam." These are their stories. Many of them were unheard, unknown, and unread—until now.

JOAQUIN AFLAQUE LIMTIACO

The following is an accumulation of facts, supported by some brief conjured conversations:

A close friend of Adolf C. Sgambelluri (Sgambe) and Tomas "Tommy" Tanaka, Joaquin Limtiaco, was a Chamorro businessman who owned a garage and a fleet of taxis in Agana in 1941. "Limty," as he was known, assisted all the American Navy men in evading the Japanese. He was one of the go-betweens, who secretly worked with Sgambe, sometimes passing messages through Agueda Johnston and on to the other loyal Chamorros of the underground network, such as Tommy, and Jose Flores. Joaquin Limtiaco always received the guarded information in Chamorro from Sgambe, usually delivered through Mrs. Agueda Johnston, the leader of the Chamorro Underground (CU) group. Only she was to decide to whom in the CU would be privileged to receive the information to be passed on. Agueda was selected because she was in a stable position and given just a bit of leeway and freedom of movement by the Japanese authorities. And, who would suspect a woman?

If Sgambe had word that there was to be a radio listening at a particular place, or some word to get to one of the Navy men, he would alert Limty, who, in turn, would usually alert Mrs. Johnston and then the message would get to the right people, thus evading or confusing Japanese searchers. For the American sailors attempting to evade the Japanese searchers, Joaquin provided guidance and occasional food, clothing, and other supplies usually obtained by Tommy or Agueda, to assist them in staying safe, relatively comfortable, and avoiding areas and people that he simply wasn't too sure about. But, everything was not in the control of Joaquin. Japanese authorities sometimes had independent searchers, unknown to members of the resistance group. Sometimes even unknown to Sgambe. They eventually found three of the sailors and executed them.

After L. L. Krump, L. W. Jones, and A. Yablonsky, were found and murdered, Joaquin was devastated. However, he then concentrated on assisting C.B. Johnston, George Tweed, and Al Tyson, and because he (Tweed) had split from the first two and was alone, he was especially concerned about him. Tweed was his most problematic sailor in hiding.

When Tweed was in his early period of evasion, the Japanese were getting pretty close to finding him. Sgambe let Joaquin know, and Joaquin went to Mrs. Johnston to discuss another hiding place. The choice was Tommy Tanaka's place. It was decided to get Tweed out of his current hiding area and to head toward upper Tamuning, where he introduced Tweed to Tommy Tanaka. Tommy took good care of Tweed, giving him canned goods of sardines, condensed milk, and other items and keeping him well hidden; but when Tweed learned that Tommy was a Nisei, he no longer trusted his benefactor. Sensing this change in attitude, Tommy no longer wanted to hide Tweed. As a matter-of-fact, he was insistent on it. Tweed needed to be moved again. Joaquin went back to Mrs. Johnston. They hatched a plan that didn't work out exactly as intended.

Actually, Tomas Tanaka wasn't a Nisei. He was the son of a Japanese man and a Chamorro woman. Tweed owes his life directly to Tommy. When Tweed fell ill with what they suspected was pneumonia, it was Tommy who took the supplies from the Dejima store, and Joaquin brought them to either Tweed's hideout or to the person hiding Tweed.

That milk and food kept Tweed alive and allowed him to slowly regain his strength.

To carry out the plan for moving Tweed, Joaquin met with various members of the resistance whom he trusted. After numerous discussions with several people, a meeting was arranged with Juan Pangelinan.

"Juan, how you doing?" (all speaking Chamorro)

"Good, Limty, good. What's up?"

"We need to move babui (Tweed). Different place. Fast!" Limty stated. "J (Agueda) says it doesn't have to be a long move, but, if it were, can you talk to Tony (Artero) soon?"

"Tony is not part of pasto (underground), is he?" Juan asked.

"No! I know, but he has big land, lots of caves, best location."

"I'll see what I can do, Limty," he paused in deep thought.

"Do it quick, Juan. It's needed now."

For a moment, Juan paused in deep thought. Finally, he spoke, "I'll take him. I know a place." Juan Pangelinan smiled a wiry smile at Joaquin Limtiaco who nodded in agreement. "I have a place in upper Yigo. Let's not involve Tony right now. He has a big family. Too many talkers."

So, it was Joaquin who got Juan Pangelinan to hide Tweed. He did hide him for about four months. Again, perhaps largely due to the loose-talk telegraph, Tweed was passed from Juan to Antonio Artero. He was to be somehow persuaded to hide Tweed. Tony was well respected and very pro-American. And, he had a lot of property.

Several months had gone by when Sgambe passed by Juan on his way to see Agueda Johnston. "Juan! Close call! Japs feel that you got 'babui.' Get up to see Tony. Talk him into accepting him. Do whatever is necessary. Tell him as long as 'babui' is safe, the Americans will return. He's our insurance package. The Japs believe 'babui' is talking to the American Navy. They're stepping up their efforts to find him. You're next on their list, but Tony . . . let us call him 'A,' is he not a safe bet to hide Tweed? But, Tweed must be more discrete. He needs to stop going to parties and stop his excursions to see his friends disguised as a woman." Sgambe paused briefly, "his outside excursions to different places must be stopped. And, Juan, you might want to go into hiding yourself," he added.

"All right, Sgambe. Consider it done."

At first Antonio Artero was dead set against having anything to do with hiding the American sailor. He and his family were safe—up on his large ranch. As long as he gave his quota of food to the Japanese authorities, they pretty much left him alone. He said he would think about it and that it would require the approval of his father. "Give me a few days, Juan. Okay?"

Tweed had been moved to Upper Tumon, to a ranch owned by Joaquin Flores. Flores had kept Tweed a short time. Then, Tweed was transferred to Tommy Tanaka. It was Joaquin Limtiaco who arranged to move him to Juan Pangelinan further north. It was Juan Pangelinan who got Tony Artero to take Tweed because the Japanese were closing in on *him*. The notice that the Japanese were beginning to suspect that Juan had Tweed would come quickly, forcing Juan to act fast.

It was about this time that the sailors Tyson and Johnston were caught and killed.

There were other things that kept Joaquin busy. Joaquin had also warned Jose Ada that the Japanese knew he had a radio, and they were going to descend on him in a few days to capture him with his radio. Jose Ada kept the radio on his property and occasionally men would gather there to listen to far away broadcast. So, Joaquin and a select few of the CU used his Hallicrafter radio to listen to the news from San Francisco or Sydney. Unfortunately, loose talk had now turned the attention of the Japanese to Ada.

The closest the Japanese came to actually catching someone with a radio was the one Jose Ada had. Keeping it secluded on his property was risky. Sgambe alerted Mrs. Johnston and Joaquin that the Japanese were going to search Ada's property for the radio. To save Jose Ada, the radio was moved off his property. Then, Sgambe and Joaquin worked out a guise of burying a whole bunch of radio parts and tubes in the ground on the property of Ada and dousing them repeatedly with salt and sea water to corrode the parts, thus saving the life of Jose Ada.

When the Japanese arrived to seize Ada and his radio, he led them to where he told them he had buried the radio after smashing it up. After he heard that possession of a radio was forbidden, he just smashed it up further and buried it. Besides, he told the Japanese, "It didn't work anyway." He told the Japanese that he did not realize they wanted him to turn in what were essentially old radio parts that no longer worked. The Japanese slapped him around a bit, but he kept his head. It worked out. The clandestine radio network of Guam never shut down.

Only the timely intervention of two members of the CU saved Jose from being caught with that radio.

Hallicrafter Radio drawing from
Hallicrafter WW II poster

Eventually, perhaps due to continued loose talk, Joaquin Limtiaco again came under suspicion of the Japanese authorities. After hearing too many conversations about the activities of locals secluding the Navy men from Japanese eyes and listening to forbidden radios, the Japanese decided to bring him in for *questioning.*

Joaquin had been *interrogated* by the Japanese before. He was familiar with their tactics. He wasn't ready for what came next. They began to brutalize him, beating him with sticks and lead pipes. When that did not work, they hog-tied him, as they called it in the American West, binding his feet and hands together, hoisting his body up off the floor, and swinging his body forcibly against the walls of the jail. They bounced him off the walls and hit him with sticks like a Mexican piñata. As the Japanese and Saipanese taunted him, he was continuously beaten unmercifully, while they laughed at his predicament.

After days of brutal torture, including *waterboarding*, the Japanese relented. They released Limtiaco, although he never broke. He did *agree* that he would personally search for the American sailors and relay to the Japanese any information he uncovered. On these conditions, he was released from the jail. Battered, bruised, and bloodied, he was grinning widely, a smirking, taunting grin through a battered and bruised face and painful split lips, as he limped away from the jail to his family wheelbarrow. That wheelbarrow had a car tire and rim as its wheel and was made of wood, with wooden handles. The family always "wheeled" Limty home from his *interrogation* sessions because he was always bruised, battered, and lashed to a point of near-death. Limty had *True Grit,* and gonads the size of coconuts. In the American vernacular, he was a hell of a man.

To call for a meeting of the CU, one would use the code words in Chamorro "tan fan boka," which in English literally meant, "Let's eat." The CU was called "Pasto" which simply meant, "the pasture." The upright Underwood typewriter used by Tweed to type the news which he called *The Guam Eagle* had been smuggled to Tweed. He received the news generally from radio station KGEL in San Francisco.

The code word the CU used for Tweed was the Chamorro word "babui," which meant "pig." No one in the underground used Tweed's actual name in conversation, but instead would say *babui*, in their repeated daily conversations. Tweed used the code name Jauquin (shortened to Quin) Cruize (sp?) or JC to sign letters or notes, mostly directed to Mrs. Johnston. To exchange information within the CU, almost everything went through Agueda Johnston as a focal point of the CU. Sgambe and Joaquin wanted to insure that Agueda's leadership of the CU was never compromised.

After Limtiaco was *worked-over* by the Japanese, and as a precaution, Sgambe was ordered by Jose Villagomez to *watch* Limtiaco to ensure that he was, in fact, searching for the Americans.

"I'll even go with him, and together, we'll search for the fugitives," Sgambe asserted to the chief jailer, Villagomez.

"Good idea, Sgambe. Make sure he's keeping his word. If not, he's a dead man," Villagomez announced.

Frequently, Sgambe and Joaquin would pretend to *search* for the American sailor, and although they knew where he was hiding, they followed supposed *leads* in different directions, misleading the Japanese.

The following is from the Guam Website, Guampedia, World War II, titled—From Occupation to Liberation:

> *There were many other heroes during the occupation period, men and women who displayed bravery and the instinctive ability to survive during a tragic period. Among them was Juan Cruz (Apu) Flores, who was tortured by the Japanese on several occasions.*
>
> *With the help of Flores and other Chamorros, including Joaquin Limtiaco, George Tweed successfully escaped capture by the Japanese and survived the war. Flores helped Tweed move from place to place in order to hide him from the Japanese. Because Japanese investigators suspected him of harboring Tweed and was being hunted day and night, Flores was careful not to be seen with his family, who were living in Inarajan. He had to sneak around at night in order to bring food to his family, or to visit with his wife and children.*

> *Towards the end of the war, Japanese soldiers arrested Flores and brought him to Tutujan (now Agana Heights). There, he found Father Duenas and his nephew, Eduardo, and Joaquin Limtiaco. The Duenas were tied to posts after having been tortured. During the night, a Chamorro interpreter from Saipan* [actually it was Joaquin Limtiaco] *advised them that they had to escape in order to avoid sure death. Father Duenas refused to leave for fear the Japanese would go after members of his family and that it would be futile to try to escape. Eduardo agreed to stay with his uncle. Father Duenas advised them to go back to their families and that he was ready to be with God.*
>
> *Eduardo Duenas was a brilliant attorney and was serving the government as chief prosecutor at the outbreak of the war. He often accompanied Father Duenas on trips for food or visits to relatives and friends. Both men were about the same age (early thirties) and very close in a large family that helped one another. In monitoring Father Duenas' movements, the Japanese police took notice of Eduardo's association with his uncle, and presumed Eduardo knew more than he revealed, generally about the whereabouts of Tweed.*
>
> *The Duenases were arrested and brutalized in Inarajan, taken to Tutujan where they met with Flores and Limtiaco, and on July 12, nine days before the liberation of Guam by American forces, the two men* [Duenas's] *were taken to Tai where they were executed by beheading.*

Father Duenas knew where Tweed was most of the time. Joaquin Limtiaco had told him. Joaquin was keeping the Father up-to-date on the progress of the war after he listened to the clandestine radio news broadcasts, and he would often relate the disposition of the American sailors. The last message Limtiaco gave him about the radio broadcast was that the Americans were invading the Caroline Islands. "They're close. It won't be long," he said to Father Duenas.

This last meeting, with Father Duenas, was one of the few times that Joaquin did not know where Tweed was hiding. He knew only that Tony Artero was hiding him. Also Juan Pangelinan, who had turned Tweed over to Tony, did not know the actual location of Tweed's hiding place. Tony even denied he knew anything at all about Tweed, even to Juan and Limty. Tragically, the Japanese eventually beheaded Juan for refusing to give information about Tweed.

The last person to be with Father Duenas, before he was beheaded by the Japanese, was Joaquin Limtiaco. He had offered to cut the Father and his nephew free from the restraints, at the risk of his own life, but both refused. The last words he heard from the Father were, "God will look after me. I have done no wrong."

Luck and deception finally failed Tyson and Johnston while hiding out on Tommy Torres ranch. In October 1942, during one of many surprise searches by the Japanese military, usually unknown even to Villagomez, Japanese soldiers descended onto the Torres ranch and dragged Tommy Torres outside to question him. Clearly, they were preparing to execute him if his answers displeased them. Facing instant death at the hands of the Japanese, Tommy relented and led the Japanese to the hiding place of the two Navy men. After surrounding the hiding place, the Japanese waited until the arrival of dawn. Both Johnston and Tyson were shot through the head at close range, killing them instantly. Tweed became the lone American serviceman still hiding on Guam, mostly under the watchful care of Antonio "Tony" Artero. Tony, as he was called by his friends, would furnish him with clothing, food, water, magazines and information obtained from various sources in the underground network. He took care never to reveal the location of Tweed, or even admit to anyone that he had him.

In addition to searching with Joaquin Limtiaco by his side, to allay concerns the Japanese might have about him, Sgambe would ask his boss, the Saipanese Jose Villagomez, to accompany them on many of those *searches*.

"By having the Jap lover at my side during many of the *searches*, it alleviated any suspicion that I was not assisting Joaquin Limtiaco actually searching for the fugitives. It seemed to be working," Sgambe would say. "I did enjoy the deception," he added.

In *Robinson Crusoe, USN*, written in 1945 by Blake Clark for George Tweed, the following passage is chilling:

> *"The patrol then enlisted some expert local aid. Villagomez, a native of Saipan, was boss at the jail. He had a partner, a half Italian named Sgambelluri who'd worked in the police department in Agana before the war and who stayed on and worked for the Japs.*
>
> *These two initiated searching operations of their own, in addition to the reconnoitering carried on by the regular patrol. I frequently heard of them passing near my lair, and I'd slip up near one of the main trails and lie in ambush, waiting for them to come along so I could end their activities. I had decided that if I threw their bodies into the sea the Japs would not know what had happened to them. I never saw them."*

This detail from Tweed's own words may give the reader some idea of how dangerous a life Adolfo Sgambelluri and certainly Joaquin Limtiaco lived and how mistrusted and despised Sgambe was to the vast majority of the inhabitants of Guam, during and right after the liberation by the Americans. Tweed, the man he was protecting, wanted to kill him. There were others too. Joaquin Limtiaco and Sgambe were often together *searching* for Tweed, usually in areas they knew he wasn't.

Tweed's continuous presence on Guam became an ordeal for many Guamanians and an irritation to all Japanese officials. Most Japanese were convinced that Tweed, a communications specialist, was in radio contact with the American Navy. Actually, Tweed had *obtained*, a workable commercial radio and was simply listening to commercial American radio broadcasts by Bob Goodman and Merrill Phillips at station KGEL in San Francisco. As previously mentioned, for a while, Tweed had a workable typewriter, and he would type his newspaper, *The Guam Eagle*, to distribute to his caretakers and their friends, thus further irritating the Japanese. In a way, George Tweed was taunting the Japanese at the risk of his caretakers.

Many Chamorros were subjected to *waterboarding* and other more brutal forms of interrogation about the whereabouts of Tweed. Some were killed. Joaquin was almost caught in possession of the *The Guam Eagle* newspaper at one time.

Eventually, Tweed became a cause célèbre to the Guamanians and a "stick in the eye" of the Japanese, who had to find and kill the sailor to save face. Conversely, the Guamanians had to protect Tweed, as he represented the American military that was defying the Japanese. To the Chamorro, Tweed and the Chamorros hiding him were smarter than the Japanese. It was almost like a game, a deadly serious game, and it would continue until Tweed was picked up by an American destroyer a few days before the invasion of Guam by the Americans.

Interestingly, the Chamorros seemed to take great pride in knowing where Tweed was, furnishing items for his use, or actually keeping him. Unfortunately, this *Chamorro pride* caused much of the ire of the Japanese as talk spread. Words like "I saw Tweed today," or "Jose has Tweed now," or "I sent some food to Tweed," or worse yet, "I know who's hiding Tweed," on the Chamorro "telegraph" caused many problems. That's one of the reasons Tony Artero never admitted he was hiding Tweed. He cut the *telegraph* lines.

In pain for the rest of his life, Joaquin departed Guam in the 1950s to visit an uncle in Detroit. While in the United States, he travelled across the big country and enjoyed what he saw. Later, he decided to relocate to the San Francisco Bay area. He travelled from Guam to San Francisco, via Hawaii, on a Navy transport vessel to permanently reside in the country he had served so loyally.

The series of severe beatings from the Japanese, while suspected of protecting George Tweed and others, had caused him to lose all his teeth and suffer with constant pain throughout his life, and yet he never complained about the permanent damage to his body—nor did he complain about the fact that he never received the recognition he so richly deserved from his island of Guam, or from the government of the United States of America. Due to those beatings by the Japanese, Joaquin Limtiaco suffered greatly for maintaining his loyalty to the United States and to its living symbol on Guam—George Tweed. He is a true American hero of the War in the Pacific and should be recognized as such. Joaquin Limtiaco served his country above and beyond anything imagined—for a society of captives of the Japanese.

That fact should be embarrassing to both the Guam and United States governments for not recognizing his exploits—and should be corrected.

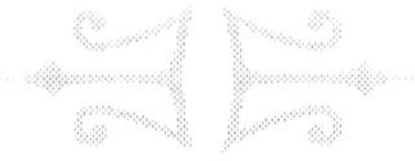

TOMAS "TOMMY" TANAKA

The following is an accumulation of developed factual data, supported by brief conjured conversations designed to support known facts:

In the late 1960s, Tomas "Tommy" Tanaka was a very successful, highly respected businessman and local politician on Guam, and he didn't get there the easy way. He had to overcome obstacles few have encountered to get where he was in his later life. His story is the story of Guam during and after the Japanese occupation.

In an article in the 30 October 1966 issue of the *Territorial Sun*, a weekly Guam newspaper, it is written that Tommy Tanaka's father, Cecilio Tanaka, ". . . had been an adventurous lad who travelled around the world at an early age and wound up in the States. He joined the U.S. Navy and eventually came to Guam." The article, written by Roy Anderberg goes on to say, "The Navy taught him to be a proficient cook, and when he married his Chamorro bride, he decided to remain on Guam. When released from the Navy, he opened a restaurant in Agana." That's the story told by Tomas "Tommy" Tanaka, regarding his father, in that interview with the *Territorial Sun* reporter.

The family sees their father and grandfather as emerging from a slightly different origin. According to Tommy Jr. and Fred, Tommy's sons, they had been told Tommy Tanaka's father, their grandfather, Cecilio Tanaka, had been a merchant seaman on a Japanese merchant vessel before the Great War, and one of his voyages aboard that merchant vessel brought him to Guam. While on shore-leave on Guam, he got into a bit of trouble in a bar-fight and emerged from the Agana jail only to discover his vessel had sailed without him. He was marooned. But, being the adventurous soul that he was, he didn't despair; he liked Guam and the Chamorro people and decided to remain.

Regardless of the origin of Tomas "Tommy" Tanaka's father, and regardless of the means of his arrival on Guam, Cecilio eventually married a Chamorro by the name of Rosa Santos-Santos. But getting married on deeply Catholic Guam was a bit more complex. He had to have a Christian name in order for the Catholic Church to allow him to marry his Chamorro bride. His birth name of Kitamura Tanaka would have to be changed; therefore he chose the name Cecilio. One of his children was Tomas (Tommy to his friends) Tanaka, was born on 15 October 1915, to mixed-race parents—Japanese and Chamorro— just before the Americans entered the Great War (WW-I).

Tommy's dad, Cecilio, died when Tommy was six or seven-years-old, and he was raised by his mother.

Tommy grew up on Guam and considered himself American. After all, it was an American island, and those born on Guam were American Nationals. Tommy eventually married Josefina Maria Camacho in 1939, and they had a one-year-old son, Thomas, by the time the Japanese invasion came. Two more children were born to "Fina" and Tommy, Vivian, in 1943, and Fredrick, in 1945.

While the Americans controlled Guam, Tommy and his young bride had settled into life on the American island as American Nationals. It was a good life. When the Japanese invaded Guam in 1941, twenty-three-year-old Tommy was a jack-of-all-trades clerk and bookkeeper at Mrs. Riye Dejima's general store. She was a Japanese National living on Guam.

As the occupation began, all westerners were segregated and confined; the Japanese divided the remaining residents of Guam into two groups.

The Chamorro made up one group and mixed-race individuals made up the second group. The Chamorro were sent on their way to their homes with instructions as to how life was to be for them on Japanese controlled Guam. Mixed-blood Tommy was initially confined by the Japanese with Japanese-Chamorro, Philippine-Chamorro, Korean-Chamorro, and other mixed-blood residents, until Mrs. Dejima, vouched for him and he was released.

Tommy found himself between the classic devil and the deep blue sea. The Chamorros didn't trust him because he was *Japanese*, and the Japanese didn't trust him because his dad, who had been on Guam under the American Navy and had been away from Japan for many years, was—in their view—Americanized. As the Japanese settled into the occupation of Guam, Tommy went back to work in Mrs. Dejima's store, selling, stocking, keeping the books, *and* keeping a secret diary. He kept it on bits of scrap paper in a jar hidden at his home. "Fina" and Tommy would keep the jar "wrapped inside the leaves of a banana tree" (1966 *Territorial Sun*). The assumption is that Tommy would write down what he saw and heard throughout the day, and when he got home, he would place those scrap papers inside the jar.

⁂

The Japanese policeman, along with his Saipanese (Northern Chamorro) interpreter, entered the general store, just as Tommy had started to work. *"You!"* (speaking Japanese) He pointed at Tommy standing behind the counter. *"Outside, now!"*

Tommy was surprised and bewildered. He didn't know what was being said, and for a brief few seconds, he just stared at the Japanese policeman.

Swiftly, the Japanese man reached across the counter and slapped Tommy forcibly across the face with his open left hand as he drew his pistol with his right hand. Tommy was stunned.

"You, get outside! You bow to Japanese officer!" The Saipanese spoke in Chamorro.

Tommy quickly bowed, as the pistol was pointed straight at his head.

Remaining bent-over, he rushed from behind the counter, across the floor to the doorway, and stopped just outside the doorway, still crunched in that position. He knew not to look directly at the Japanese.

"You have radio?" The Japanese man asked, as the Saipanese man repeated the question.

"No sir," Tommy responded, while still bowing.

Tommy had a radio, but it had been well hidden. Joaquin Limtiaco and Sgambe had found the perfect hiding spot and had told Tommy he didn't need to know where it was located. "It was better to know little or nothing, rather than too much of everything," they had said to Tommy. He was now grateful.

The policeman hit Tommy across the side of his head with the pistol. Tommy grimaced, almost fell, and reached with his hand to feel his face.

"You no Japanese, you American," the Japanese yelled, as the interpreter screamed the same words in Chamorro. The Saipanese slapped Tommy's hand away from his face.

Tommy was bleeding, but he kept his hands to his side and remained in a bowing position. He was certain he was going to be shot, and instantly, thoughts of his wife and child flashed through his mind. He was frightened beyond belief.

"Where radio?" (in Chamorro)

"Sir, I do not have a radio," Tommy responded (in Chamorro) weakly, as he began to shake uncontrollably.

"What is going on here?" Mrs. Dejima had stepped onto the porch from inside the store. *"Sir, this man works for me. His father was a loyal Japanese. This man is loyal to the Japanese government. I can vouch for him. He has done nothing against the Japanese,"* she spoke quickly, and a bit sternly, in Japanese.

"He has radio," the Japanese remarked. But, it almost sounded like a question.

"No, Sir, he does not have a radio. I know it to be true. He does not have one. He has never had one," she spoke convincingly.

The Japanese policeman holstered his pistol and slapped Tommy across the face with his open hand.

Tommy continued to quake uncontrollably.

The Japanese policeman spun on his heel, bowed slightly to Mrs. Dejima, and walked away—followed by the Saipanese.

After he was accosted and threatened the first time, Tommy became paranoid about having the diary and would later destroy it. However, as time went by, he seemed to be "underneath the Japanese radar" and he went back to work, both in the store and with the underground. Due to his job, he had access to food and clothing. Therefore, he was asked by the underground to furnish such items for the six American sailors hiding on Guam. Without hesitation, he did just that. He had several very close friends, including Sgambe, Jose Flores, and Joaquin Limtiaco. All were members of the *Guam Chamorro Underground* (CU) or *Resistance Movement.*

Later, in his deadly game of cat and mouse, Sgambe asked Limtiaco to ask Tommy if he would keep George Tweed for a while because the Japanese were getting mighty close on Tweed's tail. Mighty close! Sgambe and Limty were very concerned.

Tommy agreed. He kept George Tweed for a while on the Castro property, and later, he would move him to a secluded area in Tamuning. Sgambe said when he and Limty got Tweed to Tommy's place in Tamuning they secreted him behind a building (where the current Boy Scout building is located) and instructed him to stay put. Then, the three of them went off to chat and drink some tuba, celebrating their successful move of Tweed. When they returned, Tweed was gone. He had slipped out and walked to Agana *to see a friend.* He returned a few hours later to a tongue lashing from Limty and Sgambe.

The situation remained static until Tweed became concerned that a—*Japanese person*— was hiding him from the Japanese. Tommy could sense the attitude change in Tweed and asked to be relieved of the responsibility. Besides, he didn't like Tweed's habit of disappearing occasionally, going to parties, driving through Agana at night, and in general, putting everyone at risk, including himself.

Tommy continued to pass very helpful and highly critical material to the sailor. He didn't personally like him, but he *was* a symbol of America, and Tommy continued to support his daily needs of food and drink, magazines from Mrs. Johnston, and razor blades. Tommy's wife, Josefina, pointedly asked Tommy, "Why are you doing this?" She was very concerned about their young child. "You are jeopardizing our very lives," she finished.

"He is a human being!" was Tommy's reply, and that was that. It was enough of a reason for Tommy Tanaka.

Before the war, Tommy and his wife had a Halifax commercial radio. It was a fairly new one, a Skyrider-Diversity model which was two complete receivers installed side-by-side. This particular radio allowed someone to connect two antennas to the radio, which counteracted the signal-fading. When the Japanese outlawed possession of radios, Tommy hid his, with the assistance of Joaquin Limtiaco. But when word spread that Tweed wanted a radio, Tommy allowed Joaquin to send Tweed the radio. As stated in the *Territorial Sun*, in October 1966, this particular radio *was to play an important part in the history of Guam. . . And, for most of the war, this radio kept Tweed and the Guamanian's up to date with the true conduct of the war, . . .* That radio is the one Tweed used to listen to news broadcast, and which allowed him to produce his "newspaper." The paper was his way of snubbing the Japanese—a very dangerous snubbing. That "newspaper" distribution almost got several members of the underground killed.

Table Model Hallicrafter Skyrider-Diversity model, DD-1 1937-1940
Photo from Hallicrafter Website

Tweed had someone distribute his one-page "newspaper," and a copy of it ended up in Limty's home just as the Japanese raided the home to beat up on Limty again. Only the swift action of Jose Flores, ripping up the "paper" and disposing of it in the toilet, saved Limtiaco from instant beheading.

Tommy's big contribution to Tweed occurred when Tweed got sick. Almost everyone privy to the situation thought it was pneumonia. So did Tweed. It was the intervention of Tomas Tanaka which saved Tweed's life. Tommy would smuggle canned cream, coffee, corned beef, tuna, and whatever he could find from Mrs. Dejima's store to give Tweed the nourishment needed to ward off the sickness. And, it worked. Tweed essentially owed his life to the supplies provided by Tommy.

There are those on Guam who thought Mrs. Dejima was aware of Tommys' taking items from the store. Others disagree. Whether or not she knew, we will never know. She apparently died in the late 1980s. Her daughter is said to be living in Hawaii. It is rumored the jewelry and approximately $11,000 in U.S. currency she supposedly buried on her store property as the Japanese invaded is perhaps still buried—somewhere! Then—perhaps not!

Like many others, Tommy came under the watchful eyes of Japanese authorities, and the loose talk of some locals caused him to once again become one of their "punching bags." This time, it would be pure torture and extreme brutality. Even with Dejima's protective cover, Tommy was tortured because he was now *suspected* of knowing the whereabouts of Tweed. He did, but, he never divulged anything. He also decided to destroy his secret diary, fearing the Japanese would find it and exact reprisals against his family. The Japanese took special interest in punishing Tommy. They taunted him, beat him, hog tied him, and then beat him while he was hanging by his thumbs, standing on his toes in the jail—sometimes for hours.

Eventually, Tommy was sentenced to be beheaded as a *spy* who had *given* comfort to the *enemy* (the sailors). Only the forceful and timely intervention of Mrs. Dejima prevented the sentence from being carried out. Though Tommy never relented, he was physically and psychologically devastated from the numerous beatings. And, as they came for him, yet again, to take him to the jail for interrogation, he retreated into a state of withdrawal and isolation. As he was standing on the tips of his toes, with his thumbs ratcheted in a vise-like grip of twisted wire suspended from a ceiling rafter, he simply shut-down his cognitive consciousness. As blows were delivered to his body, time and time again, he retreated further into a self-created inner void. He didn't feel the cigarette burns to his body; he struggled as the water hose was inserted into his mouth with full torrents of water forced down his throat until he vomited it back up, again and again. It didn't faze him. He was in a survival mode. He was so withdrawn that later he even contemplated suicide, to the horror of his wife. But, he survived. He persevered. Tommy survived in this withdrawal state for weeks. Eventually, he regained his composure, until he was devastated again, this time by the American Navy.

Tommy Tanaka was a loyal American, giving support to the underground. Adolf P. Sgambelluri said, "My dad's most trusted confidants were Joaquin Limtiaco, Tommy Tanaka, and Mrs. Agueda Johnston."

He never relented, never broke—never betrayed his country. But his country betrayed him. His greatest desire after all he went through for his country was to join the United States Navy. After the war, he tried. He very badly wanted to enlist. Not only would they not take Tommy as a sailor, they would not even take him as a Navy steward. But they were still taking American black men (it was still a lily-white, segregated Navy), Chamorro, and Filipinos as Stewards. He was, apparently to the American Navy, a Jap, not eligible for enlistment. Because of the perceived nationality of Tommy Tanaka, the authorities apparently were never aware of his underground activities, and he was also suspected, again based on his "nationality," of subversive activities. They never searched for the truth. His father's ancestry was apparently enough for the Navy.

That decision and the Navy's rejection devastated Tommy and is even affecting his descendants to this day. "The one thing that really devastated my dad was his rejection to join the U.S. Navy. They would not let him join," so stated his son Thomas "Tommy" Tanaka, as we sat down with him for interview. "After all he accomplished for the United States, the American

Navy, and the sailor Tweed, the Navy rejected his effort to become one of them—an American sailor."

He continued his life overcoming obstacles one after another. Because of his perceived ancestry of Japanese, and apparent ignorance of his Chamorro blood-line, "*he was constantly thwarted in his attempts to start a laundry and an ice cream shop,*" according to the 1966 article in the *Territorial Sun* newspaper. It took a deception to get his first business up and running. He asked, and a friend agreed to "front" for him, and he opened a gas station in 1946. Then he built and opened a hamburger joint with an ever-popular soda-fountain included. He was now off and running. He became a stock-broker, opened other businesses, and eventually turned to politics. He won a seat in the Guam Legislature in 1964, after having been defeated in 1960. Tommy didn't know the word *defeat.* But, he did know the word *perseverance.*

Tomas "Tommy" Tanaka is one of the unsung heroes of Guam and of World War II. He is a giant of a man, who deserves belated recognition from Guam, from the Department of the Navy, and from the United States of America.

JUAN UNPINGCO PANGELINAN

The following contains a believed to be true account, and very brief conjured conversations designed to support these known facts uncovered by research:

Adolfo Sgambelluri (Sgambe), B.J. Bordallo, Joaquin Limtiaco (Limty), and Joaquin Flores, approached the farm of Juan Pangelinan, in north-western Guam, in late 1942. These men were part of the CU group designed to confuse and defy the Japanese authority on Guam during the Japanese occupation. Juan or John, as he was sometimes referred to, was a recently retired U.S. Navy sailor. He was a Chamorro of Guam, who had joined the Navy initially as a steward to serve his country and to see the world. He ultimately became a water-man keeping the boilers of steam-powered ships working to propel them across the waters of the world. As a Chamorro, like the Filipinos, American black men, and other so-called minority race peoples, these men were sailors who performed menial tasks, while serving in very limited capacities usually considered beneath the status of lighter skinned American sailors. But, it was a way for young men of Guam to see the world and be paid for doing so.

Six American sailors had refused to surrender to the invading Japanese forces and were considered criminals by the Japanese authorities. Each had a death sentence on his head to be carried out immediately upon capture. In addition, anyone caught or suspected of assisting or harboring these sailors would be subjected to the same fate, as would the immediate family of the offending party. Keeping any of these sailors was an automatic death sentence—if caught.

Juan had retired from the Navy in 1932, and had returned to his family farm to resume his first love—farming and ranching. His farm bordered the farm of Antonio Artero, and he soon settled into the life of a farmer, a large-farm farmer, on Guam. He was also a member of the American Legion Mid-Pacific Post. Life was good. His life on Guam was interrupted when the Japanese invasion came to its shores.

Like several other large-farm owners, he was required to continue to maintain his farming and ranching, but now for the benefit of the Japanese authorities. He, like the other large landowners, received no payment from the Japanese, but they were required to provide them with food products. For almost a year, he had fulfilled his requirements and had been left pretty much alone. As long as he continued to provide his quota of foodstuff, things remained static for him and his family.

Now he was being asked to shelter one of the sailors.

He was about to make a decision that would ultimately cost him his life.

As a former Navy man, he felt a loyalty to the United States. Even though he was now subjected to Japanese rule, somehow he knew America would prevail in this war. But, his isolation prevented him from receiving information derived from the secret radio reception produced by members of the underground. These men visiting his ranch were members of that clandestine group—the CU.

They briefed him about the Coral Sea and Midway naval battles and of the American Marines fighting the Japanese in the Solomon Islands. He knew where the Solomon Islands were, and he knew they were a long way from Guam. Still, he had this inner feeling of allegiance to the United States that outweighed his hesitance to jeopardize his safety—especially the safety of his family.

"I'll do it!" he replied to their request. "I'll take the American Navy man, George Tweed."

He had just sealed his fate, and he had saved the life of an American sailor.

Tweed had been moved from place to place since December 1941. Numerous families and individuals had sheltered the six sailors, some, for a week or so, others, for a day or two. Tommy Tanaka had been the last to shelter Tweed, but the Japanese were getting close to finding out about Tommy's activities. At first, he was questioned while a pistol was pointed at his head. Later, the Japanese brutalized and tortured Tommy Tanaka, and Limty and Sgambe knew that Tweed had to be moved, again—and quickly.

Sgambe, Limty, and John breathed a collective sigh of relief.

One of the problems related to sheltering the Navy men was the pride that many Chamorros had in defying their Japanese occupiers. They bragged about it. It was a status thing. Even some, who had no knowledge of the sailors, would brag that they had seen them or that they had furnished them food or clothing. Indeed, the Chamorro *telegraph* was a big problem.

Another problem was George Tweed himself. He didn't like to stay in one place. He often left his hiding place without anyone knowing it. He once drove a car through Agana, and at least once, he attended a party at a private home. Then, there was the *Guam Eagle,* which was often discovered by Japanese authorities, and it inflamed their desire to capture and kill Tweed and anyone assisting him.

Juan Pangelinan sheltered Tweed for a period of about four months. He constructed a shelter for him near his ranch-house, but it was far enough away for it to be secluded and not easily seen or stumbled onto inadvertently. He kept him fed adequately and furnished him with clothing.

In early fall, the Japanese were looking mostly at the isolated North of Guam more and more. Sgambe warned Juan to be prepared to move Tweed if necessary.

By the beginning of October 1942, the Japanese were getting bits and pieces of information leading them to believe that Radioman George Tweed may be hiding out on the ranch of Juan Pangelinan. The fact that Juan was a former sailor in the American Navy added to their suspicion.

Sgambe picked up on the information that the Japanese were planning a surprise raid on the ranch and alerted Limty and Joaquin Flores. The three of them travelled up to Juan's property to warn him. It appeared, at the time, that the raid was hours, not days away. They notified Juan he needed to get rid of the sailor. Get him off his property. Now!

"Juan, we talked to Tony, some time ago. He was reluctant to even talk to us at that time. He only said he would talk to his father. Other than that, we have had no contact with Tony. But, you need to do something, today," Flores stated.

"I'll think of something. If they find any evidence he has been here on my ranch, they will kill me and my entire family," Juan replied.

"Perhaps Tony's brother would hide him," Limty stated.

"Look, you three get outta here. What if the Japs are on the way now?"

"I think they'll be here early in the morning, John," Sgambe explained.

"Then I have today and tonight. You guys take off. I'll handle it," Juan insisted.

Juan was in a controlled panic. The Japanese could be only hours, or perhaps minutes away. His *guest* had been ill for the past few days. Tommy Tanaka had been furnishing him with canned milk and Juan had given him fresh fruit and meat, but the sailor had lost weight, and become feverish off and on. Other than drinking lots of milk, he had not consumed much of anything. Juan seemed to be caught between that same rock and the same hard place. But, he had to act. The lives of his family depended on it.

First, he moved the somewhat frail-looking sailor to his own bed in the ranch house. Then, he painstakingly removed the shelter he had built for Tweed. Removing any evidence of the sailor's presence, he washed and properly stored all bedding, utensils, clothing and food. Finally, he swept the area clean and eliminated the obvious trail from his ranch house to the shelter.

It was afternoon by the time he loaded George Tweed into his bull-cart and took him onto his neighbor's property, secluding him comfortably in the grass and tall bushes alongside the trail. He returned the bull-cart and the animal to his ranch, put both away properly, and trudged off toward the Artero ranch house. It was about an hour before sunset.

He had a plan. The only plan he felt would continue to safeguard his *guest*, and protect his family from Japanese style *justice*. The plan was to simply give his neighbor no choice but to accept the sailor and to seclude him somewhere on *his* vast property. It was a plan which worked—Tony suddenly had custody of Tweed.

It was several weeks later, and only once, when he asked Antonio how his *guest* (Tweed) was doing.

"I don't know what you are talking about, Juan," was Tony's reply.

Juan knew what he was talking about. In fact, he continued to see and chat with Tweed occasionally, as Tweed would leave his hiding place once or twice a month and return to Juan's ranch house just to chat with his former landlord and his family. He especially enjoyed talking with Jesus, Juan's teenage son. George Tweed simply didn't like being alone.

The morning after Juan Pangelinan transferred Tweed to Antonio the Japanese showed up at Juan's ranch and searched his property. Finding nothing, they departed without comment. Juan felt he had *dodged the bullet*. Later, when Tweed began to show up for his visits, Juan worried that someone may see him and he cautioned his family to never talk of these visits.

Months later, as the Americans intensified their bombardment of Guam—they threw bombs and rockets from airplanes, and huge shells, containing high explosives, from naval guns onto the island in obvious preparation for their invasion of Guam. Some of this rain-of-death fell near the ranches of Juan and Antonio. At the same time, Japanese forces intensified their defensive work. They also intensified their search for the sailor George Tweed. They were convinced that the radioman was communicating with the American fleet.

As previously mentioned, there had been a directive from Imperial Headquarters in Tokyo to field commanders of the Japanese army and navy; it said they should make plans to eliminate (kill) any and all allied prisoners if it appeared American military forces would prevail in battle against Japanese forces under their command. Further, the memorandum detailed some suggestions as to how to make the killings appear to be accidental, such as a barracks fire.

PRIMARY SOURCES: KILL-ALL POLICY

Intercepted and decoded by the Allies, this message from the Japanese Vice Minister of War to the Commanding General of Military Police in Taiwan explains the conditions under which Japanese commanders could execute prisoners of war without formal orders from Tokyo.

Author Linda Goetz Holmes, author of *Unjust Enrichment: How Japan's Companies Built Postwar Fortunes Using American POWs*, points out that it was not a military order, but a policy clarification, since the author in the war ministry did not have the authority to issue orders. Still, according to Holmes, the message was "transmitted to every POW camp commander in Japanese-occupied territory as well as the home islands," and widely known among former Japanese soldiers and former POWs. This memo was introduced into evidence at the post-war trials of Japanese war criminals.

The translated directive read as follows:

1. (entries about money, promotions of Formosans at Branch camps including promotion of Yo Yu-Toku to 1st Cl Keibiin - 5 entries)
2 The following answer about extreme measures for P.O.W.'s was sent to the Chief of Staff of the 11th Unit (Formosa P.O.W. Security No. 10).

"Under the present situation if there were a mere explosion or fire a shelter for the time being could be had in nearby buildings such as the school, a warehouse, or the like. However at such time as the situation became urgent, and it be extremely important, the P.O.W.'s will be concentrated and confined in their present location and under heavy guard the preparation for the final disposition will be made.

The time and method of this disposition are as follows:

- The Time.
  Although the basic aim is to act under superior orders individual disposition may be made in the following circumstances.
  (a) When an uprising of large numbers cannot be suppressed without the use of firearms.
  (b) When escapees from the camp may turn into a hostile fighting force.
- 2. The Methods.
  (a) Whether they are destroyed individually or in groups or however it is done, with mass bombing, poisonous smoke, poisons, drowning, decapitation, or what, dispose of them as the situation dictates.
  (b) In any case it is the aim not to allow the escape of a single one, to annihilate them all, and not to leave any traces.
- 3. To: The Commanding General
- To: The Commanding General of Military Police
  Reported matters conferred on with the 11th Unit, the Kiirun Fortified Area H.Q., and each prefecture concerning the extreme security in Taiwan P.O.W. Camps.

3. (The next entry concerns the will of a deceased P.O.W.).

I hereby certify that this is a true translation from the Journal of the Taiwan P.O.W. H.Q. in Taiwan, entry 1 August 1944.

Signed,
STEPHEN H. GREEN [American cryptographer]

This directive, combined with the defiant acts and apparent loyalty of the Guam Chamorros to America, caused the Japanese commander on Guam to direct that all Chamorros be moved and relocated to several *concentration* or *prison* camps in the interior of Guam.

Many of the Chamorros made the assumption, right or wrong, that they would never return alive from these *camps*. Many were actually murdered when they were removed from these camps to be used on so-called *work details*. In groups of fifteen, twenty, or thirty men and women, from several of these concentration camps, Chamorros were systematically murdered by grenades, gunfire, bayonets, and swords. It was the height of man's inhumanity toward man.

To this day, many of the survivors of the Japanese occupation firmly believe that the Japanese had planned to kill as many Chamorros as they could before being overrun by American forces.

After Antonio Artero secreted Tweed in fairly comfortable surroundings, both the Artero and Pangelinan families reached a decision to make every attempt to avoid going to any of these concentration camps. Both family heads strongly felt it would have been a one-way trip. Initially, they decided to hide in the jungle together. Both families maintained a strong friendship and felt comfortable hiding together. Being isolated in the north-west of Guam had its advantages. Most of the Japanese forces were busy herding thousands of Chamorros into three or four of these *camps* in the central and southern areas. Many Chamorros died along the way, especially the very old and the very young. Many more died after they arrived. With no food, water, shelter, or proper clothing, they simply withered away. Others were systematically murdered by Japanese forces. Not going to the concentration camp at Manenggon was a life-saving decision for the Pangelinan and Artero families, as it truly was a death camp.

The families continued their efforts to work their farms and tend their cattle, while sometimes secluding themselves in the jungle area nearby. One particular day in either late June or perhaps early July, a Guam Chamorro called by a nickname of Aleju, or Alejo, arrived at Juan's ranch where the family was staying at that time, rather than in the jungle location. He stated that he had been sent by the Japanese to *summon* Juan Pangelinan to Japanese headquarters. He explained that the Japanese wanted to pay Juan for the meat and vegetables they had taken from his farm. It was a guise, and Juan knew it.

"I have no choice," he explained to his family. "I must go. If I do not go as they asked, they will come and kill us all. If I do not return by four or five o'clock today, go into the jungle, stay in the cave. Do not return to the ranch," he emphasized.

Juan departed with Alejo. He would not be seen again until his son Jesus identified his decapitated body by the gold in his teeth and the patterned shirt he had been wearing when he departed his ranch. He was killed by beheading along with Father Duenas, the Father's nephew, Edward Duenas, and another man who remains unidentified.

Like Father Duenas, Juan Pangelinan went to his death to save his family.

Father Duenas, a loyal and devout Catholic Priest, was a thorn in the side of the Japanese occupiers during the occupation of Guam. The Japanese tortured all these men and ultimately beheaded them.

God will look after me. I have done no wrong, were the last words spoken by Father Duenas.

Pale' Duenas, along with his nephew, Edward Duenas, Juan Unpingco Pangelinan, and another unknown man were beheaded at dawn on July 12, 1944. The last person to see these four men alive was Joaquin Limtiaco who had offered to cut them free at the risk of his own life. However, Father Duenas refused because he knew that the Japanese would then come after his family. This was the same reasoning as that of Juan Pangelinan.

Juan Pangelinan was a man of great honor and integrity who gave his life to protect his family and the lives of others in his native land. He is one of the great unsung American heroes of World War II.

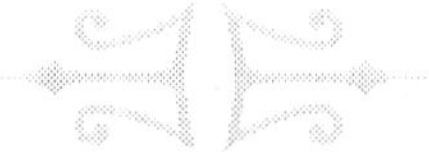

DEATH MARCH, MASSACRES, AND REBELLIONS

DEATH MARCHES

The following contains factual data revealed by research, historical data, Pacific War Chronicles, documented interviews, and actual conversations with survivors of the Japanese occupation:

Although the treatment of the people of Guam was very restrictive and immeasurably harsh, in March 1943, it became worse. The Japanese Army again took over the island from the Japanese Navy and occupation force and immediately began the institution of virtual slave labor followed by the massive relocation of the population. Things went from bad to worse. Schools were closed, and all persons over twelve years of age were forced to grow food for the Japanese, build fortifications, or construct airfields. Strict rationing of food was imposed on the civil population. Treatment of the population went from cruel to brutal. It would later get even more dangerous for the island's society of captives. Indiscriminate killings became ordinary. Group massacres would begin.

Some of the killings were unexplainable. Magdalena San Nicolas Bayani was twenty-six-years-old when the Japanese invaded. Later, she was forced to work for the Japanese. It was slave labor. One particular day, she was witness to, well . . . let her explain—*One day we were told to stop work, stand in line and we stood there without knowing what was going to happen. We were warned that whoever whines, cries, or calls out, we'd all be killed.*

> *There were three men who were standing there while some people were digging a hole in front of them. When the hole was dug, three Japanese, with raised bayonets, approached and told the men to kneel down with their hands tied behind their backs. They were told to bow their heads with their necks fully exposed. The three Japanese counted to three and the three were then beheaded right in front of us. The heads rolled down into the hole . . ..*

Stories such as this fill volumes of books and testimonials on Guam. Another such publication, from which the above was drawn, *real Faces,* 2014, is a publication of the Guam War Survivors Memorial Foundation. Frank F. Blas, Jr. is the president of the foundation. They are in a hurry to fill another similar book, to be published after we depart Guam. Also, the testimonials contained in documents developed and maintained by the Micronesia Area Research Center (MARC), at the University of Guam, are of vital importance. Time is of the essence because the survivors of the Japanese occupation are rapidly fading away. One day soon, there will be none.

In early May 1944, the Guamanians had another worry. American aircraft began to bomb and strafe Guam on a routine basis. Carrier-based aircraft and land-based B-24 heavy bombers blasted Guam, Saipan, Tinian, and Rota unmercifully. They would hit Japanese troops, Okinawan and Korean laborers, and Chamorro alike with their rain of death and destruction from the skies.

After the "Great Marianas' Turkey Shoot," so named by a pilot from the USS *Lexington,* who remarked to a reporter, "Why, hell, it was just like an old-time turkey shoot down home!" The Americans controlled the skies and the waters around the Mariana Islands. American warships prowled unchallenged, and American aircraft ruled the skies. That "Turkey Shoot" became the largest of five carrier-to-carrier battles in the history of warfare. The Japanese lost the contest, and the Japanese on Guam became desperate. They stepped up their harsh treatment of Guamanians, and soon, vicious, unpredictable, indiscriminate killings began. It was as if the Japanese had decided to leave no one alive to tell the story of what happened on Guam.

Indeed, as a reminder, about a year earlier, Tokyo had sent out a directive instructing, if the Americans were to invade their command area of responsibility, and if they felt that the Americans would prevail, they were to execute all prisoners-of-war. Erase the evidence. Some commanders complied with this directive. Wake Island serves as an example.

It would soon become crystal clear that Guam was in the sights of the American fleets, and nothing was going to stop them from invading and recapturing Guam. What to do about it became a nightmare for the Japanese.

In the days prior to the Americans' amphibious landings on Guam, the Japanese simply lost it. They lost all semblances of military order and discipline. In their fatalistic concept of death before surrender, the Americans were preparing to assist them. The American Navy roamed at will around the Mariana Islands, including Guam, blasting the island of Guam with daily and nightly bombardments. Navy and Marine carrier aircraft spewed violence from the skies with bombs, rockets, and machine gun fire. Army Air Corps B-24 heavy bombers dropped their deadly loads on a daily, routine basis. The big rifles of Navy warships threw tons of high explosive shells onto the shores. Saipan had fallen with the Japanese garrison virtually wiped out.

Just before Saipan was secured, somehow, a lone Japanese pilot from Saipan had flown his damaged aircraft to Guam, landed it safely and related to his fellow Japanese a bizarre story. He told of thousands of American ships of various sizes as far as the eye could see across the waters around Saipan and Tinian. Some of these huge ships, he said, came right up to the shore and opened their bowels to discharge hundreds of enemy soldiers, even vehicles and tanks, right onto the shore. He described the skies as being filled with enemy aircraft, so thick, he said, that they cast a shadow over all of Saipan. "They cannot be stopped," he finally blustered out. "They are coming. We are finished." He stopped talking and stared straight ahead. Indeed, they were coming. Indeed, they were finished.

The defenders of Guam knew they were next. The constant bombardments were beginning to affect the Japanese psychologically as well as physically. Bands of Japanese soldiers, some under command and some not, committed senseless indiscriminate acts of barbarism. The commanders of the Japanese garrison on Guam were prepared, if not committed, to doing anything to extract a price from the American forces destined to recapture Guam. And many of them also believed that somehow the Chamorros were in contact with the Americans, perhaps through the lone sailor, Tweed. They also knew that their lives would soon be over.

Many elements converged to create panic and spur a deeply ingrained sense of fatalism within the average Japanese soldier and his officers. They became more unreasonable, therefore more dangerous. Strong anti-western beliefs, and the bastardized Bushido Code, derived from the ancient Samurai philosophy of *death before dishonor,* combined with the cracking, wavering belief of racial superiority, added to the foreboding evolving truth of the onrushing American military and naval forces. These Americans were in-fact defeating the here to fore *invincible* Japanese forces in the Pacific. It certainly created panic.

Weeks earlier, the senior Japanese general on Guam, Takashima, had ordered that on 10 July, *all* Chamorros would be collected and marched to locations in the eastern and southern interiors of Guam. Every Guamanian man, woman, and child was to be *rounded up* like cattle on the Oklahoma plains and herded into valleys in the jungles of the interior of Guam. As mentioned, some reports suggest the Japanese believed that some of the Chamorros were in contact with the American Navy, again—perhaps through Tweed. He was still loose on the island. Other reports suggested that the Japanese planned to exterminate the majority of the Chamorro population. Genocide was being arranged by the isolated Japanese garrison. Similar to the Japanese garrison on Wake Island, they knew there was no relief on the way. They were doomed, and they knew it. But, they would go out in a blaze of glory by exterminating an entire race of people. All they had to do was to gather them together.

The largest of these valley regions was in the Manenggon Valley. Manenggon is a valley area located between the villages of Yona and Talof, across and slightly south of Yigo, on the east side of the island. For days (and nights), long columns of men, women, children, and babies estimated to be near 10,000 or more, were marched at bayonet point to these so-called *relocation camps* located not only in the Manenggon Valley, but also located farther south at Pajesjes, Atate, and Talofofo. One of these areas in the south was in the Geus River Valley near Merizo. Other than what they could carry, there was no food or water provided. The Chamorros had to abandon all their property and depart from their homes. Those who fell out on the march were killed or left to die.

The long march was not unlike the Bataan Death March in the Philippines in 1942, when American and Filipino military prisoners were marched without mercy to prison camps in the interior of the island by the victorious Japanese. In the Japanese way of thinking, to be a prisoner was to be a coward, worthy of no respect. Those who fell out due to sickness, wounds, or weakness were simply killed where they were. So it was with the Chamorro, however, there were no women and children on the Bataan march. There were no civilians on the Bataan march. On Guam, men, women, and children were included—all civilians.

In 2001, the House of Representatives paid special homage to the survivors of the Bataan Death March. In a commemorative speech in front of the United States House of Representatives, Representative Dana Rohrabacher of California stated:

> *They were beaten, and they were starved as they marched. Those who fell were bayoneted. Some of those who fell were beheaded by Japanese officers who were practicing with their samurai swords from horseback. The Japanese culture at that time reflected the view that any warrior who surrendered had no honor; thus was not to be treated like a human being. Thus they were not committing crimes against human beings. [...] The Japanese soldiers at that time [...] felt they were dealing with subhumans and animals.*

There has been **no homage** in the United States Congress to the survivors of the Guam Death March of 1944 (see: Guam's World War II Survivors Await Justice |... www.petition2congress.com/3506/guams-world-war-ii-survivors-..)

This is not an attempt to lighten the result of the Bataan Death March. It was brutal. It was barbaric. Those men who experienced it demand our respect and admiration. It is simply a manner of presenting the death march on Guam in proper perspective. It too was barbaric and brutal, but it was directed against civilian men, women, and children, of all ages, not captured military men.

Perhaps the only thing comparable to the Death March of the Chamorros on Guam, excluding the Armenian massacres during World War I, and the Jewish massacres during World War II, could be the march of Native Americans from their homes east of the Mississippi River to the congressionally designated *Indian Territory* in what is now Oklahoma. In human history, it is called *The Trail of Tears.* In United States history it is called the *Indian Removal Act of 1830.* Men, women, and children were removed from their homes and forced by American soldiers and State militia units to walk in all sorts of weather conditions, for hundreds of miles. Many men, women, and children died along the way. However, there were no plans to kill the American Indians once they arrived at their destination.

Some have suggested that the Chamorro should have resisted. But, in reviewing the overall situation, how could that happen without massive casualties among the Chamorro population. The Japanese had occupied the island since December 1941. The civil population was controlled by severe beatings for small infractions and death for greater, more serious infractions. Serious infractions that could get you killed such as getting caught listening to a commercial type radio, or worse, striking a Japanese soldier or sailor. Even not bowing to a soldier could result in a beating.

We're not talking about just a few Japanese military on the island. In June 1944, there were an estimated 18,000 Japanese army and naval personnel on the island, heavily armed with tanks, artillery, aircraft, machine guns, and naval vessels. For the Chamorro to possess a weapon was an offense demanding an instant beheading. Beheading was a common cause of death among the Chamorros during the Japanese occupation, and even while American forces were ashore, retaking the island, Japanese atrocities continued against the Chamorros.

The Guam Chamorros couldn't clandestinely converse in their own language, as the Japanese had imported Northern Chamorros from Saipan and Rota, loyal to the Japanese, to assist in controlling the Chamorros of Guam. By 1944, the Japanese had even taken the machete, a common farm implement, away from the Guamanians. Active resistance, by groups or individuals, armed or otherwise, was virtually impossible. But the impossible would soon become possible.

On the long marches to interior *camps,* the Guam Chamorros tried to take with them some food, some clothing, some-*thing* they cherished. Most thought they were going to a place of their execution. Indeed, killings accompanied the march. Anyone who fell out and could not be carried was summarily executed. Although the average Japanese soldier did not know of it, only their commanders did, it was a Japanese form of the *final solution*: Kill them all before the Americans retake the island from the Japanese. Considering the directive from Tokyo about disposing of prisoners before American forces invaded Japanese positions, it is highly probable the Japanese were preparing to carry out that directive.

The Japanese set up machine guns around the *camps* in preparation for a *killing field* of Chamorros, but the American Marines and soldiers had landed and moved so quickly and aggressively from the west and south, it caught them by surprise. As the Army closed onto the Yona area sooner than expected, the plans of the Japanese high command were interrupted. Even so, several attempts at mass executions had taken place. The amphibious assault was swift. The Americans advanced far beyond the beachhead and so quickly, it caught the Japanese completely off-guard. The Americans literally smashed through Japanese opposition.

At about this time, there was also a story circulating around of a Chamorro named Nito (last name unknown). It was said and repeated that it was Nito who sneaked up to several unoccupied machine gun positions around a *camp* in one of the valleys, and, at night, when the Japanese were napping or otherwise *doping off,* he would remove the firing pins from those guns. That's guts. Sheer guts. Total bravado.

No one knows how many died as a result of this barbaric *final solution.* The numbers were high. Ironically, the mass relocation accomplished one thing the Japanese had not planned on. It saved some Chamorro casualties from the American pre-invasion bombardments and bombings. However, to suggest that it was a trade-off would be wrong and irresponsible. While the deaths of civilians from American guns and bombs were unintentional, the death of civilians at the point of Japanese bayonets, grenade explosions, and gunfire was intentional murder. Most Americans have never heard of the Guam Death March, but, it happened.

Many Chamorros who had escaped the round-up, while attempting to find safety elsewhere, were caught and executed. Others died during massive American bombardments. By 21 July 1944, Guam had the dubious distinction of receiving the most massive bombardment from the American Navy in the entire Pacific War.

MASSACRES AND REBELLIONS

JOSE S. REYES

In the days and hours before the American Marines and soldiers came ashore and also continuing after the Americans were actually ashore, some Chamorros finally began to extract their revenge from the Japanese. They had been subjected to inhumane acts of barbarism. Wives and daughters had been raped and killed, sometimes before their eyes. Property had been taken, and many had been tortured, some executed. Believing that the Japanese had hatched plans to execute the Chamorros of his village, by taking them out in small groups to kill them, Jose Reyes believed someone needed to fight back. After two such small groups had been executed—murdered by the Japanese, one band of Chamorros armed with only one Springfield rifle, led by Reyes, captured an entire town, killing several Japanese soldiers and causing others to flee.

On 15 July 1944, the Japanese organized a *work party* of twenty-five men and five women near the village of Merizo, a village of about eight-hundred residents. The villagers wondered why most of this *work detail* was made up of many of the village leaders, the most elderly of the population. They were taken out and ordered to dig in some cave for gun emplacements. At about noon, the Japanese gave them some water and rice balls for a meal. They were resting in the cave they had been working in when suddenly the Japanese soldiers began to walk away. As the Chamorros wondered what was going on, the Japanese suddenly began to toss hand grenades into the cave. The explosions were deafening and deadly. Body parts, blood, and clothing scattered all around. Most died instantly, but some survived the sudden attack. Then, the Japanese came in with bayonets fixed. They stabbed and slashed those apparently alive and thrust their bayonets into the bodies of the dead. Manuel Charfauros survived. Felipe Santiago Cruz survived. Frank Anderson survived. Joaquina Concepcion survived. All survivors would tell their stories.

The day after that murderous slaughter at the village of Tinta, thirty more men were rounded up as a *work* detail. They appeared to be the biggest and strongest of the village men. They were killed in a similar fashion as had occurred at Faha. Some survived this massacre also. They told their story.

That left about 740 villagers. These villagers were marched toward Manenggon, and at Atate, they halted for the night. A young boy slipped out of the group to run toward a ranch house that he knew about nearby. At that ranch house, the young man found Manuel Charfauros, wounded but alive. Manuel told the young boy to return and tell the men what had happened—tell of the Merizo massacre.

The young boy did just that.

Several men then went into a nearby village looking for supplies for supper and ran into Jose S. Reyes. Reyes had survived the second massacre and had gone home to retrieve a Springfield rifle that he had hidden from the

Japanese since the invasion. Reyes collected the men about him and laid out a plan to kill Japanese. The massacres would end the men swore. Reprisals had begun.

Jose Reyes led the first rebellion against the Japanese occupying forces on Guam. When the Japanese gathered together the girls and ladies of Merizo, tied them up, and threatened to behead them—that was enough. American naval forces were already bombarding the island and Reyes knew it was only a matter of time before American Marines came ashore on Guam.

My wife was one of them, he said. It scared him, but the Japanese released everyone unharmed. That was enough. He decided to act:

> *Several successive incidents occurred shortly thereafter. First, the Japanese came into our village and selected the bigger and stronger men to go out on a supposed work detail. That night, the 15th of July, they put them in a cave and they killed most of them. It was at Tina. Some had survived the massacre. A heavy rainstorm had started and the Japanese simply didn't want to get wet. They threw some hand grenades into the cave to kill the people and went in with bayonets to finish them off. But, the rain came, and the Japanese left. Fourteen people survived.*
>
> *Pacific Daily News,* 4 July 1974

> That night one of the survivors told Reyes the Japanese took at least thirty men to Faha and killed them all. That same day, the Japanese ordered villagers to move supplies to the north. Reyes knew they would never return. However, to cap it off, on 17 July, the Japanese ordered all the young, attractive girls to attend a "*banzi*" or party. Then, they started to dig a big hole. Jose said: *I figured it was for us. I started to look for people to assist me. I found only six.*
>
> Quotes taken from an article in the
> *Pacific Daily News,* 4 July, 1974

That night on a supply trip, they planned to attack the Japanese guards. Only two of the men stuck with Reyes. The three unarmed men killed three armed Japanese guards. They took their guns, ammunition, swords, and grenades, and armed more people. Jose went to his nearby ranch and retrieved his hidden Springfield rifle. Reyes's group grew larger as they proceeded to Atate camp. They took the camp. At times, Reyes had to command people to join him at gunpoint.

Eventually, Reyes developed a sizeable force and fought back against Japanese attacks, they held their own until Marines arrived being led by Chamorro guides.

Reyes had sent six men in canoes out to a U.S. destroyer offshore that could easily be seen from land. The growing group, under Reyes, continued to attack and kill Japanese. Then, the six men returned with U.S. Marines from the 1st Provisional Marine Brigade. They led the Marines to Agat, and then to Umatac and Merizo. It took only a few days for the Marines, with the assistance of the Chamorros, to secure the area.

> *In 1974, it was Jose Reyes who was selected to be the Grand Marshal of the 21 July Liberation Day Parade. He said that the admiral wanted to publicize his accomplishment, but simply being alive was enough. He reluctantly accepted the honor as recognition of the fact that the men rebelled against the Japanese and should be so recognized and honored. Reyes was a modest man and didn't want attention focused on him.*
>
> *Pacific Daily News*, 4 July 1974

❧

There were others: Alberto Babauta Acfalle tells the story of the rebellion near Tintinghano. Several Chamorro from Tintinghano jumped the Japanese guards and killed them. They then left Atate with Carlos Chargualaf carrying a gun and Jose Gueredo carrying a sword, but they were ambushed by the Japanese, and several Chamorro were wounded. Continuing on, three men from this group, Jesus Barcinas, Jose Quinene, and Juan Garrido, past members of the Naval Insular Guard, took a canoe, and with others, rowed out to a nearby U.S. Navy warship. They were guardedly taken aboard and during questioning they told the Americans where the Japanese were—in the southern part of Guam. They offered their services as guides. Their offer was accepted, allowing a Marine landing force to come ashore without opposition near Merizo.

> Ana Acfalle says—*several Japanese were killed near Inarajan. At a place where the Japanese were killed, seven of our people left in a large canoe for the American ship. When these men did not return in three days, Jose Reyes, or Tonko, as he was called, sent out five more in a canoe with white handkerchiefs. Some wore old navy uniforms. They joined the other seven and told the Americans where to land. When we were at Yligi (sp?), the men returned from the ship with a lot of American soldiers. . .*

Mariano Nangauta also talks of the attack on the Japanese by Chamorros at Atate. The group killed several Japanese soldiers and took their guns. Mariano credits Jose Reyes as the Chamorro who led the rebellion against the Japanese. According to Mariano they killed about thirty Japanese soldiers, and most of the Chamorros in this group were from Inarajan.

These stories may be read in their entirety at the Micronesia Area Research Center (MARC), University of Guam.

In Tony Palomo's, *An Island In Agony*, Francisco G. Lujan described what happened: . . . *because of the Merizo incident, we plotted to dispose of the Japanese guards in the camp because we knew they had plans to kill us that night.*

The men had discovered a case of Japanese rifles and a box of ammunition. They armed themselves and went out hunting—hunting Japanese.

The narrative continues: *Vicente Sanchez was in charge . . . and accompanied by Antonio Cruz . . . both armed to the teeth with automatic rifles and hand grenades.*

This group of armed Chamorros killed several Japanese soldiers. They protected their families and other Chamorros, guided American soldiers and Marines engaged in combat against the Japanese, and volunteered in large numbers to join the reactivated Insular Force that had been renamed Insular Combat Patrol. They were armed and supplied by the Marines.

These stories from different people vary slightly, but it is also obvious that the Chamorros are resisting the Japanese. They were also aware that it was just a matter of time before the American forces would be on their island. They had to stay alive until that happened.

At this juncture, the Chamorros began to resist extermination. It was kill or be killed. It was do you want to live, or are you ready to die? They wanted to live.

We had planned to interview Jose Reyes. He died while we were on Guam, researching and writing. We were too late. But, it's not too late for the American government to recognize him.

ANTONIO CRUZ ARTERO

The following is an accumulation of known facts that is sometimes supported by conjured conversations designed to assist in telling a factual story:

"Tony" Artero had trudged from his ranch house, in a revolving path, eventually arriving at the cave sheltering Navy man, George Tweed. He brought some magazines from Mrs. Agueda Johnston, a few cans of milk from Tommy Tanaka, and some baked chicken from his own kitchen. He'd climb the cliff with a bag of items, stay a few minutes, and return to the base of the cliff.

During one particular visit, Tweed appeared to be in deep concentration regarding some figures and numbers he had scratched out in the dirt floor. He greeted Tony as he approached, "Tony, look at the bundle of cash I'll be getting in back-pay when I get back home."

"Wow! Five-thousand bucks," he mused, "lotta money, George."

"Yeah, lotta money. Say, Tony, what can I buy that you'd like to have? I owe you, big time."

Suddenly, the sound of thunder could be heard from the north, although there wasn't a cloud in the sky.

"Hear that, Tony?"

"I hear what sounds like thunder."

"That's not thunder, Tony. That's big guns. I think they're Navy guns. Our Navy."

"Well, we've had some planes flying over that don't look or act like Japanese planes. They fly high and don't stay long. They come in from the east, circle once or twice, and fly back toward the east. Jap planes usually come from the north, probably Saipan, fly low—and slow—then either land or head back north."

"They'll be coming, Tony. That's why I'm figuring out my back-pay. Thinking about what I'm gonna buy. Not just for me, but for you too, Tony."

"Not for me. No! I want nothing, and you certainly don't owe me anything."

"Surely you want something. Haven't you ever dreamed of getting something you've always wanted?"

I guess so, may be—but, *you* owe *me* nothing.

"You're keeping me. I owe you rent."

They both laughed.

"Think about it, Tony. What would you do with five-thousand dollars? If you had it, just pretending now, what would you do?"

"Well, if I had it, I would buy myself a Chevrolet sedan automobile. Always wanted one. But that'll never happen until this war is over. Maybe then. Who knows?"

"I'll get you one, Tony."

"Yeah. Sure. Dream on, George. It's good for you. It keeps your mind occupied."

"I'm serious, Tony. When I get outta here. . ."

Tony cut him off, "George, I, like the others who have sheltered and protected you, do this out of loyalty to America. You are a symbol of America. Some have died protecting you. I owe them. You owe them your life. You owe me nothing."

George had to recognize the gravity of Tony's remarks.

"I realize some people have died at the hands of the Japanese for my protection. Perhaps it would be better if I just gave myself up. It won't be long before the American Navy and Marines arrive here. I think. . ."

"Don't even *think* about it!" Tony was angry. "You wouldn't last five minutes with what the Japanese would do to you! You'd rat out every person who has ever come in contact with you. I don't want you to ever say that again."

Antonio Cruz Artero, Don Pascual's second son, was born 13 May 1905.

Antonio's father, Don Pascual Artero y Saez, a former Spanish Soldier, was born on 28 May 1875, in the village of Mojacar, in Almeria Province in Southern Spain. After a life of wandering and performing odd jobs from Africa to Asia, he ended up as a Spanish soldier assigned to the island of Yap. On Yap, he met and married a Chamorro from Guam, Asuncion Martinez Cruz. Once the Spanish-American War ended, and Yap was sold to Germany, he and his wife came to Guam. The couple would have seven children in the course of their marriage: Jesus, Antonio, Isabel, Maria, Consuelo, Pascual, and Jose. Asuncion Cruz died in the late 1920s, and Don Pascual married her sister Teresa Martinez Cruz, whom he had also met while on Yap. Don Pascual eventually became one of the largest land holders on Guam. His holdings came through marriage (U.S. Naval Lieutenant Commander Eugene L. Bisset's daughter Eugenia and Artero's firstborn son, Jesus). He also received payments of land in exchange for goods and services, and through acquisitions of lands by outright purchase. Eventually, his holdings became much of the northwestern land area of Guam.

Captain Eugene Bisset, as the Chamorros called him, gave half of the property he had purchased at Upi to Eugenia and Jesus as a wedding gift and sold the other half to Don Pascual. What was Upi is now Andersen Air

Force Base. The Naval Communications Base takes up almost all of the remaining Artero property.

During the war, one of Don Pascual's sons, Antonio "Tony", and his wife Josefa shielded George Tweed at great risk to their entire family. Josefa actually carried letters from Tweed to Mrs. Agueda Johnston in Agana, and, letters and notes back to Tony from Mrs. Johnston to Tweed. It was a daring and risky endeavor. One slip-up, and there would be immediate and deadly consequences.

Tweed had been secluded and cared for by numerous others before he was brought to the Artero ranch in northern Guam. Once there, he was hidden in a cave on the family property near Toguac along a remote section of shore-line cliffs made fairly comfortable and thoroughly protected. Tweed was protected by Tony for twenty-one months, and Tweed would often jeopardize that protection by sometimes departing the secluded cave for outside excursions.

Tony Artero didn't *request* to shield Tweed. He was somewhat trapped into shielding him, although some would call it *volunteered*. His neighbor and fellow rancher, Juan Pangelinan came to the Artero ranch and told Tony that some of his cattle had broken through the fence dividing their property, and that Tony needed to come out there and gather his cattle and get them back on his side of the fence.

"I need you to help me get your cattle back and fix the fence," Juan said.

"Just keep the cattle John," Tony replied. "It's late; I'll come down tomorrow and fix the fence."

"I want you to come *now*," Juan demanded.

"Alright! If you're so all fired-up about it, but, it's getting dark. Can't we wait 'til tomorrow?"

"It must be done *now*!" Juan demanded.

"Let's go, before you bust a blood vessel," Tony replied, angrily.

The two men rode a bull-cart together about a mile down a bull-cart path. As they neared a grassy clearing, Juan Pangelinan shouted, "Stop here!"

"There's no break in the fence here, Juan. What's going on with you?"

"Follow me, Tony." Juan dismounted the cart, and led Tony to a patch of grass about a foot high on the side of the path. There lay a man, dressed in tattered clothing, very skinny, unshaven, and with long hair. He was a white man.

Some accounts were that George Tweed emerged from the bushes in view of a startled Tony. All describe him as emaciated.

"Tony, this is George Tweed, the American sailor. I have been keeping him, and the Japs may suspect me and are coming to my ranch soon. I'm not sure when. Would you take him and hide him? You have much more property to hide him much better than I can, and if the Japs find him on my property, they will kill me and my family."

"What in the hell do you think they will do with me and my family?" Tony was angry.

"Look, Tony, you have many more places to hide this guy. I don't."

"I'm not getting involved with this. The Japs pretty much leave us alone as long as we give them our quota of meat and stuff. . . ."

"Alright! Alright! I thought you was a friend."

"I'm not stupid, Juan. Why would I jeopardize my family?"

"Well, at least stay with him until I go get my bull-cart to return and pick him up."

"Okay! I'll do that, but you hurry."

"I'll be right back."

Juan Pangelinan trotted down the path, jumped the fence, and began to run in the direction of his ranch house.

Antonio Artero stood looking at the very weak, sickly-looking man (Tweed had pneumonia), wondering how this guy had evaded the Japanese so long.

As time passed, before sunset arrived, Tony bent down to take a close look at the man that had caused so much trouble to not only the Japanese, but to the people of Guam. He had heard most all the stories of people being beaten and tortured by the Japanese as they desperately tried to find this American sailor. He was mumbling and seemed to be waking from a sleep. He looked pretty sick.

"Hey man. You okay?" Antonio asked.

"Who are you?" the startled sailor responded.

"I'm Tony," he replied, as he reached toward the sweating, slightly shaking, bearded man, "are you alright? Can you get up?"

"I don't know. I been feeling pretty puny. I think it'll pass though. Musta ate the wrong thing, or something," the sailor replied weakly.

"You just lie there and try to relax," Tony stated, as he began to remove his shirt, "here, let me cover you up. Looks like you got a fever."

"I'll be okay," Tweed replied in a whisper, as he appeared to drift off to sleep or unconsciousness—again.

"Just relax man. Just relax," Tony insisted as he draped his shirt over the shoulders and upper body of prostrate George Tweed, who shook slightly from apparent chills.

It began to get dark. Tweed was mumbling some incoherent gibberish. Tony waited—Juan never returned. It was an hour after nightfall when Tony realized that he had been had. Now, here he stood, next to the elusive Navy man, George Tweed, on his property, and the Japs were killing people just for information about him and those keeping him.

He had no choice; he loaded Tweed into his cart and drove home. He once verbally described that he felt it was his Christian charity that compelled him to help the sailor. As he arrived home, he told his wife to make some chicken soup and to try and get it down the sickly-looking man. Tony had received not only permission, but also some sage advice from his father. However, again, he went directly to his father to tell him what had happened.

"Son," Don Pascual said, "Pray, and follow God's advice. Then tell no one."

That is how, by most accounts, the elusive Navy man, George Tweed, came under the protection of Antonio Artero.

Tweed was picked up by the American Navy on 10 July 1944, just eleven days before the American invasion of Guam. He returned to Guam in 1945 to present a Chevrolet to Antonio Artero. That presentation, set up by the Navy and the Chevrolet Corporation, caused quite a stir on Guam. Adding to the turmoil was George Tweed's book, and previous inconsistent public statements he had made to war correspondents and magazine writers. Then, his book titled, *Robinson Crusoe, USN,* published in 1945, caused even more of a stir than the Chevrolet. Although the Chevrolet has been described as a curse by some Artero family members, it was not Antonio's desire to have it, but rather his avoidance of the insult it might cause if he might refuse it. It's a Chamorro thing. Tweed was not popular with much of the Chamorro population on Guam. And, unfortunately Tony was selected to bear some of the blame. It wasn't right, but it was the way it was. It was as believed in 1944, and into 1945. This is now the full story.

Adding to the turmoil surrounding Tweed, the United States awarded Antonio Artero with the *Medal of Freedom* for protecting Tweed. It's the highest civilian award that the United States government can bestow. It read in part: "*For exceptional devotion to the American ideal of liberty for risking his life and the lives of his family. . .*"

Yet, at the same time, the American government confiscated almost all of Antonio's family property on Northern Guam. Today, in 2015, Andersen Air Force Base and the Naval Communications Station occupy most of the property that once belonged to the Artero family. The Arteros have retained only about ten-percent of their original holdings, and the American government denies them the logical use of some of their retained property. They have never been properly compensated for the acquisition of their property. Tony's compensation, provided by the government, did not cover all of the five-thousand acres the government of the United States seized. A more blunt way of stating it is to say that they have never had their stolen property returned, or reasonable compensation paid to them, even though the thief has been identified and confessed to the crime.

Much earlier, when approached by a member of the Guam Underground (CU), and asked about harboring Tweed, Tony was very reluctant at first. He discussed it with his father, as harboring Tweed was a very dangerous task. It would be for them all.

When Tony's father gave his permission, and cautioned his son to ask God for guidance and follow his conscious, the key elements of Don

Pascual's statement to his son contained two parts. First was the suggestion that he follow the Corporal Works of Mercy, which dictates that one will have mercy and compassion for another's misfortune, and the second was more than a suggestion, it was a command that such action of mercy must be kept as a highly secretive endeavor, known only to a very select few—not to the entire family. Tony faithfully kept his word. Initially,

"If word or even innuendo gets out, Antonio, we will all be killed," Don Pascual had cautioned his son.

"I understand, father, but America is our country, and even though the Japanese occupy our island, our allegiance is to America. I will be cautious," he paused and looked at his father directly, "and we never had this conversation," he added.

"What conversation?" his father answered.

Tony took over Tweed's protection because Tweed was an American sailor who needed assistance. To many Guamanians, Tweed was a symbol of America. In a way, they were convinced that as long as Tweed was alive, the Americans would surely come back to Guam.

And they did.

Shortly after Tweed was picked up by the crew of an American destroyer, the Artero family had to evacuate their ranch to evade Japanese soldiers who were still on a rampage of indiscriminate killings, and the American aircraft were also bombing and strafing their property. Joining the family of Juan Pangelinan, they secluded themselves deep in the jungle area. It was at about this time that Juan had been summoned to Japanese headquarters and had never returned.

Initially, while aboard the American destroyer, Tweed spread different versions of his stay on Guam in several different interviews and formats after he was picked up by the Navy.

Later, days before, or just after the American invasion, the Japanese had sent Joaquin Limtiaco and Jose Flores to tell Antonio to report to police headquarters, supposedly to pay him for services rendered. They knew the real reason was to torture Tony regarding Tweed. Once they arrived at Antonio's ranch, they warned Antonio that the Japs were on to him, and advised him to remain in hiding. Limty and Jose told the Japanese that they had gone to the ranch, but it was deserted. "No one was there. It was totally deserted," they told the Japanese.

Tony then took his family deeper into the coastal jungle area. However, upon discovering that the sailor Tweed had been picked up by the American Navy, the entire family secluded themselves in the same cave that had sheltered Tweed.

Antonio kept everyone in the crowded cave on the cliff side, until American Marines grew close to their property. As the Marines approached his hiding place, they discovered the Artero family, and, accompanied by the Marines, Tony led his family into American lines. They were now safe.

Then, Antonio began his lasting quest to seek proper compensation for the family property seized by the United States government. It has never been granted. To this day. This man is one of many heroes of the Second World War. He was awarded the Medal of Freedom by the U.S. government.

Artero family 1945 Photo from Eric Forbs blog

Accompanying the photo was the following note: "Stoney, the names L to R: Carmen, Maria, Eleanor (baby), Rose, Joseph, Virginia, Franklin; L to R Back: I do not know the name of the man who is in this picture, he came with George Tweed, he and George took turns being in the picture. Next to him is our mom, Josefa, our Papa, Antonio, our sister. Josephine is between papa and our mom's mom, Maria P. Torres. Our brother Anthony is not in this picture. Good luck and God bless you with your work [on the book]."

ALASKA

The following is a factual retelling of an event in history. It relates to the story of Guam because it is the *other* American territory captured and occupied by the Japanese during World War II:

Guam was not the only American possession or territorial land captured by the Japanese during World War II. However, it (Guam) was the only somewhat densely populated American territory, containing Americans (American Nationals), captured and occupied by the Japanese. In addition to the capture of Guam and Wake Island (American possessions), Attu and Kiska, islands in Alaska, were invaded and occupied by the Japanese, and the U.S. Naval base at Dutch Harbor, Alaska was attacked twice by Japanese bombers. And, of course, the Philippines, an American possession at that time, was invaded and occupied. The heavily populated Philippines was, at that time, on its way to total independence (originally set to happen in 1944), whereas Attu and Sitka were island possessions in the Aleutian Archipelago chain of islands, as part of the Territory of Alaska. The islands were possessions of the United States as part of the Alaska Territory, even though they were very sparsely occupied. Most of the islands in the Aleutian Archipelago were, in fact, unoccupied. One of the islands, Attu, was occupied by a small group of Native Americans (42

Aleuts) and a husband-wife team, Charles (or Foster) and Etta Jones. They were teaching school for the Aleuts under the United States Bureau of Indian Affairs, and Charles was also maintaining a weather radio station. Both worked for the U.S. government.

During the Japanese invasion, Mr. Jones was killed by the Japanese during their *questioning* of his status as an American radio operator. It was a short-wave weather radio. Etta, along with the native Aleuts were taken to prison camps in Japan, for the duration of the war.

Additional information about Foster and Etta Jones has been found in a great book titled *"The Aleutian Invasion"* published in 1981. It was prepared by Ray Hudson and his students at the Unalaska High School.

Cheri Ensley writes of Etta Jones, in the article: *Prisoner from Attu:*

At age sixty-two, Mrs. Etta Jones was taken prisoner by the Japanese on June 7, 1942, at Attu. Mrs. Jones and her husband had arrived on Attu eight months before [October 1941]. She was a school teacher for the Bureau of Indian Affairs. Her husband was a radio technician and operated a government radio and weather-reporting station.

The Joneses were not really expecting the Japanese when some men debarked from a huge transport off Chichagoff Harbor. Word had come that an American ship was due to evacuate all the people on Attu. A few soldiers or sailors would maintain the radio station and continue to send weather reports. The Joneses mistook the Japanese ship for this vessel.

A short time later Mrs. Jones heard a series of rifle shots echo through the valley. Almost at once a woman rushed into her cabin and cried, "The Japs are here!" Mrs. Jones quickly looked out the window. Japanese were pouring all over the hills surrounding the valley, shooting as they came and yelling wildly. Some of the Aleut people were wounded by the haphazard fire but none seriously.

While bullets hit the cabin windows and walls, Mr. Jones continued transmitting messages to Dutch Harbor. When the Japanese were almost in the house, he walked out and gave himself up.

Right after Mr. Jones gave himself up, an officer thrust himself into the cabin and confronted Mrs. Jones with a bayonet. He poked the bayonet against her body and asked in English, "How many are here?"

"Two," Etta replied, "how many have you?"

"Two thousand," was the answer.

Early the next morning the Japanese came for Mr. Jones. He was taken to the commander for further questioning. That was the last time Mrs. Jones saw him alive. How he was killed she never learned.

After her husband was taken away, Mrs. Jones believed she lost her mind. She said she remembered little of what happened in the next few days until she was placed on a transport and taken to Yokohama.

"I have one vivid recollection," she said. "After climbing the long stairway of the ship and getting on deck, I noticed myself in a mirror. I was laughing like an hysterical fool. Perched on the back of my head was a blue knit cap. The reflection was enough to shock me back to normalcy, and from then on I remember everything clearly."

She arrived at Yokohama around June 21st. She was surprised to see a picture of herself and some Attu people in one of the daily newspapers.

The Japanese took Etta to the Bund Hotel. She was interrogated, but they were finally convinced that she had no military knowledge. She was soon joined by eighteen Australian nurses who had been captured in New Guinea. The whole group was transferred in August 1942 to the Yokohama Athletic and Rowing Club. There were no bedrooms so everyone slept on the floor. Later they were moved to a different prison camp, at Totsuka, about twenty miles outside of Yokohama. She didn't have to do any work if she didn't want to.

The Japanese were actually nice to her and called her "Oba San," which meant the aged one and was considered a title of respect.

To pass the time of day they knitted little silk bags for the Japanese soldiers to put their religious pictures in. With the little money this gave them, they were able to buy certain personal things that they needed.

Christmas was especially disheartening for the prisoners. However, their spirits were given some uplift when Red Cross packages arrived. At

Easter 1944 they received some American Red Cross boxes. However, the fate of Mrs. Jones was still not known in the United States.

The Japanese would not let the Red Cross representative visit the prisoners until July 3, 1945 by which time they realized the end of the war was near. As American planes swept over the Yokohama and Tokyo areas the prisoners came to realize that the end of the war could not be far off.

A police official notified Mrs. Jones and her companions on August 17th that they were free, but they were told they should stay inside or close to the camp because the people could not be trusted with their safety.

Four or five days later Americans dropped food and relief supplies at the camp. A little of it landed outside the camp.

"We all disregarded the police warnings and ran right out to get the packages," she recalled. "Some of the Australian girls were along the road and picking up the packages when they saw several American staff cars going by. They tried to stop them but couldn't."

On September 1, 1945, Mrs. Jones was put on an airplane outside Tokyo. She was finally headed for home. Once in the United States she was given a check for $7,371.00 for back pay as the B.I.A. teacher on Attu.

An American military force was to retake Attu in 1943, with hard fought pitch battles against the Japanese forces and the wilder weather. Most of the Japanese soldiers occupying Attu were killed by the avenging Americans. The Japanese defenders dug in for a sustained battle with the Americans on Attu resulting in a total of almost 4,000 American casualties, nearly 600 killed in action and almost 1,200 wounded in action. The weather caused additional casualties among the American invasion force. Of the 2,500 Japanese defenders, only twenty-nine survived as prisoners of war.

The Japanese attempted to build an airfield on the island, from which they could control the North Pacific, but the arriving American invasion force interrupted their plans. Although this was indeed occupied American Territory, it was now *occupied* only by the Japanese. This made Guam the only densely populated (population of around 25,000 + or -) American territory captured and occupied by the Japanese during World War II. Guam *was* and *is* an American territory that was *not* guaranteed independence like the Philippines had been, nor was it occupied by a mere 40 natives as was Attu. As a footnote: The war delayed the Philippine independence by a few years.

As Attu was being retaken by the American army force, few Americans would hear or care about this battle because it was overshadowed by the first American ground offensive against the Japanese, the battle of Guadalcanal in the Solomon Islands.

On 29 May, without hope of rescue, Yamasaki led his remaining troops in a banzai charge. The momentum of the surprise attack broke through the American front line positions. Shocked American rear-echelon troops were soon fighting hand-to-hand combat with Japanese soldiers. The battle continued until almost all of the Japanese were killed. The charge effectively ended the battle for the island, although U.S. Navy reports indicate that small groups of Japanese continued to fight until early July. In 19 days of battle, 549 soldiers of the 7th Division were killed and more than 1,000 injured. The Japanese lost over 2,850 men; only 29 prisoners were taken alive.

Attu was to be the last action of the Aleutian campaign. The Japanese Northern Army secretly evacuated their remaining garrison from nearby Kiska, ending the Japanese occupation in the Aleutian Islands on 28 July 1943.

The loss of Attu and the evacuation of Kiska came shortly after the death of Admiral Isoroku Yamamoto, who was killed by an American plane in Operation Vengeance. These defeats compounded the demoralizing effect of losing Yamamoto on the Japanese High Command.

Despite the losses, Japanese propaganda attempted to present the Aleutian Island campaign as an inspirational epic.

Army Heritage Museum "Battle of Attu."

The American attempt to retake the second island, Kiska would be almost comical, if it weren't so tragic. Unknown to the Americans, the Japanese gave up remaining on Kiska and had evacuated after heavily mining and booby-trapping everything and every place they could. The Navy pounded the island with tons of bombs and shells in a pre-invasion fashion for almost three weeks. The Army landing force poured thousands of men onto the frozen tundra suffering over 300 casualties. All casualties were from friendly fire, booby traps, and accidents. Thirty-two died and 50 were wounded by friendly fire. There were no Japanese on the island.

They had landed Canadian forces in one place and American forces in another place, and, when they met they started shooting at each other. It was a tragic situation that is seldom talked about very often by military planners. It was the classic SNAFU.

AMERICA'S RETURN

The following contains factual historical data:

By 1944 in the Pacific, massive American naval armadas, consisting of hundreds of ships, carrying thousands of Marines with their organic combined combat arms cargo of tanks, artillery, aircraft, ammunition, medical supplies, food, water, and fuel, converged on heavily defended islands. Some are coral ringed and tropical, while others are stark and barren; but each contains a fanatical foe, a foe that will fight to the death, a foe that will not surrender.

From these ships, down cargo nets, or from wells deep within the vessels, these Marines grouped inside floating iron Trojan horse-like monsters, belching cannon and machine-gun fire; they swam their human cargo toward hostile shores, under the protective cover of giant naval guns and Navy and Marine Corps aircraft. These floating steel *Trojan horses* discharged their "Spartans," from the "Age of Aquarius," disciplined, aggressive, amphibious assault forces into the face of tough, die-hard, fanatical defenders, as Marine and Navy aircraft flew overhead to provide support to the ground Marines. The issue is never in doubt. The Marines will prevail.

Again and again, they came, through Guadalcanal, Tarawa, Eniwetok, and Saipan, more aggressive, wiser, tougher, better than before. They were unstoppable. Eventually, six divisions and five aircraft wings composed of more than half a million Marines of the Fleet Marine Force struck across the Pacific in a series of epic battles, fulfilling the prophecy: "The Marines have landed and the situation is well in hand."

These men of the Fleet Marine Force were originally sent to simply "hold the line," until the war in Europe could be won, and then they would assault and drive back the forces of Japan. But these Marines were an attack force who needed to take the offensive. It was in their blood. They prevailed, and they converged on defended shores and assaulted across the Pacific, not driving the enemy before them, but killing them where they stood—all the way to the Japanese home islands. These Marines, their skilled fighting tactics and their specialized equipment were the final products of a visionary from earlier times. He was a Marine they called "Gabe." He was Major General Commandant John Archer Lejeune. He is the Marine who set the Marine Corps on the path that would eventually create the most powerful amphibious force in the world. That force,accompanied by an infantry division of soldiers, was now moving toward Guam.

On 21 June 1944, American Marines stormed the beaches of Guam followed by U.S. Army troops. In the days before and especially just hours before the landings were taking place, Navy and Marine aircraft blasted Guam; then came intense bombardment by ships of the 5th Fleet. Several battleships, each with their nine 16-inch rifles, joined in the bombardment of the island and its human inhabitants.

Operation Forager, the capture of the Mariana Islands, was concocted in faraway Cairo, Egypt by allied leaders. It was a plan for two simultaneous thrusts toward Japan. One was led by Army General Douglas MacArthur across New Guinea toward the Philippines from the South. The other would be a deep thrust straight across the Central Pacific to capture the Mariana Islands, led by Admiral Chester Nimitz with his Navy and his Marines along with a few Army troops. These islands of the Marianas were needed in order to have a base for the new American long-range, very-heavy bomber, the B-29 Superfortress for stepped-up bombing of Japan proper. And, as Nimitz saw it, it would cut Japan off from the

Philippines thereby supporting Douglas MacArthur's landing operations in the Philippine Islands.

> *The **Cairo Conference** (codenamed **Sextant**) of 22-26 November 1943, held in Cairo, Egypt, outlined the Allied position against Japan during World War II and made decisions about postwar Asia. The meeting was attended by President of the United States Franklin Roosevelt, Prime Minister of the United Kingdom Winston Churchill, and Generalissimo Chiang Kai-shek of the Republic of China. Soviet leader Joseph Stalin did not attend the conference because Chiang was attending, which could cause friction between the Soviet Union and Japan. (The Soviet-Japanese Neutrality Pact of 1941 was a five-year agreement of neutrality between the two nations; in 1943 the Soviet Union was not at war with Japan, whereas China, the U.K. and the U.S. were.)The Cairo meeting was held at a residence of the American Ambassador to Egypt, Alexander Kirk, near the Pyramids.*
>
> *Two days later Stalin met with Roosevelt and Churchill in Tehran, Iran for the Tehran Conference.*
>
> *The Cairo Declaration was issued on 27 November 1943 and released in a Cairo Communiqué through radio on 1 December 1943, stating the Allies' intentions to continue deploying military force until Japan's unconditional surrender. The main clauses of the Cairo Declaration are that the three great allies are fighting this war to restrain and punish the aggression of Japan, they covet no gain for themselves and won't involve themselves in territorial expansion wars after the conflict, "Japan be stripped of all the islands in the Pacific which she has seized or occupied since the beginning of the First World War in 1914", "all the territories Japan has stolen from the Chinese, including Manchuria, Formosa, and the Pescadores, shall be restored to the Republic of China", Japan will also be expelled from all other territories which she has taken by violence and greed and that "in due course Korea shall become free and independent".*
>
> Notes of the: Cairo Conference

At first, the discussions revolved around the first phase of Forager to be the seizure of Guam. The Americans wanted to take back American property in order to *save face* for *giving it up* to the Japanese in 1941. But, this was primarily an emotional and moral argument. Tactically, Saipan should be first because it was closer to Japan for the envisioned B-29 flights. To take Guam first would require the early B-29 flights to fly over the Japanese held islands of Saipan, Tinian, and Iwo Jima. Taking Saipan first would give the Navy a base to support attacks and amphibious landings on Tinian and Guam. Plus the Army Air Corps could start the bombing of Japan from Saipan, one-hundred miles closer to the Japanese main islands than Guam. Tactics won over morality.

The American and British political and military leaders had earlier resisted the Nimitz plan for an across the Central Pacific thrust to the doorstep of Japan. So did MacArthur who commanded the Southern Pacific forces. MacArthur was concerned that Nimitz would consume forces that could be dedicated to him in his desire to fulfill his "I shall return," pledge to the people of the Philippines. Then, into the scene flew the B-29. That's when the Army Air Corps threw their weight in with the Navy, led by Admiral King. The Air Corps was preparing to use the new weapon, the B-29, to bomb Japan back to the Stone-Age. The Marianas would put them in range of Japan proper. It would also shorten their supply lines which then travelled all the way to China, where several of the new B-29s were based. The Army Air Corps strongly supported the Nimitz plan to capture the Mariana Islands—including Guam.

Thus, the plan was modified. MacArthur would get what he needed, even a Marine Air Wing was to be provided for his landings in the Philippines. The Northern Mariana Island of Saipan would be first and Guam second. The plan was to invade and recapture Guam just a few days after the invasion of Saipan.

As usual, things did not go as planned. Two situations delayed the invasion of Guam. First, the Japanese fleet sailed into the Philippine Sea to challenge the American Navy supporting the invasion of Saipan. The Americans met them head-on and defeated them, virtually destroying their remaining Japanese naval air arm. Historians called the battle the *Great Marianas Turkey Shoot.* The "Turkey Shoot" name came from an American pilot returning from a mission, describing the event to an anxious reporter as: "It was just like a olé turkey shoot back home." The Japanese lost three aircraft carriers and 476 irreplaceable aircraft. The American Navy fleet was busy taking out what remained of the Japanese Navy and was therefore unable to support the invasion of Guam on schedule. Second, the resistance on Saipan was much greater than expected. Plus civilians on Saipan (Japanese, Korean, and Chamorro), committed suicide by the hundreds as American forces approached. The civilians of Saipan and Tinian, including the Chamorros of the northern islands, had been so indoctrinated by the Japanese since 1918, they did all they could, including suicide, to avoid the Americans.

C. Peter Chen describes the mass suicides on Saipan:

> *Unfortunately, that was not the end of major bloodshed on Saipan. Encouraged by Tokyo, thousands of Japanese civilians on Saipan committed mass suicide to avoid the shame of being ruled by the conquering Americans. Men dived off cliffs into shark-ridden waters, mothers throwing their babies against rock walls before jumping into the water to join their husbands and brothers. Even children committed suicide, holding on to grenades before they jumped off the cliffs. Nearly 8,000 civilians of Saipan died in this mass suicide. Americans watched in absolute horror, but were able to finally stop the madness by convincing fair treatment over loudspeakers. After the battle, the two sites where the mass suicide took place were named Banzai Cliff and Suicide Cliff as memorial to these fallen civilians.*
>
> WWII History.com-Mariana Islands Campaign and the Great Turkey Shoot

The invasion and recapture of Guam had to wait until 21 July instead of 18 June. Now, Guam would receive extra massive firepower thrown upon it prior to the actual landing to soften it up for landing operations. Of course, this bombardment ended up killing Japanese and Chamorro alike.

Saipan was invaded by the Americans on 15 June 1944, and the island was declared secure on 9 July. It was a tough campaign. Tinian was invaded on 24 July, and the battle raged until 1 August 1944.

The amphibious assaults on Guam began on 21 July and would involve the 3rd Marine Division, the 1st Provisional Marine Brigade, and the U.S. Army 77th Infantry Division with a Navy fleet in support. Marine Lieutenant General, Holland M."Howlin' Mad" Smith, USMC was still the overall commander of the Marianas amphibious operations. Major General Roy S. Geiger, USMC commanded the Guam landing forces. Rear Admiral Richard A. Connolly, U.S. Navy, commanded the amphibious operation against Guam.

Much later, due to the strained Marine Corps-Army relations created when Smith relieved the 27th Infantry Division commander on Saipan, some say unjustly, Smith was replaced in July 1945 by Marine Major General (later Lieutenant General) Roy S. Giger.

General Smith may not have looked the part, but he was a tough, no-nonsense, aggressive Marine. His nickname, Howlin' Mad, did not come from a Wall Street advertising firm. "Howlin' Mad" Smith is a Marine Corps legend. And, it was this same General Smith, more than any other, who actually implemented the vision of John Lejeune's amphibious Marine force.

Due to the late assembly of the 77th Infantry Division, arriving from Hawaii, the revised planned date for landing on Guam was reset for 28 July; however, the Army division quickly assembled at Eniwetok where the old hands snapped the division into operational shape. Then, the invasion of Guam was again rescheduled for 21 July.

They couldn't have been more different. The 77th Infantry Division was a New York and Pennsylvania National Guard Division. The average age was around twenty-eight years for the men of the division. By contrast, the 3rd Marine Division and the 1st Provisional Marine Brigade was mostly a bunch of eighteen and nineteen-year-old kids. These, *kids* were quarterbacking a high school football team or hanging out with their girl at the soda-fountain a year ago. Yes, some were veterans of previous campaigns, but more than usual, the Marines were from recent enlistees, toughened and disciplined by Drill Instructors and hardened by veterans of previous Pacific campaigns. These were the tough, proud, aggressive, invincible Marines. And, because they believed it, it was so. These Marines formed the point of the spear.

In the early morning of 21 July, at about 0830, Marines of the 3rd Marine Division and the 1st Provisional Brigade stormed ashore on Guam at Asan and between Asan and Adelup Point. They also came ashore between Apaca Point and Bangi Point on the other side of the Orote Peninsula. Both landings took place on the western side of Guam. The Army's 77th Infantry Division landed later to back up the Marines.

The Army division did not have tracked landing craft when they landed on 22 and 23 July on the shore between Magpo and Adofgan Point, eager to get in the fight. It took the Army two days just to get ashore due to their flat bottom landing craft hanging up on the reefs. Lacking tracked landing craft, they also had difficulty getting supplies and equipment ashore. Amphibious assault was not the forte of the U.S. Army as evidenced by a quote from their [Army] historical publications:

> *The unloading itself was a difficult operation. As a reserve division, the 77th had no LVT's. Assault divisions normally have two battalions. There were 60 dukws but these had to be reserved for cargo and to get the light artillery ashore. Consequently, plans had to be made to carry troops to the reef in landing craft, after which they would wade ashore at low tide carrying all equipment. Vehicles were to be dragged from the reef to the beach by bulldozers. The Division G-4, operating from an SC1319 (Submarine Chaser) just off the reef, was to coordinate all landings. Although the troops got ashore without difficulty, most of the vehicles drowned out in the water between the reef and beach, and practically all vehicles' radio sets, even the waterproofed, were completely ruined. One medium tank dropped in a large pot hole and disappeared from sight.*
>
> CENTER OF MILITARY HISTORY UNITED STATES ARMY, WASHINGTON, DC, 1990

But these soldiers were aware of the problems encountered by the 27th Division on Saipan. They knew that the Marines were disappointed in the performance of that particular division. They were not going to disappoint the Marines on Guam. After the island was secured, Generals Smith and Geiger praised the conduct of these men of the 77th Infantry Division.

Elements of the 1st Provisional Brigade landed at Agat, the southernmost landing site of the Guam invasion. Chamorro guides assisted the landing force.

Once ashore, the Marines and soldiers drove the Japanese before them with ferocious fighting skills. Chamorros by the dozens lent their support and experience of the island to the American forces. Napalm, first used on Saipan, became a weapon of choice from the air and on the ground, burning or suffocating Japanese defenders hiding in caves. Attacks from the skies, artillery on the ground, and naval guns from the sea reaped death and destruction throughout the island of Guam.

A dispatch from war correspondent John R. Henry describes it this way: *Howling Leathernecks and Army troops smashed into the foliage areas using rifle fire [marching fire], tanks, and squirts of flame throwers to wipe out the "sons of heaven" who were sniping and crouching in the remaining pill-boxes and trench works.*

Almost more difficult than the Japanese defenders was the rugged terrain and dense jungle on Guam. Movement forward was extremely difficult. Flanks of units frequently lost contact with the flank of adjacent units. Here is one man's description of movement forward on Guam. He was attached to the 2nd Battalion of the 305th Regiment, of the 77th Infantry Division:

> *The distance across the island is not far, as the crow flies, but unluckily we can't fly. The nearest I came to flying was while descending the slippery side of a mountain in a sitting position.... After advancing a few yards you find that the handle of the machine gun on your shoulder, your pack and shovel, canteens, knife, and machete all stick out at right angles and are as tenacious in their grip on the surrounding underbrush as a dozen grappling hooks. Straining, sweating, and swearing avails you nothing so you decide on a full-bodied lunge, success crowns*

your efforts as all the entangling encumbrances decided to give up the struggle simultaneously. Just before you hit the ground a low swinging vine breaks your fall by looping itself under your chin, almost decapitating you and snapping your helmet fifteen yards to the rear, narrowly missing your Lieutenant's head. He glares at you as though he suspected you threw it. What a suspicious nature. You untangle your equipment, retrieve your helmet, and move on. The flies and mosquitos have discovered your route of march, and have called up all the reinforcements including the underfed and undernourished who regard us as nothing but walking blood banks. We continue to push on. . . .

Guam Operations of the 77th Infantry Division,
www.history.army.mil/books/wwii/**guam/guam**77div-fm.htm

Unlike Saipan, the Chamorros of Guam were happy to see American soldiers and Marines, and the welfare of the Chamorro was a priority for the ground troops and Marines as they advanced toward the Japanese:

First to be addressed on the way were well-armed outposts like Finegayan and Yigo. Each promised casualties, blood, and delay. General Geiger employed the 77th to reduce Yigo and take Santa Rosa, and left the capture of Finegayan and the rest of northern Guam principally to the 3d Marine Division. He brought up General Shepherd's brigade to assist in the final drive. To protect the Force Beachhead Line, care for the Guamanians, and hunt down enemy stragglers in the south, General Geiger tasked the 1st Battalion, 22d Marines; the 7th Antiaircraft Artillery Battalion; and the 9th Defense Battalion, all under Lieutenant Colonel Archie E. O'Neil, who commanded the 9th.

Before moving on, the brigade had aggressively sought out Japanese holdouts, brought the fearful Guamanians into friendly compounds, and provided security for those who chose to remain in their own homes and again work their own ranches. As late as 2 August, 4th Marines' patrols approaching Talofofo Bay on the southeast coast came across some 2,000 natives, still apprehensive of the Japanese, who were directed to a compound which promised safety and at least minimum comforts. The Guamanian people in their own residential and farm areas could, however, still readily call upon the civil affairs sections for food, protection, medicine, and shelter. Such civil care was integral to the American occupation and was controlled by Marine General Larsen, who would head the garrison force as soon as the island was again under the American flag.

LIBERATION: Marines in the Recapture of Guam - www.**marines**.mil/Portals/59/Publications/**Liberation**.

With the 4th Marines over on Talofofo Bay, they were clearly within the 77th Division TAOR (tactical area of responsibility), and with elements of the 77th Infantry Division in Yigo, near where Marine Corps Drive, Guam Route # 1 is presently located, units were drifting left and right in their attacks going north. This is when the assistance of the volunteer Chamorro proved invaluable. The military quickly incorporated the Chamorros into an ad hoc scout force to assist the Marines and soldiers in traversing the terrain and locating Japanese defensive positions. Some unit commanders, probably small unit leaders (captains and lieutenants), gave M-1 carbines and ammunition to many of the Chamorro guides. "It was the least we could do," said a Marine sergeant. These Chamorro volunteer guides proved to be a very valuable asset and, with their assistance ultimately reduced casualties among U.S. forces.

It was very difficult to know where one was located during the battle of Guam. Marines on the left got tangled with soldiers on the right. Even finding the MLR (main line of resistance) became difficult. One war correspondent dropped into a fighting hole with a half dozen tired, but highly alert Marines. "How do you know when you're at the front lines?" he asked.

One of the Marines responded, "When they're shooting at you from the rear, you're at the front lines."

Even as the Marines and soldiers advanced against Japanese resistance, the atrocities against the Chamorro did not stop.

The following is a story written in Guam while researching the contents of this novel:

Today, 8 August 2015, at 0900, accompanied by my wife, Lyn, we attended one of the most poignant and deeply reverent events that I have ever been associated with or privileged to attend. It was on Guam in the village of Yigo, at the site of a mass murder of over forty young men (and perhaps one woman) by retreating Japanese forces in 1944. The full story of this event had fallen into the shadows of history, unknown, untold, and lost within the chronicles of a wartime battle by the 21st Marines, until recently.

On 6 or 7 July 1944, there were several thousand American residents of Guam called Chamorro, confined in a makeshift prison camp in the Manenggon Valley near the village of Yona, as well as several other locations on Guam. They were destined for extermination. In several such "camps" group killings had already begun. But the plans of the Japanese were being interrupted. The American soldiers and Marines were rapidly advancing against fanatical Imperial Japanese defenders. The speed of the advance confounded the Japanese command and frightened the individual Japanese soldier. Most of the Japanese forces had been driven to the northern part of Guam where they prepared to make a last stand.

On one of these days, 6 or 7 August, 1944, a group of Japanese soldiers came into this makeshift prison camp in the Manenggon Valley and randomly picked forty or forty-two young men, young Chamorros, for a work detail. They were to carry ammunition to the Japanese defensive positions farther north. One of these men told his wife as he was leaving, "If I fail to return, run into the jungle and wait for me. I will find you." He, along with the other men never came back. His wife did as she was told, and ran into the jungle only to be found by American forces a few days later. She said she was waiting for her husband. Today, she is 100 years old. She is still on Guam, still waiting for him.

Regina Manibusan Reyes, that young wife in 1944, the aforementioned 100-year-old lady, is the mother-in-law of Senator Frank Blas, Jr., mother of Tillie Reyes Blas, Frank's wife, and wife (widow) of Henry Mendiola Reyes, a Chaguian Massacre victim.

[Unfortunately, Frank Blas notified us of her death as we were researching and writing this novel. We were very sad to hear of her passing.]

For years on Guam, it was not known what happened to these men. Rumors reverberated, stories were told, but no one saw anything or heard anything. Whispered conversations about a massacre drifted, but no one knew anything for certain except some members of a patrol from the 21st Marine Regiment driving the Japanese before them.

A patrol on 8 August discovered the headless bodies of thirty men, which had been thrown onto a Japanese truck. They made a report. The next day, a second patrol discovered twenty-one additional headless bodies in a nearby field. Those Marines also made their report and continued into combat against the Japanese forces. It was a mere footnote in the chronicles of the 21st Marines on Guam. Yet, for many years, information about the discovery of the headless bodies has been part of the undiscovered-history of the battle of Guam in 1944.

In the chronicles found on the Internet at HyperWar: USMC Monograph--The Recapture of Guam, www.ibiblio.org/hyperwar//USMC/USMC-M-Guam/USMC-M-Guam-6, (Chapter 6, Into The Jungle, page 153) the following entry appears:

> *The 21st Marines, placed in division reserve prior to the start of the attack in the morning, had spent the day (8 August) patrolling. This regiment had been assigned the mission of searching the area between the 3d and 9th Marines, at the same time being prepared to support the division if so ordered. It had regained control of its 2d Battalion at 0730, but at 1800 it lost the 1st to the 3d Marines. Patrols returned late in the afternoon and reported few enemy contacts, but one such unit from 3/21*[2nd Battalion, 21st Marine Regiment] *had discovered a Japanese truck containing the bodies of 30 native men who had been beheaded. According to the official account of the incident, the Guamanians, found near Chaguian, had not been dead more than 24 hours. The next morning another patrol found an additional 21 bodies [it does not say men] in the jungle near the same village.*

When the second group was found, a local Chamorro was engaged to identify the victims by the severed heads. He did the best he could. Today, known names are honored and remembered.

It is inexplicable why this information has been so long in being uncovered in Guam. The Marines made reports of their findings immediately. That report is entered into the records of the Guam campaign for anyone to see. In addition, several combat correspondents such as William L. Worden and Al (Alvin) Dopking, both AP correspondents, along with combat photographers such as Joe Rosenthal and others, submitted dispatches to stateside newspapers, and they were published in August 1944. Additionally, Alvin Josephy, Jr., a Marine War Correspondent on Guam and Iwo Jima, wrote the book *The Long, the Short, and the Tall* in 1945 (published in 1946) about his experiences on Guam and Iwo Jima; it included mention of the Chaguian Massacre. Finally, Robert Rogers, in *Destiny's Landfall* (1995), a book about Guam and its people, also describes the same massacre in this narrative: "On 8 August, a Marine patrol found thirty dead Chamorro's, one a woman, in and around a Japanese army truck north of Yigo. On 9 August near the same area, another patrol stumbled onto twenty-one more bodies. Marine Private Joe Young described the Chamorros to combat correspondent, Josephy, who wrote a dramatic account, *The Long, the Short, and the Tall*, of the Third Marine Division battles. 'They lay in awkward positions—on their sides and their stomachs, and on their knees—like swollen, purple lumps. And none of them had heads, they had all been decapitated. Their heads lay like bowling balls all over the place.'"

The information about the Chaguian massacre was first published by newspapers in 1944 and in book form in the year of 1946, and another book published in 1995. But the important thing is that it has been uncovered, and it is now a part of Guam's World War II heritage and remembrances.

A retired Army Sergeant Major, Juan (John) Blaz (Blas), supported by Yigo Mayor Rudy Matanane, made a pilgrimage to uncover the truth of this last effort by the Japanese occupiers to exterminate the Chamorro-Americans of Guam. Assisted by graduate students from the University of Guam, they dug into the archives and memories to reveal the history of the Chaguian Massacre. Apparently, all this initial information came about due to the Guam Representative to the U.S. Congress, Robert Underwood, coming across old official photographs of the massacre while in Washington, D.C. several years ago. Initially, Representative Underwood thought the site was aboard Andersen Air Force Base, only to discover later that it is in the village of Yigo.

This massacre was part of a string of senseless atrocities committed against innocent American civilians of Guam during thirty-one months as a society of captives.

As previously mentioned, while on Guam in August 2015, Lyn and I were invited to the Chaguian Massacre Ceremony by Senator Frank Blas, Jr, who has been very supportive of our effort to compile a novel about the Chamorro Americans during and after the War in the Pacific—as have several other of Guam's residents and officials, such as our good friend and fellow Marine, Lieutenant Colonel Adolf Sgambelluri, USMC (Ret), and many, many others.

As the guest speaker of the ceremony, Frank gave the following (shortened for brevity) address:

> *Munga ma na'piniti I korason-miyu, lao hasso i ania'nan miyu kada diha. Ma dingo hit put para u fan libre. Gof piniti fina'posnia, lao man deskakansa sa man libre siha ya man gaigi yan si Yu'us.*
>
> ***Fill not your hearts with pain and sorrow, but remember them in every tomorrow. Remember the joy, the laughter, and the smiles. They have only gone to rest for a while. Although their leaving causes pain and grief, they left to be with our God.***

Pues basta tumanges, ya hasso siha gi annai man ha hamyu yan I magof siha na tiempo.

So dry your eyes, remember the good and happy times.

Pues konprende gi korason-miyu, na man ma'pos man deskansa ya mientras gaigi guinaiyan-miyu para siha siempre la'la gi halom korason-miyu todu I tiempo.

Understand in your hearts, they have only gone to rest a while. As long as they have your love, you can live their life in the hearts of all of you.

Frank spoke in Chamorro and English.

Attending this event was a good start. Still, we had a tough task before us. We realized our limitations. We were mainlanders, outsiders, non-Chamorros delving into a Chamorro society. It is difficult to be accepted and trusted as supporters of the Chamorro of Guam when so many mainlanders have been exploiters of the people of Guam. We asked simply to be able to tell their story to the reading public of Guam, the military community, and to the readers in the fifty States, District of Columbia, and the other Territories of the Union. It is a story that demands being told, and, we do intend to carry out our mission while on Guam, and thanks to many Chamorros, it will be told. Again, and again, during our many interviews with these Chamorros, we were told by virtually each and every one—"Just tell the truth."

I was shocked, honored, and humbled when I was asked to accompany the Mayor of Yigo in laying a wreath at the site of the massacre. It sent chills through my body and gratitude into my heart to approach the altar of remembrance and place that wreath on the actual ground where this horrible act had taken place, seventy-one years ago that day. I shall never forget it. I will carry that image in my heart, mind, and soul forever.

Yigo Mayor Rudy Matanane and Maj Ralph Stoney Bates
Photo property of the author

Forty-five (Marines describe fifty-one headless bodies) innocent civilian men were ordered to carry ammunition to a place on the island by their captors. Their reward was a brutal death.

We gathered to participate in a Mass for the souls of those men and to celebrate their lives in a ceremony of healing and remembrance. After the Mass, at the Chaguian Memorial Site, we had a delightful meal, accompanied by the Japanese Counsel to Guam and other residents and officials of Guam, and all resolved that healing may continue to erode divisiveness caused by past injustices. This is a true statement, forgive—yes, forgive—but it would be unforgivable to forget.

Appropriate honors were rendered; beautiful music was presented, and worthy comments were made. None more heart-rendering than those words of Senator Frank Blas, Jr., now a good friend on the island of Guam. Frank's mother-in-law is the 100-year-old Chamorro, still waiting for her husband. She still didn't know the fate of her husband. She didn't need to know. With her death, while we were on the island, she is now reunited with her missing husband. She waited for him.

But America needs to know about the people of Guam. All America does.

The story has been around for a long time. Americans need to read, and remember that story.

By the end of July, while fighting was still going on, almost 24,000 Chamorros and other civilians liberated from Japanese occupation were escorted by the American forces into transit camps to be treated medically, fed, and clothed. Relocating, reuniting, and reconstituting life on Guam would take years. But, it did need a starting point. It was crude, it was somewhat ineffective, but it was a starting point.

Were the battles of Saipan, Tinian, and Guam worth the cost? Let us read another comment by C. Peter Chen taken from several sources:

> *During the night of 9-10 Mar 1945, the residents of Tokyo really felt the impact of Americans making use of the Marianas for their war effort. 325 B-29 bombers dispatched from the Marianas loaded with E-46 incendiary clusters, magnesium bombs, white phosphorus bombs, and napalm flew over Japan; 279 of them targeted Tokyo. They successively flew over Tokyo during a three-hour window in the early morning of 10 Mar; their 1,665 tons of bombs destroyed 267,171 buildings and killed 83,793 civilians.* [This is significant when compared to the atomic bomb deaths in August 1945.] *Alice Bowman, an Australian nurse who was imprisoned in Totsuka POW camp some distance outside of Tokyo recalled: "Flames were caught in the swirling winds and danced upward, turning into fireballs feverishly feeding upon themselves. Explosions tortured the air and the shocking scene took on the spectacle of a volcano in violent eruption." The destruction was also observed from high above; pilots of latter waves of bombers reported detection of the stench of burning flesh as they flew 4,900 to 9,200 feet over the city. Unfortunately, although it was to be the largest carpet bombing raid against Japanese cities for the remainder of the war, it was only the start of a bombing program aimed at bombing Japan into*

submission. Most of these bombing missions were to be launched from the airfields in the Mariana Islands.

Sources:
Bruce Gamble, Darkest Hour
William Manchester, Goodbye, Darkness
Dan van der Vat, The Pacific Campaign
CombinedFleet.com

While American forces continued to fight the Japanese, military intelligence, and civil affairs personnel reactivated the Insular Patrol, changing their name to Chamorro Scout Combat Patrol. Volunteers poured in. Their job was to provide assistance to American combat forces *and* to locate and capture Japanese military personnel hiding behind American lines. Actually they were hiding everywhere. Thousands of armed Japanese soldiers evading being killed or captured remained a danger to anyone on the island. The Combat Patrols found many Japanese soldiers and killed most of them. They brought in very few prisoners. Perhaps it was indeed *pay-back time.*

One interesting dispatch from Guam during the last days of organized resistance tells of a lone armed Japanese soldier who had sneaked into Agana, apparently foraging for food. It was a Sunday, and a tent had been set up for a church service. They had even found an old pump organ that worked. The organ was playing and the men were singing when several Marines showed up looking for the elusive Japanese. They (the patrol) were only thirty yards from the church service when they flushed him out. Shots rang out for several seconds. The Japanese soldier lay still. The organist never missed a note and the singers never turned around. The service continued unabated.

The above story was taken from a newspaper article written on 6 August 1944, author and paper unknown.

The following is a mixture of quotes combined with author interpretation of a 1944 newspaper article. The mixture is for brevity only, not changing the gist of the article:

Perhaps one of the most unusual, inspiring, totally unexpected, and a very different story that came from Guam dealt with a Marine patrol looking for stray Japanese holdouts. The patrol came from Able Company, 1st Battalion of the 4th Marines that had been in a bitter firefight for eight contentious days. They had just moved into a cleared area for a rest, when the Company received a patrol order to proceed out again looking for the Japanese holdouts near the village of Aslucas (Note* There is no village on Guam by that name. It is assumed that the writer of the article simply misspelled or misunderstood the name of the village). It was reported that some twenty Japanese officers were hiding out in a cave in the southeast region of Guam. A Marine Lieutenant (first name unknown) Kemp was the patrol leader. A Chamorro guide by the name of Toni Sablon (Tony Sablan), a former U.S. sailor was with them. After a long march, the patrol found the cave and no evidence of Japanese. They then went to several other caves in the same area with negative results each time.

Finally deciding to bivouac near the named village, Lieutenant Kemp spoke to his Chamorro guide, "Toni, why don't you go into the village and advise them of our presence here. Also, ask if they have any food to spare—you know, fruit, vegetables, that sort of thing. It would be nice to add to our rations."

Sablon (Sablan) returned a few hours later. "Sir, I found out that the village had been the location of a prison camp where Japs held many Chamorros. The Japanese guards fled when they learned of the landing of Americans. They left everything and took off," he paused, "the elders say they will take care of the food situation and asked if you would come to the village first thing in the morning."

With flank and perimeter guards posted, the Marines had an uneventful night and broke bivouac at dawn. They hiked about thirty minutes to reach the village.

"I couldn't believe my eyes," Lieutenant Kemp was heard to say.

"There must have been some two-thousand of them. All were in their Sunday finest. The clothing was wrinkled like it had been in a suitcase forever, but it was clean. We looked like a bunch of mud rats, by comparison," the lieutenant related later.

"In the front were about six men who were apparently village officials. You could tell."

"When they saw us they began to clap and smile. Soon, they began to sing *'God Bless America,'* and then, place flowers in our button holes and helmets," another Marine said.

"One of the Chamorros in front was a Doctor Sablon (Sablan). We found out he was a relative of our guide and a graduate of the University of Kentucky Medical School. Another, Mister Flores, was a prominent merchant before the war, and there was a Father Cabroni a priest—all were in front of the numerous villagers. Nearby were two long tables laden with food and flowers. Hamburgers, rice, steaks, table silver, plates, bowls of soup, and various fruit and vegetables filled the table and the eyes of the Marines. You could hear twenty stomachs growling at the same time."

"I couldn't believe my eyes, and I could smell it too," one of the Marines remarked.

While the men began munching from the tables and eyeing the pretty Chamorro ladies, Mister Flores led the officers to a hut where a smaller version of the two tables was located. Two bottles of Canadian Club were placed on the table in front of the officers. As they gathered around the tables, Mister Flores proposed toasts to the President of the United States, followed by toasts to the United States Marine Corps. Then, toasts were proposed to all U.S. Armed Forces and the last one to Lieutenant Kemp.

Father Cabroni offered a prayer for all our casualties.

Lieutenant Kemp kept thinking they would want him to say a few words, and it made him very nervous. "This whole thing was unbelievable," he said.

Finally, it hit him—after his fourth drink of Canadian Club.

He stood and told how proud his Marines were in liberating them and restoring the freedom they rightly deserved. It was an effective talk, clearly enjoyed by everyone. "I think the Canadian Club helped a great deal also," he later said.

After another drink, he stood and thanked the entire village for being so generous to his Marines. The more Kemp drank, the more eloquent he became.

As they prepared to depart, one of the Marines remarked, "If more patrols were like this, it would be a better war."

That kind of sums it up.

"If I hadn't been there I would never have believed it," wrote Captain John McJennett, USMC, much later.

The above story taken from a newspaper article written by Captain John McJennett, USMC, 1944

On 10 August, Major General Roy Geiger, the commander of the American assault force on Guam, announced that all *organized* resistance on Guam had ceased. Yet on 11 August, a unit of the 77th Infantry Division came upon a fortified command post containing about sixty Japanese. In the firefight that followed, the Army lost eight soldiers while killing the Japanese to the last man.

American-Chamorro Combat Teams would continue to locate (and usually kill) as many of the surviving Japanese as they could find. These combat patrols would continue to operate well into 1945. During the next twenty-seven years, Japanese holdouts, hiding on Guam, would die of starvation, be killed or captured, commit suicide, or surrender. In 1972, the last Japanese soldier alive on Guam, Corporal Shōichi Yokoi, was captured by two locals out hunting. His story of survival without assistance from locals is legendary. He survived for twenty-eight years, his last eight years alone, after his remaining two companions had died on Guam. He died in Japan in 1997.

Japanese casualties were some 18,000 killed and 485 POWs. The American forces suffered 3,000 killed and 7,122 wounded. Hundreds of Guam's Chamorros were killed.

AFTER THE BATTLE OF GUAM

The following contains factual data interspersed with brief conjured conversations designed to support developed facts:

In the aftermath of the recapture of Guam, the continued prosecution of the war against the Empire of Japan was still the mission of top priority. Plans were established for the capture of Iwo Jima. All America knew that the defeat of Japan was a top priority. However, two other important missions were undertaken by the American military command on Guam. First was the relocation and care for the civilian residents of Guam, and second, was the investigation of the events of the Japanese occupation in all their conquered territories in the Pacific. This second item involved investigating possible war crimes by Japanese. Again, enters Adolfo Camacho Sgambelluri and Agueda Johnston. Both were to provide assistance to the American military and naval forces, each in their own unique way.

SGAMBE

Marine Captain Nicholas Savage was an intelligence officer with the III Marine Amphibious Force, G-2. His job was to sort out the pre-war Japanese inhabitants of Guam, the Northern Mariana's Chamorros, captured Japanese military personnel, and others—to separate friend from foe and to investigate the foes for possible criminal prosecution. He had to sort through interviews, documents, and records, such as they were, to lay the basis for trials of war criminals by a military war-crimes tribunal. The collective savagery of Japanese atrocities against captive military and civilian personnel was well known by then—but he had to somehow get down to the specifics of the island inhabitants and their Japanese occupiers. To accomplish his monumental task, he enlisted the valuable assistance of Sgambe.

In the initial stages of relocating the population of Guam, while the fighting was still ongoing, any suspects of collaboration with the enemy were simply locked up in a prisoner of war compound. All Northern Chamorros, identified by local Chamorros, were confined along with Japanese military and Japanese civilians. Also confined were locals who were suspected of collaborating with the enemy. Unfortunately, Sgambe was one of those. He was locked up with the Japanese and the collaborators.

This act of locking Sgambe up disposed of any sympathy from his fellow Guamanians. As far as most of them were concerned, he was a collaborator. Only a handful of close friends knew of Sgambe's actual role as he *worked* for the Japanese occupiers. It took Savage and his military investigators a few long days to figure it out regarding Sgambe. Savage believed that Sgambelluri was a friend, not a foe.

It didn't take Marine Intelligence long to uncover the truth about Sgambe. The Intelligence Unit sent for him.

Sgambe quickly briefed Captain Savage of the fact that several of the locals would attempt to tell the American authorities of his actual role. But, he wasn't actually sure who would come to his aide. The fighting had caused chaos, and Sgambe didn't know who, if any of his cohorts, were still alive. Over the last few days, interview after interview proved fruitful for Sgambe and for Naval Intelligence. Gradually, Savage began to realize that the activities of Sgambelluri during the Japanese occupation had been of a "double-agent," pretending to work for one side while secretly working for the other. Savage was impressed.

Several days later, as Savage and his investigators began to figure it all out, pieces of the complex puzzle gradually fell into place. It was difficult to separate what a person actually witnessed from what they had heard from another source. Whereas Japanese oppression fostered togetherness, liberation allowed for the reemerging of old rivalries. Finger pointing, accusations, jealousies, and animosities blurred a clear vision of what had gone on for the last thirty-two months on Guam.

"Sgambe, are you sure you want to go through with this? I have four or five affidavits attesting to your activities as a 'double agent.' It's clear to me. You are certainly a hero in my eyes, and in the eyes of the Marine command here on Guam, for what you have done these last thirty-two months. Captain Murphy (later Admiral John D. Murphy, director of the war trials commission) is also aware of your double role. Hell, Sgambe, he wants to decorate you."

"Captain, I have seen and heard of numerous unlawful killings, torture, rapes, and rampages by the Japanese. There's some that I don't know about, but I will. I worked for the Marines for many years as a policeman and as an investigator. Let me do it again."

"Sgambe, you have done enough. Your information will help us greatly. Go take care of your family. Let us. . ."

"I can best take care of my family by ensuring that nothing like this ever happens again. Let me help you find and punish those who became criminals, especially here on Guam, I am a Marine Corps trained criminal investigator, and there is more investigating to do."

"What do you want to do, Sgambe?"

Standing in the Quonset hut, occupied by the Office of Naval Intelligence, Sgambe pointed out the window toward the barbed wire POW compound. "Captain, you put me back in there with the Japs, and I'll get you more information than you need against these bastards," he paused, "I've seen and heard a lot already, but you put me back in with them, slap me around a bit, pull me out and '*interrogate*' me, treat me like one of them, I'll get you more than you can imagine."

"They might kill you, Sgambe."

"They have had ample opportunity for thirty-two months. I defied them all along. I got a good thing going, sir. I want to do it. I owe my people, and I owe them—the Japs. It's pay-back time."

"Okay, your call," he hesitated, "but, here. Take this. If you need to be pulled out, tie this around your neck. When we see that, we're coming in to get you out."

Captain Savage handed Sgambe a red and white checkered bandana type cloth. "Here, put this in your pocket."

"Hai, dozo! Domo arigato!" Sgambe smiled as he startled the captain by his use of Japanese. Sgambe smiled again, "You learn a lot in thirty-two months living with these Japs, Captain," he paused briefly, and looked right into the eyes of the Marine captain, "Let's get it done, before I back out," he uttered quietly.

Sgambe remained in the prison camp for several weeks, listening and observing. When he was pulled out for *interrogation,* he would pass information to the investigators. This information was invaluable to the prosecution of war crimes on Guam.

Savage's men would pretend to *forcibly* remove Sgambe from the POW compound two or three times each week. He was usually removed around 8 p.m. and returned to the compound around 5 a.m. During that time-frame—Sgambe would slip out the back door, and under cover of darkness, with assistance from Marine guards, he went home to be with his wife and kids.

Unfortunately, the numerous war crimes committed by Japanese on Guam found no defendants at all. All but just over four-hundred Japanese were killed by American and Chamorro combat units. Only a few were captured and turned over to the Marines. How many more, if any, Japanese or Northern Chamorro fell into the Insular Combat Patrol *justice system* will never be known. It is certain that many did.

On 10 November 1945, "Staff Sergeant" Sgambelluri received a letter from Lieutenant Colonel Teller Ammons, Army of the United States, U.S. Naval Military Government Unit—Guam. In that letter, he is commended for providing "valuable assistance in bringing about the trial of persons before the Military Commission." It went on to say, "The trials which have now been completed were made possible through information which has been obtained from the time of the Americans' return up to the present time." A copy of the letter is provided:

U.S. NAVAL MILITARY GOVERNMENT UNIT
GUAM

10 November, 1945

Staff Sergeant Adolfo Sgambelluri,
LSPF, Police Department,
Military Government Unit, Guam.

Dear Sergeant Sgambelluri:

For over a year now you have given me very valuable assistance in bringing about the trial of persons before the Military Commission. The trials which have now been completed were made possible through information which has been obtained from the time of the Americans' return up to the present time. You have played a very important part in compiling information upon which to prove the charges. At the time of the Americans' return, you had a tough assignment, one which cast a certain reflection on your patriotism among many people and through the necessity of secrecy it was not generally known why you were in the stockade, but now that can be told as your work has been completed in that respect. You performed your work in the highest of police tradition, and I hope that all people now understand why you were in the stockade. It was a secret mission to make possible the trial of offenders against the Guamanians during Japanese occupation.

I personally appreciate all the assistance you have given, and you have rendered an exceedingly patriotic service to your people on Guam and the Government of the United States. Now I am sure you have a complete satisfaction that you served in the best interest of the people of Guam.

I wish you continued success in your chosen work and again I wish to express my appreciation to you for your assistance.

I assure you I enjoyed your friendship.

Very truly yours,

Teller Ammons

TELLER AMMONS,
Lieutenant Colonel,
Army of the United States.

Letter property of A.P. Sgambelluri

Sgambe received other accolades, but none were made public at that time due to the secret classification of his undercover work. Many residents of Guam continued to resent Sgambe, even as he returned to work as a policeman.

U.S. Marine Captain Savage also commended Sgambe in an interview with Guampedia wherein he stated of Sgambe—*His role was entirely in keeping with his work during the occupation, risking his life in the service of his people.*

The following excerpt was taken from the same Guampedia article by Raj Sood: *According to Savage, investigating these cases, gathering information and evidence of war crimes, collecting intelligence, these activities were most demanding and vital." Savage states, "This is where Sgamby[e] (Adolfo C. Sgambelluri, late father of the current Chief of Police A.P. Sgambelluri) played an absolutely critical role.*

⁂

> The Japanese had been warned several times, over several years, that their wartime atrocities would be reckoned with. One day, they would pay for the uncivilized treatment of both combatants and non-combatants in the prosecution of their form of warfare. *The most important and impressive warning came out of the Potsdam Conference in July 1945. The United States, Britain and China joined in it–the Russians assented later–and its language was blunt: 'There must be eliminated for all time the authority and influence of those who have deceived and misled the people of Japan into embarking on world conquest. . .stern justice must be meted out to all war criminals, including those who have visited cruelties upon our prisoners. . .*
>
> www.historynet.com/japanese-war-crime-trials.htm,

An estimated 7,500 Japanese remained concealed and dangerous on Guam, the day it was announced *secured* by General Geiger. American troops and Marines, along with the Chamorro Combat Patrol, killed an average of eighty Japanese a day for the next two to three weeks, after the announcement had been promulgated. It was a cat and mouse game, with the mouse and cat equally armed, and equally dangerous. But, unlike the hiding American sailors—no one harbored the Japanese.

Even during the American invasion of Guam, the Japanese were still committing atrocities. War crimes continued unabated.

Fighting and mop-up operations were also being conducted on Saipan and Tinian to the north of Guam, at the same time Guam was being liberated.

The renamed Guam Combat Patrol, under Marine Corps command, hunted down Japanese holdouts for years, capturing a few, very few, and killing a few more. The holdouts were small groups of diehard loyalists, who were a danger to any resident of Guam, civilian or military. Japanese Lieutenant Colonel Takeda surrendered his organized force of sixty-eight soldiers on 4 September 1945, two days after Japan signed the surrender documents aboard the USS *Missouri* in Tokyo Bay, and over a year after organized resistance on Guam had ceased. The last large group of Japanese soldiers was captured in 1960, fifteen years after Japan surrendered. How many died of disease, starvation, or suicide is unknown; however the last Japanese soldier known to be alive was Shōichi Yokoi, in 1972.
On 9 March 1974, in the Philippines, Hiroo Onoda was Japan's last World War II soldier in the Pacific to surrender. He was talked into surrendering by his World War II commanding officer who had been located and flown into the Philippines from Japan to convince him that the war was long over.

The Japanese soldier of World War II was a formable soldier to fight against. He was fanatical, disciplined, and cunning. Many would fake surrender just to kill a few Americans. They would make suicidal frontal attacks directly into machine gun cross-fires. For a Japanese soldier, surrender was a rare thing, most fought to the death or committed ritual suicide. Mopping up on Saipan, Tinian, and Guam fell upon American Marines and Guamanian Chamorros. It was not an easy task. After the war officially ended, the Japanese on Rota would surrender to American forces. Sgambe would participate in all of these activities—assisting the Marines whenever and wherever he could.

A list of World War II Japanese holdouts follows:

1945–1949

* *Captain Sakae Ōba, who led his company of 46 men in guerrilla actions against US troops following the Battle of Saipan, did not surrender until December 1, 1945, three months after the war ended.*
* *Major Sei Igawa volunteered as a Viet Minh staff officer and commander. Igawa was killed in a battle with French troops in 1946.*
* *Navy Lieutenant Hideo Horiuchi volunteered as an Indonesian volunteer Army Lieutenant Colonel. Horiuchi was arrested by Dutch troops on August 13, 1946, while his wounds were being treated in a village after the battle with Dutch troops.*
* *Lieutenant Ei Yamaguchi and his 33 soldiers emerged on Peliliu in late March 1947, attacking the U.S. Marine Corps detachment stationed on the island. Reinforcements were sent in, along with a Japanese admiral who was able to convince them the war was over. They finally surrendered in April 1947.*
* *On May 12, 1948, the AP reported that two Japanese soldiers surrendered to civilian policemen in Guam.*
* *Yamakage Kufuku and Matsudo Linsoki, two IJN machine gunners, surrendered on Iwo Jima on January 6, 1949.*

1950S

* *Major Takuo Ishii continued to fight as a Viet Minh adviser, staff officer and commander. He was killed in a battle with French troops on May 20, 1950.*
* *The Associated Press reported on June 27, 1951 that a Japanese petty officer, who surrendered on Anatahan Island in the Marianas two weeks before, said that there were 18 other holdouts there. A U.S. Navy plane that flew over the island spotted 18 Japanese soldiers on a beach waving*

white flags. However, the Navy remained cautious, as the Japanese petty officer had warned that the soldiers were "well-armed and that some of them threatened to kill anyone who tried to give himself up. The leaders profess to believe that the war is still on." The Navy dispatched a seagoing tug, the Cocopa, to the island in hopes of picking up some or all of the soldiers without incident. The Japanese occupation of the island inspired a movie.

* *Private 1st Class Yūichi Akatsu continued to fight on Lubang Island from 1944 until surrendering in the Philippine village of Looc on March 1950.*
* *Corporal Shōichi Shimada continued to fight on Lubang until he was killed in a clash with Philippine soldiers in May 1954.*
* *Lieutenant Kikuo Tanimoto volunteered as a Viet Minh adviser and commander. Tanimoto returned to Japan in 1954, after Vietnamese Independence and division.*
* *Seaman Noburo Kinoshita, after his November 1955 capture from the Luzon jungle, hanged himself rather than "return to Japan in defeat."*
* *In 1956, nine soldiers were discovered and sent home from Mindoro.*

1960S

* *Private Bunzō Minagawa held out from 1944 until May 1960 on Guam.*
* *Sergeant Masashi Itō, Minagawa's superior, surrendered days later, May 23, 1960 on Guam.*

1970S

* *Corporal Shoichi Yokoi, who served under Itō, was captured on Guam in January 1972.*

* *Private 1st Class Kinshichi Kozuka held out with Lt. Onoda for 28 years until he was killed in a shoot-out with Philippine police in October 1972.*
* *Lieutenant Hiroo Onoda, who held out from December 1944 until March 1974 on Lubang Island in the Philippines with Akatsu, Shimada and Kozuka, was relieved of duty by his former commanding officer in March 1974.*
* *Private Teruo Nakamura, a Taiwan-born soldier (Amis: Attun Palalin) was discovered by the Indonesian Air Force on Morotai, and surrendered to a search patrol on December 18, 1974.*

1980S

* *The Asahi Shimbun reported in January 1980 that Captain Fumio Nakaharu still held out at Mount Halcon in the Philippines. A search team headed by his former comrade-in-arms Isao Miyazawa believed it had found his hut. Miyazawa had been looking for Nakahara for many years. However, no evidence that Nakahara lived as late as 1980 has been documented.*
* *In 1981, a Diet of Japan committee mentioned newspaper reports that holdouts were still living in the forest on Vella Lavella in the Solomon Islands, and said searches had been conducted several times over the decades, but said the information was too scant to take any further action.*

From Wikipedia: Japanese Holdouts

AGUEDA

While on Guam writing this novel, Mrs. Linda Taitano Reyes, the daughter of Marian and granddaughter of Agueda, told of a story about her mother's plans for greeting the American liberators. It seems that Linda's mother, Marian (Agueda's daughter) kept two things faithfully at the ready, waiting for the first sight of the first Americans. One was a clean, pressed, white blouse, the other - a couple of bottles of scotch whiskey. When she told her mother about her plans, Agueda did not discourage her. When young Marian first sighted the advance of some dirty, tired, edgy Marines moving on a bombed-out road through Agana, she slipped on her clean white blouse, opened her two bottles of Scotch, and advanced, smiling toward the lead elements of Marines.

At first the Marines were very wary upon seeing a well-dressed, very attractive, smiling young woman walking toward them holding two bottles, one in each hand. A few would later say, "I thought I was dreaming." The unexpected then happened.

As Marine rifles were pointed her way, she slipped and fell directly into a pool of mud, spilling some of the contents from her bottles, and splashing muddy water all over the clean white blouse. None-the-less she emerged with a mud-splashed dirty white blouse, still smiling, holding the easily seen and now easily smelled bottles, and proceeded to engage the astonished Marines in conversation. She called herself a one-woman welcoming committee.

Slowly, the Marines relaxed and began to warily talk with her. It didn't take long for her to demonstrate with a swig from one bottle to convince the Marines of her genuine hospitality, and that the contents of the bottles were genuine. She allowed her little band of Marines to each start taking a small swig of Scotch. She held the bottle to make sure that no one overindulged. She'd turn the bottle up, allow for a quick swig, and lower the bottle, as she faced the next Marine.

"They all looked like Greek Gods," Marian exclaimed to her mother later.

Suddenly, they were approached by an officer who admonished her saying something to the effect that these Marines had been on a ship for a long time and in firefights for the last few days. He said, "The last thing they need is a bottle of Scotch," or some words to that effect.

Her response was muted, but essentially she said, "I know exactly what these men need and a good shot of Scotch will not hurt them. I know exactly what the difference in swig and long draw is. I'm only offering a swig," she smiled her bright smile as she talked.

The officer returned her smile, grabbed both bottles from her hands, and held them briefly as his Marines looked on, anticipating seeing the contents of both bottles being poured onto the ground. The officer looked directly at Marian, "Thank you," he said, and took a quick swig from one of the bottles, handed both bottles back to her, and continued on his way, followed by the Marines, of course, after each had that quick swig. They claimed that it was one of the best Scotch they had ever tasted. Actually, it was the only Scotch most had tasted since Hawaii, and for many of them, the only Scotch they had ever tasted—or would ever taste again.

As the Marines walked away to continue pursuing the Japanese forces, one man looked back at Marian to see her still smiling and waving, "Who was that beautiful lady?" he inquired to no one in particular.

"An angel, asshole. We're dead, this is heaven, and she's an angel," replied a corporal.

"Get your head outta your ass, Smitty. We still got a war going on here," a sergeant bellowed.

"I liked being dead better," Smitty rejoined.

Everyone chuckled as they spread out and continued to move forward.

As the island was being secured, long before the Japanese stragglers and holdouts were rounded up, Mrs. Agueda Johnston offered her services to the United States Armed Forces by forming an American Red Cross unit out of her own funds to provide American occupation forces with a little home away from home. She became a central figure in assisting the military and the local Chamorro community in settling in together on Guam with mutual cooperation between the locals and the military. She was a strong guiding hand in assisting in establishing the first Guam USO (United Services Organization), chaperoning young Chamorro ladies to sponsored dances and outings entertaining American servicemen preparing for the invasion of Japan proper. She also visited the military hospitals to chat with wounded and sick soldiers, sailors, airmen, and Marines, offering her thanks for liberating her island. Eventually, she became the Director of the Guam Chapter of the Red Cross on Guam, and, somewhere along the way, found time to organize the first Girl Scout Troop of Guam.

But her first love was education. Agueda always knew that the future of Guam and its people would rest on an educated citizenry. She reestablished herself as an educator and as an administrator of educational institutions and programs. Educational opportunity and educational institutions expanded on the small island. As she grew older, she then turned her attention to needs of the elderly, establishing programs for the elderly on Guam that remain today. She is forever enshrined as the "First Lady of Guam." Her iconic lifetime encompassed all three ruling nations on Guam, Spanish, American, Japanese, and American again. But, in her words, she always said that she was a Guamanian Chamorro by birth and an American by choice.

Agueda died 30 December 1978. She was the first non-elected person on Guam to have a state funeral. Her funeral was attended by heads of the United States military and leaders of the government of Guam, and a total gathering of Guamanians estimated to be 2,500 people. She was 85, and a Grand Lady to the end.

BRIG. GEN. VICENTE TOMÁS GARRIDO "BEN" BLAZ, USMC (RET)

The following contains factual data:

No Marine can write a book about the people of Guam and not mention the Marines he knew through the years, who happened to be Chamorro, of Guam. One of these is Vicente "Ben" Blaz. This author had met him only once, but he is a famous Chamorro of Guam.

"Vicente G. Blar (Blas), born in Guam in 1928, to Vicente and Rita Blar (Blas)," is entered into the census record of Guam for the year 1928. The entry misspells the name Blas. Then, later, Ben corrects the spelling of his name from Blas to Blaz, which is the original Spanish spelling. Ben's parents were Vicente Cruz Blas(z) and Rita Pangelinan Garrido Blas(z).

"Ben" Blaz was 13-years-old when the Japanese came to his island as conquerors. He was 16 when the Marines liberated him. Once the island was liberated, he hung around the Marines trying desperately to emulate their actions, mannerisms, and life-style. His major problem was his lack of English language skills. He spoke mostly in the Chamorro language. One particular day, one of the Marines who had befriended him finally said to him, "Kid, learn to speak English. Listen to the radio and speak like they do."

And so he did.

After living behind barbed wire enclosures in his native land, performing hard forced labor under the brutal Japanese guards, and seeing human beings, his fellow countrymen, being beheaded for imagined infractions or for no reason at all, Ben wanted to better himself in order to put himself into a position of being able to prevent a people, any people from being subjected to such wanton barbarism by a conquering military force. As such, like many of his fellow Chamorro, his first instinct after liberation was to enlist in the United States military, after all, he was almost 18 years old, and he greatly admired the American military personnel. He made a decision that he would enlist; the navy being his first choice, but the U.S. Navy would only take him as a steward. Such was the American Navy in 1945.

So, Ben set his sights higher. He was told by many of the Americans that he should get an education, before attempting to enlist. He was being told this by men who had to forego their own education to participate in the war, and they were anxious to get back home and continue their interrupted education. Ben set his mind and his strong determination toward obtaining an education as a route into the military. He was not going to serve food to naval officers; instead he was going to be one of those officers, he told himself.

He reentered the 7th grade on Guam and two and a half years later graduated from high school. Ben still had the burning desire of wanting to be a member of the United States military, but his strong discipline delayed that longing desire again. The desire remained strong as his expectations escalated. Then, the impossible became possible. He received a bountiful unexpected gift. It was a scholarship to the University of Notre Dame. His excitement knew no bounds. It was a chance of a lifetime. But, could he compete? Could he see it through four more years before enlisting? Could he even adapt to the great big America, and its way of life? He was a Chamorro of Guam. He knew that he would make mistakes, but he would adapt and overcome any and all obstacles. His first obstacle was getting to Notre Dame.

There is an interesting story that has been told and retold, about when Ben Blaz arrived in the United States. I think it was San Francisco, but where is perhaps irrelevant. And, who knows if the story is true, or if it was told simply as a joke. The story goes like this*: In 1947, Blaz received a scholarship to attend Notre Dame. After a 22-day boat trip, he arrived in San Francisco and told a cabdriver to take him to Notre Dame. He was dropped off at a Catholic girls' school with a similar name, where he presented his papers to the nuns. They put him on a train to Indiana.* That "Take me to Notre Dame!" story has been around for a long time. So long, in fact, that it was in his obituary. So, the story is again, re-told.

While at Notre Dame, he joined the Marine Corps Platoon Leader's Class, leading toward a commission in the United States Marine Corps Reserve.

Ben became a Marine Corps 2nd Lieutenant in 1951, and after additional training he deployed to Korea where a hot war was being fought. He assisted the people of South Korea in throwing off the yoke of oppression imposed by the communist dictatorship of North Korea, and by the Chinese Communist, later in the war. This was one of the reasons that compelled him toward a life in the military. After returning from Korea, he had numerous assignments as a Marine, gradually rising in rank and assignments. He served in the Vietnam War as a regimental commander. After returning from the war, he continued to serve his country as a Marine in various capacities until his retirement as a Brigadier General in 1980. He is the highest ranking Chamorro of any branch of the Armed Forces of the United States.

Afterward, he returned to Guam and entered politics. He finally won election as Guam's Congressional Delegate in 1984. He served in that capacity through 1992. His famous phrase about Guam is: "*We are equal in war, but unequal in peace.*" It demonstrates the plight of the people of Guam in not having full citizenship rights, but full citizenship responsibilities.

Throughout his life, he espoused the plight of the Guamanian people. They lack full constitutional representation. Specifically, they do not have the same rights as a citizen of the 50 States.

He authored the book *Bisita Guam: A Special Place in the Sun*, published in 1998, and *Bisita Guam: Let Us Remember*, published in 2008.

Ben Blaz died in Fairfax, Virginia, in January, 2014. He was eighty-five-years-old.

He was a great Marine and a great statesman for the people of Guam, and for the United States of America.

Semper Fi, Ben Blaz.

OUR GUAM JOURNEY

The following contains data and conversations with the Chamorros, and others, of Guam. It factually retells the previous stories, with sometimes different views and remembrances, none-the-less tending to support the events related to the main World War II characters about whom this novel is written. Those World War II characters are some of the real heroes of Guam during the Japanese occupation. There were others. Time and resources prevented their development. This *Guam Journey* portion of the book also contains many beliefs and assumptions of the author based on the results of research and of actually being on Guam, living among the Chamorros, and being closely associated with many of these Chamorros of the island of Guam on a daily basis. Many of them are the direct descendants of those unsung heroes of the war years, depicted earlier in this novel.

After our first visit to Guam in November 2014, we knew there were stories of the Japanese occupation of Guam that would fill a footlocker. But we needed to spend more time on Guam to gather names, events, and stories together. This time, being on Guam for a lengthy stay was an eye-opener. We began to feel like many Guamanians feel. Let me explain: What follows was our first "*letter*" to the folks back on the mainland. We needed to share our experiences with someone back home, and we chose our friends, and our South Carolina Congressional representatives to relate our initial feelings and observations:

Letter from Guam: By Ralph Stoney and Linda "Lyn" Bates
"Toto, I have a feeling we're not in Kansas anymore."

In 2014, we decided to write a novel to emphasize the plight of the people of the U.S. Unincorporated Territory of Guam. We wanted to begin with the fact that in 1941, although the people of Guam were native Chamorro—because the territory was a United States possession, the native populations were U.S. Nationals. As U.S. Nationals, they fell under the protection of the United States government, and that government abandoned them, allowing them to be invaded and occupied by the Empire of Japan.

The United States acquired Guam as a result of the Spanish-American War in 1898. The Treaty of Paris ceded Guam, Puerto Rico, and the Philippines to the United States. That treaty barely passed ratification by the U.S. Senate.

The following is related to that Treaty:

During ratification [of the Treaty of Paris] in the U.S. Senate, an opposition view was as follows: Some anti-expansionists stated that the treaty committed the United States to a course of empire and violated the most basic tenets of the United States Constitution. They argued that neither the Congress nor the President had the right to pass laws governing colonial peoples who were not represented by law-makers.

Certain Senate Expansionists who supported the treaty reinforced such views by arguing:

Expansionists said that the Constitution applied only to the citizens of the United States. This idea was later supported by the Supreme Court in the Insular Cases. The controversial treaty was eventually approved on February 6, 1899, by a vote 57 to 27, only one vote more than the two-thirds majority required.

Treaty of Paris, 1898

Guam and its people are still not represented by ***lawmakers****.*

The United States government delegated the Navy Department to administer the activities on Guam, and to defend it. The United States created a naval base in 1899 and a Marine Barracks on Guam in 1901, supposedly for its defense.

Indeed, at the beginning of war with Germany in 1917, the naval garrison on Guam seized the crew of a visiting German warship, after the crew scuttled the vessel in Apra Harbor, and held them as prisoners of war. However, as war with Japan grew more certain in October 1941, the Naval Governor of Guam ordered the evacuation of all military dependents from Guam, followed by the evacuation of hundreds of civilian construction workers that were working to improve the military facilities on Guam. Through the previous decades, the Congress had disapproved almost all requests from the Joint Army-Navy Boards to enhance defensive measures on Guam.

The United States decided that Guam would be no Malta, nor Gibraltar. As defensive forces were being rushed to the Philippines, Wake and Midway Islands, and Hawaii, none was designated for Guam. Guam was surrendered to the Japanese ***two hours*** *after the Japanese had landed on the island on the 10th of December 1941, subjecting the native Chamorro to 31 months of brutality, torture, and murder, and its military and western civilian population to three and a half years in prisoner of war camps run by the Japanese. They were all sold-out, abandoned by the United States.*

After the war, in 1950, the United States gave watered-down citizenship to the people of Guam via The Organic Act, transferred the oversite of Guam from the Navy Department to the Department of the Interior, and gave the people of Guam a form of self-government. Congress still controls the final decision regarding anything enacted by the government of Guam.

Since the end of the war (WW II), Guam has changed and yet hasn't changed. Today, Guam has evolved from a 99 percent

Chamorro population in 1941 into a very cosmopolitan mixed society of Chamorro, Filipinos, Chinese, other Pacific Islanders, some mainlander U.S. people, Japanese, Russian, and Korean bloodline that call themselves first, United States citizens, and second Guamanians. Almost all are born on Guam. Chamorros make up 37% of the population today.

Yet, somewhat like, and yet unlike the citizens of Puerto Rico and the U.S. Virgin Islands, Guam remains in a situation similar to the proverbial unwanted step-child of its wicked grandmother. Its citizens cannot vote for the President and Vice President of the United States, have no voting representation in the U.S. Congress, have over one-third of its land mass fenced off and controlled by the Department of Defense, and is the only part of any densely populated American soil to be invaded and occupied by a foreign power since the War of 1812.

When we arrived on Guam in November 2014, we encountered some of the most loyal, patriotic, proud Americans ever encountered in one place. We had only stayed on Guam for three weeks to begin our book-writing project. However, in July 2015, we sold our home in order to later move to a different South Carolina location, and decided that it would be the opportune time to return to Guam to finish our book-writing project. This time it would be for four and a half months. In that we have our household goods in storage in South Carolina and currently no South Carolina mailing address, we placed a change of address to a friend's business here on Guam.

After we arrived, the U.S. Postal Service advised us that we needed to establish a post office box as our mailing address because they would not forward mail from a business address when we went back to South Carolina. We did as they advised and several things happened.

Then, American Express cancelled our insurance coverage on our rental car, flight protection, lost baggage, all travel insurance, everything. They notified us by U.S. Mail, with their mailings travelling through all the changes of addresses—***they had already cancelled our insurance—two weeks earlier—while I was driving our rental car on Guam.*** *Somehow the great and wise American Express believes that we suddenly reside as a resident on Guam and no longer were a resident of South Carolina, even though we vote, own registered automobiles, pay taxes, and have all our property in South Carolina. We had long telephone conversations with American Express' "legal eagles" to no avail. That's not all, our United Services Automobile Association (USAA) insurance company that I have been a member of for over 50 years refuses to cover me as I drive a rental car, or any other car, while on Guam. It is odd that our Marine Corps retired friend here on Guam has USAA insurance coverage on his cars and home, but USAA refuses to cover me while I'm on Guam, apparently because I do not reside on Guam. American Express thinks we are residents of Guam, while USAA believes, rightly, that we are not residents. Both refuse to provide us with insurance coverage, for different reasons. More odd-ball stuff—the military medical care on Guam for a retired military person, can be a nightmarish bureaucratic ring-around-the-rosie—Catch-22. If you are really badly sick or hurt, you may be eventually sent to Hawaii or Okinawa for treatment. As a matter-of-fact, before being assigned to Guam, military dependents must be medically cleared, or they cannot accompany their military member to Guam. We can now see why. I had a foot problem and it took me three and a half weeks to receive treatment at the U.S. Naval Hospital. I did finally see a good doctor and my foot is on its way to full recovery. I think. But, my wife, who sought medical treatment when I did, for a different problem, is still waiting, for over six weeks. Such is life here on Guam.*

Other than the very friendly people, the fantastic scenery, the scrumptious food, the very intensely patriotic citizenry (military enlistments are the highest per-capita of any place in the United States, as is their war casualty rate), the conservative and religious values, and strong family unity, especially of the Chamorro population, one should have second thoughts about living permanently on Guam, especially as a senior citizen. My wife and I considered, at one time, moving to Guam, but never got too serious about it, as these revelations began to emerge. If we were younger, and—more healthy . . . The people of Guam are short-changed in too many areas that need correcting. And, only Congress can do that. Frankly, it is my considered belief that the government of the United States sold Guam out once in 1941, and is perfectly capable of doing it again. The people of Guam have rights granted by Congressional edit, or Congressional Legislation; they do not have all the rights granted by the Constitution of the United States. It is especially acute with military veterans who reside on Guam and do not enjoy the same rights and privileges as a veteran of the 50 States, and must often be evacuated to Hawaii to receive adequate medical treatment. The VA Hospital on Guam is much too small and understaffed to provide proper care for veterans living on Guam.

These military veterans, retired and not retired, are not treated equally to the veterans of the 50 states, yet their blood was the same color, their sacrifice proportioned equally, and their dedication second to none, but they are shorted equal benefits. As Marine Brigadier General "Ben" Blaz, USMC (Retired), a Chamorro of Guam, said repeatedly, "Equal in war, unequal in peace," to describe the people of Guam.

The United States citizens living on Guam do not have the same voting rights, property rights, nor representation rights, as granted to even the newest immigrated citizen sworn in yesterday in Arizona, or Texas, or New York. That is, as long as they reside on Guam. Or, in our case, as evidenced by above writing, just visiting Guam, can cause even corporate America (USAA and AmEx) to treat you differently. Even the Navy Federal Credit Union will not grant home loans to veterans living on Guam. Also, sometimes books ordered from Amazon.com will often not be shipped to Guam as their independent book providers do not ship to "foreign countries." Their independent book providers seem unaware that Guam is part of the U.S. Postal System, and that they use U.S. Postal stamps, just like in Alabama. Interestingly, all a citizen of Guam must do to gain full citizenship rights, is to abandon their homeland and reside permanently in one of the 50 States of the United States. Then, if they return to live on Guam, they revert to having limited rights as a U.S. citizen.

The United States government confiscated private property on Guam after the war and never properly compensated many of the original owners, even to this day.

It is not only our government that treats Guam and its people differently, it is also corporate America that makes one rule for American citizens in the 50 States, Puerto Rico, and the U.S. Virgin Islands and another set of rules for the people of Guam. The island and people of Guam have done more than any other segment of a society in this great nation, for this great nation, but are treated with the most contempt by the United States government, now joined by some of corporate America. That should not be allowed.

Somewhere, somehow, sometime, and someone must address this problem with America's frontier and its American people. It is indeed "An American Tragedy," and should be an embarrassment to mainstream America, and it must be corrected.

By copy of this document, we are requesting our Congressman Harold Watson "Trey" Gowdy III, and our Senators Lindsey Graham and Tim Scott, to look into the matter presented in this document.

Respectfully,
Major Ralph Stoney Bates, Sr., USMC (Ret)

A copy of this letter was mailed to our S.C., U.S. Senators and emailed to our U.S. Congressman. As we go into the publishing stage, no reply has been received.

Guam is two things. It is a place full of loyal, hard-working, fun-loving, family-oriented Americans on an island in the vast Western Pacific Ocean, and a part of the United States of America. Guam is also an emotion, possessing a sense of abandonment, an unwanted stepchild of a wicked stepmother, possessing a raw sense of full obligations and duties *toward* its government, yet a definite sensation that a lack of reciprocal responsibilities *of* that government toward its people on Guam has and does exist.

There are those who say that Guam is a vital link in the defense of the United States against foreign aggression. It is a shield, a Paul Revere first warning. It is a place, some point out, only minutes from North Korea, China, and even Russia, as ICBM's fly. Any of these three named nations could be struck, from Guam, before their missiles reached the west coast of America. And, from Guam, anti-ballistic missiles could intercept anything heading for the United States across the central Pacific, or toward Guam. That is—*if* America wills it to be so, and if the defensive forces directly supporting Guam have more than a .30 caliber gun (with no firing pins) for defense, and the backing of a President and a Congress. Such as it was in 1941, when a Navy Governor, the Departments of Navy and War, Congress, and a President refused to defend Guam and its American people.

Reasoning and rational prevailed about the defense of Guam in the early part of the 20th Century. For years, the War and Navy Departments urged Congress to fortify Guam. Yet, rather than build the Malta or Gibraltar of the Pacific, the United States chose to abandon the island and its people to the Japanese aggressors in 1941.

By not granting Guamanians full rights of citizenship, equal protection under the law and Constitution, rights of property ownership, and other rights granted by the Constitution of the United States, such as full representation in government of the governed, America signals that the people of Guam are not equal for full protection from aggressive acts of other nations. America abandoned Guam and its people in 1941—and it may do so again.

This novel is dedicated to two things, justifying that preceding statement and introducing the people of Guam, especially those of Guam called Chamorro. This novel has been evolving through months of research from the Internet, books, magazines, newspaper articles, and other written, visual and oral material. Plus, this was the second on-site trip to Guam. When this book is published, we will have dedicated almost six months of on-site research, and eighteen months of dedicated writing.

What follows is the continuation of a timeline of the activities with people and places while on Guam developing this novel. Some portions of the following texts may have been repeated in the previous writings, but are unavoidable in telling the full story of Guam and its American people, and for presenting the full texts of the individuals involved.

MARC

We also whole-heartedly thank the University of Guam's Micronesia Area Research Center and Spanish Archives' staff for the documents they maintain that were tremendously helpful, as has Senator Frank Blas, Jr. through his War Survivors Foundation hearings and publications; however, it was the people of Guam who proved to be the most powerful exhibits of the uniqueness of Guam and its people during the occupation period by the Japanese and through today. Again, many of those people-to-people contacts were located through our good friend Sgamby. Those who provided support to us are highlighted at the end of this book.

We have interviewed several survivors of the Japanese occupation.

SGAMBY

When Sgamby would provide us with the names of sources, we would follow-up on them, but in our many long and brief conversations with Sgamby, he would occasionally, sometimes inadvertently, relate personal remembrances of his war years on Guam.

Once, he told of his mother and his brothers being marched through the night to the Manenggon Valley near Yona. "The only food we had was what we could find nearby in the jungle," he related. "Although we were on a river, the only water we had to drink was rain. The river was polluted with human waste. It was filthy. There were thousands of us there," he paused briefly. "Driven like cattle," he would add, with a facial expression that you could read, telling you that his mind had drifted back to those very days of horror, to an entire population.

They never knew what was going to happen to them at the hands of their captors. Sgamby was almost six-years-old when the Japanese invaded Guam. He was nine when he was swept up in Guam's version of the Bataan Death March.

Another story that Sgamby let slip was when we were discussing the popularity of SPAM on Guam. After the liberation of Guam, it was the American military that provided the initial sustenance to Guam and its people. Military rations were one of the means used to provide instant relief. SPAM was included in that military food package. Tons of SPAM!

SPAM came out in 1937, but it really took off during World War II. It was a popular meat for soldiers of the United States, Great Britain, and the Union of Soviet Socialist Republic (Russia). After the war, it became a mainstay for most meals especially on Pacific Islands still occupied by U.S. forces. Guam was no exception.

Sgamby related: "My mother sent me and a couple of my brothers to see if we could get one of those long tin cans of SPAM from the military. It was the really big cans of Spam, he gestured with his hands. There was a Marine supply dump (a supply storage area) nearby. So we walked up to one of the Marines."

"What you kids want?" one of the Marines asked me.

"I am looking for a can of SPAM," I said in my best eight or nine-year-old voice.

"Spam, huh?" what makes you think you can get SPAM here?" the Marine asked.

"Sir, my mom just asked me to come up and see if I can get a can, if I could."

"Where you from, kid?"

"Right over there," I replied, pointing toward our house.

The Marine looked around as if to see if anyone was within hearing distance. "Say, kid," the Marine bent down and in a low voice asked. "You have a sister?"

"Yes sir, I do."

"Is she pretty?"

"Oh yes Sir, she is very pretty."

"Here kid, you and your little friends there, get in that Jeep. I'll load it up with SPAM, and I'll take you home."

Sgamby continued his story, "the Marine placed several big, long tin cans of SPAM in the jeep and drove us home. My mother was in the front of the house holding the baby when we pulled up, and my brothers and I unloaded the SPAM from the jeep while the Marine engaged my mother in polite conversation."

"Soon," Sgamby said, "we had unloaded the SPAM and I walked over to my mother."

"Say, kid," he looked at me, while continuing to chat with my mother. He then turned from facing mom, bent down, and whispered to me, "Where is that pretty sister of yours?"

"That's her," I said, pointing to my baby sister in my mom's arms.

The Marine gave me a dirty look, excused himself from talking with my mother, got in his jeep, giving me another dirty look, and drove away. He was mumbling something about, "stupid, wise-ass kids."

Sgamby chuckled and added, "I stayed away from that Marine for a long time."

Sgamby is the reason that Lyn and I came to Guam in November 2014. We wanted to dig into his father's clandestine, double-agent activities during and immediately after World War II. As we began our research, we discovered numerous people and hundreds of events that occurred during World War II worthy of further research resulting in a return trip in July 2015.

Sgamby has been our main source of support, guidance, and direction while researching this novel. It is fortunate that our career paths through the Marines were almost identical. We both served in the infantry, we both served in combat, we both were criminal investigators and military police officers, we both graduated from the FBI National Academy, and we both served a tour of combat duty in the Republic of Vietnam.

Actually, at one time Sgamby was indirectly my boss, as he was the Director of Security and Law Enforcement at Headquarters Marine Corps, while I was a Base Provost Marshal at 29 Palms Marine Base, in California.

Truth is, this book is largely a result of our mutual relationship as Marines, and long exchange of emails, discussions, and shared memories of many, many brief and extended experiences of two Old Corps Marines.

STEFFY

No one writes a good book without assistance. We have had assistance. On our first trip to Guam in 2014, Rlene Steffy was very helpful and encouraging; indeed she spent a full day introducing us to the island and its history. We found Rlene through our friend Adolfo (Sgamby). Rlene is a recognized expert on CHamoru (a unique spelling of Chamorro) culture.

FRANK BLAS, JR.

After we arrived on Guam, Sgamby put us in contact with the Guam War Survivors Foundation, and they put us in contact with Senator Frank Blas, Jr. of Guam's Legislature, and President of the Foundation. We had a three-hour lunch with Frank at Linda's Café on Marine Corps Drive in Hagåtña. We discussed his family's previously owned property which was taken to build part of the naval air station on Guam, and later became part of the existing commercial airport. Then, we discussed several different segments of Chamorro history and the Chamorros of today. We had interesting and lengthy discussions.

It was through the invitation of Frank that we attended our first World War II memorial service on Guam at the village of Yigo. The memorial site was in a place called Chaguian where fifty-one Chamorros were bound with their hands tied behind their backs, their feet bound together, beaten, tortured, and then beheaded by retreating Japanese forces as American Marines were closing in on them. There were many survivors of the Japanese occupation attending that service, some introduced themselves to us. And, we also met Guam Senator Tina Rose Muna Barnes.

This author also had the honor of assisting the Mayor of Yigo, Rudy Manibusan Matanane, in placing a flowered wreath at the site. We were sitting about half way back in the audience, on the end of a row, when the Mayor tapped me on the shoulder and asked me to assist him in laying a wreath. Linda Reyes had informed him of our arrival.

Being there at that ceremony eventually led us to our next gathering of Chamorros on Guam, starting at the Chamorro Island BBQ.

Frank and his wife Tillie gathered with us often while we were on Guam. We enjoyed their company very much.

BUTLER/CHAMPION

But first, we visited Gerard or Gerry Champion, the grandson of Mrs. Ignacia Butler. He still owns and manages the oldest continuous business establishment on Guam, Butler's, Inc., located in Sinajana. Gerry is a pleasant man who proudly carries the legacy of the Butler trademark of honesty, integrity, and reliable customer service established by both of his grandparents one hundred years ago. While with Gerry, he told us about his grandmother and grandfather. The Butlers are highlighted in this novel.

We had a great, delicious evening meal with Gerry and his wife and son treating the occasion, just before we departed Guam.

UNDERWOOD

Next we drove out to the University of Guam to meet with the President, Robert A. Underwood, PhD. He was also a previous Guam Congressional Representative in the Congress of the United States. We explained why we were on Guam and the purpose of our book project. He stated that he was supportive. Then I asked if he would consider an endorsement, and promised that I would furnish him a copy of the manuscript once it was near completion. His response was that he would be happy to. The UOG is in good hands with Robert at the helm.

As we were discussing the massacre site and ceremony in Yigo, he related that he had come across some old official photographs of the massacre while in Washington, D.C., and said that we could take a look at them. He believes that his inquiry about the photos may have led to the beginning of the recent study about the massacre, by a group of graduate students from the University of Guam. He then related some of the stories that often revealed a lighter side of the occupation period. "Although there was much brutality, it was not all brutality," he emphasized.

It was Underwood's grandfather, James Holland Underwood who was confined with William Johnston in Japan, and brought Johnston's famous diaries home to Guam. Underwood said that his dad was a good friend of Sgambe (Camacho), our Sgamby's dad, before the war.

Doctor Underwood is very concerned about the future relationship between the United States and the areas in the Western Pacific aligned with the United States in various forms. Recently it was written about and is reproduced as follows: . . . *The Micronesia Territory is one of them. The former Guam delegate* [Underwood] *was asked to write a think-piece for the East-West Center a dozen years ago about what might happen in 2020 when funding for the compact begins to wind down. In the recent resolution, the FSM (*Federated States of Micronesia*) expressed disappointment with Washington's treatment under the Compact that they believe subordinates the FSM.*

The article reads:

> *"So I think that the United States if they really wanted to understand and continue to maintain a high capacity to generate not just military power but political influence they have to continue to understand the value that they get from their relationship with the FSM. If they haven't done so up to now, it's not a client state, it's a partner. If you look at them as a client state then you don't give them the regard that they deserve," he said.*

If not, Underwood notes that china is reaching out, and may exploit the downturn in relations. Already it has doled out free scholarships to FSM students. "When those students graduate they're not going to stay in China, they're going to go back to the FSM. And in another five years or ten years they're going to be running agencies. They're going to be operating businesses, they're going to be speaking Mandarin. And they're going to have a slightly different view of the world than they would otherwise," he said.

In his paper of many years ago, Underwood was asked to predict the future relationship. And just as he wrote back then, Underwood expects the FSM and the U.S. will stick together. A pact is too important, perhaps even more so now, as he added, "At that time it sure seemed like yeah there'll be a lot of jockeying back and forth, but in the end they will probably sign an agreement to extend it, and I still think that's appropriate."

TAYLOR

A few days later, we drove from our hotel in Tamuning to the Chamorro Market in Hagåtña (formerly Agana) to purchase some fresh fruit for our room. We parked, looked the marketplace over, purchased fruit from one of the stands, and decided to have a cold beer before returning to our hotel. As we started to walk up a sidewalk toward a small restaurant called CHAMORRO ISLAND BBQ, we were met by a Chamorro male about the age of fiftyish who, as he approached stated, "Aren't you the people who attended the memorial at Chaguian?" Then he added, "Didn't you," he pointed at me, "place the wreath at the ceremony?"

"Guilty!" I shook his hand. "That was us," I added.

He is George Taylor, and he owns the Chamorro Island BBQ. He invited us into his ornately decorated, air conditioned establishment. Inside, were all sorts of Guam photographs from the 1920s and '30s. As we walked into the restaurant, a lady sitting at the first table inside the doorway looked up at us and announced, "Aren't you the people who were up at Chaguian last week?" George then introduced us to his mother. So we met his mother and a sister inside the establishment. His mother is a Japanese occupation survivor. We engaged in conversation, consumed grill-fired chicken and beef-rib barbeque, red rice, and the hottest coleslaw known to man, and made new friends.

As we explained why we were on the island, we were promptly invited to a family gathering the next Sunday at his mom's home for a Chamorro barbeque cook-out, and to interview his Aunt and Uncle, plus his mother, and we accepted. The next Sunday and Monday a typhoon passed just north of us giving us a torrential downpour and gale force winds. No cook-out that weekend.

We would pop into George's place every now and again until the next Sunday when we drove out to the home of Maria Della Rosa Taylor, George's mother. She survived, as a young child during the Japanese occupation by working for the captors in slave labor planting gardens for food—food destined only for the Japanese. She was also required to attend Japanese school taught by teachers brought from Japan. All children of Guam were required to learn Japanese. The Japanese told them that the Japanese would be on Guam for the next thousand years. The Americans drove the Japanese out after thirty-one months.

At the family Bar-B-Que, we were also introduced to George's aunt and uncle, Ana R. and Raymundo Tores Lizana. Both are survivors of the occupation. Ana is a light skin Chamorro and she related that the Japanese were always slapping her around because of the color of her skin. They accused her of being Caucasian. "Every time Japanese saw me for the first time they would grab me and slap me, and ask what is American doing here?" She then added, "I was only three-years-old."

Raymundo, or Ray, was a teenager when the Japanese invaded, and he lived on a farm, or ranch in the countryside. "They came to our ranch and told me that I had to work for the Japanese doing manual labor. I worked one day for them. When I got home, my father said, 'Let's go. We're outta here.'"

He laughed and then slapped me on the arm. "We fled deep into the jungle. I never worked for the Japs again. Never! The Japanese used our ranch as some kind of headquarters. Every time the Japanese would come around, we would go back deeper into the jungle. We had food, cattle, chicken, and we raised food plants. We stayed hidden. There were four families altogether." He seemed to be excited that his family had evaded the Japanese. Then his tone and demeanor changed when he started talking about the death march and the Manenggon Valley *camp* containing thousands of Chamorros, very near to where they were secluded. "The Japanese had driven them there like cattle, and if anyone fell out, they were killed on the spot. It was traumatic. It could be your mother, your sister, even your child; if they fell by the wayside, they were killed."

"They had no food, no water, they were starving," he said with sorrow in his eyes and a frown on his face. "My father took only one cow, and we moved deeper into the jungle. I asked my dad, "What about our livestock, chickens, and so-forth?" His father responded, "Let the people have it. They are starving. Let them take anything they need." He paused, a long thoughtful pause, looked down and remained silent.

"What was next?" I asked.

He broke into a big smile. "I look at this hill, and there you see men with guns, they are moving toward us. Big men! 'Americanos!!' someone yells. It was the Marines!" He clapped his hands together. "I was overjoyed," he finished.

Actually, it was men from the U.S. Army's 77th Infantry Division, but here on Guam, every conversation that entails the returning of the Americans in July 1944, they use the word MARINES. I've learned not to correct them.

We had great Chamorro food with excellent company. Every time someone else arrived, another dish of food was placed on the table already laden with enormous amounts of food. Family members kept coming, all evening long. They came into the open area of the house for most of the afternoon, young, old, men, women, children, all paying homage to grandma and grand-pa, with a kiss on the cheek or a kiss on the hand. It should be mentioned that we were paid the same homage by the younger generation. We were overjoyed that we had this invitation and shall never forget it. It was genuine, spontaneous, and sincere. We indeed, had a great time—Chamorro style.

Before we departed, Ray told me that he thought that the monument located in the Manenggon Valley was located in the wrong place, stating that it should be on the other side of the river, as best as he can remember. He says he has tried to tell officials that it is not where he remembers. But, so far, no one has taken any action.

JOHNSTON/REYES

Later in the week, we met Linda Tiatano Reyes, the granddaughter of the very famous Agueda Johnston. She invited us to her home, and we had lunch with her and her husband, Kin. Linda is very involved with happenings on Guam. The organization she manages is called, PA'A TAOTAO TANO', loosely translated it is Chamorro for "Way of Life." It is charged with keeping Chamorro culture, language, and heritage alive. That is good. The Spanish tried to destroy the Chamorro culture, and failed. Some of the American naval governors also tried to destroy Chamorro culture and traditions, and failed. Then, the Japanese came. Thirty-one months of waiting for the Americans to return. And, what held the people together—Chamorro culture and tradition.

Linda shared many items with us from her grandmother and grandfather. She still has several items from her grandfather that came from either, Alabama, where her granddad was born, or Tennessee, where her granddad went to school. She has an array of photographs of Agueda, and many of her passed-down belongings.

Linda was on her way to the mainland for an operation and would return before we were to leave Guam. She and Kin were a very gracious hostess and host. The lunch was delicious. They invited us to a traditional Chamorro dance and dinner at the Sheraton Hotel. We attended the event a couple of weeks later. Getting to know and understand Chamorro culture, traditions, and history is important to the presentation of this novel.

Linda also has stated that she will assist us in conducting book signings and sales for this novel.

Before we departed Guam, we had Thanksgiving dinner with Linda and her family. She provided us with several CDs related to her grandmother, a complete copy of her grandfather's diary, and one of Chamorro culture, before we departed Guam.

ARTERO

As we continued to locate people on Guam to add to our story of the amazing Chamorros of Guam, as usual—Lyn needed to have her nails done. A nail appointment was made with the advice of Sgamby's wife, Rosie. Portia was the nail lady. Lyn met with her. They began to talk and Lyn casually mentioned the name George Tweed. Suddenly, Portia stated, "I rented an apartment from Franklin Artero. His father hid Tweed."

So, Lyn is having her nails done by a person who knew all about Tweed, and the Arteros. That nail job led us to Franklin Artero. It's a small island.

After a few telephone calls, we met Franklin Artero, one of the sons of Antonio Artero; the last man to hide the remaining Navy man—Tweed, after the other five sailors had been caught and killed. Franklin or Frank is a 30-year U.S. Army retired veteran, still fighting the U.S. government for access rights to *his* property. *His* property now lies in a small section of land along the shoreline of a U.S. Naval base in northwestern Guam. The U.S. Fish and Wildlife Service took some of the land through the government of Guam, which adjoins the Artero property and grants only *unreasonable indirect* access to the Artero beachfront property. Of course, the Artero's high plateau property, which is part of the beachfront property, cannot be accessed unless one is capable of climbing a 200-foot cliff, because the Arteros are not allowed a twenty meter access to that property from Route 3A.

At one time, as previously mentioned in this novel, Don Pascual Artero, Frank's grandfather, owned much of what is now Andersen Air Force Base and the Naval Computer Telecommunications Station. The Arteros have never been properly compensated for their land, and adding insult to injury, the U.S. Fish and Wildlife Service, and the Air Force base, requires Frank to follow archaic rules to access his costal property. It is ironic that a man, who served his government in uniform for 30 years, a retired sergeant major, now has that same government deny his property rights of access by easement. The only way that Frank can get to his property across the land now *owned* by the Fish and Wildlife, taken by the U.S. Government by seizure, is by unreasonable access with limitations. Plus, he cannot develop his property and cannot build on his property. Indeed, it wasn't too many years ago that anyone attempting to enter that private property, including Frank, had to lie in the road and be searched before entry was allowed.

Another growing concern that Frank and his family have regarding their beach-front property, is the possibility of access restriction to Route 3A that could rear its ugly head with the arrival of the Marines as part of the military build-up on Guam.

Not being a lawyer, it still looks to me, as a layman, that either easement by implication and/or easement by prescriptive access should be granted to Frank. After all, that property had been Artero property before the Americans returned to seize the land in 1944.

Frank isn't angry that the U.S. government took his dad's land for an air base and a naval base. He loves his country too much to not want them to build a military base on Artero property. He is angry because the family has never been reasonably compensated for that seizure, and because the U.S. government won't let him have unfettered reasonable access to *his* remaining property.

Frank's current property is along one of the most beautiful coastlines on Guam. Located on the property are ancient latte-stones (used as pole-like foundations for Chamorro dwelling and meeting houses), that date back thousands of years, bent coconut palms stretching over the lapping waters surging over the white sand beaches, and a view that French Polynesia wishes it had. Indeed it is pristine property. It is a small miracle that the U.S. government didn't seize that also. Not yet anyway.

Later Frank would take us out to his beach property on a beautiful Guam day that threatened rain, but it would hold off just right to maintain a clear, almost cloudless sky, until we departed the site. His property is a section of beach and cliff property covering about 200 meters along the water, and reaching back to the top of high cliffs alongside Guam Route # 3. The federal government will not let Frank, or any other family members, who have inherited adjoining properties, develop their property. They cannot have water or electricity, cannot bring equipment onto their property, cannot directly access their property, and must traverse the most unmaintained roads on Guam in order to set foot on their property. Frankly, it has all the appearances that the U.S. government is simply "jerking" the Arteros around. Antonio Artero provided a valuable service to the United States during World War II. He received the Medal of Freedom for that service. Then, the government he served took his property and has ignored almost all requests for just compensation, and reasonable access.

If this were a criminal case, it would be so simple. There has been a theft. The culprit has confessed. But the trial will never be completed because the thief and the judge are the same.

A week or so later, we were invited to meet some other members of the Artero family. Lyn and I met Franklin and his brothers, Pascual, and Victor with their wives, along with his brother-in-law Wilfred Leon Guerrero, President Emeritus, University of Guam, at the Outrigger Hotel on Tumon Bay for dinner. It was a great gathering. They were entertaining, witty, knowledgeable, and informative, regarding that which we are writing about here on Guam. The closeness of the family is obvious and a special kinship prevailed throughout the delightful evening.

Discussions evolved covering numerous diverse subjects including, but not limited to, the liberation of Guam, the Japanese occupation, the Artero property struggle, the return of a Marine combat unit to Guam (infantry, armor, artillery, and aviation assets and personnel), which is foretold as happening in 2021, and a discussion revolving around current local U.S. military attitudes regarding Guam and Guamanians. The latter subject being of keen interest to this author, at this particular time, as it dominates discussions here on Guam.

A few days later, as Lyn and I were walking around the Chamorro Village, in Hagåtña, we ran into Franklin, again. He and his wife, Margie, were purchasing (actually picking up) food for their village festival that evening, and in the unique Chamorro fashion, we were invited. To refuse, even politely, an invitation to attend a village, or even a family festival on Guam is to miss an opportunity to meet great people, and to consume some of the best food of anywhere in the world.

We drove through threatening rain across the island to the high village of Talofofo, located up in the hills overlooking the Pacific Ocean, to celebrate their patron Saint, San Miguel, or Saint Michael. We became just a bit confused looking for a Talofofo festival as we passed festival, after festival, in parks, homes and a couple of other churches. Finally, we arrived as a steady light rainfall fell on a crowd estimated to be between two and three thousand people. We witnessed a large procession of church worshipers coming down the main road towards us after having attended the village San Miguel Catholic Church Mass. They were marching in a long procession from the church, completing a half mile walk, in a circle, to the village hall, where various gargantuan amounts of foods adorned numerous tables, awaiting the arrival of the hungry masses. Whole boars, whole fish, and a whole lotta everything covered several tables. It is an annual event.

Somehow, in that large crowd, we reconnected with Frank and Margie. They are indeed becoming one of our favorite new island friends. Like her husband, Margie met us with a great big hug. We were introduced to many people, including the Mayor of Talofofo, Vicente S. Taitague, a former Navy man who seemed to be a very busy person with this big hungry crowd in this big village event. Everyone seemed to be having a fantastic time and we were grateful to have been invited.

Then, a week or so later, Frank called to see if we would be interested in attending a church Mass and cook-out at St. Fidelis Friary in Agana Heights. The Mass and festival was at Our Lady of the Blessed Sacrament Church. Lyn and I sat with a crowd of several hundred people outside, under a tarp roof, while several hundred more crowded into the church for the Mass. Then we followed the church procession around the church and returned to the now familiar food laden tables. Another great feast!

Another wonderful and delightful evening! In summary: lotsa food, lotsa fun. Chamorro style!

Franklin and Margie departed a few days later on a trip to Israel.

Upon their return, we got together a few more times. We enjoyed the company of each other very much, and especially the Gun Beach dining experience on a rain-soaked evening while observing a hundred dollar a seat performance of Chamorro dance from our ten dollar seats next door.

It's made it even harder to leave Guam. Again!!

LIMTIACO

Sgamby told us that Limtiaco's (Limty) son was on the island, and with Sgamby's assistance we located him. We called and made an appointment to meet with Joaquin Limtiaco's son and grandson on Guam. Joaquin was a close confidant of Adolf Sgambelluri's dad, Sgambe. Together, these two kept one step ahead of the Japanese authorities, while secluding the American sailors who had remained hiding on Guam during the Japanese occupation. Also, occasionally with these two was Juan Flores. Most of the work regarding, with whom, where, when, and how, the sailors would be moved and protected fell on the shoulders of Joaquin. And, it was Joaquin who was tortured and brutalized more than any other operative of the underground network. Indeed, he knew everything, and told nothing.

It was an impressive, informative, and emotional experience. Limty's son, Tony was born in 1936 and was almost six when the Japanese invaded and going on nine when they were kicked out. As he began to talk with us, he was unconsciously drifting back in time. You could tell. His voice got raspy, his breathing-more shallow and his eyes began to well-up with tears. It was obvious that he had great love and deep admiration for his father. Several times, as he was relating information about his dad, he had to stop, wipe his eyes, and clear his throat. He may have been young at that time, but he remembers. Having lunch and chatting with Tony Limtiaco, Joaquin's son, and Rob Limtiaco, his grandson, was an emotional experience. He can never forget.

"It must have been sometime in 1942, I guess," he paused briefly, and then continued. "We lived in a two-story house in Barrigada. It wasn't much. You could see from the second floor down to the first floor through cracks in the floor. I was looking down and saw a large group of men gathered downstairs with my father. The sailor Tweed was there. I remember that my father had a gun, you know, a .45 pistol strapped to his waist."

He paused again, got a smile on his face, and continued. "Later, he picked me up and put me on his shoulders, you know, around the neck." He demonstrated with his hands how a small boy would ride his dad's shoulders with his tiny legs hanging down the front of his dad's chest so the feet were about at waist level, where—there hung the gun. "My foot was resting on the gun in the holster, and I felt so big and important." We all laughed at the easily conjured image.

He talked of the Japanese invasion and how his father had collected canned goods and brought them to the home. "Together, they buried the cans on the ranch. Most of the cans were pork and beans," he remembered. "We ate a lot of pork and beans," he said, as he gestured, holding his stomach.

Then, Tony's mood changed. He swallowed hard and continued, almost in a whisper. "The Japanese later came to the house . . . they took my dad outside . . . and they beat him. . . ." he wiped the tears from his face, looked away, and continued. "They beat and kicked him in front of his family. . . I saw it." Tony choked up, and I changed the subject; but he went right back to describing the big hob-nailed boots the Japanese wore, and how—"they would knock you to the ground and then would kick you senseless. They kicked my father in front of us." He stopped and uttered, "I'm sorry." He was visibly shaking.

Remembrances are sometimes deeply troubling and gut-wrenching. This was obviously one of those times.

"That was very difficult for you," I replied and thanked him for his candor.

His son, Rob, reached over and squeezed his dad's shoulder. Later, Rob would say that he had never heard that story before.

Tony related that they were never actually hungry—because of his dad's burial of the canned goods and the produce they grew without knowledge of the Japanese. That is until they were marched into the Manenggon Valley prison camp. "We were starving then," he whispered.

Even then, he remembers a humorous event. "I had a cap, given to me by somebody. I think an uncle. I liked it and was wearing it on the march," he paused and smiled. "As we were walking or perhaps running, the cap was knocked off my head. I wanted to go back for it, but my mom said to let it go. We were running," he corrected. After a slight pause, he continued, "Once we were in the valley, we had no food, no shelter, nothing! I saw a kid wearing my cap. We had a fight, and the cap was torn apart. Neither got that cap," he laughed, "I liked that cap."

"When did you see the Americans returning to Guam?" I asked.

"It was when we were still in the prison camp in Manenggon. I looked up and saw men. Big men! It looked like they all had red hair. They were coming over a hill. The Japanese had run away, 'Americans!' someone yelled."

We paused and talked of a few other things, and suddenly, we were back on Guam in July 1944.

"There were weapons everywhere," Tony remarked. "It was after the Japanese were defeated, but there were many of them (Japanese soldiers) running loose on Guam. They were dangerous," he emphasized.

Rob chimed in, "There were so many rifles and pistols and other stuff laying around that some people started to settle old scores. There were no laws, no rules, it was chaotic," he reasoned.

Tony then told a story about his dad being with a group of friends, he thinks at the ranch after the island was *secured*. "They were drinking and talking and laughing when suddenly, they hear Japanese voices. They are nearby," he related. He then gestured as if he were holding a rifle. "My dad and the others stood up, faced the Japanese voices, and sprayed the bushes with rifle fire."

He continued, "The next morning, my brother and I had to take two of our goats out to better grazing areas. We had not gone too far when I saw a dead Japanese soldier. His guts were shot out. Nearby was a Navy Seabee unit, a construction battalion. They brought in a bulldozer, dug a hole, tied a rope around the body, and buried him on the spot," he revealed.

We continued to talk of the war years and his dad's involvement. By the time we finished talking and eating our lunch, Joaquin Limtiaco loomed as a giant of a man on the little island of Guam.

But there was more.

"Once, Dad was being beaten so much and so badly, at the police station, his friend Sgambe thought they were going to kill him. They were looking for Tweed and were sure they could break my dad. When the Japs and the Saipanese left the room briefly, Sgambe whispered to him, 'Limty, tell 'em what they want. Give it up, Limty, they'll kill you.'"

Limty managed to look into Sgambe's face, through the bruises and the open and bleeding cuts, as he emitted the deep mournful groan of a man in great pain. His lips moved, and Sgambe turned his ear to be close to his friend's mouth. Very faintly, Limty spoke, "No!" He whispered again, "No!" The Japanese and Saipanese reentered the room.

Limty protected the Americans with his very life. He knew every sailor and usually was the one who escorted them into hiding. He knew every hiding place and every person who had ever harbored them or furnished them information and supplies. Although repeatedly arrested, interrogated, beaten, and tortured, while facing death many times, he never divulged anything. Never!

All the Chamorro resisters during the Japanese occupation were brave, loyal Americans. None took more punishment, more interrogation, or more brutality than Joaquin Limtiaco. He stands as an unrecognized giant of a man in the history of the island of Guam, indeed in the history of the United States. Guam and the United States should recognize that fact. It's long overdue.

Pedro Sanchez, in his book, *Uncle Sam, Please Come Back to Guam*, quotes Joaquin Limtiaco as follows: *Tweed was a symbol of the United States which was fighting in a war for a great cause. We were determined to fight too, in our own way, and to die if necessary.*

The word *giant* pales when discussing Joaquin Limtiaco. He was every bit the Medal of Honor type if there ever was one—but, when Limty served his country, he was not in uniform.

JUAN O. BLAZ

A few days after the conversation with Joaquin Limtiaco's son and grandson, we drove to the mayor's office in Yigo to chat with Sergeant Major Juan (John) Blaz, U.S. Army (Retired). Juan immerses himself in history. He meets military tour groups and shows them around the island. He has accompanied tour groups to Saipan, Iwo Jima, and Wake Island, and is very knowledgeable of the occupation years on Guam. In short, John is a walking encyclopedia, and occasionally, he will assist the governor with military and veterans matters.

We had long conversations about the Chaguian Massacre and the final disposition of the bodies of the victims. No one knows where the bodies are buried. No one knows who, if anyone buried them. Perhaps in some archive somewhere, a graves registration unit may have provided the answer, now lost in the shadows of history.

Juan Blaz assisted us numerous times while we were researching and writing. We are deeply indebted to him for several contacts and events. We attended a neighborhood Halloween festival at the home of his sister Agnes. Every one of these young Chamorro neighborhood kids showed the same respect, to us, and all other adults, that we had received at George Taylor's mom's home weeks earlier. Also, he set up a radio talk show interview, directed us to other festivals, and connected us with numerous people. Juan was at the airport to see us off, when we departed Guam. He was and is a true friend who is very much appreciated.

We frequently encountered Juan as we moved constantly around the island. It would take another full chapter to factually relate the assistance, information, advice, friendship, and direction given to us freely by this retired U.S. Army sergeant major. As a result, he was the first to read the draft manuscript of this novel, and to offer advice for its development.

PAUL CALVO

Later, we met with former Guam Governor, Paul M. Calvo, at his place of business, Calvo Insurance. The former governor was born in 1934 and was eight-years-old when the Japanese invaded Guam. He was almost eleven when the Americans arrived to liberate them from the Japanese. He is the father of the current governor of Guam. His office walls are adorned with family photographs and several photographs from Washington D.C., which shows him with U.S. Presidents. The largest photograph is of him with Ronald Reagan.

He related several stories of his memories of the war years.

"One of the earliest memories was that the Japanese, Mister Shinohara, advised my father, 'If you want to live, you will wear cloth identification patch.' Every Chamorro had to wear an I.D. consisting of a cloth with Japanese characters written on it, pinned to a shirt or dress."

He was ordered to attend Japanese school, and as he entered the classroom for the very first time, he was forcibly slapped across the face, so hard that it knocked him down. The teacher said to him, "If you wear your shoes in this classroom again, I will kill you." Paul said he never attended school again and never forgot that Japanese teacher's name: it was *Nakahashi*. "That was my last day in school," Paul said, "we moved out of Agana to our ranch."

Another story involved his being asked to move his grandmother from one location to another. He hitched up a very mean, black cow that they owned to the bull-cart and started driving, with his grandmother sitting in the back of the cart. Before he departed, his father advised him, "Do not unhitch that cow. It's too mean." As he was driving he looked up and saw what appeared to be two large bottles falling from the sky. Not realizing what they were, he turned to tell his grandmother to "look," but she was already off the cart and inside a nearby chapel which became a makeshift bomb shelter. She apparently recognized the falling bombs for what they were. "Grandmother refused to ride with me farther. She insisted on staying in her shelter. She would not get back on that cart."

Since his grandmother would not leave the shelter, he had to actually unhitch that mean cow and ride it to his uncle's house. His uncle returned to fetch his grandmother.

Paul smiled and gestured a lot during his recitation of events, until it came to the Manenggon Valley prison camps. "It was very crowded," he said. "It was just before the American Marines came." He paused just briefly and stated with a straight face, "and some Japanese were killed . . ." he paused briefly again, and then resumed his statement, "the Marines came and they took us up into the mountains, and we ended up in Agat." He laughed slightly and continued, "some of the people went to the Yigo cemetery."

"Those were some of the experiences that I had," he concluded.

We thanked the former governor of Guam for his time, and he promised to meet with us again.

JAPANESE CEREMONY FOR WAR DEAD

The next morning, we attended a Japanese memorial service at the entrance to a couple of old Japanese command bunkers up on Nimitz Hill. The ceremony was called "Guam World War II Peace Memorial Service 2015." It was a Shinto, or Sinto religious ceremony attended by present and former members of the Diet of Japan, Guam government representatives, primarily from various mayor's offices on Guam, and a couple of *Gaijin*—Us!

It was an interesting ceremony referred to as "Japanese Soldiers Ceremony." The previous day, the same group had conducted a similar ceremony at Manenggon referred to as the "Manenggon Hill War Ceremony." We were unaware of that one. But, we were invited to the Nimitz Hill ceremony by Sergeant Major Juan Blaz. Mayor Rudy Matanane was also there. We sat with the two of them.

Manenggon, as previously noted, is where the Japanese Army marched somewhere between 8,000 and 10,000 Chamorro men, women, and children, for mass confinement, while indiscriminately killing any who fell along the wayside. From Manenggon (and from other smaller such *camps*), the Japanese would select so-called *work details*, consisting of small groups of men. They took them out, put them to work hauling ammunition, digging revetments, or excavating caves, then—the Japanese murdered them.

It is true that tourism has replaced the American military as the primary source of income for the average Guam business. Japanese makes up seventy percent of that tourism. Today's Japanese *money* replaces yesterday's *anger* over the Japanese occupation for many—but not all Chamorros. The economic profit margin of the 2000s, usurps Japanese brutality of the 1940s, for some, but not all of the Guamanians.

As the prayers echoed from the Japanese Soldiers Ceremony, for the spirits of Japanese soldiers and sailors, Chamorro civilian casualties, and American military casualties, there was no mention of what caused the vast majority of the Chamorro casualties.

I have nothing against reconciliation of old warring combatants, or old warring nations; else I would never have visited England, Mexico, Germany, Italy, or Spain. At one time, we were at war with each of them. But on Guam, there are people still alive who bear physical and mental evidence of acts of unrepentant barbarism on a helpless civilian society, held captive on Guam. While there are those who have forgiven the perpetrators of those atrocities, there are also those who have not. Perhaps their grandchildren or their great-grandchildren will, some day. Even so, forgiveness, any forgiveness, should stir remembrances. If not, what is it that we are forgiving? To forgive should not mean to forget. Forgive, but don't forget.

It was a beautiful ceremony, somewhat long, but conducted with grace. We are comfortable around groups of Japanese people; many military tours in Japan conditioned us to that trait. But, for my wife and me, it was an uneasy ceremony that day up on Nimitz Hill. I suppose it was because we had met too many people on Guam who still remember the Japanese occupation— vividly—and still display their visible and invisible scars to prove it. Some of them we had talked with just the previous day.

LABOR DAY

The next day was a Sunday, the day before Labor Day, which was set aside for a great big Chamorro style cook-out. It is the annual blowout for the people of Guam, by the government of Guam, to "celebrate the labor force."

We were at George Taylor's Chamorro Island BBQ restaurant when we were told about the event, a Labor Day picnic at Governor Joseph Flores Memorial Park in Tumon. We were invited by George's son-in-law, and advised to get there early as it fills up fast and parking could be difficult. What an understatement that turned out to be.

We departed our hotel at 0930 and drove about three or four miles to the park already teeming with people. We were lucky to find a parking place, parked, and set out to find George's family at one of the pavilions. Unfortunately, although we searched the area over, we never located them.

The event consisted of dozens or more pavilions and/or tents sheltering hundreds of government volunteers from the different departments of government, arranging tables, cooking barbeque, displaying food, setting up chairs, icing down water, other drinks and beer, and performing dozens of other services, and all the while, being just plain sociable. We had the singing of our National Anthem with great enthusiasm and gusto followed by the Guam Hymn, delivered with equal enthusiasm, and perhaps just a little bit more gusto. It is sung in Chamorro. Although we had arrived near to 10 a.m. the food was not served until Governor Calvo arrived and welcomed everyone. Then, a prayer was given to bless the food that we were about to consume. Apparently, we had left all atheists back on the mainland. Everyone sang, everyone prayed, and everyone we talked to knew our friend Adolf Sgambelluri and spoke fondly of him.

It is difficult to properly describe all the contacts we made. There were many, but, we didn't come to this event to work on the book. We came to have a good time, and to enjoy food and friendship with our friends from the Chamorro Island BBQ, whom we never located among the maze of smoking barbeque cookers, emitting some of the sweetest aromas ever inhaled.

The food was varied and plentiful. Several whole roasted pigs were a favorite. We met a lot of people, several Marines and Navy Corpsmen, some Guam National Guardsmen recently returned from deployment to Afghanistan, and many, many retired military members. None of the people that we had conversations with, did we know. They were casual, passing conversations. However, one in particular was lengthy. It was Mike J.B. Borja, who is with the Department of Land Management of Guam. We talked of the many sites on Guam where bodies or skeletal remains from World War II are often located. He related to me that it is never unusual to find implements of war, some of it dangerous stuff, almost everywhere during construction or excavations. Then, there are the ancient Chamorro sites. I'm sure Mike is kept busy.

Shortly after the conversation with Mike, a very surprising meeting took place. I was approached by the Governor's Chief of Staff, who welcomed us, and stated that the Governor wanted to meet us when he returned from an appointment a few days later. I was bowled over. I have no idea how this Chief of Staff found me in a crowd of 5,000 or more people and growing. Nor, how he knew who I was, what we were doing there, or where I was located. When I started to give him my Guam cell number, he showed me his phone list revealing that he already had my telephone number. That Chamorro network is something to be marveled.

One thing Lyn and I agreed upon, as we departed the event, is that one will **never** experience an event like this on the mainland of the United States. Why? Because here, everything was sponsored by the government of Guam, for the people of Guam, and all the non-government workers at the event were paid for their services with out-of-pocket funds. Merchants donated, people volunteered, and voices and muscles were joined in celebration of a day of enjoyment. It was literally a government (or event) of the people, by the people, and for the people. It was a fantastic day of fun, celebration, comradery, and fellowship. And it didn't cost the citizens of Guam, nor a couple of *gaijin*, a single penny. Remarkable! Something that is exceedingly rare on the American mainland.

Interestingly, we would never have known about the picnic, had not George Taylor's son-in-law invited us. And, still—we never found him.

After that great Sunday, we took a break on Tuesday evening to attend a Shell Club meeting of those people who enjoy collecting sea-shells. The end result was that Lyn finally got her golden cowries (two of 'em), now resting in her shell cabinet.

ARTERO PROPERTY

The day finally arrived for us to meet Franklin Artero at a McDonald's eatery, near the entrance to the Navy Communication's base. The restaurant sits just behind a dark blue line painted across the roadway with the words "U.S. Navy Property," written on it. So, McDonald's is on Navy property. The gate is down the road another hundred yards. We were riding with Frank. We drove through the base gate after showing our military ID cards. First, he showed us where his father grazed up to 700 head of cattle before the American military took his property away from him. Then, we drove through grassland down a road that once was a bull-cart path to the spot where his dad first met George Tweed and took him into hiding. He also showed us where his father's ranch house used to be. Then he drove us to his current remaining property on the beach. It is his—and his brother's, cousin's, and sister's—*landlocked* property.

To get there, we drove Route 3A, the worst road we have ever traversed. It's owned by the Defense Department. No one maintains it. The U.S. government won't let anyone maintain it, even though several sources have offered funds for its maintenance. That road leads to the U.S. Fish and Wildlife property located behind a gated fence. There are fences everywhere, some with locked gates. You then travel on a private road from high on a plateau down gradually to beach level to find a stretch of pristine beach-front property dotted with latte stones with their stone caps lying nearby. A small cave carved out of the limestone cliff by thousands of years of surging and receding ocean surf is located a short walk from water's edge. Fresh water drips from overhead in small, delayed drops adding to stalactites thousands of years old. Coconut, lemon, and other trees are numerous, from the base of the cliff right up to the water's edge. A large sinkhole measuring about twenty feet across contains seepage of fresh water believed to come from underground deep within the limestone cliff, flowing slowly into the sea hundreds of feet below. The presence of fresh water just under the soil was obvious from the hundred or so Monarch butterflies hovering around the bottom of the sink-hole. The beach is a combination of rocks, coral, and sand. Blue and white waves roll—and crash—when ocean waters meet coral reef, and surge toward the beach with a roar. The view to the northwest reveals Ritidian Point and sometimes the tip of the peak on Rota Island—thirty-eight miles away. The view south is of Two Lovers Point where legend has it that a Chamorro man and woman jumped to their death because they were forbidden to marry each other. The view east is directly into a high limestone cliff covered with jungle growth, except that portion of the cliff where the Air Force and Navy dumped their trash, unexploded ordnance, tires, motor oil, vehicle parts, and who knows what else onto private property (belonging to Franklin's first cousin, Tony M. Artero) for several years. Fortunately, it was declared a hazardous waste site by the EPA (Environmental Protection Agency), which brought in heavy equipment to clean the property up. The jungle will, as years go by, slowly reclaim the land. The view to the west is the vast blue Philippine Sea.

The Artero family has divided the property among themselves. However, they are prohibited from bringing any construction equipment onto their property. Any and all construction must be by hand. Franklin has constructed a bathroom facility for men and women, complete with urinal, commodes, wash basins, and running water from a catchment of rain water located above the facility on his property. He has constructed pavilion structures with eating and sitting accommodations, a small cooking facility, and quarters for his family to remain overnight at times. All constructed by hand. Some of the benches and tables were created from local Ifit (or Ifil) hardwood trees located on his property; they make some of the most beautiful and ornate furniture seen anywhere. With these creature-comfort items, trails, benches, and grooming of the foliage, he has developed a small paradise on the edge of the Philippine Sea, set against a tall, jungle covered cliff, that rises to his property on the top of the limestone plateau—which is completely inaccessible to him.

The U.S. government can and did bring heavy equipment onto the Artero property to clean up their dumped trash and discarded broken equipment. But, forbids the Arteros from bringing in similar heavy equipment to accomplish construction on their private property. The U.S. government cuts through any property in order to access. It could be to construct a fence, create a road, or perform any other act by imminent domain *rational.* It is a tragic situation created by the United States government.

RUDY MATANANE

A day later, we had medical appointments at the U.S. Naval Hospital in the morning, and in the afternoon, we visited Mayor Rudy Matanane at his office in Yigo. We wanted to get a statement of his feelings, as a local politician, about the plan to relocate thousands of Marines, hundreds of their military dependents, and dozens of Department of Defense civilians from Okinawa to Guam. The target date is 2021 for that move. We don't know if that is a starting date or a completion date. But it is a plan.

The mayor's village would be a major recipient of additional income from relocated military families living and or shopping, in his community. The mayor understands that and is supportive of the military. He has sons in the military, and his dad was a volunteer scout, armed by the American military with an M-1 carbine to hunt and kill or capture Japanese soldiers. His dad, Vicente Quintanilla Matanane, was sixteen, but good at his assignment. He was, as a civilian scout, leading and advising as he protected elements of the American invasion force during the battle to retake Guam from the Japanese. His son, the mayor of Yigo, Rudy Matanane, is no anti-military person, and he chastises those who are.

His concern relates to the much publicized reports of gross misbehavior of Okinawa-based Marines, primarily younger, junior Marines, on liberty in the local community. Publicized reports of rapes, assaults, and occasional homicides by Marines upon local civilians, have raised concerns on Guam, specifically about the seemingly overnight dramatic increase in the presence of single or unaccompanied younger Marines.

The following is from a *New York Times* article in 1983:

Assemblyman Shuzo Sakihama, a member of Japan's governing Liberal Democratic Party and a supporter of the presence of United States forces, said the murder case reflected a continuing "occupation mentality" on the part of the Americans.

As chairman of the legislative assembly's special committee on United States bases, Mr. Sakihama spearheaded a resolution demanding that the suspects to be turned over immediately to Japanese custody, that compensation be paid to the victim's family and that stricter "discipline" be enforced in the United States military.

"Crimes by U.S. military men have been on the rise recently, both on and off the bases, and this shows laxness in military discipline," Mr. Sakihama said in an interview. "It makes the existence of U.S. bases on Okinawa politically difficult."

Police statistics, however, suggest a decline in military crime since Okinawa reverted to Japanese control slightly more than 10 years ago.

The Okinawa police arrested 239 United States military suspects in 200 incidents in 1982, compared with 242 suspects in 213 incidents in 1972. The police say increased cooperation with military authorities has resulted in more arrests for minor incidents - meaning the figures reflect fewer serious crimes.

"Two or three hundred incidents a year, that's not alarmingly large in view of 32,000 active servicemen on Okinawa," said Herb Nakayoshi of the Marine Corps Public Affairs office at Camp Butler.

However, there have been 15 murders in the 10 years involving United States military personnel, in a country were violent crime is relatively rare. Japanese were victims in six of those cases.

Of course, this article is over thirty-years-old, but the concern about crime by young servicemen on Okinawa continues through today. It is only natural that a local mayor would be concerned about this.

Today, on Guam, the average military person is with the Navy or Air Force, married, with family accompanying them during their duty assignment on Guam. The Marines bring few with families accompanying them. Most are young, single Marines. It's the nature of a Marine or Army Division, or a Marine Aircraft Wing or Air Force Wing. It's a fact of life.

Another more recent article about crime (the incident is minor) by servicemen on Okinawa was published on 18 November 2012, by the Associated Press:

Tokyo—Japanese police arrested a U.S. Marine on Sunday on suspicion of trespassing on the southern island of Okinawa amid anger over military crimes and demands for stricter regulations for U.S. troops.

The incident, the second after the U.S. military had stepped up disciplinary steps last month, immediately triggered harsh reaction from the Okinawa government.

Police said xxxx Txxxxxx Cxxxxxxx of the Marine Corps Air Station Futenma allegedly sneaked into a room through an unlocked door and slept until spotted by a resident who called police.

Sunday's arrest was especially inflammatory on Okinawa, where the Emperor Akihito was visiting to attend a fisheries event.

"I'm too shocked to say anything. It's utterly ridiculous and extremely regrettable," Okinawa Gov. Hirokazu Nakaima told reporters. "I must lodge a strong protest to both the Japanese and U.S. governments. They must do something more significant."

Prime Minister Yoshihiko Noda is expected to raise the issue during talks Tuesday with President Barack Obama on the sidelines of the summit of Southeast Asian countries in Phnom Penh, Cambodia, Kyodo News agency reported.

An alleged rape by two Navy sailors last month enraged Okinawans and reignited deep-rooted anti-base sentiment on the island, home to more than half the 52,000 U.S. troops in Japan.

The case led to a curfew on all troops in Japan, but two weeks later a U.S. airman allegedly assaulted a teenager. Sunday's incident also raises questions over the effectiveness of the curfew and other disciplinary steps.

Japan has lodged a formal protest with the U.S. Embassy and U.S. military over the incident Sunday and demanded that they make sure the curfew is enforced.

> *Cxxxxxx was apparently drunk when he entered the apartment, Okinawa police official Masahiko Gishi said. Police are investigating if he broke the curfew and was drinking off-base prior to the alleged trespassing.*
>
> *On Friday, Okinawa's prefectural (state) assembly adopted a resolution protesting the two earlier cases, demanding tougher regulations and stepped-up efforts to reduce the number of troops and bases on the island. The resolution also called for a review of legal procedures for military suspects and efforts to streamline the U.S. troop presence.*
>
> *Okinawans have staged massive protests against the deployment in October of Osprey military aircraft despite opposition over safety concerns following two crashes elsewhere.*
>
> *Local opposition to the U.S. bases over noise, safety and crime flared into mass protests after the 1995 rape of a schoolgirl by three American servicemen. The outcry eventually led to an agreement to close the Futenma airfield, but the plan has stalled for more than a decade over where a replacement facility should be located.*

Okinawa continues to have crime problems. But, it is not unusual, nor confined to Okinawa. In areas around certain military installations, especially installations containing large numbers of young, single military personnel, crime rates in the communities are higher than average. The rise in the rate of crime tends to be property crimes and minor misdemeanor crimes, not crimes of acute violence.

It appears the latest plan to relocate Marines to Guam will involve mostly Marines without dependents. In short, about 5,000 unaccompanied Marines, mostly young, junior Marines, is exactly what Mayor Rudy Matanane of Yigo is concerned about.

Having served as Okinawa's Provost Marshal from 1978-1980, this author can attest to the fact that young, single male Marines tend to get into trouble from time-to-time—as do young, single college men around a college town. The area around the town or village, just outside their base (or college), tends to be the place where they "blow off steam." Through the years, I have found that the attitude and guidance of those in command of these Marines (or students) have a direct influence on their off-duty (off campus) activities. Also, joint cooperation between military and civilian police tends to usurp and mitigate instances of improper and unlawful conduct.

Guam will not experience a rapid increase in instances of criminal conduct with the Marines and should establish a "welcome to Guam" attitude within the civilian population. It is the irony of all ironies that some of the civilian populations of Guam fear the arrival of Marines whose fathers and grandfathers liberated them from Japanese oppression—while, at the same time, they welcome thousands of Japanese tourists whose fathers and grandfathers brutalized the Chamorro population of Guam for thirty-one months. Ironic indeed!

Guam should also consider that, on Okinawa, a Prefecture of Japan, the Status of Forces Agreement (SOFA) tends to be an irritant to the Japanese. Because the American Armed Forces have primary jurisdiction over U.S. Armed Forces personnel, even though the crime is committed by a U.S. Forces person, and even though the crime victim may be Japanese, custody of the criminal by the Japanese cannot occur until after indictment by Japan. That can take up to a year sometimes. Therefore, the tendency is for the Japanese media to intensify the issue.

On Guam, if a U.S. Forces person commits a crime off the military installation, they would immediately fall under Guam law and would cool their heels in a Guam jail awaiting trial. That's a big difference.

In light of that fact, there will be a greater burden on law enforcement, courts, and correctional/confinement programs on Guam. The U.S. Government should provide additional compensation in monies and/or military support to the Government of Guam. And, it would not be a bad idea to augment the Guam police with military police to assist in resolving problems with military personnel. Years ago, there were Armed Forces Police Detachments in Honolulu, New Orleans, and other locations, assisting local police departments with irritant military personnel.

On 26 April 2012, U S and Japanese officials announced the 2 nations had agreed on a plan to relocate US Marines from Okinawa to Guam. The joint statement was the latest result of negotiations between the two countries dating to the 2006 Realignment Roadmap and the 2009 Guam International Agreement. Under the original plan about 9,000 Marines would relocate from Okinawa, with about 5,000 moving to Guam. The agreement also involved possible development of joint training ranges in Guam and the commonwealth of the Northern Mariana Islands as shared-use facilities for US and Japanese forces. In April 2012, the United States and Japan decided to adjust the terms of the 2006 Realignment Roadmap by delinking the relocation from progress on the Futenma Replacement Facility and reducing the number of Marines relocating to Guam from approximately 8,000 (with significant numbers of family members) to approximately 5,000 (mostly rotational/without family members), while maintaining the overall reduction in the US Marine Corps presence on Okinawa through additional relocations to Hawaii and rotations to Australia.

GlobalSecurity.org

While in the mayor's office, we talked at some length about his dad being on Guam during the Japanese occupation. He said his mom would tell him that "they were not all bad," while his dad would say exactly the opposite. Much depended on where you were on Guam during the occupation. His mom, Ana Adriano Manibusan Matanane, worked on a crew that had a Japanese overseer who wasn't a bad guy. But she related that one time, she drifted into an area where the head honcho was a bad dude, and she almost got hurt. Her good honcho came to her rescue. So, she sees the good and the bad of the Japanese occupiers. Conversely, Rudy said to me that his dad would always say, "They were all bad." That explains why a sixteen-year-old Chamorro teenager volunteered to hunt Japanese soldiers with the U.S. Army's 77th Infantry Division and got his share of kills. For him, it was definitely *pay-back* time.

A few weeks later, Rudy told us that his Uncle Art had told him a story about his father being out on patrol looking for Japanese stragglers, who were still pretty dangerous guys. They came upon a group of them, and one of the group stated to the Chamorro Combat Patrol members, "We're surrendering." Well, Rudy's dad had heard that before. The Marines had heard it before through dozens of islands. It was always a guise, always a false statement. Many Marines had died heeding that *surrender* statement. Rudy's dad, according to Uncle Art, said, "Surrender Hell!" and opened up on them. Two of those Japanese were holding hand grenades as they died. Rudy's dad went home that night to be with his family.

Rudy Matanane is also a retired civil employee at Andersen Air Force Base. Interestingly, Andersen Air Force Base is a part of the village of Yigo. It was very obvious that Rudy is a strong supporter of the United States Military presence on Guam, while he is also a strong supporter of the citizens of his village of Yigo.

Rudy told me of one time, shortly after he retired from Andersen, he was taking several family members to the base, and they would not let him on the base. A retired federal worker, a mayor of the village, which the base is part of, cannot get on the base. Just think about what a stink would have been raised if Yigo had prevented the Andersen base commander from entering the village. Different shoe or different foot? Or just a double standard?

Rudy is very proud of his father, Vicente Quintanilla Matanane, a volunteer combat scout who is one of the many heroes of Guam during the Second World War.

TANAKA

Through Mayor Rudy Matanane and Franklin Artero, we met with the Tanakas, Thomas or "Tommy," and Fredrick or "Fred." Both are sons of Tomas "Tommy" Tanaka of occupation fame. We met at a very loud California Pizza Kitchen and talked of their grandfather and their father and his activities during and after the Japanese occupation. Unfortunately, we recorded little useable audio from the restaurant due to the background noise. "Tommy" Tanaka, like Sgambe, Limtiaco, and others in the organized resistance group on Guam looms in history as a heroic giant of a man. We had found several bits of information about Tomas "Tommy" Tanaka from MARC and other sources before we met with Tommy and Fred.

We had done our research and uncovered some differences, in historical annotations, between our findings and their recollections, primarily gleaned from their mother about their grandfather Cecillo, or Cicilio, and "Tommy's" World War II days. They learned much that they did not know, as did we. That's called research. We'll figure it out. The two sons of "Tommy" Tanaka could not have been more enjoyable and generous with their time. They are great representatives of their famous father.

Today's Thomas Tanaka remembers little of the occupation days; however, he does remember two small but significant events. He recalls being carried by his grandmother during an apparent bombardment of the island. It must have been in 1944, making him around five-years-old. He remembers her earrings. They were shaped like a bunch of grapes, tiny grapes hanging from each earlobe. "As she was carrying me up this hill, there were these explosions, and we had to fall to the ground. I remember the explosions, falling to the ground, and those earrings. Funny what you remember sometimes," Thomas related to us as we were having lunch. Almost in the same sentence, another strong, deep-rooted remembrance surfaced. "I don't know if it was at the same time as the earrings story, or another time, but I somehow remember my face, all around my mouth, I think, being almost a bluish-black from me eating these berries. I don't know what kind of berries they were, but I remember the aftermath of eating them," he paused briefly, "if that makes any sense," he finished.

It does.

Our main goal is to relate the facts about "Tommy" Tanaka and his participation with the Guam Underground and of his acute disappointment in the U.S. Navy that rejected him for service, based apparently on the racism of the time. It is a tragic, but historically factual chapter in Navy and American history.

We learned more during our second meeting for breakfast at Linda's. It was quieter. It was raining, but we had a good meal and good conversation. We met a couple of more times with Fred and his wife, Bertha, at their boutique, in Hagåtña for casual conversation.

There is no doubt that the two sons have a great love and admiration for their dad. It is the history of their grandfather that requires some correlation and potential adjustment. Perhaps! But, it has nothing to do with the activities of their father during and after the Japanese occupation of Guam. The story of an American hero, Tomas "Tommy" Tanaka, of Guam, is a story that, like the stories of Limty, Sgambe, and others, demands telling and retelling, until they become household names to all Americans.

We were invited, by Tommy (Jr.), to have Thanksgiving dinner with them, however, it was invitation number four and we had only enough time and space to make the first and second Thanksgiving invitation, unfortunately missing number three and four. Perhaps next time.

We will meet Tommy and Fred again when we return to Guam to salute all those great Americans of Guam lost in the shadows of history.

FRANK BLAS, JR. (AGAIN)

Shortly after our discussion with the sons of Tomas "Tommy" Tanaka, we met Senator Frank Blas, Jr. again—this time for lunch. We had not seen Frank since the ceremony at Chaguian, in Yigo. We met in a place called the Lemai Café, situated in an old military Quonset hut on Purple Heart Highway in Maite. It is always good to meet with someone who thinks like you do and feels as you do on a wide variety of subjects. Frank fits that bill. We discussed Chamorro culture and family traditions, the U.S. military on Guam, and the Marines pending arrival, we also discussed citizenship, specifically U.S. citizenship as it relates to Guam and other U.S. Territories, especially the issue of voting and property rights. We always learn from discussions with Frank. He is a Guam asset.

Frank has great admiration for our friend Sgamby and often speaks very highly of him. Sgamby was the Chief of Police when Frank was a policeman with the Guam Police Department. He says that Sgamby was one of the best police chiefs Guam has ever had.

Sometime later, just before our departure from Guam, we were invited to dinner with Frank and his wife, Tillie. We had a great meal, great company and fond memories. Frank and Tillie also invited us to breakfast the day before our departure.

ARTERNIO TUDELA MAANAO

A few days later, after we had lunch with Frank at the Lemai Café, we drove to the mayor's office in Yigo to meet again with Rudy Manibusan Matanane. From his office, we followed him to his uncle's home in Yigo, where we had a delightful and informative conversation with his uncle, "Art"—Arternio Tudela Maanao, a survivor of the Japanese occupation. We had a great time and enjoyed a very informative conversation with "Uncle Art." It went like this:

It was Monday, the first of September, 1930—as the sun rose on the small island of Guam, the Marines were raising the American flag over their Marine Barracks at Sumay, the Navy Yard at Piti, and the Governor's House in Agana; meanwhile the second official population and non-population census schedules for Guam were being concluded on that same day. That formally ordered census was being finished, counted, or measured, for not only human population count, but also general agricultural and livestock schedules, reporting farm products grown, raised, or under cultivation, or otherwise owned in Guam during 1929-30. In short, they were counting livestock and estimating cultivated food harvest—as well as counting people.

The Fifteenth Census Act, approved 18 June 1929, authorized a census of population, agriculture, irrigation, drainage, distribution, unemployment, and other things (to be) taken by the Director of the Census. The governors of Guam, American Samoa, and the Virgin Islands [plus Puerto Rico] each were ordered to complete a census that same year. So was the governor of the Panama Canal Zone.

In the Asan Municipality on Guam, including Asan town and Libugon barrio, the official count of humans was to be increased by one additional person that day. A boy was born to Vicente Angoto Maanao and his wife, Francisca Pangelinan Tudela. They named him Artenio Tudela Maanao. He joined the family with two older brothers and an older sister.

"Art" is now eighty-five-years old. He was eleven when the Japanese invaded Guam. He was fourteen when the Americans returned to Guam. Today he told us his story.

With assistance from Rudy, we met his uncle, Art, on a bright, clear, Guam afternoon at his uncle's home in Yigo where he lives with his wife, Anna, or "Auntie Annie," as she is called.

We arrived, by following the mayor's truck, just before one o'clock in the afternoon. As we were introduced, his uncle had a firm, warm handshake, a wiry smile, and a friendly gaze with dark brown eyes that sometimes told his story as well, if not better, than his speech. We sat at a table on his patio, and we began a conversation that took him back over a span of seventy-odd years on his island.

But, we started the conversation elsewhere. After the war, he had worked for the Micronesia Trust Territory, both on Guam and on Saipan, starting as a maintenance supervisor and later serving as a supervisor of supplies. He enjoyed his work. When he became eligible for retirement, he retired early, in 1981, taking eight percent off of his maximum retirement pay, because he retired early. He does not regret it. He said that the work was good, but sometimes the workers were so-so; sometimes because it would take his workers two days just to hang a door. "Island time," he said. We all laughed.

During our bout of laughter, Juan Blaz drove up and joined us at the table.

Then suddenly, we were back to the times that the people of Guam will never forget. The Japanese occupation of Guam still burns deep into the memories of many Guamanians. This was one of those times, and he was one of those people.

"As a young boy, I was required to work for the Japanese occupiers of Guam. My entire family was required to work for them," he stated matter-of-factly, without prompting.

"Before the war came, my father worked for the Arteros. He maintained some of their cattle. Down by Asan. Then, after the Japanese came they considered everything theirs. Everything!" he emphasized.

"One day during the occupation, my father was working to watch the cows. There was a break in the fence, and the cows came over and ate the corn," he got a sad look on his face, as he continued. "The Japanese," he paused, wiping his eyes, he looked directly at me as he began to speak of a remembrance that is still very painful to him. He swallowed, raised his hands as he sat in the chair, "They beat my father." There was a long silence.

Uncle Art was shaking.

"The two Japanese held him and beat him with a stick. A long stick, about this big, round," he gestured with his hand a motion of a person hitting with a stick, and then circled his thumb and forefinger to indicate a circle about two-inches across—the thickness of the stick.

Again, he swung his hand in a motion of a person hitting something with a stick, or club, as he continued to talk and gesture. "They beat my father across the back from his head to his feet. He was bloody and raw. He could not sit or lay on his back for over three months. They beat him so bad; they beat him until the stick broke," he concluded.

"When was the first time you ran into, or saw, or had contact with the Japanese?" I asked.

"In Asan," he replied. "I walked by a Japanese soldier, you know, a guard. I just walked by him. As I got passed him, he said, 'Hai! Or Hey! Come here,' something like that, he said to me."

"So I walked over to him, and he commanded me—'You, bow!'"

"So, I bow. You know," he gestured a slight bow.

"When I stand back up, he slapped me. Two times, you know, with the palm and immediately with the back of the hand. Slap! Slap"! He gestured with his hand. "He slap my face on one side and then on the other. The Japanese beat me up," he finished.

"At about that time," he hesitated, his eyes welled up, but he revealed no tears. He started again, this time his voice cracked, "My oldest sister," he hesitated, and began again. "The Japanese came and took my oldest sister," again, a slight pause, "for the officer." Again hesitation, it was difficult for him to speak of what happened. "I don't know what they call it. Like maids or something," he finally related.

We knew what he couldn't say.

"How old was your sister then?" I asked.

"She was eighteen-years-old," he revealed.

He choked up and hesitated briefly, "I can't remember," he explained.

"That's okay!" I stated.

He changed the subject as Auntie Annie joined us with Coke, water, and home-made munchies. She was an outgoing and lively person, a pure pleasure to talk with.

We simply got on the subject of the cows and the corn, and the Arteros again.

"Then, my father, he decides that we should go from Asan to Yigo. Just how, we don't know."

"My father asked my sister, 'hey, your friend [the Japanese officer], can he get us to Yigo?'"

"She says, 'I'll try.'"

"Officer is big guy."

"A senior officer?" I asked.

"Yes," he replied. "So she fixes it that day."

"The Japanese has an American car," he declared, "he is going to drive us."

"Now, my father has a 12 gauge shotgun. He wants to take it with him," he paused, looking straight ahead. Then, he looked directly at me.

"If the Japanese had found that gun they would have killed the entire family," he said.

"Did he take the gun?" I asked.

"Yes, he wraps it with this burlap."

"So, he broke it down and wrapped it up and buried it?" I probed.

"No! He wraps it up and put it in the trunk of the car."

"The Japanese car?" I asked, somewhat astonished.

"Yes."

"Who was driving?"

"The Japanese officer," he answered.

"So a Japanese officer, driving an American car, was driving you and your family, along with your dad's forbidden shotgun from Asan to Yigo?"

"Yes!" He emphatically replied, then added, "Through all three checkpoints where we would be searched."

"With the Japanese officer driving, we pulled up to the first checkpoint. Everyone is scared," he offered. "My mother and father are shaking."

"Did you get through?"

"Oh, yes. Then comes the second one," he said. "The Japanese guard is looking in the trunk, and we are so scared. Then, the babies start crying. They are crying very loud. The guard looks at us and said something about the babies crying and finally shouted, 'okay, okay, you go!'"

Everyone had a good laugh at the explanation and the descriptive scene painted by words and gestures.

Auntie Annie remarked, "Maybe God had the babies cry then, to save us all."

Art continued, "At the third one, the guard said, 'okay.' Maybe he figured that we had already been through two, so why bother. The car with the shotgun made it to Yigo."

"We stayed at my mothers' brother's property in Yigo. It was a farm. There, I had to go to Japanese school for about six months," he declared. "I did not like Japanese school. Had to learn to speak Japanese. *Ichi, ni, san, shie, go*," he blurted. "Never forget!"

"What happened after the schooling?"

"More Japanese came. They made everyone over twelve-years-old to go to work for the Japanese. I worked where they were building an air base. It was where the airport is now. I was the ice-tea boy. I had to deliver a big, heavy container of tea for people to get a drink. It was very heavy, about five gallons of tea. I worked about two weeks but it was a very hard job. I asked for a change to work with a pick and shovel."

"A week later, I joined my cousin with a pick and shovel and a big wheelbarrow. I worked alongside my older brothers and my father moving dirt."

We laughed as he described how he had difficulty holding that heavy load of dirt back as he descended the steep hill with his load of dirt and coral. He described how he dug his heels in, but continued to slide while holding onto that wheelbarrow.

"One day as we were riding in a flat-bed truck, an airplane appeared causing the driver to drive straight into the jungle to escape being seen by the airplane."

"On another day, when the airplane appeared, all the Japanese run and hide. We all ran with them into the jungle. My cousin said, 'Why are we hiding?' When the airplane disappeared, the Japanese began calling us back to work. My cousin said, 'We are not going back,' so we stayed hidden. We never went back to work. We lived off coconuts and all that stuff. Then, we finally got home in Yigo. My father was quiet angry. He didn't know where we had been."

"We stayed around the farm in Yigo until one day the Japanese came and told us that we were going to Manenggon. They said for one week. So, we gathered some food for one week."

"My father didn't want to go to Manenggon; he said that we will hide. It was my mother who reminded him of the babies. 'They will cry,' she said. 'The Japanese will find us and kill the whole family,'" she reasoned.

"We went together to Manenggon. We went from Yigo to Maimai and on to Manenggon. While at Maimai, one of the families made a fire to warm a meal. Jesus was always getting into trouble with the Japanese. Making a fire, any fire, was a big no, no. It was a serious crime. American planes could see the fire at night and/or the smoke during the day. When the Japanese saw it, they put the fire out, tied the couple to a coconut tree, and beat them severely. When we got to Manenggon, a Japanese soldier came and he hit me, 'Go!' he said, 'get some coconuts.'" He then paused and looked me straight in the eyes, "They're [Japanese are] mean," he declared.

"My cousin was selected to carry supplies for the Japanese. He was given two big cases of salmon and two big cases of biscuits. As he crossed a river, he dropped a case of salmon and a case of biscuits into the river. He was watching to make sure the Japanese didn't see him. Later, when he returned, he got me and we went to get the cases. There were already two young boys that had found the cases. My cousin shouted in Japanese at them, and they ran away. They thought we were Japanese."

We all had a good laugh at his word picture and his gestures.

"So you had more food for the family?" I asked.

"No! My cousin doesn't want to tell anybody. He wants to keep it just for us."

"So, I took two biscuits and put them in my pocket. I'm going to give them to my little sister. Which I did. Then, my mother said to me, 'Where did you get the biscuits?' I replied that a Japanese guard gave them to me."

"She never believed me."

"My cousin and me later went back to the creek where I stuffed myself with salmon and biscuits. I think I ate three. Then I took big drinks of water." Here, he gestured with his hands of an expanding belly. "I was so sick. I thought I was going to explode." He laughed along with all of us.

"When did you first see the Americans?" I asked.

"We saw a truck. A military truck."

"So, where did they take you? You were still in Manenggon, right?"

"Yes, they drove the truck to Agat. My sister, we found her at Agat. My whole family was together." He smiled a big smile and continued, "From there, we went back to Asan."

"So, your entire family survived the Japanese occupation?"

"No, one of my baby sisters died on the march to Manenggon."

"There were many babies that died on the march to Manenggon," I replied.

"Yes, there were many," he responded.

"What do you think was the primary reason that Chamorros survived as well as they did?"

"I think that sharing what we had was important. We shared breadfruit, but picked it before it was ready; but it was the coconut, more than anything else that allowed us to live, and not starve," he emphatically stated. "Without the coconut, we would have never survived," he added.

The discussion with Uncle Art wound down to just a few more comments as the afternoon lengthened and the food and drink dwindled, along with conversations. That is until Auntie Annie (Anna) resupplied the munchies for our trip back to the hotel.

Without prompting, Uncle Art mentioned Beatrice Flores, the young girl whom the Japanese thought they had beheaded—but she lived to be found and treated by American forces. It was the maggots eating the dead and gangrenous flesh that saved her life. She died at age seventy-three and lived right down the road from uncle Art. Her daughter still lives there.

The survivors of the Japanese occupation are fading fast. There are a few people and institutions on Guam, racing against time, to capture the memories of those who lived it. We have now joined those few people, and institutions.

One of my last questions was, "Were you afraid, during the Japanese occupation?"

His response, "No!"

Indeed, the reader must remember that Uncle Art was a young, mischievous, carefree, happy-go-lucky youngster during the occupation, so he says—until you watch his eyes as he talked, the tears he fights back, or quickly wipes away, the eyes downcast as he changes a storyline adding a bit of color to an emerging thought that he suppresses, the eyes—they tell another story.

PATTI ARROYO

A few days after our conversation with Uncle Art, Juan Blaz called to relate that he had set up an interview with Patti Arroyo of K-57 Radio/TV on

Guam. The interview was posted on the Internet in Guam, at the following on-line address:

http://www.pacificnewscenter.com/pnc-k57-interviews/6042/ Major Ralph "Stoney" Bates, Sr. and Sergeant Major Juan Blaz with Patti Arroyo. 8 October 2015.

It was a good thirty minute interview on the air. Patti asked a lot of insightful questions. She is a very good interviewer. I gave her a copy of *A Marine Called Gabe* and *Short Rations For Marines.* Juan Blaz sat with us through the interview, which yielded great results arriving in the form of an email from an Anthony Ada, to tell me that he had heard the interview and wanted to meet with me to talk about his dad. We would meet Tony, his sister Rose, and her husband later.

CARMEN

On 20 October 2015, I met with Carmen Artero Kasperbauer, who was born in 1935, at her family home in Agana, Guam. The Artero ranch home, in the northwest of Guam, was in 1941, just about a good city block from where we were sitting as we talked. We were sitting on a U.S. Navy base, at a McDonald's eatery, having a cup of coffee and chatting about her World War II experience. Her remembrances of the events early in her life are from her experiences as a young child during the Japanese occupation of Guam.

She was born to Antonio Cruz Artero and Josefa Torres Artero, the second oldest of seven Artero siblings at that time. It was Antonio Artero, or Ton, as he was called, who sheltered the U.S. Navy man, George Tweed, for twenty-one of his thirty-one months hiding from the Japanese on the island of Guam. This eighty-year-old lady who was sitting in front of me, walked with the assistance of a cane (due to recent surgery), and was as lucid and spry as I somehow expected her to be.

We had talked on the phone earlier to arrange the meeting. Our contact was arranged by Mayor Rudy Matanane, and through Fred Tanaka, one of the sons of Tomas "Tommy" Tanaka, of World War II fame.

Carmen was six-years-old when the Japanese invaded Guam and almost nine-years-old when the Americans retook the island from the Japanese. In that we were writing a novel about the Japanese occupation of Guam made her eye-witness story valuable to us. It was valuable in that she qualified parts of her story by distinguishing among things that had been *told* to her, from those things she *believed* were happening at the time, or what she actually *saw* or *heard* directly and clearly remembered. Her memory is good, as she explained, "Because most of the events were so traumatic."

We had a long recorded conversation that day, and we met again on 16 November 2015, at the home of Carmen and Larry Kasperbauer, to go over my notes, and to make adjustments for clarity, and, where necessary, to avoid any possible conflict. The second meeting was also recorded to assist the author in writing the finishing touches of her story.

Carmen was living on Guam with her parents and siblings until she was almost seventeen-years-old. At sixteen, she departed for the mainland (as everyone on Guam refers to the fifty United States) to finish high school, attend college, get a degree in nursing, marry, and start a family. Then, as we have heard so often, she and her husband and family returned to Guam, well—she returned, he relocated to Guam—after sixteen years of living on the mainland. After she returned, she was a nurse for a while, then an elected Guam Senator (Legislator).

Carmen entered politics due to the many inequities in citizenship between being a citizen on the mainland and being a citizen on Guam. Both locations offer American citizenship but not equal citizenship. As an example, when she applied for a nursing position with the U.S. Naval Hospital on Guam, she was told, "Oh, honey, you should have applied while you were on the mainland. Now that you're here, you are a Guamanian. Your pay and benefits will be half that of someone who had applied while living in the States," that comment and that fact made her very angry.

The inequities between a citizen living on Guam and a citizen living on the mainland, or Alaska or Hawaii, are stark, and one of the leading causes that is driving the younger generation further and further away from loyalty to America—something that will never happen to the older generation who were either present during the occupation or whose fathers and mothers were present here. Their loyalty is sealed in concrete, but their disappointment in the American governments' treatment of the people of Guam grows stronger as each year passes.

As we started our discussion, Carmen told how her dad's mother and father met. Her grandmother was a Chamorro from Guam. There was a severe influenza epidemic on Guam brought to the island by ship in the late 1800. Her great grandparents died leaving behind all their children. Shortly after the epidemic, her grandmother and her siblings left to the island of Yap with the Spanish missionary Sisters to help in their mission school. Her grandfather, Don Pascual Artero, who was a Spanish soldier assigned to the island of Yap met her grandmother there. They married and afterwards her grandmother moved back home to Guam bringing her siblings and new husband; around 1901-'02. When Spain lost Guam to the Americans, the Germans got the rest of the Marianas and many islands in Micronesia, including Yap. When Germany lost World War One, the Japanese took over the German possessions. That included Yap.

In detail, she described how her grandfather acquired property on Guam and how almost all of it was simply taken from him and/or his children by the American government after the liberation of Guam from the Japanese. She clarified that much of this information was told to her by her grandfather and father. She also described a conversation she had with her father after she returned to Guam in 1967. She was told her grandfather was to be deported to Spain, by the American authorities, because he wasn't a Chamorro but rather a Spaniard. This happened even after her grandfather told the authorities he lived on Guam since right after the American takeover in 1898, raised a family, had a business, and worked for the United States Navy; therefore, he considered himself a citizen of Guam.

He was married to a Guam Chamorro, and would have been a Guam citizen, an American National, after he moved from Yap to Guam. The Organic Act would later describe him as an American citizen.

To the Arteros, according to Carmen, this event was possibly staged because of the seizure of the Artero property by the American government and the blind acceptance of land seizure by the Chamorros, at that time, because they felt indebted by being freed from the atrocity of the Japanese cruelty. He complained. That complaint was settled in favor of the American government.

Further, her father had said to her that her grandfather's children had been given a choice of signing over their vast property holdings on Guam to the American government, or their father, Don Pascual, would be deported back to Spain. Their resolution was that they cared more for family than they did for property, and they signed the papers, transferring most all of their property to the United States government. This is the gist of Carmen's memory of the discussions she had with her father, as told to me, about the former Artero property on Guam.

She continued to explain where her grandfather's sawmill was located (across the street from McDonald's, still on Navy property) and how he used that mill to cut ifit, also called ifil or ifel, lumber for churches and homes. Her grandfather discovered that his Upi property (it is now Anderson Air Force Base) contained numerous ifit trees. The ifit grew most abundantly in Upi because it is higher plateau and cooler. When the U.S. military took the approximately 2000 acres of Artero's Upi land, they destroyed all the Ifit trees with dynamite and bulldozed them down to the ocean to build the Air Force Base. Her grandfather and his oldest son were paid less than a penny per square meter for the land. They were not paid for the ifit trees, the coconut plantation, the cattle, the concrete buildings and their homes. Ifit trees, a special hardwood tree native to much of Southeast Asia, and especially the Marianas, grew in abundance on Guam until the World War II invasion by the Americans.

Ifit is the official territorial tree of Guam and is culturally important throughout the Mariana Islands. Ifit, also called ifil or ifel, belongs to the legume or pea family (Fabaceae) and subfamily Caesalpinoideae.

Ifit is indigenous from Madagascar to western Polynesia, and is native in tropical countries such as Australia, Cambodia, Commonwealth of the Northern Mariana Islands, Federated States of Micronesia, Fiji, Guam, Indonesia, Madagascar, Malaysia, Myanmar, Papua New Guinea, Republic of Palau, Samoa, Solomon Islands, Thailand, and Vietnam. The wood from the ifit tree is often referred to as merbau.

Naval assistant Governor of Guam and botanist William E. Safford described ifit in 1905 as being the most important tree species of Guam. The hard durable wood was used as posts and pillars in houses and churches. Ifit was also popular in constructing tables and chairs, as well as constructing wooden floors, often found in the better built houses.

Guampedia: Ifit Tree of Guam

The Ifit tree continues to be important to the people of Guam. It does not grow in abundance as it did before the American invasion of 1944 and is primarily used today by craftsmen for commercial souvenir carvings for tourists.

After the liberation and being denied access to his family clan-owned property, her father went back to work for the Navy, driving vehicles or doing whatever he could to generate an income and to take care of his family. The Arteros have been and are loyal Americans, enterprising, hard-working, industrious people. They made money the hard way. They worked for it.

She described how her grandfather, in his early years on Guam, would perform some work, or provide some service, for a family with little or no money, but he would do a job or perform a service for them, perhaps surveying, providing lumber, or starting them off with a hen and rooster, male and female pig, or a cow and bull so they could get on their feet. Then he would provide a shelter for them and ask in return that they provide him a percentage of the offspring or a section of the surveyed property. He would also pay them a dollar a day. It should be noted that the average pay for a Chamorro working for the government at that time was about twenty-eight cents a day. For those working for, or having some work done for them by Don Pascal, they were happy, and he was happy. It was the classic barter system. His holdings grew in this manner, and grew even more with the marriage of his oldest son to another major landowner's daughter.

Eventually, in addition to that sawmill, her grandfather added—a slaughter-house, a meat-market, and he even grew copra, citrus trees, and coffee plants for harvesting and sale.

"My father was twenty-nine-years-old when he married my mother. He was a frugal man, and a God loving, God fearing man. He rarely spent money on simple pleasures. Occasionally, he went to the movies and would buy an ice cream. They bought what they actually needed at Butler's place."

"We were in the far northwest of Guam, so the Japanese didn't come around much. But occasionally they did," she explained. "My family had to provide them with food. Lots of food. They didn't pay for it, they just took it," she continued.

Carmen articulated that she was a tom-boy as she grew up. She liked to explore, she was inquisitive, curious, and always *pushing the envelope* [my words] for a Chamorro female juvenile. "For example, I remember, my father had a shotgun. I think it was a shotgun. He was supposed to turn it in to the Japanese, but he didn't. He kept it hidden in a hollow tree in the jungle near our house. I followed him and found out where he kept it. And, I must say, that I would sneak out there and look at the gun occasionally. I knew where it was. So I was used to seeing it."

Then, we got onto the subject of Tweed.

"I was under our house." The house as she explained, sat on pillars, giving a distance of about three or four feet between the cool earth and the floor of the house. It was a cool place for kids to sit and watch things. "I was just sitting there when our neighbor, Mister Juan Pangelinan, my dad called him John, walked up to our yard. He came to the house and told my dad that his fence had broken and that his cattle had come onto Mister Pangelinan's property. He asked my dad to come and help him get his cows and fix the fence." She paused for a sip of coffee. "Somehow I remember that. So, my dad left with him."

"Later, my dad returned home. It was later after that, when I saw my mom and dad talking, they were whispering. I was curious. Then my mom filled a big pot with water. She built a fire under the pot. We children were then sent to our room and told not to come out until morning. The next morning, I got up and went outside. I saw clothes hanging on the line. They were blue shirt and pants."

"Denims?" I asked.

"Yes, blue, like the Navy denims," she replied.

"I asked my mother, 'Whose pants are these?'"

"Oh, they are Uncle Pete's. I was washing them for him," was her reply.

"I thought it was strange because Uncle Pete only wore brown pants, and he wasn't anywhere around."

"Did you see Tweed then?" I asked.

"No. I was just curious. That's all."

"Many years later, Papa told me that they had gone to the fence that was supposedly broken, he and Mister Pangelinan, and that is when my dad saw that there was no break in the fence, he was surprised. It was then that Mister Pangelinan told my dad that he had been sheltering Radioman George Tweed. He said that John begged him to take Tweed from him and to take him to his brother's land up at Upi. My father refused, telling his neighbor that he could not jeopardize his brother and his family and that he could not endanger his own family either. Then, he got scared because he now knew that John had been keeping Tweed."

"He said, 'John, I can't allow my brother to keep Tweed, and I can't keep him because I have my wife and children to consider.'"

"He was ready to leave when this white-skin, skinny, long-haired, bearded man with sunken eyes and hollow face jumped out of the bushes. My dad said that he took one look at him, 'he reminded me of Jesus,' he supposedly said, and immediately knew that it was God's will that he care for him. 'It was as if I saw Jesus. I am my brother's keeper,' my Papa said. He brought Tweed home that night."

There was a brief pause to take a few sips of McDonald's coffee.

"I also need to tell you that my mother would take letters, notes, or something from our house to Mrs. Johnston's house in Agana. Occasionally, she would bring a letter or note back from Mrs. Johnston. She would put the letter tucked into her blouse. Each time she came across a Japanese soldier, she would be required to bow. She was afraid that the Japanese would see the letter, so, occasionally she would take the youngest child with her and hold the baby in front of her. I had gone with her on one particular trip. When we got to Mrs. Johnston's house, they went into a room together. My mother would then come out, and we waited. Then, Mrs. Johnston would come out and give my mother a paper which she would tuck into her blouse and we would leave."

"Did you ever go to Tweed's cave? Where he was hiding?" I asked.

"Yes, but much later. The entire family did."

We then returned to the previous subject.

"The Japanese were building something nearby, so they were coming around more often."

"Was it an observation platform?"

As American carrier aircraft began flying over Guam, the Japanese built a few tall observation towers in high areas in order to observe for incoming aircraft; a crude early warning system.

"Perhaps, I'm not sure what it was."

"See, because the Japanese were around more, they would just drop in and eat at our table. They would come in, sit, eat, and just go away."

"Earlier, before the Japanese started coming around, my father would leave the house two or three times a week, carrying a bag. This went on for a long time. I asked him, but it was never explained," she paused briefly, she continued, "One day my father asked me to go with him, I was excited. I trailed along with my dad, and we walked through jungle and grassland toward the coast. When we got there, there was this big high cliff. My dad gave me two folded gunny sacks and told me to gather Federico nuts and that he would be back shortly. He took the gunny sacks we were carrying from home and went up the cliff and soon he was out of sight, he always came back shortly except for one time."

She looked at me across the table, took another sip of coffee, and continued. "It was scary!"

"How long did you stay there?" I asked.

"He usually came back before I finished filling my bag with Federico. He always came back down the cliff, with empty bags folded, and we walked back home, not directly, but in a circle or zig-zag fashion. Each time, we go by a different route. I never knew where we were. When I would ask a question, he would say for me to just wait. Finally, I asked him about the bags of food. It seemed that my dad was giving away our food. So finally, I ask him, 'How come you take these bags of food up the cliff?' And, just before we got home, he stopped, looked directly at me and said to me sternly, 'If you know what's good for you, you will never ask that question again nor tell anybody about this!' He said for me not to ever tell anyone where we went. 'Do not talk to anyone about this,' he said."

"And, I didn't. I never told anyone, not even my brothers and sisters. It wasn't until I came back to Guam and talked to my papa that I first told my story on Guam."

"Did you ever see Tweed?" I inquired further.

"Only when he came back to Guam—with that car."

She then drifted back to the story.

"One day, he and I started out carrying the bags of food. We got to the cliff. He took the bags and climbed it as usual. I picked the Federico nuts and filled his bag and mine. I waited. I waited a long time. It started to get dark. We had never been out at dark. I was very frightened and started to think of all sort of things. None of them good."

"First, I thought that something had happened to him. Then, as it grew darker and darker, I didn't know if he was coming back. I thought that he had abandoned me to save food for the family. I just knew that was it."

I understood. It was a classic thought process of a young child.

"You see, all these fairy tales my mother and father had told to us kids, like Hansel and Gretel, and the big bad wolf, or the bad witch eating little kids, ran through my mind. I began to cry. The more I cried, the louder I cried. Finally, I blurted out loudly, 'Paappaaaa!! Papapa!!' Please come back!"

As Lyn and I observed and listened to Carmen describe that time and place, we both felt she was perhaps reliving it. Right there in her dining room, she welled up in tears but recovered, then, she continued her story.

"'Hush! Child, hush!' my papa whispered loudly as he descended the cliff to my location. He grabbed me by both hands, bent down to look me right in my eyes, and stated very sternly, very seriously, very directly to me,

'Carmen, if you do not be quiet, the Japanese may hear us. If they do, they will find us, Carmen,' he was very serious, 'if they find us here, they will kill us. Then they will go to our home, and they will kill our entire family.'"

"I stopped crying."

Carmen said, she told her papa she thought he had left her.

"Carmen, I would never leave you," he explained. "Carmen, there are Japanese about. If we run into any of them, and I have this food bag, I can explain that my daughter and I are fixing the fence. This is why we have food with us. That is why you come with me."

"In 1967, when I returned to Guam, I asked my father what he and Tweed talked about for so long up in the cave on that day that I got scared."

"My dad said that he discussed several things with Tweed. At first, Tweed wanted to surrender to the Japanese. My dad said he told Tweed that it would not be a good idea that Tweed surrender. He told Tweed that, if the Japanese got him, they would torture him, and he might break and tell who was caring for him. If that happened, a lot of people, including the Artero family, would be killed, Papa said. Much later, they were discussing Christmas, and Tweed got on to buying a Chevrolet for my dad. Apparently, when Tweed did return to the States, he tried to buy a Chevrolet from the various dealers. They explained that cars were very scarce, and they could put him on the waiting list. As they heard more and more about why he wanted the car, one of the dealers finally proclaimed, 'Mister Tweed, you are not going to buy this car. Chevrolet will buy this car.'"

"That car was supposed to be a symbol of appreciation to the Chamorro people. It became a curse for the Arteros."

After that, Carmen explained how the family avoided the march to Manenggon by hiding in the jungle. "Papa felt that if we went with everyone to Manenggon, we would all die. Instead, he chose to hide the family. We spent a lot of time in our hiding place," she said.

She then went on to explain how men came looking for Juan Pangelinan while both families were sometimes hiding in the jungle, and at other times, tending to their ranches. "They wanted Juan to come to Japanese headquarters so they could pay him for work performed and for food furnished to them from his ranch. It was a trick, and we all knew it. But Mister Pangelinan said that he would go with them. He said that if he didn't go, the Japanese would come and take his entire family. They would all be murdered. He went with them, and we all cried. Everyone, including my father cried for a long time knowing what was going to happen to him. He never returned."

"Later, when we went back to our ranch house, these same men showed up. They ask my father, just like with Mister Pangelinan, to accompany them to Japanese headquarters to be paid."

"My father got angry and told them off. 'What did you do with John?' He was angry. Then they threatened my father, one with a machete. I was watching and listening under the house, I ran to the tree where papa was hiding his gun. I snuck back. Their back was toward me but papa saw me. I ran to him saying, "papa! papa! Look I found a gun! The two men were so shocked as Papa grabbed the gun from me and leveled it at the two men, and said, 'Tell me what happened to John and the truth as to why are you here! Look! The Americans are almost here!' The men told papa that Mr. Pangelinan was killed along with Father Duenas and others. Papa seemed to think about it for a few seconds. I was sure he was going to kill them. So were they. My papa said, 'I will give you ten minutes to get off my property, then—I'm turning my dogs loose on you.'"

"The men began to run. Papa called the dogs. I don't know if it was a minute, five minutes, ten minutes, or what. My papa said to the dogs, 'Sic 'em, and the dogs went after the two men."

"My papa said that he was going to take one last bag of food with him and would be back shortly. He departed, and within an hour or so, he came back. He was smiling and laughing. He hugged my mother and was overjoyed. He kept saying, 'He's gone, he's gone!' I learned later that the U.S. Navy had picked up Mr. Tweed."

"Papa then said for everybody to gather some clothes and food and follow him. We climbed the steep cliff to the cave that had sheltered George Tweed."

"It was very crowded. We ran low on food and water. But, everyday my papa and mama would have us pray. The airplanes were flying over us constantly, and these big explosions would sometimes rock and shake our hiding place. One particular day, I got so upset. I had become really sick because I was so thirsty. I grabbed my mother's rosary and threw it against the wall of the cave. I shouted out, 'God is not listening to our prayers.' Then, I stormed out of the cave. I went up on top of the cliff lookout and walked over to the edge and looked out to the ocean."

She got this astonished look on her face, her eyes grew large, and then, with a shrug, she stated, "I had no idea what I was looking at. There were ships on the ocean as far as the eyes could see. The ocean was filled with them—big ones, little ones, all kinds of sizes. I stood there dumfounded. There were these tiny little ships all lined up moving toward Guam. I just stood there amazed even though I didn't know what I was looking at. It was a sight I'll never forget," she stated.

"You were perhaps watching the invasion of Guam by the Americans", I remarked.

There was a brief pause. "When did you first see the Americans?" I asked.

"That same day, I think. As I was looking out at the ships on the ocean and up in the sky at all the airplanes, I heard my older cousin Chu calling from below, "Nunu! Nunu! (My father's nickname)The Americans are here!" I looked down. I saw him, climbing up to us. He was leading two big men with big helmets and guns over their shoulders. He was hiding from the Japanese with grandfather and the rest of the Artero family in the jungle below the cliff.

From where I was, I could also see papa at the mouth of the hideout with the shotgun. My cousin yelled up to papa, "Here are two Americans!"

"Papa pointed the shotgun at Chu and the two men and said, "Is this a trick? Are you bringing the Japanese to us to save yourselves?" I saw Chu made the sign of the cross and said, 'In front of God I am not lying!' Papa then said, 'Tell them to take their hats (helmets) off.' When they did, my dad yelled—'Yes Mama, these are Americanos!'"

"It was a joyous day. We cried and cried. We were so happy. Everyone was crying. We were so relieved. The Americans were back. We were saved."

The two soldiers called on their radio to tell the ships and airplanes to stop bombing and shooting into where we were hiding. After we came down to the clearing, my mom went up to one of the soldiers and asked what day it was, then she came back and hugged me tight crying as she said, Mamie, today is your birthday!" It was August 8, 1944, the day I turned nine-years-old.

"They took us through the lines to the Catholic Cemetery in Pigo where the Americans had established a camp. They called it Camp Bradley. It was still dangerous. Japanese were all over the place. Still fighting. We stayed there until the soldiers created a safe place in Tutuhan for us to move there (that place is now called Agana Heights by the U.S. military).

"By the way, after the war, as I was listening to Papa explain much about the war, he burst out laughing. I asked him what was funny, he said, 'my shotgun that I was hiding and you found and gave to me, it was very rusty and had no bullet! But it saved our lives.'"

As observers, writers, and researchers, it became obvious that Carmen was reliving the events of the time, as she remembered them, or was told of them, and relayed them to us. We are very grateful to her for sharing her story with us for inclusion in this novel.

"BUCK" CRUZ

This is a story of a Marine, Master Gunnery Sergeant Ignacio "Buck" Cruz, USMC (Ret).

Many stories are told of the Japanese occupation of Guam. This novel relates several of them, but one in particular is told through the eyes of another fellow Marine. To introduce the reader to this Marine, this author chose to use the excellent recorded words of Robert A. Underwood, a noted educator, a previous Guam Delegate to the U.S. Congress, President of the University of Guam, and all around good guy. The occasion is the retirement of Master Gunnery Sergeant Ignacio "Buck" Cruz, USMC (Ret), from the position of Mayor of Merizo, Guam:

On Tuesday, 10 October 2000, Robert Underwood spoke publically of him:

Mr. Speaker, I would like to take this occasion to commend a municipal leader, a former Marine, and a fellow educator. The Honorable Ignacio "Buck" Cruz, the mayor of Merizo, is a native son who has unselfishly contributed years of valuable service to his home village of Merizo and the island of Guam. Mayor Cruz has chosen to retire at the end of his term later this year.

The son of Ramon Padilla Cruz and Justa Santiago Cruz, Mayor Cruz was the youngest of six children. Born in the village of Merizo in 1927, Mayor Cruz had the experience of attending Japanese school during the island's occupation in World War II. He later attended the University of Guam where he majored in Psychology and Sociology. Prior to graduating with honors, Mayor Cruz was a model student who was listed in the Who's Who Among Students and Universities and Colleges in America.

Mayor Cruz worked as a teacher prior to enlisting in the United States Marine Corps in 1951. While in the Marine Corps, he enrolled in a number of professional military courses including the Staff Non-Commissioned Officer School and the Officers Basic Extension Course. Having been a Marine Corps Drill Instructor, Mayor Cruz also holds the distinction of attaining the rank of Master Gunnery Sergeant, the highest enlisted rank in the United States Marine Corps.

As mayor of the village of Merizo, he also served as Chairman of the Merizo Municipal Planning Council Foundation and as a Notary Public in and for the Territory of Guam. Mayor Cruz is a Knight of Columbus in the 4th Degree and, in the past, has served as a parochial school teacher. He has occupied leadership positions in a number of civic organizations. He served as president of the Guam Club of Hawaii, the Guam Society of Norfolk, and the Hafa Adai Club of Okinawa. In addition, he chaired the Board of Directors for the Guam Senior Citizens Division and the Guam Environmental Protection Agency as well as the Merizo Elementary School PTA, the Merizo Water Festival and the Boy Scouts Troop Committee of Merizo. Mayor Cruz has also represented the island of Guam in national and international conferences. In 1985, he was the Guam representative to the United Nations Conference in Bangkok for the 3rd Asian and Pacific Ministerial Conference on Social Welfare and Social Development. In 1986, he represented Guam in the American Society on Aging's 36th Anniversary Meeting in San Francisco and the Pacific Gerontological Society's Conference on Aging in Hawaii.

After years of distinguished and dedicated service, Mayor Cruz has chosen to step down and retire. His achievements and service to the community have resulted in great benefit to the island of Guam, more particularly, the people of Merizo. He is a role model, a leader and a great representative of his island home. I join his wife, Maria, their children, and their grandchildren in celebrating his accomplishments throughout his long and successful career. On behalf of the people of Guam, I commend his achievements and congratulate him on his well-earned retirement. Si Yu'os Ma'ase, Mayor Cruz—So stated Doctor Robert Underwood, during the retirement ceremony of Mayor "Buck" Cruz.

From public records we researched while on Guam, we gleaned a little more about "Buck" Cruz.

He was born 20 July 1927. He was a teenager when the Japanese invaded Guam. He was forced to work in the fields growing and harvesting food for the Japanese, while also attending Japanese schools, as required by his captors. He was seventeen-years-old the year the Americans came back to Guam. As the Americans pounded the island in preparation for the amphibious assault, the Japanese were in a panic. They lost the ability of rational reasoning and attempted to wipe their dirty slate clean. They chose mass relocation and group extermination of many members of the populace of Guam, the Chamorro.

Acting under some kind of ancient, medieval, barbaric concept, they marched at gunpoint thousands of civilian residents into several valleys on the interior, and systematically, in several of these locations, murdered entire groups of men and women. Young Cruz's brother, brother-in-law, and father, were marched into a cave called the Tinta Cave with about thirty other Chamorros, supposedly for *protection* from American bombs and shells. Once inside, the Japanese gave them food, and as they were eating, the Japanese gradually withdrew from the cave and then began to throw hand grenades into it.

After the explosions ceased and the smoke cleared, they went back in and bayonetted all the survivors they could find. Miraculously, twelve people, including "Buck's" brother and brother-in-law did survive by feigning death. Unfortunately, his father did not survive. After witnessing uncivilized acts of brutality and surviving until just days before the island was liberated, Buck's dad lost his life to wanton murder.

Later in his life, "Buck" Cruz enlisted in the United States Marine Corps. As a U.S. Marine, he served his country honorably, rising through the ranks to the highest enlisted rank in the Marine Corps, and continued to serve his country, his island, and the people for many years as a resident of Guam.

The tribute delivered by Doctor Robert Underwood, and the researched public records, reveal a well-deserved tribute to this Marine.

Semper Fi, "Buck," Semper Fi.

While on Guam, we sought an interview with "Buck" Cruz, and with the assistance of Piti District Mayor, "Ben" Gumataotao, we were able to visit him at his home in Merizo.

It was a long drive from our hotel to the Village of Merizo, on the southern coast of Guam. As the reader has observed, "Buck" has held many important positions through the years. But, as we entered his home, the first thing we noticed was a large poster on the right side of the entryway, an enlarged photograph of his wife and him; he was dressed in the formal Marine Corps dress uniform with master gunnery sergeant chevrons and medals. It catches the eye immediately as a poster reproduction of a prior Marine Corps birthday portrait. Above the poster was an array of Marine Corps covers (hats); He was wearing one of them.

This retired Marine is eighty-eight-years-old, friendly, gracious, and most helpful to our cause. The first thing he asked was, "Would you like to meet my wife?" Of course, we said yes. He took us into a bedroom that was very quiet except for the hum of the air conditioner unit. His wife was bedridden, comatose-like, a nurse by her side. She lay there, eyes open, looking up at the ceiling. She was unresponsive. "Buck" was proud of his wife. He wanted to have us meet her. We understood. Quietly, we departed the room and went to his porch to sit and talk. "Buck" loves his wife, and he loves our Marine Corps.

He talked to us about many things. He was proud to be a Marine. We talked of his Marine Corps career. It is impressive. "Buck" is a proud Marine forever. He had also been the mayor of Merizo for nineteen years. He is proud of his accomplishments in office, but in conversation, he tended to dwell on his Marine Corps career. On several occasions, I'd ask him about the massacres at Tinta and Faha. His dad was killed by the Japanese. Actually, his dad was murdered by the Japanese. Still, to this day, he will not talk about that tragic loss. He tends to either direct the conversation to another subject, or simply ignore the question as if he had not heard the question.

We went out together, Lyn, "Buck" and me, to purchase a lunch.

As we got into my car to drive to a restaurant, he said, "Wait, please." He got out of the car and stated, "I got to go tell my wife where we're going."

We drove to a restaurant, ordered food, and sat. Then "Buck" said, "I've got to order another meal to go. It is for the nurse."

I added the meal to our order.

"Buck" Cruz is one of the most thoughtful and caring persons we have ever met, bar none.

Then, we returned to his residence.

For a long time, we sat and chatted with this "Old Corps" Marine and former Merizo mayor, with a lifetime of public government service and dedication to the United States of America and to the people of Guam.

We had given him a copy of *A Marine Called Gabe.* As we prepared to depart, he couldn't find the book. Apparently, the nurse had placed it somewhere. We had to search and find the book's location to make sure he had it, before we could depart his residence. He wanted that book!

As we were preparing to leave, he offered to send a plate of food with us. We politely refused. He then asked if we wanted to take a chicken. A fresh killed chicken. They were running around the yard. Again, we politely refused.

"I feel bad that I can't give you something to take with you," he said. It's a Chamorro thing.

We explained that we lived in a hotel and really didn't need anything. As mentioned, Buck is a very generous and caring person.

One could count on two hands the people of Guam who *do not* know of "Buck" Cruz. He is a national treasure. We are fortunate to know him and to have sat with him as he reminisced about his life. This man, this Marine, this Chamorro, this American, has dedicated his life to one goal—service to his fellow man.

As we backed out of his driveway, past the large sign on his front lawn facing the main road, that read "BUCK CRUZ," we remarked, You know, that sign says all it needs to say. On Guam, the name Buck Cruz says it all.

Researcher Lyn Bates and Retired Marine Sergent Major
Buck Cruz at his home in Merizo, Guam
Photo property of author

ANTHONY ADA

In the aftermath of the Patti Arroyo interview, we received an email from Anthony Ada. He relayed information about his dad being in the Guam Militia after the invasion of Guam by the Americans. We agreed to meet at George Taylor's Chamorro Island BBQ. He said he would bring his sister.

His sister Rose and her husband Leandro arrived first. We had long conversations about a variety of subjects. It seems that most all the Ada family, at an earlier time, had joined the Navy as cooks or stewards. This was before integration of the Navy. An important item discussed was when Rose said her husband's grandfather had built the Lujan House in 1910. She also told of George Tweed, the American sailor hiding from the Japanese on Guam, once staying at Leandro's grandfather's ranch. Leandro's grandfather's name is Jose Lujan or Luhan.

> *Lujan House, Also known as the Guam Institute, the Lujan House is one of the few remaining pre-World War II houses in Hagåtña. The house was built in 1911 by Jose Pangelinan Lujan and was first used as a residence. In 1928 the Guam Institute, founded by Nievas M. Flores in 1922, moved to the Lujan House. Students paid a monthly fee of $1.00 in order to attend this private school.*
>
> Guampedia.com

The walls of the house were very thick, made from coral and limestone. He was nineteen when he built the house, and he had another house in Agana, which disappeared during the American bombardment. It was located in what would become the middle of Marine Corps Drive today.

"The military took his land, and he was never paid for it," Rose said.

She has also heard that the Chamorro of Saipan and Tinian have received repatriations from the United States, plus Commonwealth status, while Chamorros of Guam have received very little. That makes her very dissatisfied.

She told of one of the Japanese Catholic Priests who tended to befriend her dad's family during the occupation. On one particular occasion, the Japanese were going to kill her father because they believed he was hiding Tweed. Of course, he was, but, it was the intervention of this Japanese Priest that saved her dad.

She talked further about her father and mother during the occupation. She said they didn't talk much but when they did, it was told as a "day-to-day horror." Her mom described the march to Manenggon carrying her infant baby who had died in her arms. She continued to carry her child. Her mom told her, "People would say to me, 'Why aren't you crying?'" She said her mom responded, "Why should I cry—I should have cried while she was suffering."

Anthony arrived joining the discussion as we were talking about repatriations, the political status of Guam, the use of DDT on the island by the American military, and the seizure of land. These were thoughtful and informative discussions.

Tony did email me with several attachments that he thought would be helpful in our research. We are grateful for that. They are helpful. Thank you very much, Tony.

WILLIAM RAY GIBSON

William Gibson of Radio/TV K-57 interviewed me on Veterans Day to highlight this book, and to discuss an article I had written about the shortchanged veterans of Guam. He called me at 0830 in the morning because he had read an on-line newspaper article that I had written for the Greenville News, of Greenville, South Carolina. During the interview, others joined the radio discussion about the shortchanged military veteran of Guam, when compared to the military veteran of the fifty States. We raised quiet a ruckus.

We also learned of a lawsuit filed in federal court in Chicago that very day about Guam's status, and of not being allowed to vote for President and Vice-President. Neil Weare, the attorney filing the lawsuit, was one of the people on the air with me during that Radio/TV interview.

After the interview, Juan Blaz, who had become a good friend, stopped by our hotel room to return the manuscript he had read at my request. While giving us a run-down of his opinions, which were highly positive, he said that he had two people he felt we should meet. As a matter-of-fact, he felt pretty strongly about it. They were Carl Gutierrez and Joe Ada. Both were former governors of Guam, and Juan had worked for both of them from time to time. He respected both of them and felt they would be a valuable asset to Lyn and me for our book writing project. We agreed, and Juan set it up. Then, I called both men the following day, and we arranged meetings:

CARL TOMMY CRUZ GUTIERREZ

A few days later, we met for lunch with former Governor Carl Gutierrez and his wife, Geri, to discuss the book project. Both were delightful companions, who provided us with valuable contacts and additional information related to our writing project. Both are survivors of the Japanese occupation and survivors of the Guam equivalent of the Bataan Death March—the death camp in the Manenggon Valley of 1944.

One of the first things I learned about this man, Carl, was that he was the keynote speaker at a recent Marine Corps birthday gathering of the Ex-Pat Marine Association in Angeles City, Pampanga, Philippines. He delivered a stirring and memorable address at their birthday dinner that will measure the man more than any writing that I am capable of producing. His talk with those Marines is included in its entirety as follows:

ExPat Marine Association Celebration of the
240th Birthday of the United States Marine Corps
Keynote Address by:
Carl T. C. Gutierrez, Former Governor of Guam
November 8, 2015

Good evening, Mabuhay, and Hafa Adai, as we say in Guam!

It is quite an honor to be here this evening with all of you as we celebrate the 240th birthday of the United States Marine Corps. When I was first asked by the ExPat Marine Association to speak at this event, I accepted without hesitation. Although I am an Air Force man myself, I feel inextricably connected with the Marines.

As you probably know, Guam had a Marine presence since the early 20th Century, with the Americans having claimed Guam after the Spanish-American War in 1898. Since that time, many familial ties have been established between Marines and Chamorros, much like there have been with Filipinos.

But more than that, I, as a Chamorro, feel inextricably linked with the Marines, and will forever be grateful to them, because of the liberation of my island of Guam from the Japanese Imperial forces on July 21, 1944.

If you would indulge me for a few moments, I'd like to share with you a little bit about my personal history and that of my wife Geri, who has accompanied me this evening. I was born on October 15, 1941. When I was not quite 2 months old, just hours after the attack on Pearl Harbor, Guam was invaded by the Japanese Imperial Forces, who occupied our homeland for the next 31 months.

I really have no memories of the occupation, but have heard what has been passed on by my elders. In the waning months of Japanese control of Guam, the brutality escalated. Concentration camps were set up at various sites throughout the island. My family, who resided in the central village of Agana Heights, was forced to march with hundreds of other families to the internment camp at Manenggon.

I was 2 years and 9 months old by then. My parents later recounted the experience with such emotion that I can almost envision it: my mom and dad alternating between carrying me, my three older siblings, and my infant brother as they made the long trek of about 10 miles from Agana Heights to Manenggon; the scorching heat, followed by the torrential rains, which made treading upon the red clay dirt slippery and precarious; the cruelty displayed by the Japanese soldiers toward those who slowed down or even collapsed from exhaustion – the elderly, the weak, and even the children.

When we finally arrived at the camp site, life consisted of simply surviving – of scrounging for food, but yet always finding enough to share with others, as is our Chamorro way; of bathing in the same river where from which we drank; of witnessing atrocities that betrayed humanity.

For my immediate family, I guess you can say we were lucky, because we all survived the ordeal. But for many others at Manenggon – not to mention the many more at the other massacre sites in the island – they were not so lucky.

Listen, for example, to the story of a beautiful young woman, just 27 years old – a mother of three daughters, ages 8 years, 7 years, and 15 months. Her name was Hannah Chance Torres, the daughter of a Chamorro mother and a Caucasian father. She had fair skin, reddish-brown hair, and from every account I've heard, she had a fiery spirit that captured both her Chamorro and Irish roots.

She and her family were also on this forced march to Manenggon. The date was July 15, 1944. Those who marched alongside Hannah have said that her appearance, which was more American than Chamorro, caused her to stand out, attracting the attention of the Japanese soldiers.

Her husband, Felix, was pulled away and made to march separately with some other men. So with the assistance of the women in her clan, Hannah and her two older daughters trekked along, while Hannah carried her infant daughter.

As you might imagine, her steps eventually slowed from exhaustion, and she fell several times in the slippery terrain. This, coupled with her Caucasian look, enraged the soldiers – so much so that they began beating her. While she was crouched down and doubled over, she cradled her infant child in her arms, her own body shielding her baby from the blows of a saber.

Once the soldiers relented, Hannah's sister-in-law rushed to take the crying infant, while the other women helped Hannah, limping and beaten, walk about three more miles to a resting spot at the camp site.

There, a few short hours later, Hannah died from massive internal bleeding – just 6 days before the Marine invasion that liberated Guam.

That 15-month old girl, whose life her mother protected at the expense of her own, grew up to become an equally beautiful and spirited woman who, 19 years later, would become my wife. Our family's tragedy is not unique – hundreds of families have stories just as painful about the forced marches and the internment camps, the disappearances of loved ones during the war, the use of beheadings, and systematic murder of the leaders of the village of Merizo.

And while our marches were certainly miniscule compared to the horrors of Bataan, as with everything else in life, it's all relative: For us in Guam, our population went from 25,000 before the war to about 22,500 after the massacres, in which 10% of our entire island population was decimated. So yes, the atrocities here in the Philippines were certainly bigger in terms of the sheer numbers, but the blow to Guam was, for us, just as horrific. The brutalities witnessed and experienced still haunt those who lived through them, and still evoke so much emotion even for those of us who have only heard the stories.

I mentioned earlier that I really have no personal memories of the occupation. But I will tell you this – my very first memory, the image that I recall when I try and go back into the furthest reaches of my mind – is of being carried away from Manenggon upon the shoulders of a Marine.

I was less than 3 years old and suffering from a hernia, and that Marine – who might as well have been God himself as far as I was concerned – placed me on his broad shoulders and carried me the entire way to Agana Heights. This is what I meant when I told you I feel inextricably linked with, and thankful to, the Marines.

For me and for my people – especially those of us who experienced the liberation of Guam – we will forever be grateful. Guam continues to remember and honor the United Stated Marine Corps, even naming our main thoroughfare Marine Corps Drive.

I believe that my personal gratitude to the Marines is what inspired in me a desire to live a life of service – service to my country and to my island. I chose military life, enlisting in the United States Air Force just one hour after my graduation from South San Francisco High School.

After my time in the Air Force, I embarked on what became a 40-plus year long career in public service – as a senator and speaker in the Guam Legislature for several terms between 1973 and 1995, and as Governor of Guam from 1995 to 2003. In various ways to this day, I continue in my efforts to advance the causes of Guam and our region, nationally and internationally.

My father, who passed away when I was 16 years old, had a mantra that he always repeated to me and my 10 siblings. In Chamorro, it goes: Maseha hafa na estao na gaige hao, cha'mu malelefa ginen manu hao magi. Translated, it means: No matter what station or stature in life you achieve, never forget where you came from.

Tonight, as I stand before you proud and honorable Marines, I want you to know that I have never forgotten that you – the Marines – are a large part of where I came from. You, the Marines, brought my island back from the clutches of enemy occupation. You, the Marines, carried me – a weak, scrawny, and sick toddler – on your shoulders away from the horrors of a concentration camp. You, the Marines, inspired me to choose a life of service to my country and my people of Guam.

And like most things in life, Guam's relationship with the Marines is coming full circle, as our island prepares to welcome you back. We recognize the important role you will once again play in protecting our island and our region, in a time when, both regionally and globally, our nation faces new and ever-evolving security threats.

And so I thank you, personally and on behalf of a grateful Guam and a grateful Chamorro people. Si Yu'os Ma'ase and Happy Birthday, Marine Corps! Oorah!

His address to those Marines reflected his distant remembrances of that lone Marine who carried him on his shoulders to safety on Guam. Those memories remain deeply rooted in his mind and in the character of the man.

We could have sat and talked about the Marines for an hour, but there were other things, other views I needed to hear. Carl discussed his views based on his long-time government service as a senator from 1973 through 1986. After his reelection in 1989, he continued to serve in the senate until he was elected Governor in 1994. He served two terms as governor from 1994 through 2003. He has deep insight and accumulated wisdom regarding Guam and its people as they seek their place in the sun for their beloved island. He provided us with observations from his many years as a public servant, and shared some obstacles that he had encountered through the years.

He began service to his country right out of high school by enlisting in the United States Air Force serving from 1960 through 1965. He married Geri in 1963. It was a wise decision.

Like Carl, Geri survived the horror of the Japanese occupation and the death camp. It is heart-rending to read and to hear of her mother's death at the hands of the Japanese occupiers. As Carl has noted, there were many similar stories of this nature. Many are recounted in the pages of this novel. It is so unfortunate that the American government tends to reward some survivors of the War in the Pacific, while denying rewards—or even recognition, to other survivors of that war. The Chamorros of Guam fall in the latter group, as this book demonstrates over and over again.

Geri Gutierrez, at a Mañenggon Reflection Ceremony of 9 July 2011, stated the following:

When I was first approached to give a reflection for today's ceremony, I was both honored and admittedly a little daunted. Although I am a

Mañenggon survivor, I was just 15 months old during the internment in this valley. Merely an infant. I have no memory whatsoever of the time I spent here. Unlike other survivors who have spoken about their experiences here, I have no such memories to share. But that is not to say that my life has not been indelibly marked by the atrocities committed here 67 years ago.

For just as I have no memory of being interned here, I also have no memory of my mother, who died here at the hands of Japanese soldiers at the age of 27, beaten to death while she cradled me in her arms. I have only the stories told to me by my elder relatives and other survivors who witnessed the events. I have been told many times throughout my life about this beautiful, strong-willed, vibrant woman named Hannah Chance Torres who not only gave me life, but who protected my life until the end of hers, shielding my infant body from the blows of a bayonet while her own body bore each strike.

Many of us here today are mothers. All of us here today have a mother. So I'm sure you all know or can imagine how deep the loss of a mother is – particularly without any memories of her to cling to. Throughout my life, in spite of the pain, the longing to know what it must have been like to be embraced by my mother, to know her scent or to know her touch, the one thing that I have clung to . . . the one thing that could not be taken from me . . . is the comforting reality that she existed. That I exist because of her. And, that there has to be a lesson not just in her death, but in the suffering endured at the hands of enemy forces by all our people during the years of occupation and the atrocities here at Mañenggon.

While I don't presume to know any of life's grand secrets, I do know this: her story, my story, their stories need to be recounted, recorded, and passed on – not so that we can wallow in this tragic part of our history, but that we can ensure that the legacy we leave our children is complete. Part of this is the urgency with which we must transmit to our children the need to always be watchful and stand guard against any injustice.

We all know that here at home, many wrongs have yet to be made right, including our ongoing struggle for Chamorro self-determination and for war reparations, to name but two. We have a sacred obligation to inspire in our children a passionate refusal to be treated as irrelevant, especially in our own homeland.

For those generations born after the war – and even for some of us who lived through it – it is hard to imagine as we gather in the peaceful breeze of this valley, on this soil, beneath these trees, beside this river, that events so horrific and unthinkable could ever have happened here. But they did. And while there is certainly much to be said for putting the past behind us, it would be a tragedy in itself to allow the truths of our history to die with those who experienced them.

I look at my grandson Liam, who is the exact age I was during the Mañenggon march. I think of his life and the lives of my other grandchildren – Lily, Livia, and Seth – and what lessons they must learn from the tragedies of the occupation. Just as our mañaina have passed on their memories and wisdom to us, now we, who have become the mañaina, have an obligation to ensure that their memories and wisdom do not die with us.

I am among the youngest of the Mañenggon and occupation survivors. Eventually, the days will come to take me away. But what I hope to impart to my grandchildren and to all our island's post-war children, is this: Whatever role you fill in life and in our community, remember that you are part of a legacy. Take seriously the legacy which you in turn will leave. I hope that I will live to see the day that we Chamorros finally self-determine our political status. I hope to witness other victories of social justice in my lifetime. And above all, I pray that my legacy, and the legacy of my contemporaries, will be that of changing our beloved Guam for the better. It is that legacy that never dies.

"Changing our beloved Guam for the better." Those words from Geri Gutierrez, artfully describes the purpose, and the intent of this novel.

Reflecting on the words of Carl and Geri, caused me to reflect on a long ago memory. I don't know why. I have occupied many roles during my lifetime, the latest being that of an author. But one of my roles in particular leaps out at me right now. Why? Again, I have no idea. It just does. It was when I served as a Marine Corps Drill Instructor at Parris Island. Our Marine Corps was changing at that time because of a tragic incident at a place called Ribbon Creek. Drill Instructors were under a lot of scrutiny, and many so-called *changes* were being implemented. Even the code or creed of the DI was changed. While I was in the DI School, we were told that we had a new drill instructor's creed. A creed that, they said, was a bit more scholarly and more descriptive of our duties and responsibilities than the old one. It wasn't!

At this point in my life, I can't even remember what the new creed said. But, I do vividly remember the old Drill Instructor's Creed which was the sum product of an older and somewhat wiser group of Drill Instructors that I had the pleasure of serving with. These were the World War II and Korean War veterans. Some were actually pre-World War II Marines. Oh, I remember it well. The old drill instructors creed went something like this: *Make damn sure that no man's ghost will ever say—if he had only done his job!* Now I remember why. As the author of this book of Guam and the Chamorros of Guam, it is my fervent hope that no persons ghost will ever say, of this novel and its author, *if he had only done his job!*

During a long conversation with Carl and Geri, Geri mentioned that family members buried her mother beside one of the rivers in the Manenggon Valley. After the liberation, like many of the Chamorros who had lost loved ones, efforts were undertaken to locate the remains of family members in order to provide proper burial. Unexplainably, as the body of Geri's mother was unearthed alongside that ancient river in the Manenggon Valley, the body had not decayed. Intact, it was removed and properly reburied in a proper graveyard, with a proper service. Apparently, it was the red clay of that river bank that played a part in the preservation of her mother's body.

JOSEPH FRANKLIN ADA

A week before we departed from Guam, former Governor Joseph Ada, as arranged, stopped by our hotel room for a meeting. We wanted to get his views of the U.S.-Guam relationship based on his years as a public servant for the people of Guam. It was an enlightening meeting.

> *He was elected as the Lieutenant Governor of Guam from 1979 to 1983 and was the fifth Governor of Guam from 1987 to 1995. Prior to becoming governor, he was a member of the legislature and while in office was selected as the Speaker of Guam's Legislature from 1975 into 1979.*
>
> www.digplanet.com/wiki/**Joseph_Franklin_Ada**

"Basically, the federal government tied the hands of Guam. While insisting that Guam could not advance politically until it advanced economically; then, the federal government prevented economic growth of Guam in numerous ways. One way it obstructed economic growth was the restrictions placed on anyone entering Guam (or leaving) in the post war era," he explained.

For years, even after the passage of the Organic Act, giving so-called self-government to Guam, the U.S. Navy required anyone desiring to enter or leave Guam to obtain the permission of the Navy. Everyone! Even my good friend Lt Col Adolf Sgambelluri, USMC (Ret), as a newly minted second lieutenant, attempting to return home to visit his parents while enroute from Quantico, Virginia, to his first duty station on Okinawa, had to get *permission* from the U.S. Navy—to come home to Guam. Then, in order to continue his travel to Okinawa, he had to have *permission* from the Navy to depart Guam. It was economic strangulation. That's how absurd the rule was.

Joe Ada further explained that sometimes events move in strange ways. He related how the economic strangulation rule that the Navy had in place was lifted. Not by design. Not by plan. Not by Congress. But, instead—it was by the absurdity of the rule itself.

Joe tells the following story: After the implementation of the Organic Act, the President of the United States continued to appoint governors of Guam. Soon to be President John Kennedy had planned to appoint William "Bill" Partlow Daniel, of Texas, as governor of Guam. This new potential governor appointee decided to make a quick side-trip to visit Guam to see what he was getting into, since he had already planned to visit friends nearby while on vacation in Australia. So, a side-trip to Guam, from Australia to nearby Guam, was included in his "vacation" plans. He concluded his visit with his friends, and as he prepared to leave Australia for Guam, he was prevented from making his flight because he needed *permission* from a N*avy bureaucrat* in Washington D.C., before they would *allow* him on Guam. Not only was clearance from the Navy required, but clearance via the CIA and the FBI was also a part of that Navy clearance process.

This made the new potential governor appointee of Guam angry. Very angry! It took him just a few weeks, going through his friend, then the Secretary of the Navy, John B. Connally and also through his own brother, Price Daniel, who was then the Chief of Staff to Senator Lyndon Johnson, who was soon to be the Vice President of the United States, and ultimately all this information and these conversations converged into the Oval Office where the new President, John F. Kennedy, signed an executive order instantly eliminating the requirement for *permission* to enter (or leave) Guam.

Guam Governor Daniel once described the previous Navy *Clearance* policy as, "Iron Curtain mentality, and totally un-American." Further, he stated, "Guam was the most tightly controlled territorial possession in American history."

Texas Governor Price Daniel, brother of Guam Governor "Bill" Daniel, was instrumental in winning the crucial twenty-four electoral votes for the Kennedy-Johnston ticket in 1960.

Two lessons were learned here: first, with the elimination of the Navy's required permission to enter or leave Guam, economic development could now begin for Guam; second—don't mess with Texas!

Joe Ada explained that as long as Guam is dependent on the U.S. government for its existence economically, conditions will never allow Guam to grow. He spent his two terms as governor growing the economy of Guam through tourism and educational development. His progress was restricted by several issues, especially by the Jones Act, which according to many, is basically a protection racket for labor unions in the United States, and the failure of Congress to allow for a political status of Guam's own choice.

Perhaps no other man can, will, or has, matched Joseph Ada's record for educational and commercial-economic development for Guam. He approaches both subjects with a passion. As we discussed his two terms as governor of this Territory, we could actually feel his fervor for Guam and its people.

Today, he continues, through association with the University of Guam, to work enhancing the ability of the people of Guam to attain achievement through academic development. His desires are to improve both the programs and the physical plants to reach these goals.

He had some color to add to the conversation also. He told how, several years ago, he had met and entertained the king of Tonga who was on Guam at the invitation of the U.S. Navy and U.S. State Department. For several years the king was in a process of attempting to get some economic assistance from the United States government to no avail. The gathering was related to the Pacific Island's Nation's Conference meeting in Hawaii. Tonga is an independent island kingdom in the Pacific.

Joe Ada was the Speaker of the Guam legislature and was asked, by the State Department, to host a dinner for King Taufa'ahua Tupou IV. While attending the dinner, the King related to Joe the story of how he obtained assistance from the U.S. It seems that the USSR (Russia) had approached Tonga with a desire to *assist* the island kingdom economically—of course, in exchange for *something.* That *something* was a naval entry permit (a base) for Soviet navy ships cruising in the Pacific Ocean. They wanted a dock in Tonga. When the United States learned of the possibility of Soviet warships docking in Tonga, it was then, after that Soviet offer to Tonga, that Tonga could get just about anything it wanted from the United States government.

Before we departed Guam, we had lunch with the former governor. He is a likeable, sincere, and dedicated man. He is still a man with a mission, and that mission is—enhancing the quantity and quality of education for all the citizens of Guam.

One cannot help but to love and respect both the man and his objectives. Truly—a great leader!

We had given the former governor a copy of our unfinished manuscript. He read it in two days and had many laudatory remarks about the content. Joe gave us a very strong verbal endorsement for our novel. His words to us were "This is the best book I have ever read that properly describes Guam and its people." Or, words of similar meaning, and it meant a great deal to us, especially coming from Joe Ada.

JESUS TORRE PANGELINAN, (JUAN PANGELINAN'S SON)

While meeting with Carl and Geri Gutierrez, Carl stated that there was one other important person we should meet, an occupation survivor, who might assist us with our book project. It was Jesus Pangelinan. But, we didn't know the person or the connection to our book writing project. We believed that we were meeting with a Jesus Pangelinan, a World War II survivor. That's all. We agreed, and Carl made a telephone call from the table and talked to Jesse Pangelinan.

So, it was set up for us to talk with Jesus, through his son, Jesse. All we knew was that we were going to get to talk with a survivor of the Japanese occupation. Someone that Carl felt important for us to meet.

On the week of our departure from Guam, we met Jesus's son, Jesse, at a gas station alongside Marine Corps Drive, across from the Governor's Complex, and followed him up towards Nimitz Hill, taking several winding side roads through the awesome natural beauty of the island. Green foliage and fragrant flowering plants consumed the landscape as we continued to rise in elevation. We entered a maze of tropical growth that surrounded our vehicle and captivated our senses until we emerged at a modest home somewhere on the ocean side of Nimitz Hill, in Maina Village.

As we gathered at his home with several family members, we met his dad, Jesus, and asked him to please recount his experiences during the Japanese occupation. He began to talk.

What began as an interesting and informative conversation, slowly emerged as a vital link in the chain of characters contained in our manuscript about the times of the Japanese occupation of Guam. The trip-wire came as Jesus made the statement "My father had kept the sailor, George Tweed, for four months before turning him over to Antonio Artero." Without realizing it, until that very moment, we had been directed to the location of the son of the beheaded Juan Unpingco Pangelinan, the neighbor rancher of Antonio Artero.

Antonio Artero had the distinction of harboring the sailor George Tweed for 21 of his 31 months. Juan Pangelinan, who had secluded the sailor Tweed for four months, had to turn Tweed over to Antonio Artero because the Japanese were preparing to search his ranch for the elusive sailor. It was at that specific point, we suddenly realized we were talking to Juan's son, Jesus Torre Pangelinan, who went on to give us an eyewitness account from the eyes of a fourteen to seventeen-year-old boy about Tweed, the Artero family, and his own family, the Pangelinans, of 1942 through 1944 Guam. It was an eye opener.

Lyn blurted out, "Oh my God."

I reached over and took Jesus by the hand and stated, "I had no idea who you were, until now."

"We have found the missing link in our story. It's the icing on the cake," Lyn stated as we sat around the kitchen table.

For the past few months, at several times, in several locations, from several people, they would say to us, "If you can locate him, you should talk with Unpingco. No one could direct us to Unpingco. Until now!

Jesus and Jesse both explained that Juan was often simply called Juan Unpingco. Things began to fall into place.

Our interview continued.

This enlightening interview tended to solidify previous interviews with others regarding the unsung heroes of World War II Guam. Sure, there are some differences; but the purpose of our many interviews was not, and is not, to emphasize the differences in recollections by survivors of the Japanese occupation.

This contact was vital in that the facts as viewed by Jesus, regarding his dad, Juan Pangelinan, reveals a belief that his father went to his grave to protect his family, without disclosing the location of George Tweed or the names of the people who had been harboring Tweed.

These Chamorros of Guam, during the Japanese occupation frequently died maintaining the secrets of members of the CU (underground), the clandestine radio listening locations, and of those who were safeguarding the American sailors hiding from Japanese authorities who were diligently and desperately searching for them.

The following is taken from –paleric.blogspot.com/...history-**father-duenas-beheaded**.html

flickr.com

> *After several days of torture, having been arrested by the Japanese on July 8, Father Jesus Baza Dueñas was taken early on the morning of the 12th, along with his nephew Edward Dueñas, to Tå'i where the two were beheaded, along with one Juan Pangelinan and an unidentified man.*

❧

Juan Unpingco Pangelinan was born in 1894. He was eighteen when he joined the U.S. Navy in 1912, served through the Great War, and ultimately became a water-man in the boiler section of U.S. Navy ships. He retired from the Navy in 1932, after serving twenty years, and returned to farming—his lifelong love. His family farm bordered the farm of the Artero family in north west Guam. It was on that farm that Juan Pangelinan was asked to shelter the Navy man George Tweed. Juan was visited by Adolfo Sgambelluri (Sgambe), B.J. Bordallo, Joaquin Limtiaco (Limty), and Joaquin Flores in late 1942. These four men were members of the CU. Since Juan Pangelinan was a retired Navy man, he felt an obligation to keep Tweed. The Japanese had been closing in on Tweed in the Upper Tumon area, and he had to be moved again. Tweed was moved often.

Juan brought Tweed to his ranch.

George Tweed was one of six American sailors who chose to hide in the jungles of Guam to await the return of the American Navy after the surrender of Guam to the Japanese—only Tweed survived. The evasion of these six Americans, with the assistance of the local Chamorros, infuriated the Japanese. Eventually, assisting the sailors became a deadly game, a deadly serious game. If you were *suspected* of assisting or of knowing the location of the Americans, you were severely beaten and tortured. If you were *caught* assisting or hiding the Americans, you were killed.

Juan knew the risk and accepted the responsibility. It would cost him his life.

"My dad had asked me to hitch up the horse and wagon. I was excited because he usually took me with him. But, this time, he told me to stay. I was not allowed to go with him," Jesus said.

"What was happening?" I asked. "Your dad went down to Tumon to get Tweed?"

"Yes," he responded. Then, he hesitated.

"He brought Tweed to our house. Initially, he stayed inside the house. Then, my dad built a shelter for him away from the house," Jesus finally replied.

Then he continued, "We kept Tweed for three or four months. He stayed in a shelter my dad built for him about 100 yards from the ranch house," Jesus said emphatically.

"After the liberation, the Navy questioned me about George Tweed. They wanted to know all about who, where, and what happened to Tweed. I told them all I knew. Then, they asked me, 'How do you know that it was three or four months that Tweed was with you? You have no calendars.' I replied that the [full] moon comes around once a month and we had three or four moons, while Tweed was with us."

We all laughed at his simple yet obvious reply to naval investigators.

"After Antonio took Tweed from my dad, and after three or four months had gone by, we asked him often if he still had Tweed."

"His response was, 'No. He's gone. We don't know where he is.'"

Jesus chuckled and continued. "We still knew where Tweed was, because he kept returning to our ranch. He doesn't stay in one place. We know where he was, because he was telling us where he was. He was with Antonio. We didn't know exactly where Antonio was keeping him," Jesus emphasized. "But, Tweed would often visit our ranch while he was hiding on Antonio's property."

"One day," Jesus continued, "this man comes. He was a Chamorro, a Guam Chamorro. His name was Aleju, or Alejo. Something like that. It was a nickname. He *summoned* my dad to come to Japanese headquarters."

He strongly emphasized the word *summoned* on several occasions.

"My dad knew what was happening. He just wanted to protect us. Before he left with this guy, he said to us, 'I'm a *caballero* [gentleman]. So I have to go.' Then my dad said, 'I know what the Japs want. If I don't go, the Japs will come and kill my family. So I have to go.' Then he added, 'between four and five o'clock, I want everyone to go to the cave.' So, we all, the Arteros and my family, we all go down to the cave."

"Where is this cave that you went to?" I asked.

"Down at what they call Bare-Ass Beach. It's on the Navy base now," he responded.

"Where the divers go down this long trail to the beach, on the Navy base?" Lyn asked.

"Yes, we hide there a week or so. Then, we went back up to our farms."

"Is that where the sign is that says that you can't go down to the beach without permission from the Navy?"

"Yes, that's it," he confirmed.

"The mosquitos ate us alive when we tried to go down that trail," Lyn stated.

"Describe the cave," I asked.

"It's a big cave. It's flat inside. It's on the trail down to Bare-Ass Beach. Where people went naked," he explained.

Again, this garnered chuckles from us all.

"We had to give about sixty percent of our production of our farm to the Japanese. The Japanese were giving some of the food to the comfort women who were housed in the place where the governor's complex is now. Then, believe it or not, the comfort women would give us some food. You know, rice, sugar, that kind of thing. Then, we would provide food to Tweed."

"So, in essence, in a way, the Japanese were feeding Tweed," I commented.

"Yes!"

Again, we all had a good laugh at that ironic situation.

"In my opinion, it was Tweed's job to find the location of the Japanese defenses so he could tell the military about it." he stated.

"The American military?"

"Yes!"

"Did he do that?"

"I have no idea. I know that a ship or something picked him up, much later. I have no idea of what he said to them."

Jesse broke into the conversation after I made a remark about Juan being a true American hero. He protected not only the sailor Tweed, but also his own family and the Artero family, by willingly going to the Japanese essentially to be executed. He knew what was going to happen to him.

Jesse said, "My granddad was executed on the 12th of July—before the American invasion. If he had said anything about anyone hiding Tweed, the Japanese would have acted immediately to follow up on the information. They had killed my granddad, and they still didn't have Tweed," he reasoned.

Indeed, if Juan had told of the location of Tweed, the Japanese would have followed up on the information before killing their captive.

This discussion now entered into a highly emotional event in the life of a fourteen to seventeen-year-old Jesus Pangelinan, being told again by an eighty-five-year-old man reaching back over seventy years, as if it were an event of just yesterday. His mind was sharp.

"After my father went to Japanese headquarters, we never knew where he was. He had disappeared. It was after the liberation that we found out that he had been killed by the Japanese," Jesus responded.

"I went to the place," he hesitated. "I went to where they had buried them with my brother, Jose, my sister, Delfina, and my step-mother. I dug up my father. I recognized him from the gold teeth and his shirt," Jesus elaborated through tears and a shaking voice as he revealed the emotional events that occurred sometime after the executions by beheading and the American invasion of the island. The executions were on 12 July. The American landings were on 21 July. The American front lines would have reached the Pangelinan and Artero properties around the end of the first week, or beginning of the second week, in August.

"I saw him," he said while crying.

"Your father was executed at the same time that Father Dueñas and his nephew were killed, wasn't he?" I asked.

"There were three along with my father," he responded.

"When did you go and identify your father's body?"

"It was a few days, a couple of weeks after the liberation," Jesus responded.

Then we got back onto the subject of Tweed when he was staying with different people in the south of Guam. Actually it would be in the middle part of Guam, before he was picked up by Juan to keep. Tweed rarely stayed put in one place for very long.

"I have always thought that Tweed must have been collecting information on the disposition of the Japanese defensive positions to relay that to the Americans after they picked him up," he stated.

"Did he?" I asked.

"I don't know," he replied.

"You know, Jesus, your dad sacrificed himself. He gave his life to protect his family, actually to protect everyone who had safeguarded Tweed and the other sailors," I remarked.

As we were preparing to depart his home, I stated to everyone listening, "Juan Unpingco Pangelinan is a hero of World War II. He should be recognized by the government of Guam and of the United States as a man who willingly gave his life for his fellow countrymen during the Japanese occupation of Guam."

We departed the home of Jesus Pangelinan with the promise to communicate with Jesse and his wife, Elaine, in the future as we began to enter this portion of the manuscript into the novel, and move toward publication. We exchanged frequent emails.

The participation of Jesus Pangelinan in developing this novel is extremely valuable. We were fortunate to have been placed in contact with him only hours before we were scheduled to depart Guam.

Authors Note: Many times in this novel, we have mentioned, and repeated for the readers, different people see and hear the same events that take place, and record them differently in the recesses of their minds. As human beings, we can only do the best we can to recall the facts as we believe they were lived.

Rational people have explained that there are many conflicts among the memories and stories of Guam's war survivors. That is perfectly normal. It is not that one person is telling the truth, and that the other person is not. It is because people see and hear things differently, and they remember things differently. We also discussed how sometimes first-hand accounts become diluted by conversations with people who have heard or viewed, or developed, slightly different versions of long ago events. Both believe their versions to be true. And, as they saw, heard, and experienced them, both are indeed truth—to the person telling the story.

As an example we have talked to people on Guam who insist that there was no underground network, no active resistors to the Japanese occupation authorities. Others have described the active underground network in some detail. Both believe what they say to be true. The truth is that there was an active underground network. We have the evidence, but we do not chastise those who believe that it did not exist. Perhaps, in their remembrances, from their location, they never heard or saw anyone or anything that would have supported a belief that an underground secret resistance group (CU) did exist. We simply present the facts as those we talked with presented them. We made no changes, no editorial comments, and no judgements.

GUAM TODAY

The following contains factual data and the opinions and recommendations of the author:

Looking at the history of Guam in a more focused way, one may assume that modern Guam can be traced back to the passage of the Organic Act in 1950. Up until that time Guam had been *ruled* by the United States Navy since 1898 (except for the 31-month Japanese occupation), and by the government of Spain since 1565. At one time, before the Spanish ruled Guam, these natives of Guam, people called Chamorro, had been a somewhat isolated and totally independent society and culture, different from any other in what is now called Oceania, or the Pacific Ocean Region. But, since the permanent arrival of the Spanish, the Chamorros have been a captive society, ruled by outsiders who subjugated and governed them as they saw fit. Spain ruled these islands of the Marianas for just over three-hundred years. The Americans followed the Spanish in 1898, and then the Japanese captured the island from the United States in December 1941, and brutally ruled by barbaric military force until the return of the Americans in 1944. All of them, Spain, America, Japan, and America again, *RULED* Guam, and the Chamorros of Guam, by military and naval force, until 1950.

However, it should be noted, that when the American military and naval forces liberated Guam, it ended forever a particular lifestyle of the Chamorro of Guam, and began a lifestyle that continues to evolve today. Of course, the Organic Act propelled that lifestyle forward.

> *The Guam Organic Act of 1950, (48 U.S.C. § 1421 et seq.) is a United States federal law that predesignated the island of Guam as an unincorporated territory of the United States, established executive, legislative, and judicial branches, and transferred federal jurisdiction from the United States Navy to the Department of the Interior. For the first time in almost four hundred years of foreign colonization, the people of Guam had some measure of self-governance, however limited.*
>
> Guam Organic Act, Wikipedia

Other than granting limited citizenship to the people of Guam and allowing for a form of self-government, the people of Guam do not have the same rights as the people of the fifty States of the United States and the District of Columbia. They have the same obligations, duties, responsibilities, and requirements but not the same benefits or rights. They are pretty much in the same position as the thirteen original British Colonies of North America as 1775 approached. One exception is that U.S. troops are not quartered in private homes, but when military exercises are held, drawing Air Force personnel, soldiers, sailors and Marines from throughout the Pacific and CONUS, they do fill up the hotel rooms.

Where we stayed in the Oceanview Hotel, over half the rooms were occupied by military personnel. It begs the question—why is it that although a third of the island is occupied by the military, yet hotel rooms that would normally be used for tourists (or authors) must be rented to military personnel? What happened to barracks, bachelor officer and bachelor non-commissioned officers quarters on military installations? We viewed dozens of empty barracks and houses on the naval communications base, empty. Perhaps even dilapidated, but why not fix 'em up?

In my Marine Corps days, we often lived in tents (like Operation Strongback in 1958 Philippines) never dreaming that one day someone would rent expensive civilian hotel rooms for a military exercise), perhaps that's what they call *progress*. Very expensive progress.

Another interesting revelation discovered while researching was the intent (actually, the action) of the Gerald Ford Administration to grant Guam Commonwealth status. It is an interesting fact that tends to reveal fiefdoms within Presidential Administrations. And those fiefdoms tended to ignore even Presidential directives, in order to keep Guam subjected to Department of Defense and/or Department of the Interior control, rather than sharing equal control with the citizens and government of Guam. **This is scary stuff!**

> *A United States federal inter-agency task force carried out a study in 1973-74 to look at Guam's political status at the same time the US was negotiating commonwealth status with the Northern Mariana Islands. Known as the "Guam Study," in 1975 the task force recommended that Guam become a US Commonwealth as well. Their recommendations, however, were shelved without the people of Guam knowing about it until 30 years later.*
>
> *Secretary of State Henry Kissinger sent the report to President Gerald Ford. After Ford had reviewed it, Kissinger, in a memo with the report, said that the President agreed with the recommendations and instructed an Under Secretaries Committee to:*
>
> *". . . seek agreement with Guamanian representatives on a commonwealth arrangement no less favorable than that which we are negotiating with the Northern Marianas. If, however, Guamanian representatives prefer a modified unincorporated territorial status, we will be willing to accept such an arrangement."*
>
> The Secret Guam Study

You will find some in the U.S. government who will say that the Guamanians rejected the commonwealth status. As I talked with

many people on Guam, the situation seemed to be that the people of Guam did not want commonwealth status *with* the Northern Marianas, but as a *separate* commonwealth with only Guam. People in the U.S. government should have remembered the occupation years and the deep resentment many Guam Chamorros have for the way they were treated by the Northern Marianas Chamorro. Time may heal this rift. But, in 1974, thirty years after liberation, it had not healed. American policy makers tend not to be great historians. They should have known.

Kissinger's memorandum instructed the Under Secretaries Committee to implement the policies set forth in order to give effect to these objectives:

* *Retain US sovereignty over Guam, and, in particular, to maintain US control over Guam's foreign affairs and defense and preserve US military basing rights to Guam.*
* *Enable Guam to move toward complete self-government in internal affairs under a self-drafted constitution consistent with the US Constitution in order to enhance prospects for Guam's continued close relationship with the federal government, and for long-term stability of the island.*
* *Help promote the material well-being of Guamanians in order to maintain stability on Guam.*
* *Enhance the prospects for the ultimate integration of Guam with the Northern Marianas if this accorded with the desires of the majority of Guamanians.*

  [Guamanians still were blistering over the so-called Northern Chamorro collaboration with the Japanese in the subjugation of Guam Chamorros during WW II, therefore they rejected this.]

The directive specified:

". . . the Assistant Secretary of Interior for Program Developments and Budget should develop and implement a negotiating approach that will

> *give effect to the above instructions, and should organize a US negotiating team that will include representation from the Departments of State and Defense as well as the Department of Interior."*
>
> *The directive also ordered that Congress be kept informed of significant developments in the negotiations with Guamanian representatives.*

This federal study and its outcome are the subject of a book titled *The Secret Guam Study* by Howard P. Willens and Dirk A. Ballendorf, printed by the Richard Flores Taitano Micronesian Area Research Center, University of Guam, and the Northern Mariana Islands Division of Historic Preservation, Saipan in 2004.

The memorandum by Kissinger and all the supporting documents are included in the book *The Secret Guam Study* as appendices.

The book is basically about how President Ford's 1975 approval of commonwealth status for Guam was blocked by federal officials in his own administration.

After Ballendorf filed a FOIA (Freedom of Information Act) request for the documents related to the Guam Study, he waited almost three years with no reply, other than acknowledgement of the receipt of his request, before filing a lawsuit.

In 1973, the Department of Defense was concerned with growing resentment of citizens of Guam as to their status as second-class citizens. A 1973 Nixon Administration interagency group meeting of 17 December, held the Department of Defense partially responsible for the misunderstandings between the military and civilians on Guam.

I can certainly understand that.

The Guam Study was sent to President Ford in August 1974, as a twenty-nine page executive summary, a 196-page full report, and thirteen annexes. In summary it says:

> *This is a study of US National objectives, policies, and programs to identify prospective courses of actions by which US interest in Guam*

may be most effectively fostered. The core of the problem will be finding means to assist Guam in planning and achieving the goals and aspirations of a local community while at the same time enabling the United States to maintain its relationships in the area and appropriate military posture on Guam.

This report was marked "URGENT!"

It was never implemented and never revealed to any citizen or government entity of Guam until the report was obtained by Dr. Ballendorf in 2003. For thirty years, the government of the United States kept secret from all on Guam, that they had been offered commonwealth status by an American President, and that is a tragedy.

As one can see, many aspects of the future of Guam and its citizens are out of the control of the government and the people of Guam. Apparently, the Department of the Interior, for reasons that can only be guessed, simply failed to move forward on a Presidential directive. It apparently hid the documents from any eyes, until a lawsuit from a big man (Dirk Anthony Ballendorf) on a small island (Guam) was filed. What are the reasons for this? What is it that Administration bureaucrats were or are hiding?

Dirk Ballendorf spent the better part of his life in Micronesia and the Marianas. He contributed much enlightenment into the "forgotten society of the Pacific Americans," and I have used much of his pioneering contributions to broadcast this information to the audience of this book.

Another interesting development: Several years ago, Washington bureaucrats developed a plan to relocate all or most all of the Marines then on Okinawa and their dependents, plus the usual strap-hangers referred to as Department of Defense civilians, to Guam. It was a half-baked, idiotic, short-sighted plan concocted without logic or merit.

First, it would have increased the population of Guam almost 25 percent overnight. Perhaps that Georgia congressman was right. Maybe it would have *tipped-over.* Second, other than on the islands of Tinian and Saipan in the Northern Marianas, there are not sufficient maneuver-style training grounds on Guam for most of the Marine-style field exercises required to maintain combat readiness. Combined arms exercises of naval gunfire, artillery barrages, tank firing, night flares, helicopter and Osprey flights, and the general shake, rattle, and roll of maneuvering Marines would drive the tourists and their dollars away. And it would add to the shaking of the earth already caused by numerous small earthquake tremors. Third, the already crowded road system and other critical infrastructures on Guam would have been overwhelmed. Fourth, if all Marine aviation assets on Okinawa were relocated to Guam, it would put tremendous distances between Marine Corps aviation assets at the Marine Air Base in Iwakuni, Japan and the relocated Marine aviation assets on Guam. And, in the same vein, it would increase the distance to redeploy to hot spots such as the Korean peninsula.

Fortunately, rethinking the situation has caused a somewhat less ambitious plan to emerge. Today, as this novel is being written, a plan has surfaced to redeploy roughly 8,000 Marines, around 1,800 dependents, and nearly 800 DOD civilians from Okinawa to Guam, Hawaii, and Australia, but the Marines would rotate onto and off of a float force, between various locations in the Western Pacific region. These Marines would come from Okinawa, various Marine Corps Air Stations, Camp Pendleton, and/or Camp Lejeune. Only 5,000 would actually be stationed on Guam. Overall, it's not a bad concept of returning the Marine Corps/Navy striking power to a lethal maritime naval force, capable of projecting its power wherever needed. But still, little Guam would assume an additional role as a much more expanded forward edge of defense for the United States. At least today, the Department of Defense and other U.S. government agencies *talk* to the government of Guam, but they still *do* what they want to do. Regardless!

If Guam were a commonwealth, things would be, or should be, different.

However, there is a 2011 Programmatic Agreement dealing with land and cultural sites on Guam that has been signed by DOD (military), Northern Marianas, and Guam officials and may mitigate future problems between the military and local citizens, if Congress doesn't intervene to change things. There is no signature of a congressional representative on the document. As such, Congress has not approved the document. Congress has the final authority.

How Guam will move, or be moved into the twenty-first century is one of the great mysteries and a great ongoing debate on Guam. That same debate should be on-going in the United States Congress, but it isn't. No one really cares. Guamanian citizens are confused. On Guam, there are those who wish to maintain the status quo as an unincorporated territory of the United States, while others would prefer to become an incorporated territory of the United States, leading toward commonwealth status—and perhaps eventual statehood. Some prefer statehood, not just for Guam but all of Micronesia and the Marianas, and there are a few who would prefer total independence for Guam. The last plebiscite held on Guam seemed to prefer commonwealth status.

The following few paragraphs were found on the Internet under the Free Dictionary: the free encyclopedia.com/Unincorporated, and is reproduced to clarify the point:

The United States holds three territories: American Samoa and Guam in the Pacific Ocean and the U.S. Virgin Islands in the Caribbean Sea. Although they are governed by the United States, the territories do not have statehood status, and this lesser legal and political status sets them apart from the rest of the United States.

The three U.S. territories are not the only U.S. government land holdings without statehood status. These various lands fall under the broad description of insular political communities affiliated with the United States. Puerto Rico in the Caribbean and the Northern Mariana Islands in the Pacific Ocean belong to the United States and have the status of commonwealth, a legal and political status that is above a territory but still below a state.

The United States also has a number of islands in the Pacific Ocean that are called variously territories and possessions. U.S. possessions have the lowest legal and political status because these islands do not have permanent populations and do not seek self-determination and autonomy. U.S. possessions include Baker, Howland, Kingman Reef, Jarvis, Johnston, Midway, Palmyra, and Wake Islands.

Finally, land used as a military base is considered a form of territory. These areas are inhabited almost exclusively by military personnel. They are governed largely by military laws and not by the political structures in place for commonwealths and territories. The United States has military bases at various locations around the world, including Okinawa, Japan, and Guantanamo Bay, Cuba.

A precise definition of territories and territorial law in the United States is difficult to fashion. The U.S. government has long been in the habit of determining policy as it goes along. The United States was established through a defensive effort against British forces and then through alternately defensive and offensive battles against Native Americans. From this chaotic beginning, the United States has struggled to fashion a coherent policy on the acquisition and possession of land.

The U.S. Constitution does not state exactly how the United States may acquire land. Instead, the Constitution essentially delegates the power to decide the matter to Congress. Article IV, Section 3, Clause 1, of the Constitution provides that "New States may be admitted by the Congress into this Union; but no new State shall be formed … by the Junction of two or more States, or Parts of States, without the Consent of the Legislatures of the States concerned as well as of the Congress." The same section of the Constitution gives Congress the "Power to dispose of and make all needful Rules and Regulations respecting the Territory or other Property belonging to the United States." Under International Law the United States and other nation-states may acquire additional territory in several ways, including occupation of territory that is not already a part of a state; conquest, where allowed by the international community; cession of land by another nation in a treaty; and accretion, or the growth of new land within a nation's existing boundaries.

Through various statutes and court opinions, Congress and the U.S. Supreme Court have devised a system that gives Congress and the president control over U.S. territories. Congress delegates some of its policy-making and administrative duties to the Office of Insular Affairs within the Interior Department. The president of the United

States appoints judges and executive officers to offices in the territories. Congress devises court systems for the territories, and the Supreme Court may review decisions made by territorial courts.[Guam has two court systems, the federal courts and the Guam Territorial Courts, just like Alabama has the federal courts and the Alabama state courts.]

Congress may pass laws governing a territory with due deference to the customs and sensibilities of the native people. [Here it is described how Guam is supposed to be treated; however, how Guam is actually treated is markedly different.] *Congress may not pass territorial laws that violate a fundamental constitutional right. Such rights have not been defined concretely by the Supreme Court in the context of territorial law, but they can include the right to be free from unreasonable searches and seizures, the right to Freedom of Speech, and the rights to Equal Protection and due process (Torres v. Commonwealth of Puerto Rico, 442 U.S. 465, 99 S. Ct. 2425, 61 L. Ed. 2d 1 [1979]).*

The above is a noble, civilized statement. But again, such is not, and has not always been practiced by the government of the United States in dealing with the people of Guam.

Persons living in U.S. territories do not have the right to vote for members of Congress. They may elect their own legislature, but the laws passed by the territorial legislature may be nullified by Congress. Each territory may elect a delegate who attends congressional sessions, hearings, and conferences in Washington, D.C. These delegates may propose legislation and vote on legislation in committees, but they may not participate in final votes.

Restated, the people of Guam are not governed by legislation voted on by a people's representative.

U.S. territories have less political power than do U.S. commonwealths. Commonwealths are afforded a higher degree of internal political autonomy than are territories. Congress and the commonwealth work together to fashion a political system that is acceptable to both parties. By contrast, Congress tends to impose its will on territories. Commonwealth status once inevitably led to statehood, but such a progression is no longer automatic.

In November 1997, a report was submitted by the United States General Accounting Office to the chairman of the Committee on Resources in the House of Representatives. It was titled U.S. Insular Areas, Application of the U.S. Constitution. Excerpts are as follows:

Guam: Proposed legislation to grant commonwealth status to Guam, first introduced in the 100th Congress by former delegate Ben Blaz in 1988, was introduced in each subsequent Congress, but no formal action, beyond referral to committee, was taken on any of the bills. Delegate Underwood again has introduced in the 105th Congress the bill to grant Guam commonwealth status. Upon approval by the Congress, the act would be submitted to the registered voters of Guam for ratification. The United States would agree that no provision of the act would be modified, nor any subsequently passed federal law, rule, or regulation made applicable to Guam, except with the mutual consent of Guam and the United States.

The proposed legislation sets forth requirements for a constitution to be drafted and adopted by Guam, including a provision permitting the Chamorro people — the indigenous people of Guam — to exercise the right of self-determination. The bill would permit the President to delegate to the Governor of Guam the total or partial performance of functions currently handled by federal agencies. The bill would require the United States to consult with Guam on specific foreign relations and defense matters affecting Guam. In addition, the United States would assist Guam in becoming a member of or participate in regional and international organizations, and would permit Guam to enter into reciprocal trade and tax agreements with other countries. Under the bill,

Guam would remain outside the customs territory of the United States and would continue to have duty-free access to U.S. markets. Also, the bill would grant Guam, subject to coordination with federal agencies, control over immigration and, generally, would authorize it to enact and enforce all laws regulating or affecting local employment. In addition, the bill would create a commission to study and propose modification to existing federal statutes and regulations applicable to Guam.

This report, like others dealing with the legal status of Guam and its people, sits gathering dust on some shelf, in some basement archives storage facility, somewhere! Congress should get off its assets and start discussing this bill. It has lingered too long in history's dustbin.

To those who wish for Guam to be independent, consider it very cautiously and carefully; independence without the political and military protection of the United States would be setting up a situation where Guam would become more than a gleam in the eye of China and Russia. And, perhaps even the Philippines. Those who advocate for total independence for Guam should start taking language courses in Chinese and/or Russian to prepare for their dream to come true. If the United States Congress doesn't oppose it, those who choose to remain on Guam will need to master one of those languages.

But, let's be realistic, the United States is never going to give up Guam. It may continue to subjugate its people, it will continue to seize private property for military use, but it's not going to give up the territory. It might not even grant it commonwealth status. Congress and the American people choose instead to ignore the **people of Guam**. They either do not know of the tremendous sacrifice these people made for this United States during the Second World War, nor are they aware of the faithful contributions the young men and women of Guam continue to make to the Armed Forces of the United States—or they choose to ignore it.

It is believed by some that Guam does not have adequate U.S. military and naval power for the defense of Guam, nor the Western Pacific basin. Can the United States defend Guam and its people from China's new

"Guam Missile" or from China's rapidly developing offensive naval power? Does it have the capability of defending against North Korea's emerging ballistic nuclear missiles production program? Both countries point their spears toward Guam.

> *September 8, 2014: China recently revealed (apparently by accident) the existence of the DF-26 IRBM (Intermediate Range Ballistic Missile.) This one appears to have a range of 3,500 kilometers based on the earlier DF-21. There have been reports of such a missile since 2007 and the DF-26C appears to have been in service for several years. The DF-26C is notable because it has the range to hit American military bases in the Central Pacific island of Guam.*
>
> http://www.strategypage.com/htmw/hticbm/20140908.aspx

It has been said that some Patriot Anti-Missile batteries have been located on Guam for defense against a small-size missile attack, but retaliatory capability appears to be sorely lacking. If Guam does not have the ability to retaliate against an attacker, the attacker may be emboldened to act without even the slightest hesitation. Such is the concern regarding the dwindling strength of the United States Armed Forces**. If America cannot defend its frontiers, how can it defend its mainland? Does the Roman Empire ring a bell?**

Since the early 1900s, the Army and Navy of the United States, now joined by the Air Force, recognized the strategic usefulness of the island of Guam. It is the Congress of the United States that has ignored the vast potential and importance of Guam. But, along with the military significance of the island, is the value of having its people, the civilians of Guam, supporting the military forces that occupy its island. Conversely, the military stationed on Guam must treat the civilian population of Guam as equal partners, concerned with the future of Guam *and its people*. The U.S. military and the people of Guam share a small island. Emphases on the word share.

On another note, it should also be understood that the Japanese of the 1920s through the 1940s were a militaristic, anti-western society. This is not true of the current citizens of Japan. They tend to be more westernized than their fathers and grandfathers. They visit Guam in gargantuan numbers and spend money as if it was their last day on earth. Many seem unaware of the activities of their fathers and grandfathers. That is, until they visit places such as the War in the Pacific Museum. I have observed them wandering through the museum. They seem strangely casual and indifferent, as they see the photographs and hear the audio of the atrocities committed by the "Sons of Heaven." They depart either quietly, somewhat reflective, or seemingly still indifferent to the ancient history of Guam.

This author has had bouts with indifference here on Guam, not mine, but the indifference of others who should be anything but indifferent—some of them our own military and naval leaders assigned to Guam.

As a retired Marine, an author of two books, co-author of a third, I, along with my wife, assumed the challenge of yet another writing, and publishing project: This time, an odyssey to Guam.

This new publication is not intended to be an indictment of policy makers of the American government that seems to relish illegal entry into the United States to make new citizens, while at the same time, rebuffs constitutional citizenship for the most brutalized, loyal society of Americans ever in the history of the United States—the citizens of Guam. Instead it is intended to awaken the citizens of the fifty states, the District, the commonwealths, and the territories to the injustice perpetrated by some in the American government and its population in 1941, 1945, and possibly even today. This government abandoned an entire society of Americans on the island of Guam to the Japanese military invaders and allowed that society of Americans to be beaten, starved, murdered, and isolated for thirty-one months of horror. Yet, that same society maintained a strong loyalty to the America that had abandoned them. That is a fact, and America has never repented—nor have the Guamanians forgotten.

During this writing project about the Chamorros of the Second World War, I remind the reader, the senior military commander on Guam refused several requests to meet with her. She rebuffed me—totally. This Admiral apparently wanted no part of any discussion regarding the citizens of Guam, past and present. The reason still eludes me. Who knows! All this retired Marine and author can say about the situation is that—never, after numerous respectful requests for a brief conversation—have I been dismissed so peremptorily in my military career, active and retired. Marine and Army generals (and Air Force Lt Col's) have been much more receptive to my literary requests.

However, I must admit that the admiral's public affairs officer did offer for me to submit questions to him. He would present them to the admiral, and respond to me. I did reject the offer.

With that said, there is another interesting area that periodically came up for discussion. We have often been asked, "Who is financing your writing project?" The answer is my wife and me. We have expended thousands of dollars from our personal savings and devoted months of time to travel to Guam to conduct research, and interviews, exploring facts and opinions about a tragic time in American history. Some have asked, "Why?" Our response—why not? If not us—then who?

During the rule of Navy governors, the Navy did not always consider the feelings or desires of the population of Guam as it exercised its authority to make rules for everyone on Guam, military and civilian. After the enactment of the Organic Act, the military and naval forces simply withdrew behind their numerous fences; they had a tendency to ignore the civil population of Guam while maintaining its military force in readiness. They developed a siege mentality. Based on our time on Guam, it still appears to be the clandestine intent of the military and naval command located on Guam, to continue to look at the people of Guam through *their* fences.

Throughout the first half of the 20th century, the Navy that controlled Guam, through its appointed naval governors, flip-flopped on how the native population was treated. Even today, military commanders in senior positions on Guam, or in control of military and naval forces on Guam, seem to vary in their deportment toward the civil population and civil matters. Thus, the foundation remains for an attitude toward Guam and the Guamanians emanating from that siege position.

After the United States wrestled Guam from the Japanese in 1944, and onward through the 1940s, the military and naval forces on Guam took what land it wanted; they cut roads where they were required, leveled communities or villages as necessary for military cantonments and facilities, and in general did as they saw fit without regard to the civil population. Interestingly, the civil population understood that while there was a war ongoing—these actions were necessary for final victory.

But, after the surrender of Japan, there should have been more interest in locating property belonging to locals and compensating them in some degree, for their seized property. There should have been a more comprehensive investigation of the activities of the local population during the occupation. The heroic deeds of certain members of the Chamorro, and part-Chamorro, population would have astounded the average investigator, had they explored it further. But, they apparently didn't. The United States should have bestowed appropriate recognition on those who risked everything in their overt demonstration of loyalty to the United States. The Sgambelluris, Limtiacos, Tanakas, Flores, Arteros, Butlers, Pangelinans, Reyes, Johnstons, and others lives were always in great danger. Some escaped undetected; some were caught and severely punished, and some were murdered. Unfortunately, they wore no uniform and sometimes had no witnesses. They often acted alone, and each held to a firm belief that America would return to their island to liberate them. That is why, for Guam, the 21st of July, not the 4th of July, is their Independence (Liberation) Day. They also celebrate 4 July.

When America returned to lift the yoke of oppression, the people of Guam celebrated and supported any and all activities of the U.S. military on Guam. **But, as time went by, and the war ended, the people of Guam felt there was insufficient recognition for the contributions of its people. They had delivered in blood, sweat, and tears for the United States during the Japanese occupation, and after, as they supported the American liberating forces; therafter the United States *rewarded* them by giving them exactly what they had given the Virgin Islanders and Puerto Ricans decades' earlier—limited citizenship, by passing the Organic Act of 1950. Guamanians, like Puerto Ricans and Virgin Islanders, became hapa-citizens of the United States. Their wartime sacrifices virtually ignored..**

One of the other previously unincorporated territories of the United States, the island of Puerto Rico (now a commonwealth), has an interesting citizenship status. Certain citizens of Puerto Rico may also be citizens of Spain, and The European Union, as well as the United States, all at the same time:

> *Puerto Ricans are natural-born citizens of the United States. The current population is about 3.6 million people. The territory operates under a local constitution, and its citizens elect a governor. Puerto Rico lacks voting in the U.S. House of Representatives and the U.S. Senate, both of whom have plenary jurisdiction over it under the Puerto Rico Federal Relations Act of 1950. A 2012 referendum showed a majority (54% of the electorate) disagreed with "the present form of territorial status," with full statehood as the preferred option among those who voted for a change of status. Following this vote, the Legislative Assembly of Puerto Rico enacted a concurrent resolution to request the President and the Congress of the United States to end the current status and to begin the process to admit Puerto Rico to the Union as a State. As of 2015, Puerto Rico remains an unincorporated U.S. territory.*
>
> *In legal terms, Puerto Ricans that acquire the Spanish citizenship with the use of the certificate* [of Puerto Rican citizenship] *would possess four citizenships recognized in Europe: those of Puerto Rico, the United States, Spain and the European Union (automatically granted along that of Spain). On September 23, 2013, Representative Manuel Natal Albelo presented a bill that would render official the international recognition of the Puerto Rican citizenship through the Secretary of State, pursuing more rights within the international community.*
>
> Puerto Rico - Wikipedia

Another unincorporated territory of the United States is the U.S. Virgin Islands. Similar to Puerto Rico and Guam, the population has limited rights as U.S. citizens:

> *The U.S. Virgin Islands are an organized, unincorporated United States Territory. Even though they are U.S. citizens, the U.S. Virgin Islanders, like Guam and Puerto Rico residents, cannot vote in*

presidential elections. U.S. Virgin Islands residents are able to vote in presidential primary elections for delegates to the Democratic National Convention and the Republican National Convention. Unlike persons born on the mainland and naturalized citizens who derive their citizenship from the Fourteenth Amendment of the U.S. constitution, those born in the U.S. Virgin Islands derive their U.S. citizenship from Congressional statute.

At the national level, the U.S. Virgin Islands elect a delegate to Congress from their at-large congressional district. The elected delegate, while able to vote in committee, cannot participate in floor votes.

At the territorial level, 15 senators – seven from the district of Saint Croix, seven from the district of Saint Thomas and Saint John, and one senator at-large who must be a resident of Saint John – are elected for two-year terms to the unicameral Virgin Islands Legislature.

The U.S. Virgin Islands have elected a territorial governor every four years since 1970. Previous governors were appointed by the President of the United States.

Wikipedia, USVI

One of the great concerns on Guam, and in other U.S. Territories, is that one day, for some compelling reason, the Congress of the United States may change the citizenship status of the citizens of these Territories. Indeed that could be forthcoming, as evidenced by the reproduced document following:

Obama: Citizenship not a fundamental right for Virgin Islanders
By ALDETH LEWIN (Daily News Staff)
Published: August 18, 2014:

ST. THOMAS - In a legal brief filed last week, the Obama administration took the position that citizenship is not a fundamental right of people born in unincorporated U.S. territories.

The federal government maintains that Congress has the legislative discretion to grant privileges to those born in the territories as they see fit.

The brief was filed in response to a lawsuit about citizenship rights for unincorporated territories that is pending before a federal appeals court.

The lawsuit is Tuaua v. United States, and it is about American Samoa's citizenship rights. While the situation in American Samoa is different than in the U.S. Virgin Islands, the outcome of the litigation could impact citizenship rights for Virgin Islands residents as well.

The United States took ownership of the Virgin Islands in 1917, and citizenship was granted through an act of Congress in 1927. Congress has not made the same decision for American Samoa and residents born there are considered "non-citizen nationals."

Neil Weare, lead counsel on the lawsuit, is president of "We the People Project," an organization that works to achieve equal rights for residents of U.S. territories and the District of Columbia.

The federal government's response to the Tuaua lawsuit says the law clearly states that citizenship for outlying possessions of the United States gives people born to non-U.S. citizen parents the classification of nationals, but not citizens. Changing that status is up to Congress,

U.S. Attorney Ronald Machen Jr. said,

"The responsibility of Congress to govern this nation's territories has long been recognized and respected by the Courts."

The federal government references a Virgin Islands case in making its defense.

"In fact, the Third Circuit held in Ballentine v. United States, 486 F.3d 806, 813-14 [3rd Circuit 2007], that Congress was within its authority to determine that the U.S. Virgin Islands was unincorporated and therefore a person born there was not automatically a citizen who could vote in U.S. presidential elections," Machen said.

St. Thomas resident Krim Ballentine has filed multiple cases over the years about citizenship issues, challenging Congress' ability to confer citizenship on people born in the Virgin Islands. In 2007, a federal judge found that Ballentine, a U.S. citizen born in Missouri, lacked standing to bring that particular issue forward.

Weare said the Obama administration's arguments create two classes of American nationals - those with the protections of citizenship and those without.

"It's hard to believe that in the 21st century the Obama Administration is defending two separate classes of Americans," Weare said in a written statement.

In the Virgin Islands, people born in the territory are full U.S. citizens. While living in the Virgin Islands, residents have limited rights, such as not being able to vote for the president and not having a voting representative in Congress. However, when a Virgin Islander moves to one of the 50 states, all those rights are immediately restored.

Rather than citizenship for the territories being a constitutional right, a century-old legal precedent called the Insular Cases makes citizenship legislated by Congress.

The concern is that Congress has the power to turn citizenship for territorial residents on and off. However, if Congress did take away citizenship rights for those born in the U.S. Virgin Islands, it would not affect those already granted citizenship. It could only affect those born after such a decision might be made, according to legal precedent.

If the Tuaua case is won, Virgin Islanders could have a constitutional right to citizenship that cannot be given or taken away by Congress.

If the case is lost, nothing would change for Virgin Islanders.

The lawsuit currently is pending before the Washington, D.C., Circuit Court, a federal appeals court.

It previously was dismissed by a judge in the District Court. Weare expects arguments in the case to be heard later this year.

In May, V.I. Delegate to Congress Donna Christensen, former Gov. Charles Turnbull and other leaders from other U.S. territories filed an amicus brief supporting the Tuaua case.

The men and women of Guam live day-to-day as the forward edge of America's defense posture, yet they are the trailing edge of our nation's commitment to full freedom as American citizens. To America today, **Guam is vital—but, its citizens seemingly are not.**

The status of Guam and other U.S. territories was established by a series of Supreme Court decisions referred to as Insular Decisions—over 110 years ago. The Wright brothers had not flown from Kill Devil Hill in North Carolina, the Titanic had not hit the iceberg, television was not broadcasting, and Al Gore had not invented the Internet. Times have changed.

When these insular cases were heard and ruled on by the Supreme Court in the early 1900s, the Supreme Court was reflecting the social norms of the times. As an example, Yale professor Simon Baldwin, at the time of expansion stated—"*[It would be unwise] to give . . . . the ignorant and lawless brigands that infest Puerto Rico... the benefit[s] of [the Constitution].*" This gives us a good idea of the state of mind of the significant majority of American society at that time. Again, times have changed. We need to look at the status of the citizens of our territories—with a more modern, comprehensive, and enlightened view.

It is the Congress of the United States that needs to act by enacting legislation to expand the doctrine that the Constitution of the United States applies to all American citizens, to include the American territories. After all, this is interesting, if that citizen of Guam moves to any state, they are made whole, with full constitutional rights. Then, if they move back to Guam, they lose them, again.

As a U.S. territory, Guam is unique. It is the only densely populated American land invaded, captured, and occupied by a foreign power since the War of 1812. Its population suffered through thirty-one months of brutal repression and acts of barbarism while maintaining a clandestine—yet overt loyalty to the United States. Many paid for that loyalty with their lives. That historical fact has not been lost on post-war and future men and women of Guam, as they enlisted and continue to enlist in the United States military in greater per capita numbers and die in greater per capita numbers than any other slice of the American population. There is no greater love, no greater devotion to America and American ideals than is found on this small island.

Yet, while their rights are limited, their obligations are not. Let me repeat—*to America, Guam is vital, but its citizens are not.* And, another repeat, in the early 1900s, the Supreme Court was reflecting *the social norms of the times.*

At the turn of the 20th century, normal "group think" and conversations regarding issues of race and citizenship were very different from those issues of race and citizenship today:

> *Imperialism presented a difficult constitutional problem. Until the 1890s, the acquisition of new US territory was always considered "preliminary to its organization as new states, to be admitted to the Union on the basis of "co-ordinate equality'." Now, for the first time in American history, "sizeable populations [were] being taken under our flag with no wide anticipation that they would ever be accepted into statehood." Imperialists responded to such considerations by insisting that the federal government had a long-established right "to acquire new territory - by purchase, treaty, or war," and that such "colonies might be governed as Congress saw fit without assuming either future statehood or full application of all constitutional rights to the native." In short, the Constitution need not follow the flag.*
>
> *It wasn't until sometime later that the Supreme Court decided the Constitutional issue implicit in imperialism. In the "Insular Cases," the Court upheld the legality of what had taken place. It created a doctrine of "incorporation," which stipulated that the United States first had to "incorporate" the territory in question in order for the Constitution to be applicable. The Court found, though, that none of the newly acquired territories had satisfied this doctrine, and decided that the*

Constitution does not follow the flag. The people of the newly acquired territories are not automatically entitled to the same guarantees of the Constitution as US citizens. The Court's rulings confirmed what many had suspected: that the US government never intended to consider any of the colonial acquisitions for eventual statehood.

Reflecting an intense national discussion on the question of American imperialism, the debate in the US Senate over ratification of the peace treaty with Spain was likewise heated. On February 6, 1899, it barely approved the treaty by a vote of 57-27, just slightly more than the two-thirds majority needed for ratification.

To the astonishment of his colleagues, and to the gratification of his imperialist foes, William Jennings Bryan–the Democratic party's 1896 presidential candidate, and an acknowledged "pillar" of the Anti-Imperialist League -- decided at the last minute to renounce principle and support the treaty. His betrayal was based on what turned out to be a gross political miscalculation. He reckoned that if the treaty were ratified, imperialism would be a potent issue in the forthcoming election campaign, which he could then exploit to his advantage. He therefore used his considerable prestige to ensure ratification, a move that, by all accounts, was decisive in this close vote.

But the "Great Commoner" had reckoned wrongly, and went down to defeat once again in the presidential election of 1900. Benefiting from a revived economy, and taking credit for the impressive imperialist spoils of the recent war against Spain, McKinley coasted to a relatively easy reelection victory. While historical "what ifs" are by nature speculative, it is intriguing to imagine the course that American policy -- and world history -- might have taken if Bryan had let conscience, and not expediency, be his guide in February 1899. At any rate, the story of America's great transition from an inner-directed republic to an imperial power provides timely lessons for Americans today.

The Fateful Year 1898: The United States Becomes...
(www.ihr.org/jhr/v13/v13n4p4_Ries.html)

America was different in the 1890s than it is today. We need to repeal, rethink, and revise this nonsense of half-citizen status to make the Constitution of the United States apply fully to all Americans.

One of the irritating decisions of courts and Congress affecting the people of Guam is the inability to vote for President and Vice President of the United States. That same situation affected the citizen-residents of the District of Columbia, also not a state. So it was *fixed*:

For Guam:

> *The Attorney General of Guam argued that American citizens residing in Guam had a right to participate in presidential elections. The Court of Appeals for the Ninth Circuit disagreed, stating that the Constitution "does not grant to American citizens the right to elect the President. . . . Since Guam is not a state, it can have no electors, and plaintiffs cannot exercise individual votes in a presidential election. There is no constitutional violation." Attorney Gen. of Guam v. United States.*

For Washington, D.C.:

> *Amendment XXIII of the Constitution provides that the District of Columbia shall appoint electors who "shall be considered, for the purposes of the election of President and Vice President, to be electors appointed by a State . . . .*

So, it was *fixed* to allow the citizens of one non-state, the Washington, D.C. area, to vote for President, but for the citizens of Guam, it was not *fixed*.

It is almost unbelievable that in the 21st century, we continue to have two different types of citizenship in and of the United States, and that these types of citizenship were initially established in the 19th century.

Another restrictive measure that affects Guam adversely is the Jones Act, which makes goods more expensive and less available to the residents of states and territories outside the Continental Limits of the United States or CONUS. It has a big impact on far-away Guam.

> *The Jones Act, also called—The* ***Merchant Marine Act of 1920—*** *has a specific effect upon noncontiguous parts of the US, such as Puerto Rico, Hawaii, Alaska, and Guam as it prevents foreign-flagged ships from carrying cargo between the mainland and these locations. Foreign ships inbound with goods cannot stop at any of these four locations, offload goods, load mainland-bound goods, and continue to US mainland ports. Instead, they must proceed directly to US mainland ports, where distributors break bulk and then send goods to US places off the mainland by US-flagged ships.*
>
> Wikipedia, The Jones Act

This Act prohibits ships from delivering goods into the port of Guam directly from the country of origin unless it happens to be the United States. Pineapples grown and harvested in the Philippines, must be sent to a U.S. mainland port and then delivered to Guam by a U.S. flagged vessel, crewed by U.S. merchant seamen. This 1920s law has outlived *its union protective umbrella* and should be repealed.

And, this needs repeating lest we forget—the people of Guam were abandoned and left to suffer greatly during the Japanese occupation—for just being Americans. America owes a debt to those men and women of Guam. It has not yet been paid, by anyone, Japan or the United States.

In 2020, it will have been one hundred years since the Jones Act was passed. It has served its purpose. Enough, already!

Another abuse of the people of Guan that occurred during World War II was the use of young Chamorro females as "comfort women" (sex slaves) by the Japanese. Yes, their numbers were small, compared to the Korean women used for the same purpose; but Japan has apologized to the Koreans:

> *Japan has apologized to South Korea and will pay about $8.3 million as compensation for its use of Korean "comfort women" who were forced to work in Japanese brothels during World War II.*
>
> *The deal—which was announced after a meeting in Seoul on Monday between Fumio Kishida, the Japanese foreign minister, and*

Yun Byung-se, his South Korean counterpart—could go a long way toward improving relations between the two countries that have been strained for decades over Japan's wartime occupation of the Korean Peninsula. After the meeting, and a formal apology from Kishida, Japanese Prime Minister Shinzo Abe telephoned Park Geun-hye, the South Korean president, to repeat the apology.

"Japan and South Korea are now entering a new era," Abe said later. "We should not drag this problem into the next generation."

It's unclear how many women served as sex slaves for the Japanese during the war, but estimates range from 20,000 to 200,000. What is clear, however, is that many of the women are now very old.

Park, the South Korean president, said Monday that nine had died this year alone. Forty-six are still alive in South Korea.

"I hope the mental pains of the elderly comfort women will be eased," she said after the agreement was announced.

http://www.theatlantic.com/international/archive/2015/12/**japan**-korea-**comfort**- **women**/422016/

There has been no compensation nor apology made to or for any Chamorro, past or present for the abuse of young Chamorro females of World War II. Apparently the Japanese government and the United States government prefer to "*drag this problem into the next generation.*"

There have been other abuses of land and people that remains elusive for compensation. Guam and its people have been mistreated in many ways beyond being abandoned and subjected to the abuses and atrocities of the Japanese, and the outright taking of private property for military use during and after World War II. Additionally, the American government has used Guam as its trash dump for everything from batteries and tires to radioactive particles washed from ships that had returned from nuclear test explosions at various U.S. islands in the Pacific. Cocos Island, off the southern coast of Guam, was the site of the wash-downs, cleaning, and decontaminating of the vessels to remove any nuclear contaminants clinging to the ships after they returned from atomic test sites. The radioactive waste was washed right into the ocean around that small coral-ringed island.

Read *Bequerels on the Brain* by Mark Purdey for more detailed information.

There's more! PCB contaminants, apparently from a former naval LORAN communications facility, have been distributed by various means in and around the same area of Cocos Island and are now being studied for its effects. See *Studying Contaminants in Cocos Lagoon, Guam*: Blog Post #1, posted on May 19th, 2015 in Chemical Contaminants, Coastal Pollution. Also see_Hawaii Medical Journal Nov. 2011, Suppl 2, titled Cancer Mortality Following Polychlorinated Biphenyl (PCB) Contamination of a Guam Village.

So, Guam sits at a crossroads, again. Modern travel and communications capabilities have shrunk time and space significantly. The world has changed. The people of Guam watch *Fox and Friends, CNN, and/or ABC News* late in the evening, not in the morning, but in real time. Hawaii is only a little over six-hours flying time away from Guam. Guam has five-star hotels, high-end shopping arcades, and gourmet dining establishments. It flies the flag of the United States, has the U.S. Postal Service, and offers graduate degree programs at the University of Guam. Guam has a National Guard unit that has deployed and fought for the United States in its most recent wars. **Guam is as much a part of America as Alabama and New York—with one big exception—the way the people of Guam are treated by the government of the United States. And they get away with it.**

Guam has joined the modern world. It is time for the United States to join Guam.

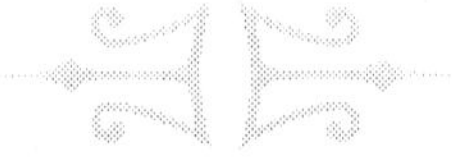

GUAM—THE FUTURE?

Electronic Warfare Overview (From FM 3-36 US Army Field Manual) *1-7:*

In any conflict, commanders attempt to dominate the electromagnetic spectrum. They do this by locating, targeting, exploiting, disrupting, degrading, deceiving, denying, or destroying the enemy's electronic systems that support military operations or deny the spectrum's use by friendly forces. The increasing portability and affordability of sophisticated electronic equipment guarantees that the electromagnetic environment in which forces operate will become even more complex. To ensure unimpeded access to and use of the electromagnetic spectrum, commande-plan, prepare, execute, and assess EW operations against a broad set of targets within the electromagnetic spectrum. The targets are electronic media, motors & generators, position/navigation/timing systems, personnel, networks, communications, ground sensors, electrical fuses, space based sensors and relays, maritime sensors, commercial communications, airborne sensors, and infrastructures—are all targets.

What follows is the substance of imagination, and a very real possibility:

It happened just at sunset. The phones went dead, computers seized, refusing to function, traffic and other outside and inside lighting systems went dark, airport and port functions came to a standstill, and most battery operated devices went silent and still. Initially, confusion reigned, and people congregated, talking in small groups, confused, concerned, attempting to use various electronic devices to communicate with someone, anyone—to no avail. As darkness began to envelop their island, panic began to enter the thoughts and actions of the bewildered population. Some automobile headlights, of older automobiles in isolated locations, lighted the immediate areas, as did old-fashioned flashlights. Both projected weak, intermittent light beams, as if the batteries were dying. At Gun Beach, the LP gas grills continued to cook food while patrons stumbled around the pavilion attempting to utilize their hand-held devices that would only function in a weak flashlight mode.

In the South, the mayor of the Piti District, "Ben" Gumataotao, had started to walk from his office as the world went dark around him. He stopped, confused. "Why did all the lights go out?" he asked aloud. Suddenly, a loud screeching, like a thousand fingernails scraping across a thousand blackboards, amplified a thousand levels, penetrated his ears causing him to clasp his hands over his ears and bend over double, falling to the ground. Totally disoriented, he screamed in pain.

Suddenly, a low hum, almost a whine, replaced the searing screech. He regained his composure while still sitting on the ground. The humming seemed to be emanating from above him. He looked up into the dark, moonless sky. At first, it appeared that the sky was falling. Large dark objects were descending all around him. He couldn't make out what or who they were. The skies appeared to be full of descending shapes as far west as he could see—All the way across to the Guam Navy Base.

"It's happening again!!" he cried in the darkness.

In the North, at the air force base, emergency reactions to the blackout and loss of all communications were underway. Most of the personnel were off-duty. On-duty crews were moving toward predetermined locations. On the duty ramps, containing ready aircraft, ground crews were attempting to start ground vehicles and equipment to no avail. Except for direct landlines, all communications were inoperative. Security police were attempting to run or walk to their predestined security positions, as their motor vehicles would not start.

Suddenly, a sharp pain permeated the ears and eye sockets of every person outside of sheltered environments, as a shrill penetrating screeching seemed to descend from somewhere above in the dark sky, enveloping everything and everyone caught in its lure. Those outside fell to the ground covering their ears with their hands, some screaming in pain as they withered around as if searching for protection from whatever evil had descended upon them. Just as sudden as the screeching had appeared, a deep humming emanated from above gradually replacing the shrill screeching that still seemed to be inside them. Out over the dual runway areas of the base, black clouds emerged from the moonless sky, dropping in black billowing shapes on the flat ground. They filled the skies.

As a man stepped out onto his balcony of the dark Oceanview Hotel in Tumon, he looked out between the Japanese Lotte Hotel and the American Westin Hotel at the darkened Tumon Bay below. He saw only blackness. He reentered the room, picked up his Night Owl Optics Tactical Night Vision Goggles, stepped back out onto the patio, flipped the battery operated device to ON, put the straps over his head, and adjusted the glasses.

Looking out into the nighttime Philippine Sea, he drew a sharp breath as he saw what appeared to be six to seven dark shapes, perhaps a thousand or so yards from the coral shoreline. He readjusted the goggles and looked again. It was submarines on the surface of the water. Figures were emerging from them and entering vehicles on the decks of the large submarines. One by one, they were actually jumping into the air and flying low across the water and coral, moving toward the hotel area of Tumon. He quickly searched the area to his front, finding the crafts landing all along the heavily populated shoreline below him. Men with guns were emerging from the crafts now occupying the San Vitores and Gun Beach Roadways in Tumon. He looked farther south to see what appeared to be hundreds of these flying contraptions going over the Sheraton Hotel and the Guam Hospital, heading toward the capital, Hagatna and the farther away Nimitz Hills. Alarmed, he reached for his cellular phone. It was dead.

U.S. Navy submarine submerging off the Guam coast in front of the Oceanview Hotel
Photo property of the author

He noticed what appeared to be large, silent, darkened aircraft moving slowly in the skies above him as he stood on the balcony. He rushed through the apartment to the rear balcony-walkway. Scanning the skies above the cliff, he could see paratroopers emerging from the aircraft over the area of the Won Pat Airport. Hundreds of black clad men under black billowing parachutes could be seen descending until they were out of sight beyond the top of the cliff.

The American island of Guam, so long ignored by the American government, was being invaded by the Chinese Navy. They struck silently, massively, and quickly—with no warning.

The Chinese opened their attack with a cyber shockwave disrupting or eliminating all computer and other digital systems, followed by a two-wave attack. Electronic warfare was the military action involving the use of the electromagnetic (EM) spectrum to include directed energy (DE) to control the EM spectrum while applying conventional military force against the military defense on Guam. This was not limited to radio or radar frequencies but included visible infrared, invisible ultraviolet, and other less frequently used portions of the EM spectrum. The proverbial kitchen sink was thrown onto Guam, including self-protection, standoff, and escort jamming, and anti-radiation attacks. Properly applied EW enhances the use of many air and space functions. Cyber and electronic attacks on Guam were followed immediately by enhanced conventional invasion forces—in overwhelming numbers.

In the far Western Pacific, Guam was vital to the defense of the United States, but the Chinese decided to attack and neutralize it by capturing it before ground forces, in the form of U.S. Marines, pending relocation from Okinawa, could be in place to defend the island. They made full use of the electromagnetic spectrum and directed energy to control the spectrum, to attack their enemy, and to impede enemy counter assaults via the spectrum. The purpose of the Chinese electronic warfare was to deny the Americans the advantage of countering the electronic spectrum. On isolated Guam, they were highly successful.

Like the Russian takeover of the Crimean area in Ukraine a few years earlier, the invasion will be opposed by angry shouts of disapproval and little else. The American President will condemn the action and voice harsh sanctions, while the Chinese gain control of the key location that controlled the Western Pacific region.

Electronic warfare (EW) was highly developed by the Chinese. It was directed from air, sea, land, and space by manned and unmanned systems, and targeted humans, communications, radar, or other assets. In this case, it worked perfectly.

Guam was captured in just a few hours on 10 December, following this elaborate electronic warfare attack disabling all but the most primitive devices and vehicles. They would take over and control military and naval installations and population centers. Each military unit had a specific target to control with a plan of minimum loss of life to the civilian population of Guam.

It was a classic and ironic repeat of December 1941.

Long standing feuds over Pacific areas of water would be settled quickly, in favor of the Chinese. The Japanese would protest to the United Nations. Philippines would remain silent. The Americans would demand a withdrawal. The Chinese would control Guam and the Western Pacific Ocean. The American president was overheard in a conversation stating, "We don't want to start a World War over a small isolated island in the far Western Pacific."

Guam and its people became a society of captives—again!!

Ben awakened from his dream in time to dress for work, and arrived early as usual at his small office. On the way, he thought of his bad dream last night, wondering if such a thing could actually happen. It was a classic and ironic repeat of December 1941. He shook it off as just a dream. A bad dream.

Later that morning, as Ben watched a portion of the news, although not knowing what the subject matter was, he overheard the American President in a conversation with a reporter saying, "We don't want to start a world war over a small isolated incident in the far western Pacific Ocean. It's not in our national interest," he stopped what he was doing in order to pay close attention.

AFTERWORD

Around 17 July 2015, in and around Greenville, South Carolina, all of the people that we knew and associated with wished us safe travel, and wonderful experiences. And, they bade us to have a great time as we departed our recently sold home in Taylors, South Carolina. As we drove away, there's no doubt some of them mumbled under their breath, "I think they're crazy doing this."

Well into our seventies, we sold our home, placed our worldly goods in storage, boarded a commercial aircraft, and flew off to the distant island of Guam for a five-month stay. Our intent and purpose was to finish writing this book about the people of Guam, especially those who had experienced the Japanese occupation during World War II. We had to apply quality time in order to dig deeper into the times and the people of then and now. And, we had to experience the day-to-day activities, discussions, dreams, and desires of a unique people by being up close and personal with—the Chamorros of Guam.

We were on a mission. It was a mission of telling a seldom told story to the American people of the fifty states, the District of Columbia, Puerto Rico, the U.S. Virgin Islands, Samoa, and most importantly, to the victims, the Americans of Guam.

We had started our quest initially to write about only one particular Chamorro, Adolfo Camacho Sgambelluri, the father of one of our very good friends and a fellow Marine, Adolf Peter Sgambelluri. We had known Sgamby for many years. When he submitted a short story about his dad to be published in my first book, a compilation of short stories titled, *Short Rations For Marines*, my wife and I developed an interest in Adolfo Camacho Sgambelluri, known as "Sgambe." We were also drawn to Guam and to the Chamorros of Guam.

That interest is what took us to Guam in November 2014 to begin our research. That research expanded dramatically to include the entire American National and citizen population of Guam during the War in the Pacific in World War II. Ninety-plus percent of that population were Chamorros.

Several years ago, I began writing in earnest— starting with feature articles appearing in newspapers and magazines, such as Police Chief and the Marine Corps Gazette. That led to writing and publishing of books. As mentioned, my first book, *Short Rations For Marines*, was an anthology of fifty-two short stories written by thirty-seven different writers. My second book was an historical-fiction about John Archer Lejeune (pronounced luh jern), a former Commandant of the United States Marine Corps. That book is titled *A Marine Called Gabe*. Then, my third work was to edit and to finish writing an unpublished manuscript developed by a Marine Corps Master Gunnery Sergeant (Retired), now deceased. It was published with the title *Back Step,* by under the authors name, Burnard Winburn.

Writing this particular book was a very unique challenge. To the casual reader, it might seem insignificant, but most career military persons will get the drift. Being a career Marine, it was arduous for me to criticize the country that I have fought for and defended for so many years. Many of my friends died to serve its national goals. It is still the country that I love, and I feel strongly about upholding its honor and its traditions, especially its military traditions. But, this country, did in fact, abandon the Americans of Guam in 1941.

In order to highlight the abandonment of an entire population of Americans by the government of this United States, I had to zero-in on—who or what—of and in—this country, *caused* the abandonment of these human beings, the Chamorros of Guam. Who decided to let these people go under the claws of militaristic Imperial Japan without a fight? Perhaps the statement that the *United States* had abandoned Guam and its people is just too simplistic. Those American Marines and sailors on Guam in 1941 wanted to defend Guam and the Chamorros of Guam; they would have fought and died defending them, but they were prohibited from doing so. Those Marines, sailors, and soldiers who liberated Guam in 1944 wanted not just to liberate, but to rescue, protect, and care for those Americans of Guam. The American fighting man will defend Americans anytime and anywhere, unless prohibited from doing so by higher lawful authority.

The decision to abandon Guam was made at the highest level of lawful authority. To discover that fact required peeling back the layers to discover who or what was responsible for the policy and plan to abandon that American island and its American people. Discovering that it was certain particular elements of the United States government that made the decision made writing about it easier. Someone, a person or persons, made the recommendation or decision, apparently approved by the President, that Guam and its population would not be defended in the event of war with Japan. Guam and its people were written off.

The primary war plan for a war between the United States and Japan was titled War Plan Orange, which the previously mentioned Marine Lt Col Earl "Pete" Ellis had worked on during the 1920s. But, since 1924, things had changed internationally, and things had changed frequently.

During the Interwar period, the Joint Planning Committee (which later became the Joint Chiefs of Staff) devised a series of contingency plans for dealing with the outbreak of war with various countries. The most elaborate of these, War Plan Orange, dealt with the possibility of war with Japan.

In light of the events of the late 1930s (the outbreak of the Second Sino-Japanese War, the Molotov-Ribbentrop Pact, the German conquest of Poland and Western Europe) American planners realized that the United States faced the possibility of a two-front war in both Europe and the Pacific. War Plan Orange was withdrawn, and five "Rainbow" plans were put forward. Unlike the earlier colored plans which had assumed a one-on-one war, the Rainbow plans contemplated possibility of fighting multiple enemies, and the necessity of defending other western hemisphere nations and aiding Britain.

THE MEMORANDUM:

The memorandum built upon the conditions described in the Rainbow Five war plan. It described four possible scenarios for American participation in World War II, lettered A through D:

- *A - Defend the western hemisphere*
- *B - Go on the offensive in the Pacific against Japan while remaining on the defensive in the Atlantic*
- *C - Fight equally committed in both the Atlantic and Pacific*
- *D - Go on the offensive in the Atlantic (against Germany and Italy) while remaining on the defensive in the Pacific.*

The memorandum, which was submitted to Roosevelt on November 12, 1940, recommended option D, from which it gets its name ("Dog" was D in the Joint Army/Navy Phonetic Alphabet).

"I believe that the continued existence of the British Empire, combined with building up a strong protection in our home areas, will do most to ensure the status quo in the Western Hemisphere, and to promote our principal national interests. As I have previously stated, I also believe that Great Britain requires from us very great help in the Atlantic, and possibly even on the continents of Europe or Africa, if she

is to be enabled to survive. In my opinion Alternatives (A), (B), and (C) will most probably not provide the necessary degree of assistance, and, therefore, if we undertake war, that Alternative (D) is likely to be the most fruitful for the United States, particularly if we enter the war at an early date. Initially, the offensive measures adopted would, necessarily, be purely naval. Even should we intervene, final victory in Europe is not certain. I believe that the chances for success are in our favor, particularly if we insist upon full equality in the political and military direction of the war."

en.wikipedia.org/wiki/United States_color-coded...

The above document was part of a lengthy memo written by Chief of Naval Operations, Harold Rainsford Stark in November 1940. Stark is, to this day, a highly controversial figure for many of his decisions that tend to be historical decisions. For example, he apparently ordered unrestricted submarine warfare against Japan on his own initiative without involving the civilian leadership of the U.S. government. He is also believed by many to have withheld information about Japanese intentions from Admiral Kimmel at Pearl Harbor, yet he blamed Kimmel for not being prepared for the attack by the Japanese. Stark was later subjected to a court of inquiry regarding the Pearl Harbor event.

One must also assume that this memo was seen and approved by Frank Knox, the Secretary of the Navy, before it was "approved" by President Franklin D. Roosevelt. However, the reader should keep in mind, as previously stated, Stark had issued directives without approval from higher headquarters. This assumption must therefore be taken with some reservations.

The memo by Stark also suggested that until hostilities broke out, the U.S. should adopt policy A:

Until such time as the United States should decide to engage its full forces in war, I recommend that we pursue a course that will most rapidly increase the military strength of both the Army and the Navy, that is to say, adopt Alternative (A) without hostilities.

> *The strategy of Plan Dog gained the support of the army and implicitly of President Roosevelt, though he never formally endorsed it. Thus at the end of 1940 a powerful consensus for strategic focus on Germany developed at the highest levels of the American government. At a meeting on January 17, 1941, Roosevelt concluded that the primary objective must be maintenance of the supply lines to Britain and ordered the navy to prepare for the escort of convoys. A few weeks after the Attack on Pearl Harbor, at the Arcadia Conference, the United States adopted the recommendations of the memo in the form of the 'Europe first' policy. Although the United States did not go entirely on the defensive in the Pacific as the memo recommended, throughout the war the European theater was given higher priority in resource allocation.*

The memorandum was declassified in February 1956.

It wasn't the Navy or the Marines on Guam that decided not to fight the invaders. Somewhere, much higher up the ladder of responsibility that particular blame lays. The highest decision maker of course was the President of the United States. When Stark wrote that memo, he wrote it to the Secretary of the Navy Frank Knox. Copies also went to other persons within the government. This memo is referred to by historians as the *Plan Dog Memo.*

The content of this memo and the content of several replies to this memo, briefly mentions Guam and other islands and atolls. But, it never mentions defending Guam. It does mention defending Manila Bay in the Philippines, and it mentions defending the Dutch East Indies (Indonesia). Yet, by not defending Guam, it left the door open for the Japanese to conquer both the Philippines and the Dutch East Indies.

We still don't know anything about any information that Governor/Captain McMillin, U.S. Navy, had been given before the Japanese attack. We know that somewhere in the command chain, above him, someone ordered Navy ships to evacuate dependents and civilian contractors from the island, back in October 1941. We know that he had received orders to destroy all confidential files, and we assume he did that. We also know that several of the activities he supposedly engaged in, or believed others engaged in, prior to and during the Japanese attack did not happen. We know that no Marines of the Marine Barracks were deployed to resist the invasion. We know that the civilian population received no warnings and were given no instructions regarding the invasion by the Japanese. Most of them were at church services when the first Japanese bombs fell on Guam. We know that there were no prepared defensive emplacements anywhere on Guam. We know that while Wake Island was receiving a Marine defense battalion and a squadron of Marine aircraft and personnel, nothing was going to Guam for its defense. The comparison and contrast between Guam and Wake Island, Midway Island, and the Philippines is both revealing and confusing.

As previously stated, Guam and the Guamanians, especially the Chamorro population, were not something or someone unknown to us. We had several months of research under our belt before departing for Guam in November 2014. So, by the time we took our second journey to Guam in July 2015, we felt that we had a pretty good handle on things. How wrong we were.

It was our association with the people of Guam on our extended second trip that tipped the scales from being somewhat familiar with Guam and the Chamorros of Guam to becoming very familiar with, or better yet, to becoming intimately familiar with Guam and the Chamorros of Guam. The first trip to Guam allowed us to meet and chat briefly with a limited number of people, but, other than our friend Sgamby and his wife Rosie, we didn't actually get to *know* anyone else in November 2014. We didn't have the time, since we spent most of our time at MARC and driving around the island, familiarizing ourselves with significant World War II events and places.

But, our second trip on the island for an extended period of time, allowed us to meet and get to know many different people and engage in more social activities, some public, such as the Labor Day picnic, and some private, such as a family gathering or a church festival. Our reliance on

Sgamby never abated, but others began to provide guidance and to tip us off to other contacts for us to gain additional information. In order to present the more accurate word pictures of Guam and its Chamorro population, we decided to become completely neutral. We crossed political, economic, and social lines and met with people who had strong differences of opinions on a variety of issues. We took no sides: we listened and absorbed, sometimes without agreeing or disagreeing, for that was our self-imposed charter. We were there to gather, not to sow.

We became close with a cross section of the Chamorro citizens of Guam. We talked with survivors of the Japanese occupation and their sons, daughters, and grandchildren. We talked with business owners, merchants, educators, government officials, and past government officials. We talked to clerks in stores, waiters in cafes, bartenders in bars and pubs, and workers in our hotel. We engaged in a wide range of subject matter over an extended period of time. Almost without exception, the Chamorro of Guam feel, at least, bewildered regarding the history of United States policies toward the island and its people. The abandoned Chamorros of World War II suffered immeasurable indignities, emotional and physical pain, the threat of death, and death at the hands of the Japanese occupiers, often because they simply remained loyal to the America that had abandoned them. Then, sometimes, simply because they happened to be in the wrong place at the wrong time, they died at the hands of their captors. In the aftermath, they have not been properly compensated, nor adequately recognized for exhibiting that loyalty under those horrific conditions.

Some of the comments heard over and over are, "We can't even vote for the President of the United States," and, "We are American citizens only because Congress allows it. What if Congress changes its mind?" We constantly heard the term hapa-citizen.

Those characteristics that set Guam apart from other overseas possessions, territories, or colonies of the United States are significant. Guam contained the only American population abandoned, literally without resistance, by its ruling government, and allowed to be captured and occupied by the Japanese Empire in World War II. After the Americans returned, it was to become a massive military and naval base from which the last year of the War in the Pacific was prosecuted. On Guam, land, belonging to members of the indigenous population was simply confiscated and used for military operations. It is the only American occupied political and geographic entity that has one third of its land mass fenced off, owned and operated by the Department of Defense. It is the only overseas American colony that was restricted from economic growth by the policies of the American government. These things are unique to Guam alone among the overseas colonies of the United States.

And, for those objecting to the use of the term colony: A colony is any people or territory [Guam] separated from but subject to a ruling power [the United States].

It is the purpose, it is the dream, and it is the hope that this book will open the eyes of the American people to the plight of the people of Guam. The Chamorro population of the Guam of 1945 exceeded ninety percent of the permanent residents, and, over time, has been reduced to thirty-seven percent today by the influx of Filipinos (twenty-seven percent), other Pacific Islanders (eleven percent), mixed race (nine percent), mainlanders (seven percent), and Asians (six percent) through the years since the end of World War II. But Guam and all the Guamanians share not only that small island, but also the dreams and aspirations that one day they may become free, full-fledged Americans, not continue to be *hapa-Americans*. But, that can only happen through the Congress of the United States, and Congress will do nothing for the people of Guam until and unless the ***people*** of the United States demand it.

Hopefully, that will happen. Soon! It's long overdue.

ACKNOWLEDGEMENTS

One of the difficulties in acknowledging those who assisted in developing a book is the tendency to overlook someone. Then, there is the unmistakable perplexing situation of just where to cut it off? Hundreds of individuals provided support and advice to us during our two stays on the island of Guam, hotel and car rental staff, guests and hosts at family and other cook-outs, and church festivals, waiters and waitresses at restaurants, bartenders (we had a few), people on the street, in stores, and in parks. There were many we just briefly ran into who filled us with knowledge we didn't have before. Lyn and I are going to run the risk of forgetting, or overstating, or just having a bad memory day, so, here goes. As we lingered in Hawaii on our way to South Carolina, we were guests of Patrick Brent and Hisako, and having dinner with them at the home of John and Stephanie Bates, we raise a glass (or bottle) and salute each of you on Guam, for your assistance, guidance, and participation:

Stoney and Lyn, Oahu, Hawaii, 3 December 2015
Photo property of author

Adolf P. Sgambelluri - My long-time good friend, a fellow Marine, Sgamby is the person responsible for generating the concept of this novel. He enabled us to move forward with this endeavor. Sgamby is a true American patriot and a well versed Chamorro of Guam. He is the man who held the lamp to light our way. Sgamby lives by the term Semper Fidelis. Semper Fi, Sgamby, and, thanks for everything.

Joey Crisostomo - Cars Plus owner, Thrifty Car Rental man on Guam. This is the man Sgambe introduced us to, who made it possible, for us to get around, for six full months of research in 2015, at a reduced rental cost, until we had a flat tire.

Derrick Quinata - Who actually **loaned** us one of his cars from SIXT Car Rental in December 2016. That loan was very much appreciated and required, for us to disseminate the word, via various mediums, of the book about the remarkable Chamorros of Guam. Thanks to the kindness of Derrick, it was made much easier.

Michael J.B. Borja - Department of Land Management, who, at a Labor Day picnic, gave us a short lesson and information on the "lay of the land," of Guam. We discussed where the bones are located.

Frank Blas, Jr. - Senator of Guam and President of the Guam War Survivors Memorial Foundation. He kicked-started us when we arrived, pointing us to the Ceremony at Yigo for those Chamorros massacred by the Japanese at a place called Chaguian. Our attendance at that ceremony allowed us to meet many people. From there, we expanded. Frank assisted us several times while on Guam. Thanks, Frank.

Tony Limtiaco - whose emotional reminiscences of his dad added a personal touch to an American hero. Tony's dad, Joaquin Limtiaco's memory, dedication, and sacrifice on behalf of all Americans and especially the six sailors of Guam are highlighted in this novel. Joaquin Limtiaco is one of the unrecognized heroes of Guam, and America. Tony told us a great deal about him. If he had worn an American uniform, he'd have the MOH.

Thomas and Fredrick Tanaka - Their dad, Tomas, "Tommy" Tanaka was a close friend of Joaquin Limtiaco and Sgambe. He was actually the main person responsible for keeping the sailor George Tweed alive when he was sick. Thomas "Tommy" Tanaka and Fred made their dad come alive in these pages. Tomas "Tommy" Tanaka is and forever will be an American hero.

Franklin Artero - who helped us delve deeply into the activities of his dad who protected the American sailor, George Tweed, and who shared with us the ongoing struggle for fairness in compensation, regarding the property the United States seized from his family. He and his wife Margie also introduced us to several church and village festivals. They truly escorted us around Guam meeting many new contacts. They are among our newfound friends of Guam.

Gerard Champion - He is the grandson of Ignacia Bordallo Butler, the person who defied the Japanese as she continued to maintain her family and her businesses, until the Americans returned to Guam. "Gerry" shared with us his many memories of his grandmother and grandfather.

Linda Taitano-Reyes - The granddaughter of Agueda Iglesias Johnston and the daughter of Marian Johnston, who graciously shared with us not only memories, but some of the actual items that had belonged to Agueda and her husband William Gautier Johnston. Linda's husband Kin and son Victor also lent us their support, and encouragement, allowing us to witness a Chamorro dance group. Linda says we will always have her support.

Rudy Matanane - The Mayor of Yigo, who afforded us the ability to look into one of the memories of one of the liberating American soldiers, as well as those of the Chamorro, regarding the occupation and its aftermath, especially his Uncle Art. Also, he shared the memory of his father as a Chamorro combat-scout for the Americans during and after the liberation. Rudy also provided us with numerous contacts and invited us to a family cook-out.

Juan Blaz - Sergeant Major U.S. Army, retired, who guided us, provided us with encouragement, and was always prepared to lend a hand. Juan paved the way for my participating in a radio show on Guam. He is a knowledgeable military-historian. Thanks for the great, festive Halloween gathering at your sister's, Juan. He is a book trail-blazer.

Rosie Sgambelluri - Sgamby's wife, and also her mother Rosario Flores Leon Guerrero – who, together survived the Death March into the Manenggon Valley. Rosie's mother told her story one more time. It appears in these pages. Rosie also took us out to the Manenggon Valley to see the monument located there. Rosie—thanks for everything.

Paul Calvo - a former Governor of Guam, owner of Calvo Insurance, and an all-round—very nice guy. He gave of his time to us for an informative interview regarding his experiences during the Japanese occupation.

Robert Underwood - the current University of Guam, President, who related a few stories of the occupation years and provided some insight into the discovery of the Chaguian Massacre. Robert is a strong supporter of this book. Thank you, Sir.

George Taylor - owner of Chamorro Island BBQ, a restaurant in Chamorro Village, who invited us into his establishment to meet his mother and invited us to his mother's home for a family gathering and cook-out. It was our first taste of real Chamorro hospitality. George also provided some of the photographs in this novel. We became regulars at George's place, an excellent gathering and eating establishment. Thanks George.

Maria Della Rosa Taylor – George Taylor's mother, whom we met in George's Chamorro Island BBQ, a survivor of the Japanese occupation; upon meeting us, she instantly invited us for a family gathering and cook-out, Chamorro style.

Ana R. and Raymundo Tores Lizana - George Taylor's aunt and uncle, survivors of the Japanese occupation, present for food and interview at George's mother's home cook-out.

Rosario Flores Leon Guerrero – Mother of our friend Rosie Sgambelluri, and a Manenggon Valley death March survivor.

University of Guam, Micronesian Area Research Center staff - The staff provided us with research material, almost instantaneously, and often. We spent a great deal of time within the walls of the MARC. Thanks, Lourdes Nededog, and Monique Storie, and all the staff at MARC.

Anthony Ramirez and Michael Cura - both of the Department of Parks and Recreation, who invited us to have Thanksgiving lunch at Lujan House during our visit in November 2014; there we met Rose Martinez, a charming conversationalist and delightful Chamorro lady. And, on this particular occasion we had our first (but certainly not our last) Chamorro food while on Guam.

Rlene Steffy - who conducted our first tour around the island, and introduced us to the Chamorro culture and tradition during our November 2014 visit to Guam. She also presented an informative production of the Manenggon Death Camp at UOG during our second visit.

Arternio Tudela Maanao (Uncle Art) - who provided us an unblemished account of his life on Guam during the Japanese occupation, told to us from his home in Yigo.

Patti Arroyo - A few days after our conversation with Uncle Art, Juan Blaz called to relate that he had set up an interview with Patti Arroyo of K-57 Radio/TV on Guam. It was a good interview, and Patti got a copy of each of my previous books.

Carmen (Artero) Kasperbauer - daughter of Antonio Cruz Artero the man who hid George Tweed for twenty-one months, of his thirty-one months in hiding on Guam. She remembers a lot of conversations with her father and grandfather, and she remembers much of what she saw and heard during the Japanese occupation. She painted a vivid word picture.

Vicente (Ben) Diaz Gumataotao – Mayor of Piti District and a survivor of the Japanese occupation of Guam. Shot through the hand by strafing Japanese aircraft, he survived several life threatening occasions, living to tell us his experiences and assisting us in locating other survivors to tell us their stories, especially Buck Cruz. He is a man of many lives. Thank you, Mister Mayor.

Governor Eddie Baza Calvo – Governor of Guam, who gave us an audience for almost an hour. We talked of the past, present, and future of Guam. He assisted us in reviewing the Programmatic Agreement between Guam and various departments of the United States Government. Eddie is a man who cares deeply about the people of Guam and their future. Thanks for your time, and your support, Governor.

Lieutenant Governor Ray Tenorio – We met with him in November 2014, as we began our initial research, and, we crossed paths several times during our second visit to Guam. We were always comfortable with Ray's support and advice. Like Eddie, Ray cares deeply for the people of Guam. Thanks for everything, Ray.

Master Gunnery Sergeant Ignacio "Buck" S. Cruz, USMC (Ret) – Marine, school teacher, Mayor (Merizo), member of the Guam Militia, and a survivor of the occupation. We met Buck at his home in Merizo, and sat and chatted with him for hours as he sported one of his many Marine Corps baseball caps (covers). Buck has accomplished many things in his life, but he is most proud of his Marine Corps career.

Tony Ada – We met Tony as a result of the radio show with Patti. Tony, along with his sister Rose and her husband, shared conversations about their dad and of the Guam of today.

Former Governor Carl Gutierrez – We joined Carl and his wife Gerri for lunch and they shared several stories related to the subject of our writing. Carl directed us to several sources contained in this novel which we would not have found on our own. Thanks much, Carl and Gerri.

Former Governor Joseph Ada – met with us at our hotel, and a few days later for lunch, to discuss his views and his record of achievements for Guam and its people. Over lunch, he gave us much insight and encouragement regarding the completion of this novel. Thanks much, Joe.

Jesus Pangelinan – Through his son Jesse, we met with him and his family at his home on Nimitz Hill. He told his story to us as perhaps he has told it many times. We listened intently as he relayed the story of George Tweed and of his own father, Juan Unpingco Pangelinan, sharing with us how keeping Tweed cost his father his life. He was firm, specific, and detailed revealing events of seventy-one years ago on this island of Guam, through the eyes if a fourteen to seventeen-year-old boy in 1943-'44 Guam. He was a treasure to talk with. Our gratitude goes to Jesus and to his son, Jesse.

Patrick Timothy Brent – From his island paradise in lovely Hawaii., he suggested an outstanding title for this novel, which we retained, and for his continued support and friendship through the years. *Domo,* PT.

William Ray Gibson – Mr. Gibson, of Radio/TV K-57, conducted an interview with this author on Veterans Day 2015, on Guam, to highlight this book and an article written by me about the shortchanged veteran of Guam.

Father Eric Forbes – Thank you, Father, for your guidance and support.

Colonel Walt Ford, USMC (Ret) – Former editor and publisher of *Leatherneck* magazine for his review of this novel and for his foreword comments. Much appreciated, Walt.

Amanda Capps – For her initial editorial review and for her encouragement for me to write and publish my first book *Short Rations For Marines.* Thanks, Amanda!

Roy Breeling – A friend, an attorney, living in Panama City Beach, Florida, for his review and comments.

Lyn Bates – My wife, researcher, spell-checker, critic, supporter, and great traveling companion. It is she that has guided me through the task of writing and completing this novel. Without her guidance, completing it would have been much more difficult, or as she says—IMPOSSIBLE!

Thanks, Lyn, and I love you. Also, I agree with you.

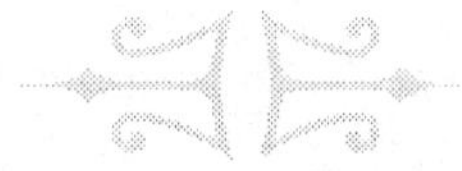

REFERENCES

In developing and compiling this novel: *An American Shame: The Abandonment of an Entire American Population*, by Major Ralph Stoney Bates Sr., USMC (Ret), in addition to on-site research, utilized these publications to assist the author and researcher in conveying an accurate word picture of Guam and the people of Guam through the years, especially those thirty-one months of Japanese occupation during World War II.

Bisita Guam: Let Us Remember, Nihi Ta Hasso, by Ben Blaz, Richard F' Tiatano, MARC, 2008

Yanks Don't Cry, Martin Boyle, B. Geis Associates; distributed by Random House [1963]

Three Volumes of -*Who's Who in Chamorro History*; the Chamorro Heritage Planning Group

real Faces, Guam's World War II Survivors, Copyright 2014 Guam War Survivors Memorial Foundation

The Recapture of Guam, Historical Branch, G-3 Division, Hqtrs. Marine Corps, 1954

Captured, The Forgotten Men of Guam – Roger Mansell assisted by Linda Goetz Holmes, 2012

Crusoe, USN Robinson, Westholme Publishing, George R. Tweed as told to Blake Clark, 1945

An Island In Agony, Tony Polomo, Copyright 1984

Destiny's Landfall A History of Guam, Robert F. Rogers, 1995

Guam 1941 & 1944 Loss and Reconquest, Gordon Rottman, 2004 Osprey Press

Uncle Sam, Please Come Back to Guam, Pedro C. Sanchez, 1979

Invitation To Guam, Tommy B. Chase, Copyright 1992, Let's Go Travel Publication

Guam 1941 & 1944, Loss and Reconquest, Osprey Publishing, 2004

The Secret Guam Study, Howard Willens and Dirk Ballendorf, MARC Univ. of Guam, 2004

The Fallen; Marc Landas, John Wiley and Sons, 2004

MARC (Micronesia Area Research Center) of the UOG (University of Guam)

Short Rations For Marines and *A Marine Called Gabe*, Major Ralph Stoney Bates USMC (Ret)

Guampedia.com, is an excellent research source in developing any facts, opinions, or recommendations regarding Guam.

Wikipedia, com, although many sources may contribute to this website, and it is constantly changing, it has provided me with information specific to my needs while developing this novel. I usually cross reference, but find the wordage specific to my needs.

Various other Internet sources, and person-to-person contact with hundreds of Guamanians..

The following individual Americans died as a result of the Japanese invasion and occupation, and the American invasion and liberation of Guam.

www.guam.net/pub/milmuseum/memorial_civcas.htm

A

Agnes Acfalle Acfalle
Carmello M. Acfalle
Carmen Babauta Acfalle
Fausto Chargualaf Acfalle
Felicidad Acfalle Acfalle
Jesus C. Acfalle
Jesus Cruz Acfalle
Juan Champaco Acfalle
Miguel Manalisay Acfalle
Rosa S.N. Acfalle
Vicente Reyes Acfalle
Juan Acosta Acosta
Pedro Acosta Acosta
Dolores Rojas Aflague
Ruth O. Aflague
Simeon Reyes Aflague
Jesus T. Aflleje
Vicente Salas Aflleje
Tommy Taitano Aguero
Balbino Guerrero Aguigui
Felix Tyquiengco Aguigui
Jesus Tyquiengco Aguigui
Bernabe Rogopes Aguon
Candelaria P. Aguon
Candelaria Perez Aguon
Catalina Borja Aguon

M

Asuncion Perez Mafnas
Joaquin Cruz Mafnas
Jose Cruz Mafnas
Juan Taisague Mafnas
Manuel Pangelinan Mafnas
Rosa Lizama Mafnas
Serafin Baza Mafnas
Serafin Cruz Mafnas
Francisco T. Manalisay
Jesus C. Manalisay
Julian Cruz Manalisay
Larry Manalisay
Prudencio Acfalle Manalisay
Julia Flores Manglona
Tomas Santos Manglona
Antonio Pangelinan Manibusan
Jesus L. Manibusan
Joaquin I. Manibusan
Jose Manibusan Manibusan
Juan C. Manibusan
Juan L. Manibusan
Juan Mesa Manibusan
Rosa Tanona Manibusan
Rufina Materne Manibusan
Soledad L.G. Balajadia Manibusan
Soledad Quenga Manibusan

Francisco A. Aguon
Francisco Santos Aguon
Jesus Aguon
Jesus F. Aguon
Jesus Gogo Aguon
Jesus Santos Aguon
Joaquin Naputi Aguon
Joaquin Santos Aguon
Jose Gogo Aguon
Jose Q. Aguon
Juan A. Aguon
Juan Crisostomo Aguon
Juan Fejeran Aguon
Juan Lizama Aguon
Manuel Lizama Aguon
Pedro Chargualaf Aguon
Pedro I. Aguon
Rosalina Duenas Aguon
Ana Q. Alig
Arthur Gifford Anderson
George Cruz Anderson
Celia Mendiola Angoco
Darlene Q. Angoco
Manuela Muna dela
Concepcion Angoco
Vicente D. Angoco
Nicolasa Respicio
Aquiningoc
Jose B. Arceo
Jose F. Arceo
Regina Crisostomo Arceo
Rosa M. Arceo
Ascension Rosendo Manley
Gabriel M. Mansapit
Jesus Maguadog Mansapit
Santiago Naputi Mansapit
Alfansiana Mantanona
Casiano Achuga Mantanona
Jose M. Mantanona
Jose Tenorio Mantanona
Juan M. Mantanona
Juan Pablo Mantanona
Juan Paulino Mantanona
Manuel Pablo Mantanona
Jose Reyes Martinez
Jesus Manalisay Mata
Vicente Manalisay Mata
Beatrice Camacho Matanane
Jesus C. Matanane
Juan C. Matanane
Jose C. Mateo
Luis Cruz Materne
Jesus M. Matsumiya
Jose M. Matsumiya
Josefina M. Matsumiya
Rafael S. Matsumiya
Tomas M. Matsumiya
Catherine Carmen McDonald
Julia Anderson Medina
Consolacion Palomo Mendiola
David Joseph Mendiola
Encarcinacion P. Mendiola
George Mendiola
Ignacio Mendiola

Segundo Gogue Arceo
Ygnacio Namauleg Arceo
Maria T. Arnold
Maria Soledad Camacho Arriola
Eugenia Vidal Artero
Pascual Cruz Artero
Rosario C. Atalig
Dolores Benavente Atoigue
Emeliana O. Atoigue
Felipe Mafnas Atoigue
Henry O. Atoigue
Joaquin Lujan Atoigue
Jose Benavente Atoigue
Juan Benavente Atoigue

B

Antonia S. Babauta
Donecio Babauta
Felix S.N. Babauta
Francisco Lizama Babauta
James Babauta
Jesus Taianao Babauta
Joaquin Babauta Babauta
Joaquina S. Babauta
Josefa Carbullido Babauta
Juan Blanco Babauta
Juan Cruz Babauta
Juan N. Babauta
Manuel Acosta Babauta
Maria Sablan Babauta
Pedro Babauta

Jesus Aguero Mendiola
Jesus Blas Mendiola
Jesus F. Mendiola
Jose M. Mendiola
Juan B. Mendiola
Juan Jot Mendiola
Juan Ulloa Mendiola
Juana Perez Mendiola
Justo Demetrio Mendiola
Manuel S. Mendiola
Maria Cruz Mendiola
Mariano Borja Mendiola
Mariano Cruz Mendiola
Pedro C. Mendiola
Pedro Palomo Mendiola
Rosa F. Mendiola
Vicenta T. Mendiola
Vicente Mendiola Mendiola
Vicente T. Mendiola
Cornelia C. Meno
Dolores Quidachay Meno
Dometro Quinene Meno
Felipe Meno Meno
Francisco Castro Meno
Francisco Delgado Meno
Jesus Chargualaf Meno
Jose Castro Meno
Jose L.G. Meno
Jose Meno Meno
Pedro Chargualaf Meno
Vicente Gogue Meno
Vicente Lujan Meno

Robino G. Babauta
Rosa C. Babauta
Rosalia Babauta Babauta
Vicente Sahagon Babauta
Bartola Pangelinan Balajadia
Joaquin Guerrero Balajadia
Jose Guerrero Balajadia
Magdalena P. Balajadia
Manuel I. Balajadia
Maria Quichocho Balajadia
Maria Blas Bamba
Rita M. Bamba
Arthur Barcinas
Dolores Tyquiengco Barcinas
Jose T. Barcinas
Jose Tyquiengco Barcinas
Magdalena T. Barcinas
Martin C. Barcinas
Martin Cruz Barcinas
Pedro T. Barcinas
Omega Elliot Barrick
Dolores T. Bascon
Antonio Camacho Bautista
Conchita T. Bautista
Francisco B. Bautista
Jose Atoigue Bautista
Jose T. Bautista
Mati S.L. Bautista
Rosa Lujan Bautista
Francisca San Agustin Baza

Antonio Mafnas Merfalen
Antonio Santos Merfalen
Gloria Santos Merfalen
Ana Cruz Mesa
Anito L.G. Mesa
Antonio Rios Mesa
Antonio Toves Mesa
Francisco Aguon Mesa
Geronimo Dela Rosa Mesa
Joaquin Mesa Mesa
Johnny Duenas Mesa
Jose M. Mesa
Manuel C. Mesa
Manuela S.N. Mesa
Maria Lukban Mesa
Maria Rivera Mesa
Rosalia Pinaula Mesa
Jose Muna
Gloria C. Munoz

N

Jesus Nangauta Nangauta
Jose Benavente Naputi
Dominica Duenas Nauta
Elisabel Taijeron Cruz Nauta
Isabel Leon Guerrero Nauta
Juan Quidachay Nauta
Mariano Nauta Nauta
Pedro Quidachay Nauta
Juan Matanane Navarro
Ana Terlaje Nededog
Emelio Charfurous Nededog

Jose A. Baza
Jose T. Baza
Maria Baza Baza
Rosa C. Baza
Rosa Taijeron Baza
Vicente Sablan Baza
Visentacion A. Baza
Jesus Guerrero Benavente
Juan Guerrero Benavente
Maria Q. Benavente
Clemente Unsiog Bitanga
Ana Limtiaco Blas
Antonio Perez Blas
Asuncion R. Blas
Francisco Atao Blas
Guido Flores Blas
Jane Flores Blas
Jose Aguon Blas
Jose Castro Blas
Juan Castro Blas
Juan Limtiaco Blas
Pedro Cruz Blas
Vicente Camacho Blas
Franklin Delano Bordallo
Dolores Cruz Borja
Jose Cruz Borja
Juan Mendiola Borja
Juan Soriano Borja
Luca M. Borja
Magdelina C. Borja
Trinidad Materne Borja
Vicente Cruz Borja

Jesus Terlaje Nededog
Joaquin Castro Nededog
Juan Perez Nededog
Juan Taienao Nededog
Juan Terlaje Nededog
Rita Terlaje Nededog
Henry Roleigh Nelson
Esther L.G. Ninete
Jose Camacho Ninete

O

Eziquuiel Ogo
Joseph Okiyama
Narcina Charfauros Okiyama
Juan Onedera
Miguel A. Ovenata

P

Jose Aguon Pablo
Josefa Pablo Pablo
Julia Castro Pablo
Ruth Camacho Palacios
Isidora Quintanilla Palomo
Maria C. Palomo
Olympia Ojeda Pablo
Antonio Pangelinan Pangelinan
David Edward Pangelinan
Emeterio N. Periera Pangelinan
Francisco Baza Pangelinan
Francisco Tyquiengco Pangelinan
Ignacio Rosario Pangelinan
Jesus Q. Pangelinan

Vicente Munoz Borja
Ana Rice Brockwell
Frank Brown

C
Antonio Duenas Cabo
Antonio Camacho Cabrera
Ignacia R. Cabrera
Jose Castro Cabrera
Clotilde Perez Calvo
Ana Mantanane Camacho
Bictornio Perez Camacho
Buena Ventura Cruz Camacho
Carmen C. Camacho
Dolores Camacho
Dolores Mantanane Camacho
Edward Eclavea Camacho
Francisco B. Camacho
Gaily Cruz Camacho
Gregorio Camacho
Jesus C. Camacho
Jesus Guerrero Camacho
Jesus S.N. Camacho
Jose C. Camacho
Jose Santos Camacho
Lucy Ann Castro Camacho
Maria Camacho
Maria Lujan Camacho
Maria O. Camacho
Ramon Eclavea Camacho
Ramon Ogo Camacho

Jose Baza Pangelinan
Jose Quichocho Pangelinan
Juan Atoigue Pangelinan
Juan Unpingco Pangelinan
Lorenzo Lujan Pangelinan
Luis L.G. Pangelinan
Magdalena Aguon Pangelinan
Mercedes D. Pangelinan
Patricia Cruz Pangelinan
Rita Lujan Pangelinan
Rosalia Indalecio Pangelinan
Roman Eclavea Parker
Pedro L.G. Paulino
Ana C.M. Peredo
Ana Bontugan Perez
Antonio Concepcion Perez
Basilia C. Perez
Candilario Lujan Perez
Dolores M. Perez
Francisco G. Perez
Francisco Martinez Perez
Jesus Finona Perez
Jesus Manibusan Perez
Juan Perez
Juan C. Perez
Juan Concepcion Perez
Margarita P. Perez
Mariquita Hines Perez
Mary Talavera Perez
Nicolasa Roberto Palomo Perez
Pedro Cruz Perez
Soledad Reyes Perez
Vicente M. Perez

Roman Eclavea Camacho
Vicente O. Camacho
Victoriano Perez Camacho
Rosita M. Campos
Beleng Carbullido
Evelyn Taitano Carbullido
Jose Santiago Carbullido
Anne C. Castro
Asuncion Rabago Castro
Bastian B. Castro
Carmen T. Castro
Concepcion Castro
Enrique Rosario Castro
Felisa Santos Castro
Felix C. Castro
Franklin Thomas Castro
Ignacio Cabrera Castro
Jesus Rosario Castro
Jose Alejandro Castro
Jose Garrido Castro
Juan A. Castro
Lourdes N. Castro
Manuela Cruz Duenas Castro
Maria Rabago Castro
Maria Reyes Castro
Mariquita Castro Castro
Ramon C. Castro
Ramon Techaira Castro
Ramona Techaira Castro
Rosa C. Castro
Sylvia Antonette Castro
Tomas N. Castro
Veronica M. Villa Ceal

Dolores T. Perona
Antonio Cruz Pinaula

Q

Carolina San Nicolas Quenga
Joaquin S.N. Quenga
Jose Taijeron Quenga
Manuel San Nicolas Quenga
Maria M. Quenga
Milagro San Nicolas Quenga
Sebastian Quitugua Quenga
Vicente San Nicolas Quenga
Antonio Manibusan Quichocho
Jesus Quichocho
Jesus Cabrera Quichocho
Jesus Indalecio Quichocho
Rosa Talavera Quichocho
Vicente Quichocho Quichocho
Carmen A. Quidachay
Dolores P. Quidachay
Jesus A. Quidachay
Jose San Agustin Quidachay
Prodencio T. Quidachay
Ramon P. Quidachay
Ramon Pangelinan Quidachay
Rosa Quinata Quidachay
Vicente Atoigue Quidachay
Vicente T. Quidachay
Felisita T. Quifunas
Agueda A. Quinata
Amadeo T. Quinata
Anastacia T. Quinata

Ana Fejeran Cepeda
Ignacia C. Cepeda
Ignacio Cepeda Cepeda
Juan Sablan Cepeda
Trinidad Cepeda Cepeda
Trinidad J. Cepeda
Atanacio Quenga Certeza
Jose Eguegan Champaco
Roberto Lorenzo Champaco
Vicente Acfalle Champaco
Maria Santos Chang
Adela B. Charfauros
Antonio Babauta Charfauros
Antonio C. Charfauros
Arthur Benedict Lujan Charfauros
Edward C. Charfauros
Felix Cruz Charfauros
Francisco N. Charfauros
George I. Charfauros
Juan B. Charfauros
Maxima C. Charfauros
Polocarpio Chiguina Charfauros
Tomas C. Charfauros
Cresencio Meno Chargualaf
Jesus M. Chargualaf
Jose S.N. Chargualaf
Jose T. Chargualaf
Juan R. Chargualaf
Lorenza N. Chargualaf
Luis Nangauta Chargualaf
Vicente Cruz Chargualaf
Vicente S.N. Chargualaf
Virginia S. Chargualaf

Daniel L.G. Quinata
Ignacio A. Quinata
Ignacio Aguon Quinata
Jesus S. Quinata
Jose A. Quinata
Jose S.N. Quinata
Ramon A. Quinata
Trinidad A. Quinata
Veronica Quinata
Vicente A. Quinata
Silvestre Reyes Quinene
Vicente Reyes Quinene
Antonio Quintanilla
Gloria Arceo Quintanilla
Ignacio Reyes Quintanilla
Jesus D. Quintanilla
Jesus San Nicolas Quintanilla
Maria A. Quintanilla
Maria Borja Quintanilla
Rosario Gomez Quintanilla
Vicente W. Quintanilla
Ana L.G. Quitano
Agustin Quitaro
Ramon Baza Quitaro
Soledad Quitaro
Ana T. Quitugua
Catalina Aflague Santos Quitugua
Jesse N. Quitugua
Jesus Concepcion Quitugua
Jesus F. Quitugua
Jose Charguane Quitugua
Maria Duenas Quitugua
Maria M. Quitugua

Alfred L.G. Chiguina
Jesus Doroteo Chiguina
Frank Untalan Colner
Eduardo L.G. Concepcion
Jesus Q. Concepcion
Joseph Gumataotao Concepcion
Juan C. Concepcion
Juan Q. Concepcion
Rosa Guerrero Concepcion
Teresita M. Concepcion
Dolores Rivera Conway
Maria Techaria Baza Crawford
Concepcion P. Crisostomo
Edwardo J. Crisostomo
Faustino Cruz Crisostomo
Felix C. Crisostomo
Francisco Flores Crisostomo
Jose Torres Crisostomo
Juan Pereira Crisostomo
Maria Flores Crisostomo
Vicente Flores Crisostomo
Vicente L.G. Crisostomo
Albert Quenga Cruz
Alberto S. Cruz
Ana Acfalle Cruz
Ana Manalisay Cruz
Antonio Castro Cruz
Antonio Cruz Cruz
Antonio V. Cruz
Beatrice Portusach Cruz
Benito Salas Cruz
Carmen Atoigue Cruz
Cristobal Leon Guerrero Cruz

Pedro Charguane Quitugua
Rita T.M. Quitugua
Tomas A. Quitugua
Vicente Charguane Quitugua
Vicente Reyes Quitugua

R

Joaquin Cepeda Rabon
Jose Perez Rabon
John Hongyee Ramas
Trinidad T. Ramas
Jose Antonio L.G. Ramirez
Ramon S.N. Rapolla
Vicente Taijito Rapolla
Antonio Perez Reyes
Francisca Baza Reyes
Francisco Junior Reyes
Henry Mendiola Reyes
Jesus R. Reyes
Jesus Segundo Mendiola Reyes
Joaquin Cruz Reyes
Jose Mendiola Reyes
Maria B. Reyes
Maria G. Reyes
Victor B. Reyes
Jose Rios
Juan Salas Rios
Carmen Cruz Rivera
Francisco S. Rivera
Herminia T. Rivera
Jesus Rosario Rivera
Joaquin Rivera Rivera
Jose Ulloa Rivera

Cristobal Padagos Cruz
Delfina Blanco Cruz
Delfina C. Cruz
Delgadina San Nicolas Cruz
Delores Cruz Cruz
Delores Jesus Cruz
Dolores Jesus Cruz
Dolores Ofrecido Cruz
Elena Cepeda Taijeron Cruz
Elena T. Cruz
Eliza Mafnas Cruz
Engracia Quinata Cruz
Felipe C. Cruz
Felix V. Cruz
Francisco Camacho Cruz
Francisco Cruz Cruz
Galo Mendiola Cruz
Gregorio Agualo Cruz
Guadalupe C. Cruz
Henrique Atoigue Cruz
Ignacio Mendiola Cruz
Isabel Cruz
Isabel L. Cruz
Jaime Quitugua Cruz
Jesus A. Cruz
Jesus Cruz Cruz
Jesus Quitugua Cruz
Jesus Reyes Cruz
Jesus Toves Cruz
Joaquin Borja Cruz
Joaquin M. Cruz
Joaquin Reyes Cruz
Joaquin Taijeron Cruz

Juan S.N. Rivera
Rosa Nego Gogo Rivera
Rosalia Cruz Roberto
Josefina G. Rodriguez
David B. Rosario
Francisco Aguon Rosario
Milagros Martinez Cruz Rowley
Jose Cruz Royos

S

Annie Sanchez Sablan
Antonio Lang Sablan
Beatrice Espinosa Sablan
Catalina Perez Sablan
Concepcion Dungca Sablan
Concepcion Espinosa Sablan
Dolores Delgado Sablan
Enrique Benavente Sablan
Epifanio Benavente Sablan
Felicita Benavente Sablan
Felisa Delgado Sablan
Francisco Benavente Sablan
Francisco Quitugua Sablan
Gregoria G. Sablan
Henry Hamamoto Sablan
Jesus C. Sablan
Jesus Delgado Sablan
Joaquin Santos Sablan
Jose Benavente Sablan
Jose Espinosa Sablan
Josefa Benavente Sablan
Josefa Delgado Sablan
Juan Rosario Sablan

Jose B. Cruz
Jose Camacho Cruz
Jose Cruz Cruz
Jose Leon Guerrero Cruz
Jose Mafnas Cruz
Jose Pangelinan Cruz
Jose Q. Cruz
Jose Taianao Cruz
Joseph A. Cruz
Juan Aflleje Cruz
Juan Benavente Cruz
Juan Cruz Cruz
Juan Leon Guerrero Cruz
Juan Quinata Cruz
Juana Q. Cruz
Luis D. Cruz
Manuel Ada Cruz
Manuel B. Cruz
Manuel Guerrero Cruz
Manuel Rojas Cruz
Marcela Aflague Cruz
Margarita Sudo Cruz
Maria B. Cruz
Maria Jesus Cruz
Maria M. Cruz
Maria O. Cruz
Maria San Nicolas Cruz
Mariquita Jesus Cruz
Olympia T. Cruz
Oscar Duenas Cruz
Pedro Castro Cruz
Pedro Ofecido Cruz
Ramon Padilla Cruz
Louisa L.G. Sablan
Maria S. Sablan
Nicolas Q. Sablan
Nicolas Quitano Sablan
Nicolas Santos Sablan
Nicolasa Santos Sablan
Pedro Castro Sablan
Pedro Gogue Sablan
Raleigh Carbullido Sablan
Raymond L.G. Sablan
Rosita Carbullido Sablan
Segundo Flores Sablan
Vicenta Benavente Sablan
Vicente Sablan
Vicente Guerrero Sablan
Vicente Palomo Sablan
Vicente Santos Sablan
Agapito Nauta Salas
Angel Jesus Salas
Anthony Taijeron Salas
Antonio San Nicolas Salas
Antonio Taijeron Salas
Felix Mesa Salas
Felix S. Salas
Francisco Cruz Salas
Francisco Javier Salas
Jesus Chargualaf Salas
Jose Santos Salas
Juan Blas Salas
Juana Blas Salas
Maria Delgado Barcinc Salas
Ricardo Eustaquio Salas
Rosario Q. Salas

Ricky Cruz
Roque Namauleg Cruz
Rosa A. Cruz
Rosario Aflague Cruz
Rosario L.G. Cruz
Rosario P. Cruz
Rosita Sablan Cruz
Santiago A. Cruz
Simona Charfauros Cruz
Teddy Flores Cruz
Thanas Joseph Cruz
Thomas Cruz
Vicenta L.G. Cruz
Vicente Agualo Cruz
Vicente Taianao Cruz
Vicente Terlaje Cruz

D
Petronilla Bodestin Damian
Clemente Aguigui De Gracia
Lorenzo Aguigui De Gracia
Lorenzo Aguon De Gracia
Felisa L.G. Dela Rosa
Alfonso Delgado
Ana Cruz Delgado
Jesus M. Delgado
Jose Mendiola Delgado
Nicolas Mendiola Delgado
Olita Babauta Delgado
Silvano Mendiola Delgado
Josefa C.A. Denorcey
Doroteo D. Diaz
Jose Flores Diaz

Soledad Aquino Salas
Vicente S. Salas
Carlos S.A. San Agustin
Ignacio Crisostomo San Agustin
Joaquin Crisostomo San Agustin
Jose S.A. San Agustin
Antonia A. San Miguel
Rosario A. San Miguel
Adela C. San Nicolas
Ana P. San Nicolas
Candido A. San Nicolas
Candido Aguon San Nicolas
Catalina Jesus San Nicolas
Concepcion S.N. San Nicolas
David Cruz San Nicolas
David Sablan San Nicolas
Eugenio Taijeron San Nicolas
Fidel Concepcion San Nicolas
Francisco L.G. San Nicolas
Gregorio Aflague San Nicolas
Jesus Atoigue San Nicolas
Joaquin C. San Nicolas
Joaquin Limtiaco San Nicolas
Joaquin Mata San Nicolas
Joaquin P. San Nicolas
Jose Chaco San Nicolas
Jose Gogo San Nicolas
Jose Limtiaco San Nicolas
Jose T. San Nicolas
Juan S. San Nicolas
Juan Santos San Nicolas
Leus S. San Nicolas
Maria Concepcion San Nicolas

Julia T. Diaz
Zacarias G. Diaz
Francisco G. Diego
Vicente S.N. Diego
Ignacio Materne Dimapan
Rosario C. Domingo
Margarita Quidachay Dudkiewicz
Ana P. Duenas
Antonio Concepcion Duenas
Antonio Cruz Duenas
Antonio S.N. Duenas
Carlos Santos Duenas
David Santos Duenas
Delidonia Lujan Duenas
Eduardo Camacho Duenas
Emiliana Perez Duenas
Flora P. Duenas
Francisco Baza Duenas
Frankie Reyes Duenas
Jesus Baza Duenas
Jesus Duenas Duenas
Jesusa Santos Duenas
Joseph Santos Duenas
Juan D. Duenas
Juan Mendiola Duenas
Juan Torres Duenas
Juanita S. Duenas
Milagros M. Duenas
Paul Reyes Duenas
Pedro Baza Duenas
Pedro L.G. Duenas
Peter Reyes Duenas
Vicente Delgado Duenas
Maria Limtiaco San Nicolas
Olimpia Taijeron San Nicolas
Pedro R. San Nicolas
Ramon L.G. San Nicolas
Regina Diego San Nicolas
Rosa Aflague San Nicolas
C.A. Sanchez
Francisca Q. Sanchez
Jesus Q. Sanchez
Joaquin A. Sanchez
Jose T. Sanchez
Juan A. Sanchez
Maria A. Sanchez
Maria Q. Sanchez
Rosalia Camacho Sanchez
Domingo Q. Santiago
Ed Igos A. Santiago
Gregorio Chargualaf Santiago
Hilarien A. Santiago
Jose A. Santiago
Maria A. Santiago
Petra A. Santiago
Vicente Q. Santiago
Alvina Q. Santos
Aniceto De Gracia Santos
Antonio Borja Santos
Antonita Wusstig Santos
Carlos Mariano Santos
Clemente Degracia Santos
Dolores Chargualaf Santos
Eneceto Degracia Santos
Enrique Blas Santos
Francisco Blas Santos

Jesusa Babauta Dumanal
Jose Guevarra Dumanal
Pedro G. Dumanal
Rosalia Q. Dumanal
Thomas Q. Dumanal
Franklin Herrero Dungca

E
Alfred Miner Eclavea
Lecirio Miner Eclavea
Florenza Miner Eclavea
Juan A. Elatico
Tomasa M. Elatico
Antonio Cruz Elliott
Antonio Ramon Elliott
Victoria Manibusan Elsas
Annie English English
Domingo T. Espinosa
Grecia Tomasa Espinosa
Jose T. Espinosa
Jose Tyquiengco Espinosa
Juan Taitano Evangelista
Pedro Taitano Evangelista

F
Carlina Alvarez Faustino
Sabino Taitano Fausto
Antonio Champaco Fegurgur
Enrique Fegurgur Fegurgur
Carmen A. Fejarang
Ana C. Fejeran
Dolores Cruz Fejeran

Fredes Duenas Santos
Gregorio Borja Santos
Guadalupe S.N. Santos
Honaria Santos Santos
Jesus De Gracia Santos
Jesus Santos Santos
Jesus T. Santos
Jesus Villagomez Santos
Joaquin Camacho Santos
Jose Quenga Santos
Jose Quichocho Santos
Josefa Santos
Juan Cruz Santos
Lourdes A. Santos
Margarita S. Santos
Maria Santos
Maria Borja Santos
Maria Herrero Santos
Maria Perez Santos
Melva Pangelinan Santos
Nicolas Camacho Santos
Pacita Santos
Pedro Cruz Santos
Rosita Borja Santos
Soledad Arriola Santos
Tomas De Gracia Santos
Vicente Sablan Santos
Vicente Salas Santos
Herman E.F. Scharff
Magdalena Nora L.G. Shimizu
Gregorio C. Siguenza
Gregorio Cruz Siguenza

Enrique Cruz Fejeran
Tomas Perez Fejeran
Trinidad Cruz Fejeran
Rosaria Acfalle Fejerang
Vicente Q. Fejerang
David J. Fernandez
Isabel Pocaigue Fernandez
Jose Pocaigue Fernandez
Josefa Duenas Fernandez
Joseph Taijeron Fernandez
Maria Taijeron Fernandez
Roque Q. Fernandez
Rudy D. Fernandez
Salome Camacho
Fernandez
Santiago Lujan Fernandez
Manuela Salas Finona
Maria Fegurgur Finona
Alfred G. Flores
Angel L.G. Flores
Angele T.G. Flores
Antonia N. Flores
Candelaria Sablan Flores
Dolores Duenas Flores
Exequiel U. Flores
Jose S.N. Flores
Maria Q. Flores
Ana Borja Francisco
Johnny L.G. Francisco
Vicente Cabrera Francisco
Luisa M. Franquez
Guadalupe Santos Freegord

Lorenzo Taitingfong Siguenza
Rita Garcia Soriano
Sandra M. Stanley
Carmen B. Garrido Stemburg
Gregorio S. Sudo
Josefa Santos Suzuki

T

Ana C. Taijeron
Antonio Soriano Taijeron
Elias Santos Taijeron
Gerohimo L.G. Taijeron
Juan Jesus Taijeron
Juan Soriano Taijeron
Maria L.G. Taijeron
Maria Lujan Taijeron
Juan S. Taijito
David Quitugua Taimanglo
Francisco M. Taimanglo
Cerilio Tajalle Tainatongo
Maria Castro Tainatongo
Jesus T. Taisipic
Jose Taitingfong Taisipic
Florentina C. Taitague
Jose Cruz Taitague
Jose Delgado Taitague
Thomas Babauta Taitague
Vicente Quidachay Taitague
Carmelita Santos Taitano
Francisca Santiago Taitano
Frank L. Taitano
Joaquina L. Taitano

G
Angela Cruz Garcia
Eduardo Flores Garcia
Francisco Mesa Garcia
Jaime Flores Garcia
Jaime Mesa Garcia
Joaquin Flores Garcia
Juan Cabrera Garcia
Juan Flores Garcia
Ignacio Chargualaf Garrido
Jesus Garrido
Joseph L. Garrido
Ramon Garrido Garrido
Tomas Sablan Garrido
Vicente B. Garrido
Vicente Chargualaf Garrido
Andrew Garrison
Beatrice Q. Gofigan
Vicente San Nicolas Gogue
Asuncion Castro Guerrero
Felomena Lizama Guerrero
Jesus F. Guerrero
Juan M. Guerrero
Patricia T. Guerrero
Regina S. Guerrero
Vicente F. Guerrero
Anthony R. Guevara
Dobres Q. Guevara
Antonio Leon Gumataotao
Rita L. Gumataotao
Teresa Naputi Gumataotao
Vicente Ungacta
Gumataotao

Ramon Pangelinan Taitano
Rose Taitano
Vicente San Nicolas Taitano
Francisco Borja Taitingfong
Jesus Borja Taitingfong
Josefina C. Taitingfong
Maria Sablan Taitingfong
Rosa Cepeda Taitingfong
Vicente Borja Taitingfong
Gregoria C. Tajalle
Gregoria Chargualaf Tajalle
Gregoria Tajalle Tajalle
Jesus A. Tajalle
Jose Chargualaf Tajalle
Vicente Azaro Takae
Carmen D. Tedpahago
Manuel D. Tedpahago
Manuela D. Tedpahago
Angel M. Tedtaotao
Juan M. Tedtaotao
Rita F. Tedtaotao
Edward S. Teilge
Gino Tenorio
Gonzalo Gumataotao Tenorio
Jesus Namauleg Tenorio
Juan Quitugua Tenorio
Magdalena Atoigue Tenorio
Vicente Gogo Tenorio
Vicente Gumataotao Tenorio
Anthony J. Terlaje
Francisco S. Terlaje
Jesus C. Terlaje
Juanita T. Terlaje

Angustia Taitano Gutierrez
Maria Taitano Gutierrez
Rosa Diaz Gutierrez
Thomas Cruz Gutierrez
Juan Concepcion Guzman

H
Ana Cruz Hernandez
Jose Benevente Hernandez
Josefina Rivera Hernandez
Juana Rivera Hernandez
Jesue S. Herrera
Jose Taiano Herrera
Vedot Cruz Hocog
Mariquita Perez Howard

I
Jesus Iglesias
Jesus Mendiola Iglesias
Jose Iglesias
Manuel Pangelinan Ignacio
Juan Indalecio Indalecio
Rosario Rojas Indalecio
Vicente Indalecio Indalecio
Antonio G. Iriarte
Maria Iglesias Leon
Guerrero Iriarte
Rita C. Iriarte
Tomas Leon Guerrero Iriarte
Jose P. Isezaki
Juan P. Isezaki
William D. Isezaki
Francisco Hedesoboru

Maria Reyes Terlaje
Miguel Aflleje Terlaje
Vicente Reyes Terlaje
Rosalina Degracia Tolentino
Tomasa Degracia Tolentino
Ana Leon Guerrero Topasna
Ana S. Topasna
Isidoro E. Topasna
Jose A. Topasna
Juan E. Topasna
Juan Inocencio Topasna
Juan Q. Topasna
Pedro Aguon Topasna
Apolonia Ada Torre
Antonio Untalan Torres
Fred Santos Torres
Hannah Chance Torres
Jesus Taitague Torres
Joan Torres
Juan Taitague Torres
Julia Aguon Torres
Rosa Franquez Torres
Antonio Quichocho Toves
Frank Ellis Toves
Jesus Cruz Toves
John Toves
John S.N. Toves
Johnny T. Toves
Jose S. Toves
Juan S.N. Toves
Juan Toves Toves
Nicholas Cruz Toves
Pedro Lujan Toves

Ishizaki
Cevera Santos Iwatsu

J-K
Jesus Perez Johnson
Carmen Kamminga

L
Felix Santos Laguana
Ignacio Ignacio Laguana
Jesus Cruz Laguana
Teresita Cruz Laguana
Diana Sablan Leon Guerrero
Felix Camacho Leon Guerrero
Ignacio S. Leon Guerrero
Jesus Garrido Leon Guerrero
Jose S. Leon Guerrero
Josefina M. Leon Guerrero
Josefina Sablan Leon Guerrero
Juan Salas Leon Guerrero
Justa Baza Leon Guerrero
Mariquita M. Leon Guerrero
Matias De Leon Guerrero
Rita Franquez Leon Guerrero
Rosa R. Leon Guerrero
Vicente San Nicolas Leon Guerrero
Damian Castro Limtiaco
Rosa Aflague Limtiaco
Ursula Ignacio Limtiaco
Caridad T. Lizama
Carmen N. Lizama
Gregorie T. Lizama
Gregorio T. Lizama

Pedro Meno Toves
Ramon S. Toves
Ramon Siguenza Toves
Rosa Cruz Toves
Tomas Santos Toves
Clemente M. Tuncap
Carmen Chargualaf
(Garrido) Tyquiengco
Francisco Babauta Tyquiengco

U
Dorotea Cepeda Ulloa
Felix Ungacta Ungacta
Felipe Aguon Unpingco
Isabel C. Untalan
Jose Castro Untalan

V
John Cruz Van Meter
Josefina C. Vanderly
Francisco Taitano Velasco
Sebastian Taitano Velasco
Joaquina Campos Vergara
Antonia U. Villagomez
Jose C. Villagomez
Cresencia E. Villanueva

W-Y
Anna Cruz White
Maria Cruz White
Francisco Borja Won Pat
Louisa Camacho Wusstig
Manuel C. Wusstig

Karidat Lizama
Vicente De Leon Lizama
Dometro E. Lujan
Jesus San Nicolas Lujan
Jose C. Lujan
Juan Espinosa Lujan
Maria Santos Lujan
Mariquita L.G. Lujan
Ramona Ulloa Castro Lujan
Rosa E. Lujan.
Rosa Barcinas Yamanaka
Rosalia L.G. Lujan

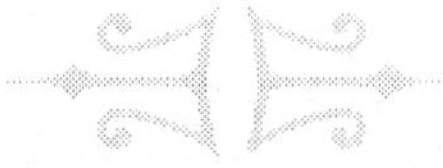

POST SCRIPT (REVISED DEC. 2016)

One never knows what the future may bring. Even in my wilder dreams, during my early contacts with Guam, did I ever think that one day I would write a book of the people of this small, peanut shaped American island. But, it happened. I did write about it, and them. There has never been, in the history of the United States, a more compelling and tragic event than the abandonment of an entire American population of men, women, and children to the ravishment of an evil Empire, the Imperial Japanese Empire of 1941. And, then continue to hold them at arm's length since the 1944 liberation of the island by America's armed forces.

I pray, trust, and hope that I have done the people of Guam justice. They deserve it. And, that it resonates with all other American people and their lawmakers, plus the brave resolute American military and naval personnel assigned to or pending assignment on Guam. The Guam situation described in this book requires understanding and needs a resolution. It needs closure. It needs amending. It needs fixed. Otherwise, America may, sooner rather than later, suffer the loss of long standing, dependable support among most of the American people residing on Guam. Only the Gerald Ford Administration seemed to understand that fact. But, so far, since the Ford Administration made its effort at resolving the situation, it has been an ongoing ignorance, a national ignorance, about Guam and its people. That too, remains an American shame.

After writing and publishing this book, we returned to Guam in December 2016, to promote the book. That promotion was a rousing success, and a bitter disappointment. For the, at large, Chamorros of Guam, it was a hit right off the bat. It was the networking and media publicity that created the groundswell of interest, resulting in a sellout of all the books brought to Guam. Before we arrived back on Guam, with an advance copy of the book in his hand, the governor of Guam spoke to Guam's military veterans on Veterans Day of his approval of its contents. When we arrived, we were enthusiastically received back to Guam. Many of our Guam friends welcomed us with the phrase, "Welcome Home!" And then the downside emerged. One important military facility and another U.S. government organization flatly rejected the book. It was a disturbing wall of censorship. Not just on Guam.

But, the people of Guam, average Guamanians and most definitely the University of Guam, led by its President, Doctor Robert Underwood, radio and television stations, newspapers, and survivors of the Japanese occupation, along with their descendants, flocked to our side. The book sold like free pancakes at an IHOP after church on Sunday. The people of Guam definitely did not ignore us. The Agueda I. Johnston Middle School praised our work, as they accepted a copy of the book for their library. The book is alive and well on Guam.

The rejection of this book by U.S. government institutions and facilities, while being embraced and lauded by the local population, is symptomatic of the gulf slowly seeping into minds and hearts here on Guam, as sabers rattle in their sheaths in this region of the world. If those swords are drawn, it is best to have a cast of Guamanians, as they did before, substantially supporting the U.S. government, rather than standing idle, or worse, rejecting America's forces in readiness on this bastion of America's defense, in these trying times.

Does the government of the United States not see a parallel between the British North American Colonies of the 1700's, and the United States Colonies of the 2000's? Eventually, the British citizens of America rebelled against not being considered equal to the citizens of Great Brittan. News flash: the United States Virgin Islands, Puerto Rico, Samoa, Northern Marianas, Federated States of Micronesia, and Guam, each being Colonies of the United States, are not treated equal to the citizens of the United States. The Constitution of the United States does not follow the flag. It is as simple as that.

Also, it should be noted, while we were promoting and selling our book, something else good happened, driven by Guam's U.S. Congressional Delegate Madeleine Bordallo and assisted by Guam Governor Eddie Calvo and Guam Senator Frank Blas. Finally, in December 2016, after waiting 75 years, the U.S. Congress passed the War Reparations for Guam Act, in the 2017 National Defense Authorization Act. Finally, the U.S. government recognized the tremendous sacrifice the people of Guam made during the War in the Pacific of World War II. However, they failed to appropriate sufficient funds for it. Instead, it appears they will, in a way, let Guam pay for it, again. That is, unless the Trump Administration provides additional funding for the bill. It is long overdue, and sadly most of the war survivors have simply faded away. Most of that society of captives on Guam died waiting for some recognition, some compensation, and some acknowledgement for this abandoned population of Americans, ever loyal to the country they loved, the United States of America.

The passage of the Guam War Reparations Act, included in the Defense Spending Bill of 2017, is a first step on a long march toward eventual justice. Guam has *given* more of its soul *to* the United States of America, than has been *received* in justice, *from* the United States of America.

Left to right are, Guam Governor Eddie Calvo, the author Stoney Bates and Lyn, discussing Guam's future and the pending relocation of Marines from Okinawa to Guam. The governor was very gracious and supportive of the book project and wished for us smooth sailing as we completed our research. Photo property of the author

At the age of seventeen, Ralph Stoney Bates dropped out of high school and enlisted in the United States Marine Corps. He was a drill instructor at Parris Island when he met and married his wife (Lyn) of over fifty-five years. He has served in "every clime and place," including the Republic of Vietnam (1967-'68), and the 124th session of the FBI National Academy. He retired from the active Marine Corps after twenty-six years.

He is also a retired deputy sheriff.

He holds an associate degree from Los Angeles City College, a bachelor's degree from Sam Houston State University, and has been an instructor at various colleges and universities.

An American Shame, is the culmination of six months on the American island of Guam, over a year of intensive research, and reflects his admiration for the Chamorros of Guam, and his incomprehension of their treatment by the United States government.